I060663E

THE STOLEN GOSPELS

BOOK 1 OF THE STOLEN GOSPELS

THE STOLEN GOSPELS

Brian Herbert

WordFire Press
Colorado Springs, Colorado

Published by
WordFire Press, an imprint of
WordFire Inc
PO Box 1840
Monument CO 80132

ISBN: 978-1-61475-034-5

First Trade Paperback Edition: January 2012
Printed in the USA

www.wordfire.com

DEDICATION

For Jan, with all of my love and admiration, and my great appreciation for your special contributions to this novel and its sequel. You are the most powerful and interesting woman I have ever met.

ACKNOWLEDGEMENTS

Over the years there have been numerous advisers and editors on this project, and the suggestions of Kevin J. Anderson, Robert Gottlieb, Matt Bialer, Martin H. Greenberg, John Silbersack, Mary Alice Kier, and Anna Cottle have all been greatly appreciated. I am also grateful to Rebecca Moesta-Anderson, for her work on this novel.

INTRODUCTION
The Stolen Gospels

The Stolen Gospels has a long history as a writing project, going back to the mid 1990s. By then I had read a number of books about the early centuries after Jesus Christ, when the gospels of His remarkable life were being assembled and religious leaders debated over what was to be included in the *Bible*, and what was to be omitted from it.

By 1995, I had read a number of feminist religious books that had been referred to me by my cousin Marie Landis, a fellow author (with whom I collaborated on occasion) and an admirer of Mary Magdalene. Marie said to me that she might be related to Mary Magdalene, and she was quite knowledgeable about the legendary woman's history. She argued against the characterization of Mary as a prostitute, and when I researched this I discovered that she was right, because I found proof that the facts of her life had been distorted for centuries, and it was only through the flimsiest of evidence that she had been characterized as a fallen woman.

At the time, I had also read about the discovery of buried papyrus codices at Nag Hammadi, Egypt in 1945–bound volumes that included ancient Christian religious texts that were not included in the *Bible*. These comparatively recent discoveries contained gospels suggesting that Mary Magdalene was much closer to Jesus Christ than most people had previously imagined. Many of the passages extolled the virtues

of women much more than did the *Bible*, which in contrast contained verses calling for wives to be ruled over by their husbands

(Genesis 3:16), for women to remain silent in the churches (1 Corinthians 14:34–35), and for women not to teach or to usurp authority over men (1 Timothy 2:12).

The Gnostic Christians were considered heretics by other Christians of the time, and in the midst of this conflict, and the concern of all Christians about being persecuted and tortured by the Romans, someone hid the Nag Hammadi codices, so that they would not be destroyed.

The Nag Hammadi discovery included religious works (the Gospel of Philip and the Gospel of Mary) that described tension between Mary Magdalene and the Apostle Peter, and his displeasure over how Jesus favored her. This led me to wonder if Mary Magdalene had actually been a full-fledged apostle of Jesus, a concept that had been suggested by a number of other researchers, but which had not been widely accepted.

I also began to wonder if the gospels of women had been suppressed by influential men in the early Christian church, purposefully excluding feminine writings in favor of those written by men. It seemed probable, and this troubled me, because I believed in the feminist cause, and in the advancement of women. I was married to a strong woman, Jan, and my mother (Beverly Herbert) had been the role model for the strong and elegant Lady Jessica of my father's classic novel *Dune*, arguably the most famous and most admired female character in all of science fiction. In fact, by the fifth and sixth books in the Dune series, Frank Herbert had women running everything, ruling numerous planets. The heroines were the Bene Gesserit Sisterhood, and they competed with their own dark side, women who had gone rogue from the organization to become the deadly Honored Matres.

The strong and interesting women in my father's writings—as well as my own experiences and observations—had been instrumental in my feeling that the world needed more female energy, because men had wreaked such havoc throughout history with their endless violence and mistreatment of the planet. Male-incited wars had killed millions of people and caused extreme environmental damage, so it seemed to me that the males of the human species had proven their inability to govern peacefully, and our planet could not stand any more of it.

With all of this in my mind, in late 1995 I started brainstorming a new novel with my brilliant and creative wife, Jan. We envisioned a sci-fi religious thriller that we entitled *The Stolen Gospels*, an immense story that would ultimately be divided into two novels, to include *The Lost Apostles*.

In science fiction, it is common to ask the question "what if?" and to extrapolate kernels of information to the extreme. Jan and I began with the assumption that Mary Magdalene had actually been an apostle of Jesus Christ, and because of the many women who were known to be in the company of Jesus, we wondered if He might have had other female apostles as well. What if, in fact, He had twelve female apostles in addition to the twelve known male apostles? From this assumption, we postulated that there had been a series of events that buried information about those female apostles in the dust bins of history, and only came to light many centuries later when the female apostles of Jesus were reincarnated, and began dictating their authentic gospels—gospels that were being formed into a new *Holy Women's Bible*. Our title for the novel, *The Stolen Gospels*, was a natural outgrowth of the postulation that the sacred religious texts of women were stolen from them by men many centuries ago—and the corollary that this was a huge loss to all of humankind.

Soon the new novel began to take shape, as I wrote chapters and scenes and discussed them with Jan. By late 1996, I sent a copyrighted draft of the novel to my literary agent, Mary Alice Kier. She made suggestions for improvement, and after I completed two rewrites, she submitted the book to a number of publishers. All of them turned it down.

In 1997, I began talking with Kevin J. Anderson about collaborating on new Dune-series novels, and we made arrangements with the William Morris Agency to represent us on new book proposals. I provided Kevin with a copy of the manuscript of *The Stolen Gospels*, and he gave me additional suggestions for improvement, as did my new literary agents at the William Morris Agency, Robert Gottlieb and Matt Bialer. With that input, I hurried to write yet another draft in an attempt to publish the novel by the year 2000, which had been declared a Holy Year by Pope

John Paul II to commemorate two thousand years since the birth of Jesus Christ.

But even more publishers declined to publish the next draft of the story, making me wonder if it was too long or too radical and controversial in its feminist viewpoint and theological presentation, complicated by the fact that it did not fit neatly into any one literary genre—it was a sci-fi religious thriller with elements of fantasy, and was not like any fictional work that had been published before. My agents referred the novel to the well-known editor and publisher, Martin H. Greenberg. After a careful reading, Mr. Greenberg and his staff provided additional suggestions for improvement, which I began incorporating into the manuscript—when I had time between new Dune-series novels with Kevin, and a number of my own other solo novels and non-fiction books.

Through it all, the Gospels novel project slowed down, and by 2004 I had yet another agent, John Silbersack, who worked at Robert Gottlieb's new agency, Trident Media Group. After I divided the story into two parts, John found an interested publisher, who sent me a contract, but that contract was never signed and we did not move forward with them.

Now, sixteen years after beginning this ambitious project, I am pleased to finally present both novels—*The Stolen Gospels* and *The Lost Apostles*—in e-book form. I hope you will find the story interesting and thought provoking, especially in the context of the strong female characters I like to include in much of my fiction, and the religious elements contained in a number of my other solo novels, including *The Race For God* (1990), and the three-volume *Timeweb* series (2006–2008).

This is the epic, heroic story of the brave women who might have been apostles of Jesus, and of the men and women who protected them from harm. . . .

Brian Herbert
September 10, 2011

Other Books by Brian Herbert

The Stolen Gospels (Book 1 of THE STOLEN GOSPELS)

Sidney's Comet
The Garbage Chronicles

Man of Two Worlds (with Frank Herbert)

Sudanna Sudanna

Prisoners of Arionn

The Race for God

Memorymakers (with Marie Landis)
Blood on the Sun (with Marie Landis)

Timeweb (Book 1 of THE TIMEWEB CHRONICLES)
The Web and the Stars (Book 2 of THE TIMEWEB CHRONICLES)
Webdancers (Book 3 of THE TIMEWEB CHRONICLES)

Dreamer of Dune

Forgotten Heroes

Hellhole (with Kevin J. Anderson)

DUNE Series (with Kevin J. Anderson)

House Atreides   *The Butlerian Jihad*
House Harkonnen   *The Machine Crusade*
House Corrino   *The Battle of Corrin*

Hunters of Dune   *Paul of Dune*
Sandworms of Dune   *The Winds of Dune*

The Road to Dune   *Sisterhood of Dune*

Part One

VOICES

But I suffer not a woman to teach, nor to usurp authority over the man, but to be in silence. For Adam was first formed, then Eve. And Adam was not deceived, but the woman being deceived was in the transgression.

—1 Timothy 2:12–14, *The New Testament*

Prologue

July 9, 2033

At her office in Salonika, Greece, Dr. Katherine Pangalos read an e-mail concerning two mysterious babies in the care of her non-profit international medical organization. Within hours of birth, the children—both girls—were babbling, making peculiar, complex sounds that seemed very similar.

Over her computer's speaker system Pangalos listened carefully to the recorded sounds: rhythmic and fluid for short stretches, but halting and clicking much of the time, like a language in the process of formation. Definitely not normal baby talk, her doctors were saying, and she couldn't help but agree.

Utilizing a high security encrypted Internet line—which Pangalos normally employed for other purposes—she contacted a renowned linguistics expert who could be trusted, and the startling truth began to unfold. . . .

Chapter 1

We must await the proper moment to reveal our incredible secret, when all is in readiness. If we come out too early, an eruption of fear and suppression will destroy our movement.
　　　　　　　　　　　　　－Report of the Commission on the She-Apostles

February 7, 2034 . . .

An orderly queue of seventeen robed women moved across the cobblestone plaza toward a weathered stone church. Second in the procession, a stocky black woman, Dixie Lou Jackson, heard the ancient tower bell ringing, a melancholy throb carried on a cool afternoon breeze. She shivered. It was winter, in the Macedonian mountains of northern Greece.

Around them rose the other structures of Monte Konos, a secluded mountaintop monastery that had been abandoned during Turkish raids in 1827. For centuries before that, it had been a sanctuary for a form of chauvinist monasticism in which only men were permitted to participate. In all that time, no women had been allowed to set foot on Monte Konos, not even female animals.

Of course, all that was changed now.

At the church entrance Dixie Lou and her superior, Amy Angkor-Billings, stepped into shadows on one side while their companions filed past them through arched double doors. Each door featured a large, carved Byzantine cross. Nervously, Dixie Lou looked up at the cerulean sky, wondering if an enemy might detect them here with an orbital surveillance satellite. If that happened, the consequences would be disastrous.

She hurried inside with the others.

* * *

The tall, broad-shouldered man moved through the underground corridor with athletic grace and power, a deportment that stemmed as much from his intense attitude as from physical prowess. Vice Minister Styx Tertullian wore wire-rimmed glasses and carried two jet-ball pens in his shirt pocket. His straight blond hair was overly long, so that it fell around his eyes.

He passed the door to the bustling, all-male secretarial pool, then continued on through the plex-bubble of the communications pod and into the honeycomb-walled concrete and steel office core, the most heavily protected section of the bombproof office complex. The air filtration system in the facility had been designed to keep the interior atmosphere clean in case of military attack, but dust still got through from a sandstorm that was raging outside. The equipment had never functioned properly, just one of numerous construction problems and cost overruns in this four-year old network of concealed subterranean structures, in eastern Washington state.

As Styx approached, a guard in a silver-and-black Bureau of Ideology uniform nodded to him. Styx stopped at the guard station and pressed his face against the cool surface of an identity plate. Lavender light washed across him, reading his epidermal cell patterns and retinas, while imparting a slight tingle to the skin. He felt a pin prick as a DNA sample was taken from his cheek, and seconds later the clearance bell rang, permitting him to continue on his way. No person, not even the Minister himself, was exempt from such procedures.

This morning the Vice Minister had important news for his boss's ears only, and was hurrying to make his report. Styx's ear-implanted phone went off, making his skin tingle. A subconscious link told him it was Minister Nelson Culpepper himself, exactly the person he was going to see anyway. Seconds after the call, Styx walked into the Minister's opulent reception area, where an electronic secretary registered his presence and transmitted the information to the inner office.

"Come in, come in," a voice boomed across the intercom system.

Styx hurried into the office, and blurted out in his high-pitched, whining voice, "I have exciting news, Minister!"

But as he entered he saw a holo-projection of the broad-faced President of the United States, Lowell Markwether, dancing in the air in front of Culpepper's desk. With a crafty smile, Culpepper motioned for Styx to take a seat, which he did, in one of the deep armchairs off to one side.

At the press of a button, Styx caused a cup of steaming hot coffee to pop out of a slot in the table next to him. It was the best coffee he had ever tasted, a blend of the finest beans in the world, brewed through enhanced methods that produced a cup of java that tasted just as good as it smelled. He waited for it to cool down.

A fat man with a youthful face, the Minister looked like an oversized child. He wore an impeccable silver-and-black uniform with gold buttons, each of them a Christian cross. The flag of the Bureau of Ideology hung on a pole behind him, a silver banner with a black cross in the center.

"I need more funding," Culpepper said to the President. "Another four billion dollars."

"Four billion more?" the holo-form responded. "How many favors do you think I owe you?"

"This is a time of special need, my friend, and I promise a quid pro quo when you're up for reelection. We need more military equipment and intelligence resources. Our female foes have been—mmm—quite troublesome."

The President's holo-form faded to half-strength, and Styx saw him leaning to one side, his lips moving but not projecting sound to the distant BOI office. Undoubtedly, Markwether was conferring with his ever-present older brother, Zack, a US Army colonel who was in charge of White House security, a man not visible in the holo-projection of the virtual meeting. Intelligence reports indicated Zack Markwether, while brilliant and in many respects more qualified than his brother for high office, was not well-liked by the White House staff, in part because of jealousy over his access to the President, but in larger measure due to Zack's inability to get along with high-level White House staffers. He had an arrogant way of swaggering around in his uniform and white gloves, sometimes even wearing aviator-style sunglasses indoors to prevent people from seeing the direction of his gaze. He was, to say the least, eccentric.

In a few moments, President Markwether's beefy holo-image brightened, and he twitched nervously as he stood up straight. "Coming up with that much money isn't easy, after the billions we've already obtained for you. We can only skim so much, you know."

"Get it done anyway," Culpepper demanded, "and don't waste my time with weak-kneed excuses. Pull strings, knock heads, threaten to kill their families if you have to. Whatever it takes. I don't care how you get the money, just get it, and do it fast."

The President shook his head in dismay.

"Don't let me down," Culpepper said, in the most ominous of tones. Abruptly he ended the virtual meeting, and the holo-projection faded, as if intense sunlight had burned through a layer of fog.

"He'll get the money for us if he ever wants to run for office again," Culpepper said. He grinned, revealing cigarette-stained teeth that seemed out of character with his otherwise spotless appearance.

The ultra-conservative BOI was not relying on any one source of income. They were in constant contact with wealthy right-wing investors around the world, people who did not want the radical, upstart women to make any more headway. Through its web of carefully tailored relationships, the BOI was able to fund its own paramilitary and political operations in secrecy. In fact, the public had no idea that this powerful group even existed.

"I've got some nice dirt on President Markwether if you ever want to use it," Styx said. "On the campaign funds he diverted for his own personal use, and other irregularities."

"I thought I told you to get rid of that stuff," Culpepper said. "We run an upstanding Christian organization. Trading favors is one thing. Blackmail is quite another."

"Yes, sir. I'll delete the files from our data base."

"Don't make me say it again. I don't like to repeat myself."

"You can count on me, sir. I'll take care of it." Actually, Styx intended to conceal the information, burying it in deep computer encryptions where no one could find it. He had gone to a great deal of trouble to build files on a lot of important people, and he was certain that they would prove to be valuable one day. He even had one on Culpepper himself, who claimed to be so squeaky clean. What a hypocrite!

Styx sipped his coffee, waiting for an opportunity to discuss another matter he had on his mind.

Culpepper coughed from sandstorm dust, and with a flurry of expletives that would make a longshoreman blush, he cursed the building's air filtration system. He paused to take a drink of water from a bottle, while his subordinate spoke quickly, excitedly: "Sir, I have incredible news!"

With a scowl, Culpepper thumped the bottle down on his desk. "It'll keep. I have a more important matter to discuss with you."

"But Minister, this is something you—" Styx fell silent, after detecting a look of disapproval on the fat man's face.

"Don't forget. *I* called *you* here."

"Of course. I'm sorry." The Vice Minister stared at a wall-displayed projection of the storm topside, while sand pummeled the rural Bureau-controlled town up there.

"You know how I feel about United Women of the World," Culpepper said, his voice raspy, as it sometimes became when he was upset. "I'd like to blow them off the face of the earth."

"That's exactly what I came to discuss with you, sir! The Legions of Eve, those shameless sinners in silk and chiffon. Just wait until you hear what I—" Styx fell silent again, shifted uncomfortably on his feet.

"Blast those harlots," Minister Culpepper said.

The UWW—run by rabidly militant females—was the Bureau's archenemy in every country on the planet, waging behind-the-scenes battles that the blissfully ignorant general public never even heard about. The UWW's secrecy was obtained through similar methods to those utilized by the BOI, and it was reported that the troublesome women forced all personnel to take oaths of secrecy and to undergo unbreakable, deep hypnosis—thus preventing information from leaking. Some sort of witchery, Styx thought; one of many proofs that the UWW was in league with the devil. In any event, their Svengali methods didn't work entirely. The BOI, through its contacts, knew some of the bizarre, heretical acts they were committing, stirring up susceptible women, claiming certain passages in the Bible were the result of political machinations, and were not true gospel.

"Listen, Styx. I've got a line on Billings, a way we can get to her."

Styx caught his breath. This was indeed more significant than his own report. The Minister was referring to the diabolical Chairwoman of the UWW, Amy Angkor-Billings herself.

"That's excellent, sir," Styx said.

Culpepper struggled with his raspy voice. He started to speak, then cleared his throat several times and drank more water. "We'll have to move quickly," he said, regaining his vocal ability at last. "Tomorrow she's leaving for the Greek city of Salonika to meet with a doctor."

"She's ill?" Styx asked.

"No, the doctor—Katherine Pangalos—is a wealthy eccentric, and according to intelligence reports she's a big UWW contributor. Billings is probably going there to pick up a hefty check."

"Greece is unstable," Styx said. It was a phrase the BOI used, meaning the organization didn't have much political influence on a particular government, and it was suspected that the UWW did.

"Unstable, yes," Culpepper said, "making what I have in mind a bit more difficult. But we have guerrilla forces in Macedonia, the same people we used in Turkey and the Ukraine."

"Ah yes, our legendary Night Fighters."

"Exactly. I want you to mobilize them for a covert operation."

Styx: "Mmmm. To assassinate someone?"

The fat man smiled. "You're quick, Styx. You'll make a fine Minister one day." Then he asked, "Now what is it you wanted to talk about?"

"One of Billings' closest associates, Dixie Lou Jackson."

"The black witch?"

"Uh huh. As luck would have it she's vulnerable, too. Before joining the UWW she conducted a goddess circle in a Seattle suburb, and now she's going back for a guest appearance at a related group."

"When?"

"Tomorrow evening. It's in a private home owned by an associate, near Lake Washington."

"That *is* interesting, and Styx, luck has nothing to do with it. God is moving the heretics into position for us."

"For two commando attacks, sir?"

Culpepper nodded. "We'll stage the Seattle raid from here. You lead it. Our Athens office will handle the other one."

Styx's narrow, bespectacled face grew warm with anticipated pleasure. Having been trained as a US Marine before joining the Bureau, he enjoyed using weapons and often participated in surprise raids. "Praise the Lord," he intoned. "Demon blood will flow."

* * *

140 miles west, in Seattle . . .

Within the privacy of her bedroom, surrounded by holo-photos taped to the walls, an auburn-haired teenager replayed her phone messages and heard the disturbing words again: "I'm gonna kill you for what you did, girl."

Lori Vale didn't recognize the muffled male voice that came through speakers in her ceiling, and no name had been left; but based upon what her friends were saying, she suspected who it was—Chad O'Kray—a twenty-year-old street punk who had provided her with a place to stay after she'd run away from home the month before. On probation for a drug offense, he'd been charged with a felony for harboring a runaway, since Lori was a minor. According to rumor, he'd been blaming her for his legal troubles, but she wasn't sure why.

Hearing a door close downstairs and the familiar footsteps of her mother as she prepared to leave for work, Lori snapped her fingers to erase the message. The threat didn't frighten her in the least, and she would take care of it herself.

* * *

Across the world, inside the centuries-old Greek church, Dixie Lou Jackson sat somberly with her fellow councilwomen, in a half-circle of black leather chairs. They watched Amy Angkor-Billings as the elegant woman took a seat in a high-back red leather chair facing them.

"Immense changes are in the wind," Amy said, "a shift in the cosmos from male to female energy. The destructive forces of men are waning—"

On a table by Dixie Lou a computer screen was on, a coded Internet connection that linked them with United Women of the World contacts all over the world—cells run by women who were capable of activating secret paramilitary forces on short notice. Peripherally, she watched the screen scroll.

"Praise be to She-God!" the women intoned.

A petite Cambodian with a regal profile and narrow, slanted eyes, Amy had removed her dun-colored monk's robe, revealing long, jet black hair secured in a pony tail by a golden clasp. As befitted her high position she wore a gold dress with the green-and-orange design of the UWW on her lapel—a design that merged the traditional Christian cross with a sword.

"As all of you know," Amy said, "Dixie Lou and I will be away for several days on separate trips."

"A prayer for your safety," said Kaiulani Maheha, a large Hawaiian woman.

The councilwomen bowed their heads in silence for several moments and made cradling motions with their arms, as if holding babies. Then, in unison, they looked up.

On a high pedestal behind the council loomed the white marble statue of She-God, representing all the heroines of history, or "herstory," as Amy preferred to call it. On the statue's upturned palms rested the Sword of She-God, a magnificently tooled blade with a jeweled Christian cross for its hilt. Of unknown origin, it was the subject of legend in the UWW, and the organization's most important religious artifact. It was a design repeated on banners draped around the inside of the ancient building, partially covering streaky gray-and-black walls. Dixie Lou smelled the musk odor of burning incense.

Some of the councilwomen still wore their robes—even with blouses and slacks beneath—because the dun robes, while lacking style, compensated for this inadequacy by offering warmth.

Dixie Lou blew on her hands and rubbed them together. The church's heating system had not been working well, and was scheduled to be inspected the following day. She put the coldness out of her mind, an ability she had that enabled her to set aside pain and personal discomfort.

Glancing around, Dixie Lou noted that most of the councilwomen had lowered their eyes in deference to their Chairwoman, as if Amy were the She-God incarnate. Dixie Lou did not do that. As always she gazed with intelligent, dark brown eyes at the tiny Asian woman, looking steadily at her as if she were no more than any another female. Amy didn't seem to mind, and had supported the promotion of Dixie Lou to number two in command.

Their all-important project was centered across the cobblestone plaza in the ancient Scriptorium Building, once occupied by monks for the copying of manuscripts. In that place the council had set up computers, recording equipment and the most accredited biblical scholars and linguists in the world, female and male, who toiled to compile an extraordinary, earthshaking new work.

At the moment, however, Dixie Lou had something else on her mind, a vivid, recurring image. Upon the internal screen of her memory appeared the face of a black man she had shot to death five years ago in Seattle, on a cold, rainy night. It was one of several justified killings she had committed in her lifetime. Now she recounted all of the violent episodes in her mind, as she sometimes did for enjoyment.

She caught her breath, because this time a strong new image dominated the others. She envisioned a shadow enshrouded room where people slept. In her right hand she held a knife, and she brought it down over and over, stabbing the sleepers. She smelled the metallic odor of their blood.

Suddenly her mind roiled and whirled in confusion—for she had never killed anyone in that manner.

Chapter 2

It is said that Jesus Christ showed his feminine and masculine sides equally, by simultaneously wearing long hair and a beard.
—The Alternative History of Jesus, UWW Press

"You'd better be in school when I call, young lady," Camilla Vale shouted, from the base of the hall stairs.

Leaving her bedroom door closed, the fifteen-year-old didn't respond. Lori wore red-and-white pajamas, and having been awake for a few minutes, she sat on the edge of the bed. Her microdisk music player was on, but not loudly. Taller than most girls at Seattle High, Lori had long auburn hair, lavender eyes, and a heart-shaped face, with soft features. She had her father's height, not the stunted body of her mother, whom she loathed.

"Do you hear me, young lady?"

Lori turned up the volume on the microdisk, and her room filled with the throb of Sister Moon, one of the new space-rock groups.

Moments later—predictably—her door slammed open (with the handle hitting a dent already in the wall), and her mother roared in.

"Turn that music down!" she commanded.

Lori did so, but as she went to sit on her bed again she shot a contemptuous glare at the small, feisty woman, who wore brown slacks and a beige sweater. Camilla Vale could be so difficult at times, without any understanding of the problems of being a teenager.

"I'm going to call your school in an hour," Camilla said, "and you'd better be there. If you aren't, I'll send the police after you again."

"Oh, right. Like they're your personal cops—the Camilla Vale Police Patrol. I could run away again and they wouldn't start searching for days."

A hurt look crossed Camilla's face. A woman of slumping posture, she had a small nose and light brown hair. As she sat beside her daughter she said, in a voice suddenly fragile, "You should appreciate what I do for you, dear. All the hours I work to put clothes on your back and food in your belly, and this is the thanks I get?"

"You're so out of touch, Mom, I can't even talk to you." She blinked her long eyelashes, shook her head. "All I ever hear is the same old garbage, over and over." Lori felt a little guilty over these harsh remarks, but not enough to apologize. Her mother wasn't that old, but couldn't seem to remember what it had been like to be a teenager.

"Get ready for school," Camilla snapped. She glanced at her watch, left hurriedly. Lori heard the front door close. Her mother worked in a clerical position, as she'd done for years.

The videophone jangled, and Lori waited to read the caller identification screen before touching a button to answer. The video screen went on. It was her best friend, her rainbow-colored hair cut short and jagged.

"Hey, Alicia," Lori said, speaking first.

"How's it going?" Alicia asked.

"Wonderful. Some guy left a message threatening to kill me."

* * *

In a previous incarnation, the two-story stucco building had been a convent for Roman Catholic nuns. Now it housed families . . . the surviving parents and siblings of the special children. Situated on a hillside outside Salonika in northern Greece, it commanded a stunning view of the Aegean Sea. Over the years, many of the red roof tiles had been replaced, so that they didn't quite match, and there were discolorations and streaks on the stucco exterior walls.

It was mid-afternoon, with the fresh aroma of the saltwater beach in the air. An old woman stood on the balcony of the second floor library, her age-spotted hands resting on the sun-warmed iron railing. Dr. Katherine Pangalos watched as a sleek black Mercedes—her personal limousine—passed the guard station and pulled onto a paved circular driveway in front of the building. Her own elaborate villa, built in the eighteenth century, graced an adjacent property, beyond a grove of olive trees.

Before her chauffeur could go back and open the rear door, it swung open and a small woman stepped out, carrying a dark briefcase. Despite her lofty position, Amy Angkor-Billings preferred doing things for herself. Dr. Pangalos went inside and crossed the library to an elevator that would take her down to the main level. Personally, she'd been blessed with servants since childhood, and couldn't imagine what life would be like without them. But Amy, from her impoverished upbringing in Cambodia, came from an entirely different background.

As the aged doctor awaited the elevator, she thought about how curious it was that two women of such divergent backgrounds—herself and Amy—now found themselves on the same path. The she-apostles were responsible for that . . . the unusual babies they had gathered from around the world. Some six months ago, Katherine's own non-profit medical organization had brought the first two children to the UWW's attention—babies born to poor families in backward countries. Babies who babbled a strange language . . . ancient Aramaic.

This alone had been astonishing, and the translations even more so, revealing the existence of others like themselves . . . highly unique female children.

It turned out that the eleven children they had so far—who called themselves "she-apostles"—were not all the same age, and that one more had not yet been born, but soon would be. The first two children had told Katherine's people where ten others could be located, and what their birth names were, or would be, when born. Armed with this information, Katherine had dispatched operatives to bring them in, by ruse or even by force if necessary. In the process, people had been killed, including two sets of parents. The UWW leadership had not wanted this to happen, but they had to locate and gain control over all of the she-apostles by any means.

Now they had all of them, with the exception of one.

Not surprisingly, this was the first thing Amy asked when they met in the foyer of the building: "Any news on Martha yet?" She was referring to Martha of Galilee, so named by the other she-apostles. Voices could be heard in another room: the families were gathering.

Katherine held onto the smaller woman's hand in a long, warm handshake. "We think she's somewhere in Mexico. You heard about the problem, I assume?"

"Yes," Amy said as they separated, "the difficulty of translating from Aramaic–several villages with similar names–"

"We're narrowing it down. I've dispatched teams to five peasant villages in the central highlands of Mexico. Something is bound to turn up."

The epicanthic folds around Amy's green eyes tightened. "With only one to go, we can't let her slip through our fingers."

"I understand how important she is. I'm sparing no expense."

"And we all appreciate that. Too bad you can't take a tax deduction for your contributions."

"No matter. Money is no object." Heiress to a huge shipping fortune, Katherine seemed to have an endless supply of money.

Amy followed Katherine through a wide doorway into an immense, high-ceilinged room that had once been the dining hall of the convent. Men, women, and children were seated in chairs . . . the surviving birth-families of the she-apostles. As the two women entered, a hush fell over the assemblage.

Amy climbed three wooden steps to a stage and crossed to a podium. On an adjacent table, she set down her briefcase and opened it, with four clicks of the air latches.

"I've brought holo-recordings of your children," she said.

Presently the audience grew quiet and listened as Amy set up a projection machine on the podium and adjusted the transmitting ball on top. "I'm sorry we can't leave anything with you," Amy said. "We've explained the security problems to you." She touched a button, and a little girl's voice came on, a fifteen-month-old toddler speaking in Aramaic.

"This is Gina Michelli," Amy explained, concealing the child's apostolic name, Veronica, and the related information about her. That she-apostle, like the others, had renounced her birth-name when she began speaking Aramaic. Such facts had not been revealed to the birth-families . . . only a made-up story that the children were special, and the subject of a top-secret government study.

Now Amy stretched the truth even further when she gazed from the podium down at the parents—an overweight Italian couple in the front row—and said, "Gina says she loves you, and misses you." In reality, the children seemed to have passed over a threshold, rising above familial concerns to a different level, one that affected all of humankind.

A woman beside them translated Amy's words into Italian, and tears began to stream down the mother's face. She said something, which was in turn related back to Amy: "She wants to know when she can hold her baby again."

"I'm sorry, but I can't provide an exact time," the Chairwoman replied.

This was true, because in this room only she and Katherine knew that the Italian baby and ten others formed the core of a rigorous academic research program, with no end in sight. In order to maintain secrecy, the families were forced to live here under guard for an indefinite time. With all of her wealth, Dr. Pangalos was providing them with amenities that rivaled a luxury resort, including a health club and swimming pool, meals prepared by world-class chefs, tutors for their other children, and even high-security Mediterranean cruises. This former convent had, in effect, become a velvet-lined prison for the families. They were not permitted to send or receive any type of mail or correspondence, to make phone calls, or to receive visitors.

As the first child finished speaking and Amy began playing a recording of the second, she paused, having heard something . . . the sound of breaking glass, followed by loud footsteps.

Suddenly men in silver-and-black uniforms burst into the hall, carrying automatic rifles. They sprayed the ceiling with bullets, and their leader shouted, in English, "Everybody on the floor, face-down! Now!"

Amy touched a button on the holo-recorder, destroying it. Smoke curled out of the machine.

* * *

In separate caves rimming the top of Monte Konos, monks wearing dirty, frayed robes murmured the Prayer of the Heart, over and over: "Lord Jesus Christ, have mercy on me, a sinner . . . Lord Jesus Christ, have mercy on me, a sinner. . ." The sun, low in the sky, splashed golden hues across the mountains of northern Greece.

These men—a handful of religious hermits—had inhabited the caves long before United Women of the World took over the mountain. The council had allowed them to remain, considering them non-political and unthreatening. Two of the monks (who called themselves "musers") earned food and simple personal articles by telling fortunes to the women, while others performed manual labor around the facility. There was no shortage of work needing to be done.

At the conclusion of his prayer one of the monks emerged from his primitive home and climbed a short distance up a rock, in cool shadows. Dipping his hands in a small natural bowl, he drank rainwater. Then he gazed uphill, at the streaked gray-and-black stone buildings of the ancient monastery, with its Byzantine arches and domed rooftops. The sun, just dropping below a mountain peak behind him, was glinting off window panes on the top floor of the Scriptorium Building.

Inside that structure, the women who controlled the mountain were particularly busy. He wondered what they were doing in there.

Chapter 3

Q: "What did the Divine Spirit say, after creating Adam?"
A: "What a huge disappointment. We need to improve on this!"
—One of Amy Angkor-Billings' oft-repeated jokes

Shortly after dinner, Lori stood in the small kitchen of her mother's two-bedroom house, staring at a flier on the counter, a green piece of paper with bright orange lettering on it. The notice from the Golden Goddess Society, sitting on top of a pile of mail, said something about a surprise speaker at the next meeting. The teenager sighed. Her mother got involved in so many oddball things, always having to do with women's issues.

Just as she was about to move the flier aside to go through the letters, Lori felt a peculiar tingling sensation in her fingertips when she touched the green paper. Handling another piece of mail, she didn't get that feeling. Hesitantly, she touched the flier once more, and got the tingling again. It must be static electricity, she decided, clinging to the fiber structure of the paper.

Just as she was wondering how far-fetched this sounded, her mother came in and announced, "You're going with me to the meeting."

They argued all the way to the car, and across the airbridge spanning Lake Washington. . . .

"I don't see why I have to go with you," Lori said. She slouched in the passenger seat as her mother drove the old Chrysler. Angrily, the lavender-eyed teenager glanced sidelong at her mother, who still wore her office clothes—a brown tweed suit with narrow lapels that were at least ten years out of style.

"It'll be good for you."

"A goddess circle? Don't make me laugh."

"Watch it, young lady." She glanced with disapproval at Lori's short red skirt and tight pink blouse, which revealed her blossoming figure. Her long auburn hair was secured in a pony tail.

Fiddling with the strap of her purse, Lori gazed out the window. The old car rolled along a winding street on the west side of Mercer Island, an upscale suburb of Seattle. Expensive waterfront and view homes were set in the midst of evergreen trees, with BMWs, Mercedes, and Rolls Royces parked in driveways. The moon was full and bright.

"Oh, like I don't have a right to have an opinion, Mom? This is America, isn't it? Land of the free?"

"If you hadn't abused drugs and alcohol, I wouldn't worry about leaving you at home."

"I've been through therapy." Lori stared at her own brown leather purse, which contained, in a zipper pocket, a plastic baggie of marijuana.

"And you relapsed."

"A couple of lousy beers. Big stinkin' deal." She felt stressed, wanted to roll a joint and smoke it.

Lori was street-wise, tough and sassy. When she ran away from home the month before it was her second time, after which she'd gone to weekly counseling sessions with her mother. Lori's friends were a major concern for Camilla. She called them "users, losers, and abusers."

"If I have to, Lori, I'll put you back in the rehab center."

"It's easier to get drugs in there than it is outside, do you know that?"

"You're not staying out all night with boys any more, either, young lady."

"Oh, like I'm gonna sneak off while you're at the goddess circle."

The car hit a bump, causing the glove box to pop open, revealing a .38 handgun inside. Reaching over, Camilla slammed the little door shut. Lori's mother knew martial arts and the use of weapons . . . said she had almost been raped once, and refused to ever let it happen again. She regularly took Lori to target practice, showing her how to fire this handgun and a rifle, and had enrolled her in advanced *t'ai chi chuan* and beginning *karate* classes.

"Lori, you have to build back my trust," Camilla said. "You've let me down too often, and each time it hurts. I've been looking forward to this meeting, and I swear you're not keeping me from it."

"Do you want me to be a lesbian, like you?"

"That's not true and you know it!" As Camilla glared at her passenger, the big car veered, before she corrected the steering.

"You don't like men."

"I've never said that." Because of Camilla's burst of anger, her hands gripped the steering ball so hard that they seemed welded in place.

"Oh *right*, like you have sweet things to say about Daddy. Try to think of something good about him, Mom. Just one little thing."

"There isn't much. He did not treat his family well."

"That's a tired tune. Same old generality, without details."

Steering the heavy car around a corner, Camilla nudged the accelerator. The old engine sputtered, then finally caught hold, just when it seemed about to expire. Exhaust fumes seeped into the passenger compartment.

"You're too gullible around men, Lori, too trusting of them."

"*Men*? Mom, I'm only fifteen. I date guys my own age, or maybe a year older."

"Yeah, and I know what you do with them."

"You're paranoid, Mom, do you know that?"

"You must think I'm stupid. I know you're sleeping with them."

"Oh really? Well maybe I made up things in my diary because I knew you'd sneak and read it."

"I never said I read your diary."

"Then what's this talk about sleeping with boys? Where'd you get that crazy idea?"

"I have my sources."

"You're so secretive, Mom. It makes me sick. Dark secrets about Daddy, unrevealed sources of information about me. You're never honest with me."

"That's uncalled for, Lori. You know I love you."

"You're overprotective."

The rain and wind from an afternoon storm had let up, but the roadway was strewn with small branches and evergreen boughs. Lori wondered what it was like to live in elegant, sprawling homes like those she saw out the window. In her own household, money was always tight, since her mother was a single parent with only a clerical position. Lori thought it might be nice to live another way some day, just for awhile.

"I'll do whatever it takes to save you," Camilla vowed. "I feel like I'm fighting for your life."

"I'll bet you're lying about Daddy," Lori said, ignoring her mother's words. "You probably drove him away by being frigid."

"That's better than dressing like a whore. Your skirt is too high and you wear a pound of makeup."

A headstrong girl, Lori removed her safety harness and lifted the door button. The dented passenger door creaked open, and she tried to get out of the car while it was rolling. With surprising strength her mother grabbed her by the arm and jerked her back inside, then pulled the car over to the side of the road.

"You could have been killed, Lori!" Camilla said. She cried for a moment, then reined in her tears with a burst of anger.

"I don't care."

"Put your safety harness back on, young lady. *Now.*"

With furious energy, Lori complied, because she didn't really want to die. She had only opened the door of the moving car for dramatic effect. In reality, Lori Vale always thought she had something significant to do with her life, that one day she would be involved in a really important activity. At this point, though, she just didn't know what form that might take.

Ever since Lori's younger years—and in many respects she considered herself quite *old* now—she had felt things instinctually, as if able to sense another realm, or a form of energy that others did not detect. It was not a subject she liked to discuss with even her closest friends, and certainly not with her own mother, because she feared people would laugh at her. For now, she preferred to keep it as her own little secret. The ability served her well on occasion, enabling her to detect the motives of people, whether they were out for their own interests or if they were true friends. Or so she thought.

Camilla opened a small packet containing a moist towelette, and used it to remove makeup from Lori's face, while the girl grimaced and tried to turn away. "Where are the earrings I gave you?" her mother demanded. "I told you to wear them tonight."

"I don't know." Lori was lying. The pearl-and-gold earrings (a gift on her last birthday) were in a pocket of her skirt.

Muttering an epithet under her breath, Camilla pulled back onto the road. Several minutes later she slowed to read a street sign, then grabbed her notes from the seat beside her, concerning the location of the meeting. She flipped on the dome light. It cast a yellow glow.

"This is it," she announced. "West Glen."

"Whoopty-doo."

Camilla switched off the interior light and turned onto a narrow street, which climbed sharply. At the top of the hill the road curved left. "That must be it," she said, pointing to a beige colonial with three dormers.

As they pulled into a space in front of the house, Lori noted a neatly edged lawn, with rhododendrons and azaleas in winter dormancy, their leaves curled and stiff. The home featured large windows, which she guessed must provide a fine view of Lake Washington and the tall buildings of the Seattle skyline. Two late model imported cars were parked beside the driveway, along with a new off-road hovercraft. The garage doors were open, revealing a Cadillac and a Mercedes.

While walking to the house, Lori noticed that the sky was a wash of gray-black with a sprinkling of visible stars. A cold wind whipped across the moonlit waters of the lake. A chill ran down the girl's spine, but she didn't know why. She stared up at the house, and women who were visible inside at a second floor window, milling around, talking.

Something rustled in the bushes.

Camilla let out a cry.

"Just a cat," Lori said, watching a gray-and-white feline, illuminated in yard lights, as it scurried across the lawn and disappeared into the backyard.

The pair climbed brick steps to the creaky, wooden front porch, where Camilla rapped a brass lion's head clapper mounted on the door. The soft tones of women's voices could be heard inside.

But no one answered.

A peculiar feeling came over Lori, an odd mixture of fear and excitement.

Camilla rapped again, but still no one came to the door.

With a splash of headlights across the porch, a green sports car pulled into the driveway and squeaked to a stop behind one of the open garage doors. An exotically beautiful dark-skinned woman emerged and climbed the steps to the porch. Without a word she opened the door and stepped inside.

The woman hesitated, looked back. "Are you going to join us?" she asked.

"We rang the bell and knocked," Camilla said, "but no one answered."

"I'm sure it's all right to go in," the woman said. She glanced at her watch. "They're about to begin."

Trying to sort out her feelings, Lori went inside with the others.

* * *

In the front passenger seat, Styx felt the throbbing heartbeat of the V-Warrior attack helicopter as it bore him westward. The Cascade Mountains of Washington State lay in moonlight below, with their craggy tops casting fantastic shadows across the nightscape, as if the mountains were living creatures that had been frozen in time by the ice and snow.

The aircraft looked like an ordinary transport chopper, but it had concealed gun ports and missile launchers. It was not one of the stealth aircraft that the Bureau had, because none of them were available on short notice for this mission. It didn't matter to Styx; this disguised attack craft was all they needed.

Glancing back into the rear compartment, he saw the eight members of his squad sitting motionless, with the portholes beside them letting in moonlight that glinted off the silver portions of their uniforms. They wore black helmets fitted tightly to their heads like second skins, with their eyes concealed behind narrow slits.

Styx's heart matched the iciness of the night as he thought of the Satanic women who would feel his wrath tonight, especially Dixie Lou Jackson, second in command in the UWW, just as he was in the BOI.

"Bring her in alive if you can," Culpepper had ordered.

But that wasn't Styx's intention, and the men in his squad were fiercely loyal to him. He would do whatever he pleased.

Chapter 4

They want a reversion to the mythical days of when we didn't talk back as much, when women were little more than slaves to the interests of men.

–Amy Angkor-Billings, United Women of the World

In central México, Consuela Santos was filled with fear. A young peasant woman whose father tilled the land and whose mother cooked and cleaned for the local parish priest, Consuela had shamed her parents by bearing a child out of wedlock. She and her baby—now five months old—still lived with them in their small adobe house, but so religious were they that they had not spoken to her in weeks.

It had been an unseasonably warm day, but now Consuela pulled her thin *rebozo* around her shoulders to ward off the night wind, and held her baby close, wrapped in the long scarf. She passed the town *cantina*, moving through dim light cast through an open door and windows, and heard the drunken patrons inside, laughing and talking loudly. Across the street were the cloth-draped merchant stalls of the *mercado*, which only a few hours before had been the bustling center of commerce for three villages, but which now lay dark and quiet. She smelled the spoiling remnants of fruit, vegetables, and fly-encrusted meat, and saw a mangy, swaybacked street dog eating scraps.

From fear she could hardly catch her breath. Holding the bundled child securely, she turned onto a narrow cobblestone street, hurried up broad stone steps and entered the village church, pulling her *rebozo* over her head and uttering a prayer as the cool darkness of the interior enclosed her. She kept glancing back, to make sure no one followed. People were looking for her child. They called themselves doctors and claimed they only wanted to help, but she knew better.

Her baby had been making strange sounds, and she suspected something evil had possessed her, something that could only be purged in this holy sanctuary.

The people who sought little Marta were not really doctors; that was only a ruse to make her let down her guard. They were too intense and she saw something in their eyes. Deception and malevolence. In reality they were servants of the dark prince—Satan—and wanted her precious child for their secret, unholy purposes. She felt this in the deepest core of her being, and that they had put a spell on Marta.

Consuela knew her demonic pursuers wouldn't dare enter the church. As the heavy wooden door closed behind her and she stood in the vaulted Spanish sanctuary, she breathed a deep sigh of relief. On her right, red votive candles burned, flickering at the kiss of a slight and ghostly breeze. Townspeople had lit them, to pray for friends or family members.

With her heart beating rapidly she hurried along the main aisle, past the rows of pews to the altar. Towering beside her, a statue of the crucified Jesus was flanked by the smaller statues of two women, one the Virgin Mary, and the other the Virgin of Guadalupe, patron saint of México. Before the latter, she knelt and prayed. The saint's face was benign, and seemed to gaze down on Consuela and her baby compassionately, giving them personal attention and protection.

Behind her, three other people knelt inside the high-vaulted building, praying silently in the dark-wood pews. Upon passing them she'd noticed Bibles in their hands. No one escaped her scrutiny now, because of the extreme danger.

In Consuela's arms, her baby made the strange, unholy sounds again, this time too loudly. Putting a hand over her child's mouth, she muffled the blasphemy that she could sense, but could not comprehend.

The black-robed parish priest slipped out of a door behind Consuela and glided past her, going toward a door that led to the bell tower. She almost called out to him, but decided not to. He was Father Matteo, who employed her mother to cook and clean.

The baby whimpered, and continued the muffled, abhorrent sounds.

Out of the corner of her eye, Consuela saw the black-robed priest pause and gaze back at her. He had a puzzled expression on his weathered face, which was half in shadows and half in the flickering yellow light of a candle.

The baby kicked and thrashed, and went into a screaming, crying tirade.

Hesitantly, the priest approached her.

Behind Consuela, she heard the heavy door of the church slam shut, and felt a hot breath of outside air.

At the head of the aisle, looking in her direction, Consuela saw what appeared to be a large woman in a white dress. She couldn't make out details of the face. The woman began walking toward her. She was carrying what might be a medical bag, but it was white, not the customary black. Her lapels were starched and stiff. Her shoes squeaked on the tile floor.

Consuela looked at the priest, and saw his hand go into a pocket of his robe as the big woman approached. He appeared to be afraid of her.

Does he have a weapon there? A priest with a gun?

She didn't know why she was thinking so strangely, so conversely to everything she had been taught in her life. She was twenty-four years old and had always been a good Catholic; it was in her blood, as much a part of her as the child she held so tightly in her arms. Her faith had always been her anchor, providing her with strength and constancy and the knowledge that her life was connected to something more important than her solitary, meager existence. But her faith was a broad white sail as well, linking her with an ethereal wind that guided all humankind on a heavenly course.

How did this holy man fit into such a structure?

Her pulse drummed and thrummed in her ears.

Keeping his hand in his pocket, the priest moved briskly toward her.

By now the other figure—approaching from the aisle—had halved the distance to Consuela. Out of the shadow-face of this person emerged two burning red embers for eyes, like fiery fragments wrenched from the bowels of Hades.

The priest reached her first and placed a hand on her shoulder. He smelled of fear. Sweat glistened on his brow. "My child," he said in their native Spanish, "you are troubled, and I—"

Consuela wasn't looking at him. The other figure neared, moving slowly, inexorably, and the terrified peasant woman no longer saw ember-eyes, replaced instead by a white visage and the palest of albino orbs, staring directly at her. She wondered if all this was only her imagination, if she was trapped in a wild kaleidoscope of the mind, a spinning, topsy-turvy nightmare. For some reason she felt a threat not only from this person but from the priest. She didn't trust either of them. The priest's grip tightened on her shoulder.

The woman reached into her white bag.

Consuela bolted and ran out a side door into the night. The church was no longer a sanctuary. It had been invaded by evil, an extension of the entity that was trying to destroy her child.

Shouts and gunfire sounded behind her, and a bullet struck the door frame as she ran into the street, but neither she nor her baby were hit. Dogs barked frantically.

A man screamed out in agony. It sounded like Father Matteo.

She didn't dare look back.

* * *

A tiny nun in a black habit hurried through the grand corridor, her smallness and simple garb contrasting with the exquisite craftsmanship and immensity of scale around her . . . the Italian marble floor, the ornate mirrors, gilded walls, leaded glass, and vaulted ceiling, the paintings of Christian religious scenes by renowned masters, the sculptures of famous popes and cardinals. On the third finger of her left hand she wore a golden band, signifying the sacred wedding vow she had given to her blessed savior, Jesus Christ.

At a Gothic entrance portal she stood before two Swiss Guards who wore sixteenth century body armor with royal purple and gold leggings and red headdresses. Each man carried an automatic rifle. It was shortly after 7:00 AM in Vatican City.

Beneath the folds of her robe the nun carried a glass message cylinder, which she brought forth and displayed for the guards. One of the guards looked it over, then waved her in with a jerky motion of one arm.

She passed through into a waiting room that featured intricately designed blue-and-white mosaic tiles. Two more Swiss Guards stood at another door, which led to the papal offices.

The door to the inner sanctum swung open, and an angular, ruddy-faced man in a white vestment emerged, walking toward her energetically. Pope Rodrigo held one hand on a golden cross that dangled from his neck. He ushered her in, smiling broadly. "Ah, Sister Meryl," he said as they walked together into his enormous, exquisitely appointed office, "It is good to see you!"

This nun was from his own home city of Segovia, Spain—and he liked her so much that he always came out to greet her in this fashion. They knew many of the same people, and often shared stories and gossip.

"And you as well, Your Holiness." She bowed. "May I say, you are looking especially well today."

"You have brought me another recipe?" he asked, knowing full well that only official business was carried in such a manner.

She giggled, revealing a toothy smile. With a diminutive mouth, smooth skin, and clear brown eyes, she appeared much younger than her sixty-three years.

Accepting the cylinder from her, he brought forth a sparkling diamond key and opened it. The cylinder twisted into two sections. He removed a slip of parchment from one of them and left the sections on his desk.

"Mmmm," he said as he read. "Minister Culpepper again, but this time he isn't asking for money."

She nodded, and despite her familiarity with the pontiff she maintained her place, not asking any questions.

"It seems he has a twelve-year-old grandson who wants to embark upon a career with the Church. The boy's father is a manufacturing executive, taking a position in Rome."

"I see," Sister Meryl said.

"Culpepper says the boy is bright and a fast learner." Then, with a heaving sigh, the Pope set the parchment on an ornate side table. "In four years—when he's sixteen—we'll set him up as a clerk while he attends seminary."

"Do you have any orders for me?" she inquired.

"Yes," he said with mock seriousness. "Wear my robes for awhile and deal with all the important people who want favors."

* * *

Half an hour later, Sister Meryl sent a coded e-mail message to UWW headquarters, informing them what had occurred that day in the papal offices. From minuscule to large details, she had been providing them efficiently for more than two decades. The week before, she had transmitted other records on the Roman Catholic Church, updating information that the UWW already had on the religious organization's real estate holdings and other assets all over the world. This was absorbed into the burgeoning UWW data base, along with similar facts on every other religious group on earth.

Sister Meryl wondered what the UWW did with all of it, and what their plans might be, although she believed in the group because they advanced the cause of women. Lately she'd been hearing intriguing rumors that the female leadership had embarked upon a top secret project. She liked their energy. The United Women of the World, in contrast with the Catholic Church, was dynamic and in a constant state of flux.

Chapter 5

The omissions of recorded history are substantial, and sometimes the process of recovering lost information takes surprising turns.
—Report of the Commission on the She-Apostles

As they entered the house, the woman introduced herself as Su-Su Florida, a real estate agent. "Do you live near here?" she asked Camilla.

"Across Lake Washington—in Seattle."

The woman's brow wrinkled and she gazed down her nose, as if she considered the Vales interlopers from an inferior social class. "Oh," she said, and hurried down the hallway.

Camilla and a hesitant Lori followed. The teenager absorbed everything around her. She sensed something very peculiar here, but was unable to identify it. Her stomach was turning over.

Incense burned on William and Mary side tables, which had Christian objects arranged on them, including Rosary beads and angel candle holders. A small painting of Jesus Christ adorned one wall of the entry, and across from that a large painting of St. Joan of Arc depicted her in a suit of armor, leading the soldiers of the French Dauphin, Charles VII, into battle.

The visitors entered a tastefully decorated living room, featuring deep cushion Queen Anne chairs, a Chippendale sofa, and a Goddard desk. A large painting of the crucified Jesus hung over the fireplace. Women were moving furniture out of the way, with a short but muscular black woman of around forty directing the work. She wore a loose-fitting white gauze dress with dangling bracelets of oversized black beads, and an unusual necklace: a gold cross with the lower portion of it shaped like a sword blade. Her hair was braided, clasped on one side by a wood and leather barrette. From the lobes of her ears hung large gold earrings, and glittering golden boots covered her feet.

"Welcome to my associate's home, everyone," she said, in a soft Southern drawl. "I'm Dixie Lou Jackson, the surprise speaker." In her hands she held the statuette of a woman.

A murmur of excitement passed through the room, but Lori didn't know why. "She's second in command of the UWW," Camilla said, "an umbrella organization for this goddess circle and others like it around the world."

This still didn't provide much information to Lori. The UWW? She'd never heard of it. Apprehensively, she stared at Jackson, and held gazes with her for a moment. Dixie Lou gave her a hard glare, but only her eyes were unfriendly. The rest of her face smiled.

Lori felt a sick queasiness in the pit of her stomach.

The teenager glanced to her left at an Early American side table where a large *Bible* lay, with pink tabs sticking from the pages. Beside that lay an open notebook with the handwritten heading, "Quotes Detrimental to Women," and beneath that were biblical references. She noted one, Genesis 3:16: "And thy desire shall be to thy husband, and he shall rule over thee."

She had read passages from the *Bible* and even liked them, but didn't recall seeing that quotation or the others that were entered on the pages of the notebook. They made her think.

Flipping pages, she found an especially intriguing entry: "Jesus did not say that women are to be subordinate." It had no attribution, so maybe it was the finding of one of the women in this house.

Her mother tugged at her arm. "Come on Lori. They're getting ready for the meeting."

Dixie Lou directed the attendees to sit on the floor in a circle. One of them was an elderly blind woman, guided by a German Shepherd dog. Lori overheard the woman saying the animal used to be a police dog.

On the floor at the center of the group, a round piece of dark-stained oak was placed, upon the surface of which Jackson arranged candle holders of glass, pottery and pewter that depicted female themes, including little girls, mothers with babies, and female angels and goddesses. In the middle of the candle arrangement she placed the statuette of the woman, which Lori now noticed held a tiny weapon in her upturned palms, a sword that looked like a modified Christian cross—matching the one hanging from the neck of the hostess.

Su-Su Florida and a dark woman in a sari (she might have been East Indian) lit the candles. The electric lights were dimmed low, giving the room an eerie, funereal appearance. A shiver coursed Lori's spine. The women found their places and sat quietly. Camilla did the same, and forced Lori to do so as well, despite her protestations. Through a window she could see a large saffron moon hanging low over the city of Seattle and its brightly-lit high-rises that cast glittering reflections on the lake.

The discontented teenager set her purse on the floor beside her, and folded her arms across her chest. She tried to analyze her feelings. Angry with her mother, she didn't want to be here. A dark, disturbing sensation of danger crept over her, and a growing curiosity about these eccentric women, which she struggled to fight off. Part of her wanted to disrupt their meeting and get herself tossed out.

It grew quiet in the house except for a little whimper from the guide dog, which stood stiffly across the circle from Lori, looking in her direction. Dixie Lou held what looked like a black plastic remote control for a VR-TV set. She pressed a button, and dulcet, ethereal piano music seeped into the room. After a minute, the music faded.

Glancing at her watch, Dixie Lou asked, "Shall we begin now?" She gazed at Lori, who sat cross-legged beside her mother.

The attention disturbed Lori, and she looked away. On a side table across the room, she noticed pots of herbal tea and ceramic mugs. She smelled something acrid, like the residue of marijuana smoke on clothing, and wished she could get to the stash in her own purse in order to relax her nerves. She thought the source of the odor might be a middle-aged woman near her who wore a cotton dress with a batik print and a bead necklace. An overage hippie by all appearances, she was the type Lori's friends derisively referred to as "granola," based upon a common food they were said to favor.

Lori considered teasing her mother, telling her there was a marijuana aroma in the room, but Dixie Lou distracted her by pressing the transmitter and saying, " Unless someone objects, we're recording this."

No one spoke up.

In a corner of the room, the red light on a holo-recorder blinked on.

Dixie Lou spoke for several minutes about a women's issue that bored Lori, since she didn't care much about such matters. Why should she? Adults didn't understand the problems she was going through as a young woman, so why should she pay attention to their concerns? She'd rather be with her friends when they gathered at a waterfront park in the middle of the night, or at their pool hall and bowling alley hangouts. She missed Jeremy, a boy she'd met at a party the week before, and with whom she'd grown close in only a few days. She thought he was cute, and liked his hip way of talking and the tiny pearl earrings he wore on both ears.

Most of all she missed her best friend, Alicia Koppel. For more than two years they'd been inseparable, and had shared the endless problems of growing up. Now she needed Alicia more than ever, but couldn't reach her.

In memory she heard Alicia's voice, saying in street slang, *"Hey dopegirl, you high-flyin'?"*

Then Lori noticed the dog had come around behind her and was sniffing at her purse, whimpering again. It had been a police dog.

No! Lori thought. *Get away from me*!

The dog pawed the purse, and Lori pulled the bag away, holding it on her lap.

"Bobo was the top drug-sniffer in the department," the blind woman said.

Thinking fast, Lori said, "I had some food in my purse today, and he probably smells it." She nudged the animal away, and reluctantly it returned to its master.

The "granola" woman—despite the aroma around her—appeared to be of no interest to the dog.

Without looking, Lori knew her mother was staring at her, and the teenager felt her face burning. Maybe she could get to the bathroom and flush the stuff down the toilet.

Dixie Lou asked everyone to hold hands, which Lori refused to do, and instead she kept her arms folded across her chest. Jackson uttered a strange prayer to an entity she called "She-God," which she described as "all-powerful" and "the hope for womankind." Then she asked those in attendance to identify themselves by name and occupation.

She-God? Comparative Religion was one of the few classes Lori had enjoyed in high school (and she'd done well in it), but she'd never heard of a deity by that name. She wanted to tell herself it was just another absurdity in a long line of ridiculous things in her mother's life. But Lori wasn't so certain this time.

One by one the attendees identified themselves, with Camilla going first, providing a bland description of her secretarial job for the Fort Lawton Army base in Seattle, in a civilian secretarial pool. The participants moved around the circle away from Lori, and a wiry woman with dark hair said she owned an herbal pharmacy in the suburbs, with exotic ingredients imported from all over the world. The sari-adorned woman, with a pinched face and tiny eyes, spoke of a She-God temple— whatever that was—in her backyard, and said she sold handmade religious paraphernalia. Su-Su Florida made a pathetic, thinly veiled sales pitch for her high-earth orbital excursion agency, and another woman said she was a family counselor.

When Lori's turn came, last among the visitors, she announced in a firm voice, "I'm a hopeless cigarette junkie."

"Lori!" her mother whispered, as embarrassment reddened her face.

Then Lori proceeded to light a cigarette, fending off her mother as she did so.

All around the circle, the women glared at the rebellious teenager and whispered to each other. Even the blind woman seemed to be looking at her disapprovingly, with eerie white, sightless eyes.

"Lori, give me that cigarette!" her mother insisted, in full voice.

With a slight smile, Dixie Lou picked up the statuette and approached the errant girl. She knelt down, face-to-face with Lori. The teenager blew a puff of pink, scented smoke in the woman's face, as her mother groaned in displeasure.

"I'm sorry she's being like this," Camilla said. "Perhaps we should leave. She didn't want to come tonight. I've been having trouble with her."

"What brand of cigarette is that?" Dixie Lou inquired of Lori, in the calmest of tones.

"Pink Paradise."

"I've told her a thousand times not to smoke," Camilla said. "I just don't know what I'm going to do with this girl."

"Regular or light?" Dixie Lou asked, still focused on Lori.

With a perplexed expression, the girl replied, "Regular."

"My favorite. May I have a drag?"

Before Lori could reply, the woman had the cigarette in her hand and was inhaling deeply from it.

"But let's do this afterward, okay?" Dixie Lou said. She dropped the cigarette into a flower vase, where it fizzled out in water. "We'll smoke and have a nice little chat, OK, Lori? So you're a hopeless addict, eh?"

"Yeah. I'd have my lips sewn onto a giant cigarette if I could."

"You're awful, Lori," her mother said. "You used to be such a nice girl. Always respectful and a good student. I don't know what's come over you."

"You do have quite an imagination," Dixie Lou Jackson said to the girl. "Maybe it'll make you famous someday."

Lori considered lighting a second cigarette, but resisted the urge. Instead she took a deep breath and stared back into the woman's dark brown, impenetrable eyes, a gaze that bored into her.

"A most interesting young woman," Dixie Lou observed, at long last. "An old soul, I suspect, despite the clever subterfuge she's putting on for us."

Lori squirmed. She felt warm, uncomfortable, didn't like this woman for some reason, and it had nothing to do with the fact that she was black. Lori knew a lot of street people, of many races, and made no superficial judgments about them—not based upon skin color or any other aspect of their appearance.

An old soul? Maybe she's right. And maybe I don't like the way she looks too closely at me.

Dixie Lou's cimmerian eyes glistened. "We're here this evening to discuss women's issues, Lori. And it's about time, too. For thousands of years people have been talking too much about men's issues, and the world has suffered for it. Have you ever noticed that most women are less violent than men, less aggressive, less destructive? Women are even better drivers, so they get lower insurance rates."

Lori didn't respond. *What kind of weird talk is this?* she thought.

Dixie Lou continued: "If we're so much better than men, why do you suppose we haven't been more important throughout history?"

Lori shrugged. She felt perspiration on her upper lip, wiped the moisture off.

"Because men are physically stronger," Camilla suggested. "Because they—bully us, dominate us."

"Precisely," Dixie Lou said, "because we've been pushed, slugged, slapped, stabbed, beaten, raped, and shot for thousands of years. But I'm here to tell you we won't be treated that way anymore."

Lori didn't respond, but her mother and others murmured assent.

"Remember, Lori," Dixie Lou said, "you can do anything if you set your mind to it. You can accomplish *anything.*"

"We're just as good as men are!" a woman exclaimed.

"Better!" Dixie Lou shouted.

A murmur of assent passed around the circle, which consisted of fourteen women and Lori.

"Do you know who this is?" Dixie Lou asked, pointing to the statuette of the woman.

Lori shook her head, smelled the burning wax of the candles.

"It's She-God, representing all women since time immemorial. We'll discuss what She's holding later this evening."

Momentarily, Lori focused on the tiny sword. Again, she wiped perspiration from her upper lip.

Returning to her original place, Dixie Lou spoke briefly about herself. Without elaboration, she said she was an executive, and that she had not led a goddess circle for a long time. And she asked, "Why do you suppose we're all here?"

Lori saw blank faces looking back at the group leader.

"To feel better about ourselves," Su-Su said. "We've been pounded down by the system."

"And who runs the system?" Dixie Lou asked, rhetorically.

"Men!" several women said, simultaneously.

In the distance, Lori heard what sounded like the rhythmic throb of a jet helicopter.

"Some of you have attended these circles before," Dixie Lou said. "But such experiences pale in comparison with what lies in store for womankind!"

Lori found herself staring at the statuette, which stood amid the burning candles. The figurine was strangely familiar, something that . . . or representing something that . . . lay just beyond the reach of her memory.

"Men have written most of the history books," Dixie Lou was saying in the background of Lori's awareness. "But think of this: What about *her*story books? Instead of history, written by men about men, herstory is *our* story, the tale of female journeys written by us. Much of our past is veiled in mystery, because men have perverted and destroyed the truth. They have rewritten it in order to maintain themselves in power, making themselves look good at our expense."

Lori didn't fully agree with what she was hearing. Sure there had been abuses by men against women over the centuries. Every intelligent, liberal-thinking person knew that. But she liked boys and one day she would like men. Besides, things had gotten better for women, hadn't they? Weren't most American men treating the ladies in their lives with respect now, as equals?

She sighed, wished she knew the truth about her father, not the distorted, incomplete version told by her mother. She didn't know where he was, if he was alive or dead. All such inquiries she'd made to her mother had been rebuffed. She missed him, remembered fun they'd had together when she was small . . . before he went away.

As Lori watched, Dixie Lou adjusted the position of the statuette.

Suddenly something surged in the girl's mind, a powerful but unformed and unclear thought.

She locked gazes with Dixie Lou, and a violent shudder passed through the black woman, whose dark eyes were open wide in shock and fear. Dixie Lou pulled her hand away from the statuette, and her lips moved without making a discernible sound.

The noises of the helicopter grew louder, a throbbing, vibrating intrusion. To Lori, the craft seemed to be passing directly overhead at very low altitude. Almost too close, it seemed.

Dixie Lou snapped to awareness. Her gaze darted around wildly, like a trapped animal.

The noise grew louder still, and remained that way for several moments. Then a percussive explosion shook the house, followed by the thunderous crash of glass, and the glare of bright lights outside. Through the window Lori got a glimpse of a helicopter. A uniformed man knelt on the running board, firing an automatic rifle at the house. Another man behind him hurled something that crashed through a kitchen window. A second explosion rocked the house.

Camilla scrambled for cover, pulling Lori with her. The girl grabbed for her purse, but dropped it.

Screams filled the air, and the guide dog barked. Something heavy landed on the roof. Men shouted outside, amidst the helicopter noise and gunfire.

"What the hell is going on?" the blind woman cried out. Then she screamed as the front door burst open, followed by a burst of gunfire that tore through her chest and face. Her horribly mutilated body thudded to the floor. Another woman wailed, "Oh God, I'm dying! Who would do this to us? Why?"

Concealed from the gunmen by a couch and desk that had been moved aside for the meeting, Camilla and Lori crawled toward the hallway behind them. Bullets shattered a glass-fronted Victorian cabinet, and Camilla complained of pain in her lower legs. Then something exploded by the right side of her head. She crumpled to the floor.

"Mom!" Lori cried out. She saw two men in the living room, carrying automatic rifles. Silver-and-black uniforms with caps, and black cross insignia on the lapels and arms.

Fighting tears of rage, she dragged her mother into the hallway and then into a large hall closet, pulling the door shut behind them to form a dark cocoon.

Lori's heart raced. She felt her mother's wrist, checking for a pulse. It was erratic.

"I'll be okay, sweetheart," Camilla assured her, struggling to speak. Her voice faded. "I'm . . . fine."

Lori suppressed a sob. She felt the wrist again. The pulse was slow.

"Mom!" she husked. "Mom!"

No response.

How badly was she hurt? There wasn't enough light to see, and the girl was afraid to poke around on the head, for fear of exacerbating the injury. Her mother's legs had been wounded, too, so Lori worried about a severed artery. Hurriedly, she removed her own long cotton stockings and tied one tightly around each of her mother's thighs, hoping these makeshift tourniquets would slow any loss of blood.

Sticky wetness covered the right side of Camilla's head, a definite wound, so this was the side Lori kept up, atop her lap. It seemed to her that the wound would bleed less this way. She prayed it was only superficial.

Hugging her mother tightly, she wished she hadn't been disrespectful to her. Camilla was unresponsive, breathing irregularly.

"Mom, can you hear me?" Lori whispered.

Still no answer. The breathing became more erratic, then settled into a regular pattern.

Oh God, Lori thought. *Please don't let my mother die! Take me if you must, but not her!* She remembered seeing the blind woman hit by gunfire and falling. And many of the others. They had to be dead. It was so horrible, so senseless.

The thickly-carpeted closet was devoid of objects. Desperately, Lori felt in the darkness around the edges of the rug. Lifting a corner she found a smooth, hard surface beneath. There was no hatch leading to a crawl space, no escape.

An explosion rocked the house. Shouts came from another room, and more gunfire. The dog started barking again, then gunfire sounded and the animal yelped.

"Four minutes!" someone called out. Lori couldn't tell if it was male or female. The voice was peculiar, a high-pitched whine.

She heard the voice again, a little farther away this time, shouting commands. This person seemed to be in charge. Gunfire rang repeatedly.

A woman cried out: "Save us, oh She-God!"

She-God again? Lori didn't understand. Dixie Lou had said the entity was all-powerful, and what else? She couldn't recall.

Cautiously, she opened the closet door, but it bumped into something. She pushed harder, saw that a woman's body was blocking the door. Squeezing out through the opening, she identified Su-Su Florida on the floor, not moving. Blood ran from her side, pooling on the hardwood beneath her.

Feeling the woman's carotid artery, Lori detected no heartbeat at all.

"She's dead," a voice said, startling the girl. Turning quickly, she saw Dixie Lou Jackson, who had emerged from another doorway. Blood ran down her face, from a deep gash high on her forehead. "That way,"

Dixie Lou said, pointing to a closed door at the end of the corridor. She gave Lori a shove in that direction, but the girl resisted.

Going back, Lori dragged her mother out into the corridor, while Dixie Lou protested, trying to get her to go the other way. Dixie Lou went ahead.

Struggling with the almost lifeless weight of her mother, the teenager made her way to the door just as Dixie Lou opened it. Breathing hard, the UWW officer leaned against the door jamb.

The door opened into a garage, but not the one in the front of the house that Lori had seen upon arrival. On the side of the house, then? At the rear? In the confusion she had lost all sense of direction. The small garage, illuminated by an overhead bank of lights, contained only one vehicle—a sleek, black van with tinted windows and mirror-like tires and wheels. Everything high-gloss.

"Help me into the van!" Dixie Lou said.

But Lori pushed by her and pulled her mother toward the vehicle instead. Cursing and muttering at the teenager, Dixie Lou stumbled behind her, and closed the door behind them.

Lori tried to open the rear passenger side door of the van, but it wouldn't budge.

"Get out of the way," Dixie Lou said. She touched what looked like the same black hand-held transmitter she had used inside the house, for control of the music and holo-recording system. The van's door slid open, and the rear seats folded flat into the floor.

Lori laid her mother on the floor and propped a folded blanket under her head, while Dixie Lou went around toward the driver's side door. Suddenly the black woman cried out, and fell on the concrete, face down. She twitched and groaned. Hurrying to her, Lori saw another wound, on the back of her neck.

As quickly as she could, Lori helped her into the front passenger seat and engaged the safety harness, which clicked over her the moment it was touched. Lori also had contact with Dixie Lou.

Abruptly, the teenagers neck flopped to one side. "What are you doing?" Dixie Lou asked.

Lori hesitated, because she had received a strange tingling when she touched the woman, somewhat like when she felt the paper of the goddess circle flier. She shook her head to clear it, said, "I'm going to drive. I don't have a license, but I know how anyway."

"Not necessary. Get me the remote control. I just had it a moment ago. Look outside for me."

Lori did as she was told, found the unit and climbed into the driver's seat, closing the door. She handed the device to Dixie Lou, who fumbled with it and swore, trying to make it work. Finally, she slammed it down on the console and said, "Doesn't work. You'll have to drive after all."

Fighting to remain conscious, with blood running down her forehead and neck, Dixie Lou muttered something about a homing signal they were supposed to pick up, and she must have damaged the transceiver when she fell.

Following additional instructions, Lori punched a code on a dashboard computer pad. The engine surged on, and the garage door slid open behind the vehicle.

"Let's go, let's go!" Dixie Lou said. "Drive this thing fast."

"OK." Lori put the van in reverse.

Seeing a black handgun on the console between her and Dixie Lou, Lori grabbed it. The gun, a .45 long-barrel, was heavier than her mother's .38 that she had used for target practice, and was one of the new rapid-fire automatics, but she thought she could figure it out. On the handle of the weapon she saw what looked like a sword-cross design.

For a moment, the woman met Lori's gaze, with eyes full of pain. "I hope you know how to use that," she said.

"I do." Lori released the safety and cocked the weapon, then laid it on her lap. With a silent prayer, she nudged the accelerator and roared backward out of the garage, onto a side driveway. The house was illuminated in spotlights from the helicopter, which hovered noisily overhead. Flashes of illumination came from the house as the van backed up.

From somewhere, men shouted. In the rear of the vehicle, her mother struggled to call her name, the word barely rising above the din. "Lori . . ."

"Just hold on, Mom. I'll get us out of this."

But bursts of gunfire sounded and bullets thudded into the front of the van, narrowly missing Dixie Lou. For a moment, Lori lost control of the vehicle. It smashed against a landscape rock and stopped momentarily. Then she corrected the steering, bumped the accelerator and resumed backing up.

Seeing uniformed men rush onto the driveway behind her, she opened the electric window by her, put her head out and fired at them, pulling the trigger until the clip was empty. She saw two of the assailants fall.

"Good shooting!" Dixie Lou said as Lori continued to steer in reverse, wildly.

Lori's body shook uncontrollably. Tears streamed down her face. She threw the empty gun on the console, next to Dixie Lou. What was going on here? She could not imagine.

I killed those men! It was the first time she'd ever fired a gun at anyone.

At high speed, Lori whipped the van onto a private lane that ran behind the houses. She wished she'd been able to get her mother into a safety harness, hoped she wasn't getting banged around too badly back there. The helicopter and more men could be seen in one direction, so Lori went the opposite way, rocketing past backyards and houses with the vehicle's headlights off. The lane curved down to a main street and she turned a hard right onto it, with tires screeching as she accelerated. She took several turns and side streets at Dixie Lou's instruction, and soon the whining, throbbing noise of the helicopter and the gunfire could no longer be heard. Occasional street lights illuminated the way, so she could see well enough without the headlights.

A siren sounded, and a police car raced by in the opposite direction, blue lights flashing.

"That was a BOI attack," Dixie Lou said, holding a cloth on the back of her neck. "Trained killers." She let loose a torrent of expletives.

Lori didn't know what she was talking about, but didn't care. She only thought about her mother. Now she felt a steeliness in her soul over the men she had shot, and knew she would do it again if she had to.

Suddenly a car roared down a side street and pulled directly in front of the van, without bothering to pause at the stop sign. Lori slammed on her brakes to avoid a collision.

"How do I turn on the headlights?" she asked.

"We can't use them. We must be extremely careful."

The black woman kept craning her neck to look up at the sky. Lori did that too as she drove, and listened for helicopter noises. She didn't hear any.

Calling for her mother, she received no response. The breathing remained slow. In a passing street light she glanced back and saw Camilla huddled on the floor, with the stocking tourniquets visible on her legs.

Her heart jumped when she again heard helicopter rotors throbbing.

The sound grew louder.

Following Dixie Lou's order, Lori pulled the dark van into a driveway, beneath a large tree.

The aircraft seemed to be directly overhead, and Lori saw the terrifying wash of a searchlight over the streets and houses.

She prayed.

The noise grew very loud, then diminished and disappeared.

Chapter 6

The gospels of the she-apostles were stolen from all humankind, not just from women.

    —Amy Angkor-Billings, to her biographer, December 11, 2033

In the shadows of the van, Lori didn't think it possible that soldiers had attacked a women's meeting. No legitimate authority would murder unarmed women. Dixie Lou had said they were BOI, but what did that stand for and who were they? Lori couldn't believe this was happening.

The van rolled along the freeway now, with Dixie Lou having used the hand-held transmitter to turn on the headlights. The vehicle was in a flow of traffic crossing the Mercer Island Airbridge, going west toward Seattle. Ahead, Lori saw blinking lights in the sky above the city. Big jets circling, waiting to land at Boeing Field and SeaTac Airport. She could also make out the lights of smaller craft. Thankfully she heard no helicopter sounds.

Following Dixie Lou's instructions, Lori drove through a tunnel and entered the city, with the irregular shape of what looked like a hospital visible on a high hill just ahead. A helicopter was setting down near the building, maybe a MediVac craft for emergency medical transport.

"How do we get up to that hospital?" Lori asked, for she didn't know which exit to take.

"We don't," came the flat response.

"My mother is badly injured! She needs a doctor!"

"No time for that. We're leaving Seattle."

"Not with us. I'm taking her to a hospital!"

"Be quiet!" Dixie Lou snapped. She grabbed the handgun between them, slammed another clip into it and waved it menacingly in the air.

Lori wondered who this crazy woman was, and thought back to the high-pitched voice of the leader of the raid, with its eerie, androgynous quality. Dixie Lou's enemy.

"This isn't right," Lori said. "I saved your life back there."

"Keep silent," Dixie Lou responded, "or so help me—" Her eyelids flickered, and Lori thought she was going to pass out. Then the woman did something with the transmitter, and a metallic woman's voice said over a speaker, "Locking onto signal. You are now within range."

Suddenly Lori no longer had control of the vehicle. It kept rolling, accelerating and decelerating in traffic. The steering ball spun freely in her hands without any control over the van. She stepped on the brakes, but they went all the way to the floor without slowing the vehicle.

"Damn you," Lori said, as Dixie Lou slumped against the passenger door. Reaching over, Lori grabbed the transmitter, but couldn't get the gun, which the bleeding Dixie Lou held onto tightly.

Fumbling with the transmitter, Lori couldn't get it to do anything now. The code she'd been given earlier no longer worked, having apparently been overridden.

The van navigated the left lane and merged with traffic onto the I-5 freeway, southbound. A steady stream of red tail lights followed the curve of the highway ahead of them, and approaching on the other side, a river of silver-white headlights.

Once, her mother whimpered, as if experiencing a nightmare. She didn't awaken, and Lori soothed her with gentle, loving words.

She glared at the braided hair on Dixie Lou's head, wanted to strike out at her and wished she hadn't lost control of the gun. She tried to grab the weapon again, but Dixie Lou snapped to awareness and wouldn't release it.

"Get in the back," she commanded.

As odd as it felt to Lori, since she was supposed to be the driver, she climbed back with her mother.

Locating the dome light, Lori turned it on. She could see that the right side of her mother's head was covered with blood, matting the light brown hair. Carefully, she parted the hair around the wound, revealing angry red, ragged flesh. Had a bullet entered her brain, or only grazed her? She couldn't tell, couldn't bear to look any more. Her mother didn't seem to be bleeding much around that wound or others on her legs, but Lori worried this might be because her pulse was slow and not pumping blood adequately.

"Mom," she said, "can you hear me? Mom!"

No response. Her mother's chest moved almost imperceptibly.

Tears streamed down Lori's face, and anger mounted within her. She felt like doing something crazy, no matter the consequences. If she didn't, her mother would die.

She saw the reflection of Dixie Lou's dark eyes in the mirror, staring back at her.

"Give me our ETA," Dixie Lou said.

A computer ditty sounded, while green-and-orange lights blinked on the dashboard.

"Seven minutes," the system's metallic voice said. "All is ready."

"Will they have a doctor?" Lori asked.

Dixie Lou didn't answer.

"Damn it, I asked you a question. Answer me!" Lori leaned forward and put an arm-lock on Dixie Lou's neck.

But the stocky woman hit Lori in the forehead with the handgun, stunning her and causing her to lose her grip. Reaching back, Dixie Lou struck another blow, this one on the temple and even harder.

Lori fought to remain conscious, but felt it slipping. She wanted to help her mother but could no longer control her muscles. With vision fading, she saw her mother's face next to hers, as the two of them slumped together.

"I hate you, I hate you, I hate you," Lori murmured.

She tried to envision Dixie Lou's despised face, but instead an intense darkness consumed her and she passed out.

* * *

Dixie Lou was determined to escape.

She looked around nervously as the van took an exit ramp that wound down to a surface street. At the stoplight it turned left and drove by a row of one-story buildings that were occupied by flying services and aircraft parts suppliers. It turned right, passed between two buildings.

A guard at a gate waved the vehicle through, and it accelerated onto a road that ran parallel with a private airfield. Small planes were parked on the tarmac, with larger craft visible in pools of light on the opposite side of the field.

The van came to a stop by a sleek black private jet that was as shiny as the van. No people were in evidence, no waiting doctor or medical technician for any of the injuries, including her own.

Pointing her hand-held transmitter at the plane, Dixie Lou pressed a button. A wall slid aside on the fuselage, and a staircase slid down, so that the bottom of it was only a few feet from the front of the van. Inside the plane, lights blinked, green and orange.

She stepped out of the van and was about to leave Lori and her mother behind, but hesitated. On impulse, she opened the rear door and stared hard at the unconscious teenager, who lay on the carpeted floor beside her mother. The girl, while rebellious, had been helpful, driving the vehicle for Dixie Lou when it was out of signal range for some reason. They should have been able to operate on automatic from the beginning, drawn by the aircraft's homing signal, but that had not been the case, not until they crossed over the bridge.

Touching the mother's temple, she felt a pulse—very slow and barely perceptible. Hardly any life there, but the woman might survive if she was hooked up to one of the two life support compartments at the rear of the plane.

Lori Vale saved my life, so I owe her and her mother something.

She reached in and lifted the mother out, who was small and relatively easy to carry. Inside the plane, she connected her to one of the life support systems, then went back to the van and pulled Lori out. Though Dixie Lou remained strong despite her own injury, the girl was tall, and weighed more than she'd expected—considerably more than the mother.

And as she touched the teenager, Dixie Lou felt an odd sensation, a peculiar feeling of déjà vu, that she had known her before. She could not place where, or when, but something told her it was important. With considerable difficulty the dark, stocky woman dragged the girl up the steps into the plane and laid her across a seat that folded back, with a pillow under her head and a blanket over her. She swung a safety strap over her and activated a security restraint mechanism on it.

The aircraft's interior was pale gold, with eight black leather passenger seats. On the forward bulkhead was the UWW's bright green-and-orange sword-cross symbol, which Dixie Lou focused on momentarily to give her some comfort.

There was no pilot for this aircraft, and no one with whom Dixie Lou had spoken when she called ahead. She'd been talking to the artificial-intelligence core of the plane itself, her commands transmitted via GPS and voice recognition modules to the flight systems.

The steps clicked back into place against the fuselage, thus sealing the passenger compartment. Dixie Lou heard the faint but shrill sound of jet engines, then distant sirens, which got louder by the moment. Looking through a porthole she saw the blue lights of a police car as it raced along a road parallel to the airfield.

"They aren't after us," Dixie Lou murmured to herself. She watched the car as it kept going.

Lori sat in a shoulder harness on the seat behind her, injured from being struck with the handgun by Dixie Lou. Blood matted her forehead and temple. Her eyelids twitched, and her mouth turned down in apparent displeasure.

"It won't be long," Dixie Lou promised, though she didn't think Lori could hear her. "We're taking the polar route."

The jet was rolling ahead, gaining speed. Through the porthole, Dixie Lou saw they were on the runway.

The injuries on Dixie Lou's hairline and neck had stopped bleeding, but blood had caked around them. She thought about how disarming her own appearance was, with a gentle, kindly smile and eyes that could exude compassion . . . if she wanted them to. It was all camouflage, concealing her deadly purposes.

Through a porthole, she watched the lights beside the runway blur as the jet gained speed. She felt a sudden thrust which pressed her against the back of the seat, and an emptiness in her stomach. They were airborne. The jet banked and flew north over Elliott Bay, with the tall, illuminated buildings of Seattle and the Space Needle visible out her window.

Built of composite materials, the plane incorporated the latest military stealth features into its design, so that it did not absorb or reflect natural light, thus reducing its detectable radar signature. It also emitted very little infrared radiation, noise, or vibration.

She glanced back at Lori. The girl's face was turned toward her, and the generous lips, which previously had been downturned in displeasure, now turned up a little, almost in a smile.

Maybe she knows something I don't, Dixie Lou thought.

She looked at her watch. A few minutes after eleven.

* * *

Lori dreamed she saw a brilliant point of light approaching her from space, with a dark, barely visible presence behind it . . . following the light. The linked entities drew closer.

She felt paralyzed, unable to move.

The girl cried out in terror, but no one heard her.

* * *

A while later she woke up, with an intense headache. Events were hazy to her, and nightmarish. Gunfire . . . men in uniforms . . . Had it really happened? She wasn't sure. Where was her mother?

She experienced a queasy feeling in her stomach and had the gradual, increasing impression that she was on an airplane. In the low light she thought she confirmed this, making out the outlines of a cabin interior and portholes. But through the nearest window she saw distant stars, and no lights below, only an inky blackness that gave her an odd sensation, as if she were in space, far from earth. That didn't seem possible. This had to be a jet. She heard the smooth drone of what she thought must be engines.

"Mom?" she called out. "Are you here?" She struggled to free herself from the safety restraint, but with her muddled thoughts couldn't figure it out. Touching wounds on her forehead and temple, she winced in pain.

A noise up front caused her to look that way. A hatch opened in the forward bulkhead, and a dark form emerged. The person turned and opened a cupboard on one side of the aisle. With the forward hatch still open, Lori saw it was Dixie Lou Jackson. Beyond her, through the hatch, a bank of green-and-orange lights blinked, colors like those on the dashboard of the van, like those on the strange sword-cross design on the bulkhead.

It all happened, Lori thought, as a dismal, sinking realization came over her.

She searched in the illumination of the forward cabin for signs of movement, of a captain up there, but she detected no one. Her ears strained for the sound of a voice, but she heard none.

"Where's my mother?" Lori demanded, raising her voice to make it carry.

"Welcome back, Killer Girl." Dixie Lou held up her gun, pointed it at imaginary foes and made the mock noises of a .45 automatic. " Pop-pop-pop-pop-pop-pop! . . . Pop-pop-pop-pop-pop-pop!"

"Answer me! "

Lowering the weapon, Dixie Lou said, "Guns, arm-locks, you're a tough teen, but listen up. I'm tougher."

"I asked you about my mother."

"She's in a life support compartment at the rear," Dixie Lou announced, matter-of-factly. She did something to turn up the cabin lights, then slid back into a seat just ahead of Lori's, but out of reach.

Again, the girl struggled unsuccessfully with the safety restraint.

"I activated the security lock," Dixie Lou said. "I'll let you out of it when we land. You may also have one trip to the bathroom."

"I want to see my mother!"

"She must not be disturbed. We're doing everything possible for her, with automatic medical systems connected all over her body."

Body. Lori didn't like the sound of that word. It didn't say enough about her mother, about the wonderful person she really was, even if the two of them had their differences. Numbness settled over her.

"How are her vital signs?" Lori demanded.

"Improving." It sounded like a lie, just to shut her up.

"Where are we going?" Lori asked.

No answer.

She stared at the unusual design on the bulkhead, and recalled the *Bible* in Dixie Lou's house, and the way this strange woman had displayed a statuette of She-God, whatever in the world that was. There had been black Christian crosses on the uniforms of the attackers, too. The BOI. What did it all mean?

For some reason Lori thought of occasions when, as a child, she had wanted to attend Catholic churches in the neighborhoods in which they had lived. Her mother, always an agnostic, hadn't encouraged Lori's involvement in organized religion. As a result, the girl had only been able to attend church a few times, and always alone.

Now, with everything that had occurred on this most terrible, horrendous of all nights, the girl was rekindling her interest in spiritual matters. If there truly was a God, she hoped with all the strength and power of her being that the Lord Almighty was a forgiving, loving entity, one that would spare the precious life of her mother.

And Lori Vale prayed, mostly for her mother, but also for knowledge. Who was She-God? What sort of group were these women involved with, and who were their deadly enemies?

Chapter 7

When the fragments of ancient Gnostic manuscripts from Alexandria are placed side by side with the more complete, transcribed she-apostle gospels, they do not conflict in the smallest degree. There is not one scintilla of disagreement. This is truly remarkable, and can only be due to inspiration—and to the authenticity of both sources.

—Report of the Commission on the She-Apostles

In the dimmed light of his underground office, Vice Minister Styx Tertullian studied the virtual-reality television field closely, comparing the female faces he saw in front of him with the holo-photos, and matching them with names on his clip-pad. Still wearing a uniform that was dirt and blood-smeared from the mission he'd led the night before, Tertullian sat in one of two visitors' chairs. He'd been up all night and had a stubble of beard on his narrow, bespectacled face. His superior, BOI Minister Nelson Culpepper, sat at a massive mahogany desk, glaring at him and muttering angrily.

Six of the photographs on Styx's clip-pad were of bullet-riddled female bodies. Five were of women who had been taken into custody, two with serious wounds. The attack on the goddess circle had been a military operation with split-second timing. In and out in seven efficient minutes. They had then flown to a public park where they'd abandoned the helicopter and boarded vans—vehicles that were miles away by the time the aircraft's self-destruct mechanism detonated.

The holo-recording came to an end. The virtual-reality field faded and went off. The office lights grew brighter, and for a moment Styx focused on a large clear plastic bag of articles taken in the raid—purses, scarves, a drawing of a woman standing with Jesus, a gray figurine of another woman with long hair, holding a sword-cross—the symbol of their damnable organization.

"You didn't get Dixie Lou Jackson!" the overweight Minister said, slamming a thick fist on his desk.

"She is extremely clever, and our time was strictly limited," Styx said in his high-pitched voice. He pushed his wire-rimmed glasses higher on his nose. "In the other raid we got Amy Angkor-Billings, though, the Chairwoman—"

"You had nothing to do with that operation. Your Seattle mission was a failure."

"But Jackson escaped in a van hidden in a side garage. Two of our men were hit and killed by the vehicle, and someone in the van shot two more."

"All dead?"

Styx hesitated, then: "Regrettably, yes."

"You shouldn't have lost any."

"Satellite surveillance failed at exactly the wrong time, which wasn't my fault. If the satellite had been working, we would have gotten her for sure."

"You know I don't accept excuses, Styx."

"All right." He heaved a deep sigh, raising and lowering his shoulders. "Maybe the Dark Angel helped her."

"Your failures have less to do with Satan than with your own inadequacies. Are you forgetting who we have on our side?"

"No." Styx hung his head. The Minister was getting worked up, and arguing with him would only make matters worse. Tertullian was one of nine vice ministers, each with a different area of responsibility. Aside from his own Department of Minority Affairs (which included jurisdiction over Bureau matters involving women, homosexuals and racial minorities), the other departments were Doctrine & Faith,

Education, Finance, Military Affairs, Media & Publishing, Foreign Policy, Judicial Operations, and Construction & Transport.

Another large area of concern to the Bureau was Political Affairs, but under Culpepper's watch this was not under the jurisdiction of a vice minister. Instead the Minister handled it himself, using his political contacts in high places to obtain funding. He was a master fund raiser.

"Who has the greater powers, God or Satan?" the Minister asked, revealing his cigarette-stained, yellow teeth. Originally trained in a Catholic seminary, he sometimes sounded like he was conducting Sunday school.

"Why, God, of course."

"Then you should have the advantage over Jackson, shouldn't you, since God is on our side! It must mean that the woman is stronger and smarter than you are, for she was able to thwart you."

Styx didn't respond. He was thinking instead of what he would do to the prisoners the following morning. A mere woman stronger than he? The Minister was being ludicrous, stretching a point.

"There is another possibility, of course," Minister Culpepper said, rubbing his fat chin thoughtfully. "You know what it is, don't you?"

Styx shook his head. He couldn't wait to get out of there. It was too warm and the lights were too bright. His uniform was sticking to the chair and to his sweaty thighs. He needed a shower.

"What do you suppose that possibility is?" the lumpy man demanded. "Think about it!" He lit a cigarette.

"I am, sir, but I can't imagine. . . " He felt his eyeglasses slipping down his nose, from the perspiration.

"You're in league with the Devil yourself!" Minister Culpepper sprayed spittle with the words. He half rose out of his chair, eyes bulging. "You're one of his demon-lackeys!"

"No!" Sweat poured from Styx's brow and ran down the lenses of his glasses, getting in the way of his vision. He adjusted the spectacles again.

"Admit it!"

Exasperated, Styx shook his head. Even though he was Culpepper's favorite and heir apparent, there were times when he wished he had never gotten involved with the top-secret Bureau of Ideology.

The Minister sat back in his chair, still glaring, his mouth moving rapidly as it discharged invectives like automatic weapons fire, using words that caused Styx to blush in embarrassment. An official in the service of the Lord should not employ such language! For another fifteen minutes Culpepper continued to lambaste his subordinate, finally characterizing him as an incompetent supporter of God and not one of the Devil's lackeys after all. It was only small comfort to Tertullian.

At times such as this Styx felt victimized, that perhaps he should perform his specialty on the Minister himself, doing to him what he would do to the female prisoners the ensuing morning. These were bad thoughts, of course, and he felt ashamed for them.

Forgive me, Lord, he thought, *for I am weak.*

* * *

On the main floor of the Refectory Building, where monks had eaten simple meals for centuries, women in pale gold uniforms and dun-colored robes took their early evening meals at small, separate tables. Some of the long oak dining tables remained from bygone days, but now they were set up just outside the kitchen, and used as buffet counters.

Councilwoman Bobbi Torrence, a short, heavyset woman, had just sat down alone to eat a huge salad piled high on her plate, with dark greens, black olives, and chunks of feta cheese. From a pocket of her robe she brought out a sword-cross and squeezed it tightly in her hand as she murmured a private prayer: "Thank you, She-God, for the food I am about to enjoy, and for the countless blessings you bestow upon me each day. In the name of holiness, amen."

As she took her first bite, her gaze wandered up to the high window panes along the western wall of the great hall, through which snowy mountain peaks and pale blue sky could be seen. Long wooden sticks with metal fittings on the ends leaned against the wall, used for opening the windows on warm summer days, allowing the entrance of breezes that blew across the valley. Months remained until they would be needed again.

Suddenly a young woman in a white surplice hurried over to a nearby table where two other councilwomen were eating, and whispered in the ear of one, Deborah Marvel. A slender woman in her fifties with short blonde hair, Deborah set down a coffee cup she had been holding and stood up, with her dinner companion.

Over her head, Deborah lifted a hand, with three of her fingers forming a "W." It was the sign for an emergency council meeting.

From all around the Refectory, women in robes rose to their feet and streamed out of the building.

* * *

Alone in the passenger compartment of the jet and unable to free herself of the safety restraint, Lori heard Dixie Lou's voice through the closed door of the forward cabin. The girl picked out some words, enough to know that Dixie Lou was discussing the attack with someone on the radio. She also spoke of switching scramble codes, an apparent security measure to prevent unwanted interception of their communications.

Lori had no watch, and Dixie Lou would not answer her questions. It might be mid-afternoon, since they had been flying in daylight for hours, but Lori wasn't sure. After a night that didn't seem to last very long, they had flown over large expanses of snow and ice, and an ice-choked sea. This suggested to her that they might be on a polar route, which could explain the rapid disappearance of the darkness, and the apparent movement of the sun. Only in the past couple of hours had she seen unfrozen lands and towns beneath the clouds.

Lori hoped her mother would survive her injuries, but felt a seeping, deadening realization that told her otherwise. Though she had prayed and prayed for her mother's recovery, that head wound looked very serious.

She fought back tears, told herself to be strong. Her forehead throbbed with pain. An untouched sandwich lay on the seat beside her. She should be hungry by now, but was too upset to eat.

The looming tragedy involving her mother made Lori think of another loss, the disappearance of her father more than twelve years before, when she was only a small child herself. He had been there one day, but not the next. Her mother said he abandoned his small family, but Lori remembered her mother moving her to another apartment at around the same time. It was all muddy in her memory, but recently she had been wondering if her mother had told the truth. She didn't want to think badly of her now, though.

But to Lori it had always been a disturbing mystery. Had her father been killed, or was he still alive and out there somewhere at this very moment, thinking about her and wanting to see her again? She hoped for the latter.

Searching her memories as she had done so many times before, she recalled three or four years ago in Seattle, when she'd found an old leather suitcase on a shelf in the garage. Inside were rent receipts for an apartment in Washington, DC, and other papers . . . in her mother's name. There were also papers showing different names in different cities, details that Lori could not recall afterward.

Catching Lori with the papers, Camilla had grabbed them angrily and burned them in the fireplace. To Lori, the reaction was inexplicable. The suitcase disappeared soon afterward, but she remembered seeing the initials ZM etched on top, by the handle . . . not her mother's initials, or those of anyone Lori knew. Who had they belonged to? Lori's father?

Had something happened in Washington, DC that broke up the relationship between her parents? Had her mother moved away, gone back to her maiden name—or taken another one to avoid detection—and hidden their daughter from him? Had they ever actually been married? Her mother had never answered that question, leaving Lori with doubts.

With Lori's father out of her life, she and her mother had moved a number of times, but the girl couldn't keep the events in order. She only remembered crying and calling "Daddy" over and over, and her mother shouting that Lori was not allowed to mention his name in her presence again. A rule that the defiant, stubborn girl never followed.

Now a memory fragment came to the troubled teenager, one that was familiar since she had reviewed it so many times before: Daddy wearing aviator-style dark glasses, outside in bright sunlight. Smiling, he had lifted her onto his shoulders, holding her arms tightly around his rough-textured neck while she laughed and giggled. He carried her around piggyback, making her feel taller than he was.

Then she saw the scowling face of her mother, and the fun ended abruptly.

Chapter 8

Let your women keep silence in the churches: for it is not permitted unto them to speak; but they are commanded to be under obedience, as also saith the law. And if they will learn any thing, let them ask their husbands at home: for it is a shame for women to speak in the church.
—1 Corinthians 14:34–35, *The New Testament*

The sleek black jet banked to the right, and through a starboard window Lori saw the forbidding terrain of a mountainous region below, with craggy, snowy peaks and sheer rock walls that dropped off to winding rivers and wide green plains. The sun hung low in the sky, casting long shadows across the landscape. As the jet descended below the highest mountain tops, a barren, rocky valley became apparent, with a narrow ribbon of highway and an arched stone bridge that spanned a ravine. The plane passed over the bridge and set down on a straight section of highway. After the landing, the aircraft taxied onto a side road and came to a stop at the base of a cliff, with the engines still running.

A hatch opened in the passenger compartment floor by the forward bulkhead, and Dixie Lou stood over the hole, looking down. Holding her black transmitter, she pressed buttons on it. Each time she did so, the plane moved a little like a big toy, first forward, then to the right, then back.

"OK," Dixie Lou said, finally, and she pressed the transmitter once more. The jet engines shut down.

Lori heard men's voices, coming from beneath the craft.

"Hurry it up," Dixie Lou said to them, a tone of command. She stepped back from the hatch, and moments later four large men poked their heads through and looked aft toward Lori. The men boarded gingerly, and Lori saw that they were muscular Caucasians of around thirty, in pale gold uniforms that bore green-and-orange shoulder patches with the sword-cross design on them.

"Medical assistance is required, M'Lady?" one of the men inquired, looking at Dixie Lou. He bowed to her.

Dixie Lou pointed toward Lori, and the men moved to her side. Lori saw her slip a handgun into a pocket of her dress. "The girl's mother is back there," Dixie Lou added, pointing toward the rear. "On life support."

Carrying a medical kit, the shortest of the men leaned over the tilt-back seat where Lori sat. He cleaned the injuries to her forehead and temple, causing her to grimace in pain, though he said they appeared to be only superficial. Then he opened a package and removed what looked like a flat white sponge, which he placed against her head. It stuck there, covering the injured areas. Lori felt soothing coolness, but she was a little dizzy. She heard the other men behind her, talking in low tones.

"How are you doing?" the man asked Lori. "A little better?"

Lori nodded.

"That's good," he said. "We knights live only to serve." He smiled, stepped back.

Knights? The comment intrigued her, but she didn't ask about it.

She looked back toward the rear compartment, saw her mother lying in the midst of medical equipment, and heard the men say they were preparing to move her. Lori made a sudden move and tried to go back there, but was restrained by the knight with her.

"You can see your mother tomorrow," Dixie Lou said, as she looked on. "But not now. She needs to get better first."

"Are you a doctor?" Lori wanted to know, struggling unsuccessfully to free herself from the man's iron grip. "What qualifies you to say I have to wait?"

"I outrank you."

"I'm not even in your organization."

"Just do as I say. I don't have time to argue with you."

"What if she dies before tomorrow?"

"She won't. Her vital signs have stabilized."

The knight escorted Lori down a metal staircase that took them out of the aircraft and through a rock-lined opening at ground level. Dixie Lou followed, and the three of them reached a metal platform which joined another staircase that led underground, to a second platform. Here Dixie Lou tried to take Lori's arm, but the girl shook her off and stood on her own. A tubular railing ran along one side, and beyond that was a narrow gauge train track with dark tunnels at either end. Overhead, Lori saw a network of steel girders and struts.

"We're a mess," Dixie Lou said, gazing in a small mirror she had brought from her pocket. She wiped dried blood from the cut on her cheek, arranged her braided hair. "We'll get you a room where you can rest and clean up."

Dixie Lou handed the mirror to Lori, who accepted it with a scowl and attempted to do something with her own long hair. It wouldn't settle down, and stuck out at the sides. The medical patch looked silly on her head, but she was feeling a little better, no longer dizzy.

"My mother was shot in the head. How can you say she's going to make it through the night?"

"Medical science can work miracles now."

"I hope you're right."

Two blocky female guards in pale gold uniforms moved from behind them to the front, and stood on the platform by the tracks. They pointed small electronic devices at the tracks and the platform, casting beams of light that Dixie Lou said were for a security check.

With a low hum, a rail car emerged from one of the tunnels and came to a stop at a platform gate.

Dixie Lou held Lori back while the guards inspected the car. After pronouncing it fit, Lori followed the black woman onboard and they sat side-by-side on a wide seat, with Lori ordered to sit by the window. The gun in Dixie Lou's pocket pressed hard against Lori's hip. The guards stepped onto exterior running boards on each side of the car.

"We're going to spiral up the inside of a mountain," Dixie Lou said as the rail car got under way with a smooth, metallic whir. "This is an old Greek monastery that's been converted to our uses. It's called Monte Konos."

"Spare me the history lesson," Lori said. But she thought, *We must be in Greece.*

"You're too smart to learn anything, eh? Well, people like you wear numbers across their chests. That German Shepherd back at the goddess circle was a retired police dog, and it sniffed drugs in your purse. What did you have in there?"

"Like I said, I had food in the purse earlier, a hamburger and fries. They were in wrappers, but maybe some of it spilled and I didn't notice." As the rail car jostled Lori against the stocky woman, she felt intermittent tingling, and a sense of foreboding.

"You think you're a good liar because you got away with it a few times, but don't try it around me anymore. I grew up on the streets, girl-child, and I saw a lot better liars than you. I know you had something illegal in that purse."

"Right, a burger laced with heroine. It's one of the pictures on the wall at the fast food joint."

"You have a smart mouth."

"If you don't want to hear it, send us back to Seattle." Lori felt very tired, and angry.

"Get used to this place," Dixie Lou said, a suggestion with a hard edge. "It's your home now."

The rail car entered what looked like a miner's tunnel hewn from solid rock. In dim light from lamps alongside the tunnel, Lori saw water dripping down the walls, and the air entering the car smelled musty.

"What are you gonna do with that gun in your pocket?" Lori asked. "Shoot me and toss me out in a tunnel?"

"Don't tempt me. No, I'm grateful to you for killing those soldiers and driving the van, and because of that I'll give you some leeway. But I warn you, don't push me too far."

Lori sensed that this was no idle threat, but she wouldn't back down to anyone. She was tired of adults making a big deal about a little marijuana. She liked the drug, and beer, too. They relaxed her, buffered her from the pains and cruelties of the world. What harm could there possibly be in that?

"If you're so grateful, let us go home," Lori demanded.

"You know too much."

"What? I don't know anything. And neither does my mother."

"Both of you know more than you realize."

"Well whatever, we won't talk."

"I can't risk it. Besides, *you're* in danger from attackers now. Here we live with constant high security, but it's always been that way at Monte Konos. They used to lift monks in and out on baskets that hung off the side of the cliff. They also built secret passageways and stairs honeycombing the mountain."

Lori stared blankly out the window, listened to the metallic drone of the rail car.

Dixie Lou pointed ahead, waggling a stubby finger. "We're coming up on the remains of one. Look right and left at the next wall lamp, and you'll see where our rail tunnel was cut across an old foot path."

At the lamp, Lori looked, and saw ancient, dark passageways going in either direction. The walls of the tunnels, including the larger one the train passed through, were streaked with black. Curling her upper lip in revulsion, she said, "What is this moldy old dump, anyway? Did you get a deal on the rent out here?"

Dixie Lou spoke calmly in response, but her charcoal eyes flashed anger. "For centuries Monte Konos was a monastery where only men were allowed. We thought it was appropriate for us to do something entirely different here. Besides, this is a very remote place, beyond the prying eyes of the BOI."

"The BOI?"

"The Bureau of Ideology. An international terrorist organization of men, masquerading as Christians. We prefer to call them the Bureau of Idiots."

"Your mortal enemies, I presume?"

"The sarcasm in your tone has been duly noted. In case you're interested, our UWW—United Women of the World—is half a century older than the BOI. We date back to the nineteenth century and the women's movement led by Elizabeth Cady Stanton. Our founder was a friend of Stanton's—Josephine Angkor, ancestor of our current Chairwoman."

"Why did the BOI commandos attack an undefended goddess circle?"

"The Bureau claims to advance Christian causes, but in reality that translates into benefiting *men*."

"So it's the men against the women?"

"Basically, it's always been that way—and it's come to a head." Touching a button on the wall, Dixie Lou lowered all the window shades, blocking the view of tunnel walls.

"You're just a bunch of male bashers, aren't you?" For a moment Lori focused on the cut across the black woman's cheek.

Leaning close and exuding foul breath, Dixie Lou snarled, "Lori Vale. Such a sweet-sounding name for a young troublemaker."

The rail car continued to spiral up the inside of the mountain. Lori wanted to be anywhere but here. She considered trying to grab the gun that pressed against her hip and breaking free, thinking back to when she almost jumped out of the old Chrysler her mother was driving. Now, as then, she didn't care if she got hurt; she just wanted to escape.

An orange EMERGENCY STOP button was on the wall not far away. She could lunge for it, bring the rail car to a jolting stop and leap off. But she didn't know where she would go, and reasoned that any attempt would just cause Dixie Lou to either kill her or put tighter restraints on her. Even more importantly, she didn't want to risk a reprisal against her mother.

"I'm always edgy when I don't have a cigarette," Lori said, but I'm not going to ask *you* for anything."

"If you're nice to me, I might be able to get you a couple of packs." She rubbed one of her oversized gold earrings.

Lori's eyes burned. "They were in my purse. Not drugs, just cigarettes."

"Foolish child! What do you think cigarettes are?"

Lori glowered at her, refusing to admit that she had a point.

From the seat beside her, Dixie Lou studied her for several moments, while Lori held her own gaze. "We'll talk about your attitude tomorrow," the woman snapped.

Lori shook her head in dismay.

She heard an explosion. A video screen flashed on in front of Dixie Lou, and a female voice reported: "Trouble in Sector Three! Tracks destroyed!"

In the tunnel ahead, Lori saw the orange glow of fire.

Alarms sounded. The rail car jerked to a stop, then backed up at high speed, slowed, and darted into a side tunnel. Another explosion followed, closer this time, and the car rocked.

The car sped through another detour, and abruptly all lights went out as it came to a hard stop. The sound of heavy doors could be heard, closing. Two thumps.

The car was bathed in light as a hatch opened in the ceiling. A stairway snapped down and Dixie Lou led Lori up it. They were in a large, rock-hewn chamber, with low natural light entering through a plexed-in hole at the top. The plex was leaded panes. Female security guards encircled them. They exchanged odd three-finger salutes.

Accompanied by the guards, Dixie Lou led Lori out of the cavern, which narrowed into a tunnel. Their footsteps echoed off the walls of the ancient corridor.

"Monks started carving these passageways nine hundred years ago," Dixie Lou said, her voice agitated. "Feel the rock floor, rutted from all the feet that have crossed over it."

With the rubber bottoms of her jogging shoes, Lori felt a rut that curved upward on each side where the walls of the passageway joined the floor. For a moment she thought she heard voices, like the eerie medieval chanting of monks, but soon it passed like a gentle breeze, and she ascribed it to her imagination. Here and there, bright halogen light fixtures had been placed to illuminate the way, modern technology cohabiting with the past.

They reached a rock staircase that led upward, with rutted, chipped steps. In silence, Dixie Lou climbed, followed by the American teenager.

Lori heard the muffled sounds of gunfire, and overheard a guard telling Dixie Lou that her security forces were mopping up the saboteurs.

"We can never relax here," Dixie Lou said to Lori. "Too many strange occurrences, sabotage attempts against our heat, lights, power. For your own safety don't go anywhere without an escort. We'll set something up for you tomorrow."

"The BOI?" Lori asked.

"Can't be. If they knew where we were, they'd blow the whole mountain up. No, we think it's a clandestine men's rights movement, claiming that we don't treat our knights well. Totally preposterous!"

"Why are they called knights?"

"Because they serve our needs. The most popular are the stud knights." Dixie Lou surprised her by laughing, a wicked cachinnation that echoed off the rock walls.

At the top of the staircase they reached a cobblestone street, which led to a three-story stucco and brick building with round, concave windows. A guard at the entrance gave Dixie Lou the three-finger salute, which Dixie Lou explained this time.

"'W' for Woman," she said, demonstrating a salute as she led Lori into the lobby. A small fountain gurgled.

Lori laughed. "You've got to be kidding," she said. "Do you have signet rings and Dick Tracy watches, too?"

"I'll assume you're just tired," Dixie Lou said in a measured tone. "You've suffered a terrible trauma and can't be expected to think straight. But I warn you, don't continue to test my patience. You don't want to be on my bad side."

Saying little more, they rode an elevator to the third floor. The air was thick between them. Lori followed Dixie Lou along a narrow, stucco-walled hallway. Water stains smeared the ceiling, and dark streaks of mildew. At a heavy black door, Dixie Lou showed Lori how to operate a security panel to unlock the door.

"Remember the code numbers," Dixie Lou reminded her.

The door swung open, revealing a tattered studio apartment with simple furnishings.

"You'll stay here," Dixie Lou said. "Meals are served in the Refectory Building—three seatings for each meal. You'll find a schedule inside the apartment, and a map of Monte Konos—at least the part that isn't off-limits to you."

Lori heard a muffled, distant explosion, saw Dixie Lou stiffen.

Without another word the strange woman hurried down the hall and left.

* * *

Dixie Lou Jackson paced nervously in front of her fellow councilwomen, who were seated in a half-circle of black leather chairs on the elevated platform of the chamber. She glanced uneasily at Amy's empty red leather chair, then away. It was mid-evening, not long after the conclusion of the long flight to Monte Konos. In all that time she hadn't eaten anything. With the attack on her goddess circle and the rail sabotage here, her stomach was too upset. She still wore the white gauze dress (soiled now), the black bead bracelets, and the gold sword-cross necklace.

Behind the council, on a high pedestal once occupied by a cross of Jesus, loomed the statue of She-God, representing all the heroines who had ever walked the earth. On the statue's upturned palms rested the jewel-hilted Sword of She-God, a weapon steeped in lore and mystery. According to legend, it had been used by ancient female warriors— thousands of years ago—to vanquish their enemies. Some tales even described Joan of Arc in possession of the weapon in the fifteenth century.

"Amy hasn't reported in," a blonde councilwoman, Deborah Marvel, said in a throaty, emotion-choked voice. "We can't make contact with her or with Katherine." She was referring to Katherine Pangalos, the wealthy UWW contributor Amy had gone to visit just outside the city of Salonika. Katherine, through a circuitous chain of title, owned Monte Konos itself.

On a nearby table the Internet computer flashed images of paramilitary forces and materiel under UWW control, information transmitted in the women's impenetrable code. Below that, a message screen reported no knowledge of the whereabouts of their beloved Chairwoman.

Dixie Lou stared across the church at the empty pews and stained-glass windows. The darkness of night loomed beyond, where their enemies might be approaching. "As all of you know, the BOI attacked me last evening near Seattle. I recognized their uniforms, and thought I saw the Vice Minister of Minority Affairs leading the raid. What's his name?"

"Tertullian," Deborah said.

"Right, the wacko with the high-pitched voice." Dixie Lou slumped into her own chair, on one end of the half-circle.

"And now Amy's missing," Deborah said. "The BOI again, do you think?"

Shrugs and blank faces gazed back at her.

"And what's this I hear about another baby?" Dixie Lou asked, looking at Deborah. "A sighting in Mexico?"

"She-apostle number twelve," Deborah responded. "The last one. Unfortunately her mother ran away with her, and one of our agents shot a priest, killing him. We're combing the villages and hills, looking for her. She can't have gotten far, a poor peasant woman without resources."

Dixie Lou grunted, thinking about the sighting, and savoring the feeling that she was in command of the UWW now, because Amy was missing. Though she'd never liked the Chairwoman, Dixie Lou had played up to her skillfully, and as a consequence had been selected as her hand-picked successor, number two in the organization. Could this be the moment when Dixie Lou would accede to power? She felt her pulse quicken in anticipation, but worried about BOI involvement. They had methods of penetrating security. Had someone in this very room betrayed her and Amy?

The stocky little councilwoman also wondered if the fateful hand of She-God had moved Lori Vale like a puppet, saving Dixie Lou's life so that she could become Chairwoman.

Her gaze wandered searchingly around the half-circle and focused finally on the sharp-chinned profile of Deborah Marvel, the third most powerful woman in the UWW. Had she orchestrated the attacks? But Deborah was Dixie Lou's friend, or seemed to be. Still, Deborah was almost too strong at times, with an irritating habit of arguing with Dixie Lou and trying to get her to change her mind on certain issues. This rarely succeeded and occasionally they voted differently. Normally, however, the two women put up a solid front to the others.

Another of Dixie Lou's allies, a narrow-faced councilwoman named Nancy Winters, said, "Look at this." She pointed at the computer monitor, which had shifted half of its screen to a Level 7 security display, showing someone with credentials passing through checkpoints. Dixie Lou saw an elderly woman rushing down a passageway and up a flight of stairs. It was Dr. Katherine Pangalos, the one Amy had gone to see. Dixie Lou despised her.

The door to the council chamber burst open and the gray-haired woman rushed in.

"Katherine!" one of the councilwomen exclaimed. "Is Amy with you?"

"They've taken her prisoner," she replied, short of breath. "The Bureau—I barely got away through an escape hatch." Turning to Dixie Lou, she added bitterly, "I guess that puts you in charge. Are you happy now?"

Outraged at the characterization, Dixie Lou rose from her chair. She wasn't very tall, but made up for it with her aggressiveness. "You're suggesting that I had something to do with this? BOI forces attacked the goddess circle; I narrowly escaped with my own life."

"How *utterly convenient*, you're safe."

"Oh, and I suppose I set it all up? A BOI-outfitted helicopter, men in uniforms, the whole bit?"

"Could be done."

"Impossible," Dixie Lou said. "Unlike you, I've taken the Vow of Angkor to guarantee my loyalty." She was referring to the sacred rite of deep hypnosis initiated by the founder of the UWW, a great grandmother of Amy Angkor-Billings—an oath that all of the organization's personnel had to undergo. Katherine Pangalos, since she was a major contributor and not technically a member, had never been required to undergo the ritual. To Dixie Lou, this smacked of favoritism, of strings pulled at a very high level.

Obviously, Pangalos considered herself too good for such a pedestrian oath.

"What about you, Katherine?" Dixie Lou pressed. "They got Amy, but not *you*?" Her voice dripped with sarcasm. "How *utterly convenient*."

With a condescending expression Katherine gazed down her wrinkled nose at the small but muscular woman, and said, "Unlike you, I do not have a ghetto background. I would have no motive to betray my sisters. You, on the other hand, could be bought no matter the oath you purportedly took, and my guess is, it wouldn't take much."

Dixie Lou's cheeks felt hot, and in a fury she lunged at the old woman. Katherine's accusing, sneering face was all she saw. Before she knew it she was pulling Katherine's hair and dragging her to the floor. Though small, Dixie Lou was younger and tougher, having grown up in the inner city.

Katherine cried out.

With considerable effort, several councilwomen pulled them apart.

"Explain how you got away and Amy didn't!" Dixie Lou screeched. "You're only accusing me to deflect attention from yourself!"

"Slut!" Katherine howled.

"All your money and you couldn't protect Amy?"

"In the confusion of the attack I was able to escape, and . . ."

"Isn't that nice for *you*?"

The women glared at each other. Pangalos had bruises on her face, but they weren't enough for Dixie Lou.

"Some unfortunate things are being said in the heat of the moment," Deborah said. "I'm sure neither one of you really thinks the other is involved in these awful events. You're both upset. All of us are."

Unable to stand the erudite, finishing school expression on Katherine's face, Dixie Lou seethed. All that patrician upbringing, all the money the old woman had, and she had used it to wheedle her way into Amy's favor. If Amy didn't return, it was a two-edged sword for Dixie Lou. While she would ascend to the position of Chairwoman, that would leave an opening on the council—one that Katherine would undoubtedly fill, since Amy had promised her the first available position. Despite Katherine's advanced age, she looked as if she had quite a few years left in her. She would have to take the oath then—small consolation.

If natural processes were permitted to proceed. A big *if*, as far as Dixie Lou was concerned.

"I can't return to my home," Katherine said, as she watched Dixie Lou warily, with four councilwomen standing between them. "It's too dangerous."

"Then you'll have to stay here where it's safe," Dixie Lou said, in a sarcastic tone. "We'll do lunch."

Fear seeped into Katherine's face, which pleased Dixie Lou immensely.

"Don't let her agitate you," Deborah whispered to Dixie Lou. She patted the de facto Chairwoman's forearm, reassuringly.

Dixie Lou took a long, deep breath. She could usually count on Deborah to take her side, at least on matters of the most importance. This ex-housewife had also come from humble beginnings in America, and that formed a bond between them, a subject they occasionally discussed over coffee or a meal. Of course, Dixie Lou had omitted certain details of her own colorful biography and embellished others, never revealing the murders she had committed or the cunning scams she had perpetrated.

"I haven't caught up on my rest," Dixie Lou said, heading for the door. "If I think of anything more later I'll let you know." She glared at Katherine and added, "Remember this, too: It wasn't my idea for Amy to visit you. It was her own."

This was the truth, but in the shadowy chambers of Dixie Lou's mind she hoped Amy had not survived, for her death would open new opportunities.

Chapter 9

All my life I've sensed something deep within myself, linking me with other women. Now I know what it is.

    —The Reflections of Lori Vale (unpublished manuscript)

A golden sunrise illuminated a desolate plain in eastern Washington State, casting long shadows from the rock escarpments and barren hills as the flaming sphere became brighter, sharing its warmth with the earth.

Walking briskly up the Hill of Golgotha, Vice Minister Styx Tertullian smelled the rank, musty odor of human death and saw tiny droplets of dew glistening on clusters of three-toothed sagebrush and great basin blue sage. Overhead, red-tailed hawks and turkey vultures soared. He was thankful for God's wisdom and generosity in allowing mortals such as himself to behold such wonders. They made him think of far greater glories awaiting him in the Kingdom of Heaven. Styx wore a silver robe, with a long black stole draped over his shoulders.

In his left hand he carried a gleaming double-edged sword, freshly sharpened to a razor's edge.

To reach the eternal, heavenly reward the Vice Minister needed to remain true to his faith, as he was doing this morning while trudging up a dirt and sand pathway lined with human skulls, some of which still had skin clinging to them that hadn't been picked away by the carrion-eaters. He paused for a moment, admiring the translucence of a piece of flesh as sunlight passed through it, then continued on.

This hill was a Bureau-built reconstruction of the far-away site of Jesus' crucifixion by the Roman governor, Pontius Pilate, in collusion with the Sadducees. In ancient days the skulls had been of Christian martyrs, but in the modern version they represented something entirely different—the vengeance of the Lord against blasphemers and schemers.

An eye for an eye. Blood for blood.

The Bureau of Ideology was the agent of God.

On adjoining land, the headquarters of the Bureau included millions of square feet of underground structures, with sixty-six levels of subterranean office space, living quarters for staff, and facilities for the storage of vehicles and aircraft. To the uninformed a portion of the land looked like a small town of four or five thousand inhabitants, containing houses, businesses, a central park and six churches in a variety of architectural designs. Some employees of the Bureau—predominantly men—lived in the houses, but most, comprising in all nearly thirty thousand persons, lived in underground apartments. None of these people were married. They were the governmental equivalents of Catholic priests and nuns, married through their professions to God.

To prevent the leakage of secrets to ideological enemies, only a few employees were ever permitted to leave the area. It was five miles across barren land to the nearest boundary of the facility, which had no visible delineation and only a few plainclothed guards, since other methods of security were employed. Chief among them were implanted medical devices connected to the vital organs of all BOI employees as a condition of employment, ensuring that none of them—other than the highest officials—could approach the perimeters. If they attempted to do so, the implants were triggered and heart and brain functions ceased. Human nature being what it was, with its inherent weaknesses, attempts to escape were occasionally made, though none successfully. Regular security patrols rounded up the bodies.

On the other side of the boundary the potentially curious were kept at bay through a different but allied means, electronic signals that transmitted outward for two miles in all directions around the facility. These signals confused the brain functions of approaching persons who did not have implanted protective devices, causing them to turn around and leave without knowing why. For like reasons, aircraft did not fly low over the facility, or near it—and the Bureau had other equipment to detect and thwart drones. In addition, through political arrangements and technology, the town and surrounding unimproved land did not appear on any maps or tax rolls, and did not show up on the satellite surveillance reports of any nation.

Styx smiled to himself as he walked up the path lined with human skulls, for he believed that even if the Bureau technology failed massively, if every backup power system went out, God would still find a way to camouflage the facility, through inclement weather or other means. The *Bible* provided ample evidence of the Lord's repertoire of storms, floods, fires, and earthquakes, all employed to cleanse the world of sin and wickedness.

Some Christians didn't understand that being devout involved duties. It wasn't enough to simply identify oneself as a Christian and attend church. It took strength, commitment, and good works to gain God's attention and grace, not weakness, uncertainty, and laziness.

God is strong and energetic, as I must be, Styx thought.

Ahead, just around a bend in the path, he saw the top of a wooden cross, and the stench of death became stronger. He inhaled it, for these were his enemies and he enjoyed smelling them in their decay. Presently the cross came into full view, and then a long line of many more like it, all rough-hewn in the traditional manner. The nearest cross was not occupied, but most of the others were, with vultures perched on a number of them.

An Asian woman with short black hair, her clothes torn and bloody, hung on the second cross, her wrists and ankles having been nailed into place within the hour, so that fresh red blood still ran from the wounds. Her eyes were closed. Open sores covered her skin. Her breasts heaved in and out, fitfully.

A wooden sign posted over her head by the BOI tribunal proclaimed, in blood-red paint:

Amy Angkor-Billings

Blasphemer and Harlot

Styx stood at the foot of the cross and gazed up at her, through his wire-rimmed glasses. An immense turkey vulture sat atop the post, just above her head. Soon this magnificent predator and its winged brethren would gouge out the sinner's eyes with sharp beaks and tear the flesh from her bones with sharp talons.

Using the flat of his sword, he touched the side of her bloody face. This had once been a woman of classic beauty, with high cheekbones and an exquisite, if petite, figure.

Slowly, Angkor-Billings opened her large green eyes, revealing what at first looked like reverie to Styx, but which he subsequently categorized as pain.

Good. This *Bible*-hater deserved to suffer. Crucifixion worked nicely for such a purpose, and there were other methods from biblical teachings and stories. Sharp swords, slingshots, fire. . . .

Styx and the Bureau of Ideology were a microcosm of the Lord Himself, employing the power of the Almighty to fill the hearts of heretics with terror.

"Good morning, Amy," Styx said. He pressed the tip of his sword against skin on the inside of her thigh where it had not previously been cut, drawing a trickle of blood.

She stared at him condescendingly with green Asian eyes, as if he were vermin and she a queen. Styx loathed her, and all women who were like her. They didn't know their places, didn't recognize that woman was created from the rib of man to serve him and bear his children. Genesis 3:16 stipulated that women were to obey their husbands, and there were other biblical passages that placed them in subservient roles to men.

Maintaining pressure on the tip of the blade, he ran it up the inside of her leg under her dress, slicing the skin and causing more blood to flow.

"Your symbol is a sword merged with a cross," Styx said in a low, menacing tone. "The Sword of She-God? Is that what you call your blasphemous symbol?"

No response or emotion from Amy.

"Well this is the Sword of *God*!" he exclaimed, stepping back and raising his sword. With the tip of the weapon, which was of the finest Spanish steel and workmanship, he touched the front of her right shoulder and then her left and finally the center of her forehead. It was the sign of the cross in reverse, to eliminate any Christian blessing that might linger on this soul and body. Sometimes he enjoyed doing that, to gain the attention and favor of the Lord. It was like an excommunication.

Again he stepped back, and this time he swished the long blade through the air with his dominant left hand, coming ever so close to her face.

She didn't flinch or move a muscle.

Overhead, the vulture made a grunting sound.

Despite interrogation drugs that had been administered to her, Amy remained strangely resistant. She gazed scornfully at her silver-robed tormentor, then looked up at the heavens and smiled. "My She-God watches over me and protects me," she said.

Vice Minister Tertullian felt like finishing the blasphemer off with a quick upward thrust of the sword into her female parts. But that would be too good for her. It would allow her to escape the exquisite pain that had been ordered for her by the tribunal. Besides, he might still be able to extract information from her.

He withdrew the sword.

"Why were you talking to those families?" he demanded. "Why did you bring them all to Greece? What was on the holo-recorder you destroyed? You'd better talk, you heretic—"

Amy smiled calmly, didn't respond. She knew he was referring to the people that the BOI had taken prisoner in the raid on Katherine's compound, the birthmothers, fathers, and siblings of the she-apostles. She felt sorry for the families, but there was nothing she could do for them, nor for Katherine Pangalos. She could only hope that some of them had escaped. It didn't surprise her that none of these vile men had mentioned the children . . . at least not yet. Fearing the families might fall into the wrong hands, she'd warned them ahead of time not to talk, not to even reveal the existence of the special children . . . for the safety of the little ones. But even if they did talk, they didn't know much of anything. The UWW had lied to them, telling them only that their children were involved in a top-secret government study.

"Who owns that Greek country club setup?" Styx demanded, "We've traced real estate records to a network of fictitious corporations. Who owns the corporations?"

Again, no answer.

"The question is too tough for you, eh? All right, here's an easy one. Tell me about your paramilitary operations, how they're all tied together on the worldwide web."

Her expression didn't change.

"What are the Internet codes? Tell me!"

Amy gazed into the distance.

"We already know a lot. How do you think we ambushed you and Dixie Lou Jackson? You might as well tell us the rest."

"Internet paramilitary operations–Hmmm–Intriguing idea. I am sorry, Styx Man, but I know nothing of military matters, computers, or electronics. Women aren't good at those sorts of things, you know. . . ."

Styx seethed. For years there had been rumors of clandestine female military activity and a secret UWW Internet network. If only someone with specific knowledge would step forward. The BOI raids had nothing to do with the Internet, though. In Seattle, a Bureau operative with a parabolic microphone had picked up details of conversations involving the caretaker of Dixie Lou's home near there, and a trap had been laid. The attack in northern Greece had been made possible by an informer.

"When I feel like it, I'm going to cut off your head and toss it over there," Styx announced, with a stiff smile. With his sword he pointed toward a pile of skulls, where hungry vultures and hawks were hopping about, looking for morsels. "Unless you decide to cooperate."

"It doesn't matter what you do to me," Amy said, her voice strong and clear, "because we have a little surprise in the works for you."

"And what is that?"

"Are you really that stupid to ask?" she replied. "Just what do you think 'surprise' means? Anyway, you'll find out what we're going to do soon enough, and it will set your male chauvinist world on its ear."

"You're bluffing."

Lifting on her nailed feet to breathe more easily, Amy said, "Whether I live or die makes no difference. A process has been set in motion, and no one, not you, nor I, nor any nation, can stop it."

"And that process is?"

A smile curled at the edges of her mouth. "Part of the shocking surprise, of course."

"Lying slut."

He tried to stare her down, but couldn't. Oh, how he wanted to finish her right now, gouging out her eyes first! "Patience, Lord," he whispered to himself. "Lord, grant me patience."

Hearing voices, Styx looked back along the path he had just traversed. Guards were bringing up more women he had taken prisoner the previous evening, in the goddess circle raid. All would be crucified, including two that could not walk and were being carried.

Looking back at Angkor-Billings he saw to his horror and amazement that she was smiling beatifically, gazing heavenward. How he longed to kill her immediately! This was one of the Lord's temptations placed before him, designed to make him strong.

Vice Minister Tertullian turned away, went to the next cross, and then the next, and continued on down the line. All of the prisoners were still alive, but some only barely; a few were moaning, others were openly defiant, or staring numbly, or slumped unconscious. Most were women, but a handful of their male accomplices had been brought in as well, ferreted from their loathsome cells of sedition.

Pausing before one of the men, who was breathing fitfully, Styx spat on his bloody, hair-covered legs. What sort of man would follow women, in violation of holy law?

With a swift stroke of the blade, Styx lopped off his bearded head. It tumbled to the ground at the foot of the cross.

Two vultures hopped close to the head, peering at it with interest. Their dark, hungry little eyes took everything in.

* * *

Lori lay in unfamiliar shadows, trying to convince herself she had experienced a nightmare and was back in her bedroom at home. The jumble of events in her mind bore the earmarks of unreality. They didn't make any sense.

She heard a distant machine whir followed by silence, then a resumption of the sound, and silence again. She knew from the shadows in this confined area and the unfamiliar noises that she was not in her bedroom, not in her home. She lay on her side, with her eyes open.

She was shaking, and thought she knew why. Her street friends used to say the marijuana she often smoked with them had been laced with stronger, unknown drugs. Still, she thought she could beat it. . . .

Lori sat up on the bed, flipped on a small lamp on the side table. It cast weak light.

The room had a single dark-stained wooden door and no windows. The walls, bare of paintings or other adornment, were rough and coated with a white chalky substance that had been worn away in places, revealing a brownish-gray surface underneath.

She drank a glass of water slowly, and as she did so she tried to take her mind off her old life and the way she had been wasting her time: the drugs, the drinking, the partying and sex with boys she didn't know. Her mother—although Lori would never admit it at the time—had been right about one thing, that Lori had been going down the wrong path, and perhaps a perilous one.

She feared that her mother actually was dead, had a terrible feeling about this. She really *really* wanted something to calm her. Fumbling in the pocket of a robe, she found a pack of cigarettes one of her street friends had given her. Not the Pink Paradises she would have preferred, these were Greek, a brand she'd never heard of. Still, they would have to do. She struck a match, and with a shaking hand lit a cigarette and took a deep drag. The taste was rough, with a faint taste of menthol that more burned than soothed.

Lori switched the light off, climbed back into bed and sat up with an ashtray on her lap, smoking the cigarette, causing the ember tip to glow orange in the low illumination of the room.

I must be strong, she told herself.

* * *

On the cross, Amy blocked out the pain in her hands and ankles, from the large nails securing them to the crossbar and post. Rolling her eyes upward, she prayed to the glorious She-God, asking Her for strength. Moments later, with a mighty effort, she ripped one of her hands free, and then—trying to hold on to the crossbar with her free hand, she pulled the other hand free. Blood gushed, so slippery and painful that she could not hold on.

With nothing supporting her upper body she pitched forward, slamming her head into the base of the cross and cracking bones in her ankles, which were still bound and secured to the cross.

She went unconscious for an undetermined time, then awakened to the most intense pain she had ever felt in her life—even worse than her tormentors had originally inflicted on her. She resisted the temptation to scream out, fearing one of her enemies would hear her.

The She-God whispered encouragement to her, enabling Amy to untie her own ankles, and pull them free. Then, unable to walk and barely able to move her hands, she crawled on the dirt to a vantage point, where she could see the perimeter of the Hill of Golgotha. She had hoped to reach freedom, so that she could inspire her sisters in United Women of the World, but her heart sank at what she saw.

A high chain link fence seemed to encircle the hill, within the limited range of vision that she had. With a Herculean effort, she crawled to another vantage point on the other side of the hill, losing blood and filling her wounds with dirt.

Again she saw the fence, and uniformed, roving guards.

Knowing that she could never hope to climb the fence and escape, with her strength ebbing fast, she vowed not to let her hated enemies—especially that slimy, cruel Tertullian—get their hands on her again.

Not alive, anyway.

Crawling back the way she had come, she found a sharp spike that she had noticed on the ground, and had hoped she would not have to use. She took a deep breath, and this time did not pray or delay at all. What she had in mind would take every bit of remaining strength she had.

And all of her courage.

Pointing the sharp end of the spike at her chest, over her heart, she lunged down on it. The spike penetrated her skin, but not far enough. Rising with great difficulty, she slammed down again on the steel point, and this time felt the crunch of bone and cartilage as it broke through.

Chapter 10

Monte Konos: A fortified monastery occupied for centuries by monks, it is now considered sacred ground by the UWW, the place where they sought sanctuary from persecution, and where they worked on their earth-shaking project.

—Notes confiscated from the body of a murdered news reporter

An unusual morning rain moistened the Vice Minister's face as he hurried up the skull-lined path of the Hill of Golgotha. Dressed in a short-sleeve black shirt and black trousers, he shivered.

Little bubbles of water glistened on the broad double-edged sword that Tertullian held in his left hand, with the point of the weapon extended forward. He hadn't expected rain but liked it, for it would cleanse blood from his sword.

God had sent rain for that purpose.

Today the first wooden cross was occupied by a blonde woman who had been hung there the day before. One of the heretics from the Seattle raid. Awake, with her body shaking from a night spent out in the cold, she watched him warily.

He passed by her with hardly a glance.

Looking at the second cross, however, he felt his jaw drop. The witch Amy Angkor-Billings was not on it! Thoughts whirled through his mind. Was he on the wrong row of crosses? He looked around, got his bearings. No, this was the right place. Had she been moved? If so, by whose authority? Only Minister Culpepper could have done it without Styx's permission. But why would he do such a thing?

Just in case there had been an escape, or one was in progress, Styx sounded a silent alarm, punching a recessed red button on his watch. Within seconds he heard activity, vehicles in motion, guards running around, the shouts of men.

He began to search the hill himself. In only a few minutes, just as guards were running toward him, he found Angkor-Billings, lying in bloody dirt with a spike through her heart.

In rage and defeat, Styx howled into the rain, and kicked her lifeless form, causing it to roll part way down the hill. Like a madman, he chased the body down the hill, kicking at it repeatedly. Once, he slipped and fell, and nearly cut himself with his own sword.

Gathering himself, he rose slowly to his feet and looked uphill, where the guards were standing, looking down at him. "Put her back on the cross!" Styx shouted, lying. "She's still alive!"

Two guards ran down the hill, to do his bidding. When they were close, he said, "The witch is still alive. If either of you say otherwise to anyone, I'll kill you myself."

They grunted in affirmation.

By the time the body was secured to the cross, the rain had stopped, but Styx hardly noticed. Something more was necessary now, the task his boss had left for him because he didn't want to get his hands dirty. Despite the fact that the Minister had killed his own wife, that had been accidental, in a scuffle to keep her from subverting the secret bureau he led. Culpepper didn't really have the stomach for terminating human life, couldn't comprehend the fact that the application of violence could be an art if performed for the Lord.

Of course, this enemy was already dead. But that was only her physical form. Certain things could be done to make sure her caliginous soul was dispatched on a journey into the realm of eternal darkness. That's why he wanted her back on the crucifixion cross, where she belonged.

Taking a step backward, Styx drove the sharp blade deep into Angkor-Billings' stomach and jerked upward, like a hunter gutting a deer. At her jugular he sliced quickly and deeply to the left and then swung hard to the right so that her head was severed and fell to the ground.

Deep in reverie, he uttered a biblical passage from Second Samuel, in which Ishbosheth's head was smitten from his body. Then with his left foot he kicked the head as if it were a soccer ball. It rolled several feet, and came to rest against a stone.

A sharp pain shot through Styx's foot. It felt as if he had broken his big toe, so his shoe leather wasn't as thick as he'd thought. He cursed, then apologized profusely to the Lord.

Must remain in control, he thought. *Control at all times, in all things*.

Even in death the woman's head was still infused with devilish powers.

He set the sword on the ground and picked up the head, which contained the evil, demented brain of Amy Angkor-Billings, leader of the women's rebellion. Holding the bloody face in front of his, he looked deep into the sightless, slitted eyes.

They seemed to stare back, though he knew that was impossible.

A slight smile remained on her mouth.

"Would you like to do something more to me, Amy?" he asked.

Out of the corner of his eye, he saw the woman on the first cross watching him, her face a mask of horrified fascination.

"How about biting my finger, Amy?" he said. Cradling the head in one arm like a football, with his free hand he parted her lips and stuck his pinkie into her mouth. The cavity was moist and still warm, meaning that she had not killed herself that long ago. Blood dripped on his shirt.

"Bite down," he said. "Come on, I know you want to."

He wondered if it was true that the brain lived on for several moments after death . . . or even longer. An hour, perhaps? If so, she probably wanted to chomp down and sever his finger, just as he had sliced off her once-pretty neck.

The rain resumed, and wind whipped around the base of the cross.

"Last chance," he said, and he inserted five fingers and a thumb into her mouth.

Suddenly her lips twitched—or did they?—causing him to pull his hand away, quickly. But she hadn't bitten down.

The woman on the adjacent cross laughed hideously, and that bothered him. Still, he would have the last laugh.

He tried to conceal the pain in his foot.

He held the head by its black hair, swung back and let it fly. The bloody orb cut through the misty rain for a distance of ten or fifteen meters, bounced off a rock, and went over the edge of the hill.

He retrieved his sword and with quick, efficient thrusts into the chest of the laughing woman, he silenced her. Then he walked at a normal pace down the path. When he was out of sight of the crucifixion crosses, he limped.

Raindrops mixed with blood on the surface of the broad sword, and dripped to the ground.

He had so much blood on his shirt and pants that he intended to throw them away. It was evil fluid, and might not wash completely out of the fabric fibers.

The sword was a different matter. It would clean up perfectly and could be used again, and again. Minister Culpepper had given him permission to "deal with" all the people taken in the two most recent raids . . . He could do so any way he pleased; Culpepper just didn't want to know the details.

But Styx went to him anyway. . . .

* * *

In the hallway outside his office Minister Culpepper saw a disheveled Vice Minister Styx Tertullian approaching, his hair wild and his clothing soaked in rain and blood. The fat man ducked inside the doorway of his office and locked the door, then had second thoughts.

Not good to show fear.

As quietly as possible he unlocked the door and hurried to his desk. Just as he slipped into the chair, the door opened and Styx filled the doorway, a crazed expression on his face and a gory sword in his grasp. Water and blood dripped on the hardwood floor.

"I did it," he announced. "Sliced her head off like a . . ."

"This is not the way to deliver a report," Culpepper interjected, in his haughtiest tone. "E-mail it to me." Surreptitiously he turned a key to open a side drawer, just enough to see the handle of the .40 Magnum he kept there. He had never fired a gun but kept this one for security.

Grab it, Culpepper thought, *release the safety and fire. . . .*

He abhorred violence and loathed Tertullian's methods. Still, someone had to do those things, and he did them exceedingly well.

Scold him a little, but not too much. Don't want him going over the edge and turning on me.

"I'm not a computer whiz," Styx whined. "I'm a hands-on kinda guy."

"Nonetheless you will complete your report in the proper fashion."

The soaked, soiled man took several steps into the room, trailing water and blood. "About slicing the head off, you mean, and the blood spurting?"

"Put it in the report!"

"Are you afraid of the details?"

"Certainly not!"

"Sir, do you ever actually *read* what I write?" His voice was even higher than usual.

"Of course."

Styx came closer, a strange, demented gleam in his eyes. "I wonder."

"Get out of here!"

A vicious smile formed on Styx's face, but he backed up. He wiped the sword on his trousers.

"Don't ever come in here like that again, or I'll boot you out."

He ran a finger over the sharp blade. "Personally?"

Culpepper glared. "Clean yourself up and transmit your report."

"As you wish." The Vice Minister whirled and departed, disrespectfully leaving the door open.

* * *

The female guard in the light of the doorway was heavily muscled, with cords and sinews visible in every square centimeter of her exposed skin, making Lori wonder how she had gotten that way. Steroids, she theorized, or perhaps she was the horrible result of some mad scientist's genetic program. She looked more animal than human, evident in her dark little eyes, as she watched Lori walk across the courtyard, moving through the shadows and pools of yellow illumination cast by antique lamp posts.

Bundled in a coat she'd found in her apartment, Lori passed wrought iron chairs and tables, painted white, and exotic, leafy plantings, but without flowers, probably due to the season. Feeling better, she no longer wore the medical pack on her head. She looked up and identified her own apartment on the third floor, where she had left a lamp on in the window. The night sky was star-dusted and peaceful, but didn't impart the usual feeling of serenity, as Lori recalled with anger the things Dixie Lou had done to her and her mother.

Hearing a rustle on her left she was surprised to see a young man dressed in baggy silks and a feathered beret. He wore a short sword, and in the patio light from a ground level apartment she made out the peculiar green-and-orange sword-cross symbol on his scabbard.

"I am Prince Alexander," he announced, with a smile and an awkward bow. "At your service, fair maiden."

Seven or eight years older than Lori, he had light black skin and soft features. His pewter eyes gazed past her and only intermittently looked directly at her, not focusing on her for long. He was about her height, but she was tall for a girl.

The guard watched, but without apparent concern.

"I'm big," the young man added, "but I still get to dress up and play make-believe. My Mom says I can, and I have lots of fun."

Realizing that he must be mentally retarded even though his face looked normal enough, she responded, "Thank you, but this fair maiden doesn't require anything at the moment."

"Dixie Lou Jackson is my Mom. You're my friend, so you can call me Alex." He leaned close to her. "You have a boo-boo on your head. Does it hurt?"

"I'm fine, thank you." Lori saw the resemblance now, in the oval shape of the face, in the wide nose and the small mouth. His black hair was long and curly, puffing out at the sides from not being trimmed.

"I'm not stupid," he said. "Some people say I am because of my motorcycle accident, but they don't know all the stuff I think about."

"I'm sure they don't," Lori said, trying not to sound insincere.

"I'm not one of the stud knights, either," he added.

"Are stud knights what I think they are? Your mother laughed when she mentioned them."

"They're men who do things for women." He grinned boyishly. "You know!"

"Sexual favors?"

A nod. "They're boy toys. That's what the ladies call them. Those are the stupid men, not me. I don't have to do that."

"You're fortunate."

"Do you want to be my special friend?" he asked. "I have lots of friends, but no special friends."

Lori thought about what she was hearing. She wanted to dislike this young man because of his mother, but found herself unable to feel any animosity toward him. "Sure," she said. "I'd like that." His manner, though simple, was open and affable, and she liked his smile.

"Why are you here?" he asked.

"Your mother and I ran into some trouble, and had to leave America."

"My mother always has trouble. She doesn't have fun like I do. That makes me smarter, huh?" He removed his jaunty feathered cap and waved it through the air with a flourish. He had such a quixotic, carefree demeanor that she couldn't help laughing. He was making some sense, too, albeit in an elementary way. Maybe people who were ostensibly intelligent didn't see the possibilities in life, she thought, since they allowed too much to get in the way.

Leaning close to her, he said, "You got any stuff with you?"

"What do you mean?"

"You know. Uppers, downers, crisscrosses, angel dust, ecstasy, speed, or maybe a little weed? You wanna smoke a bowl with me?"

Startled, Lori felt her head jerk back involuntarily, as she looked at him in a different light. She hadn't expected this. "I don't have anything," she said, and this was true, because she'd lost her purse in the attack.

"That's okay. I still got part of a bag I'll share with you. I got some Marathon."

"Marathon? Greek Hash? You've got some of that?" It was considered one of the strongest marijuanas in the world, named as it was because its effects remained with the user for long periods of time.

He shrugged. "Sure, but only a coupla cigarettes I rolled myself. They're back at my castle. You wanna see my castle?"

"Is it nearby?" she asked, glancing at the guard and wondering if she could leave the complex without permission.

"Sure," he said, pointing at an apartment across the courtyard. "Right there. See my suit of royal armor outside?"

She saw it now, a hulking shadow by an entry archway. "Cool," she said.

He giggled. "Sometimes when they're looking for me I hide inside it and they can't find me. It has a hatch in the back where I can step through, and shut myself inside."

"It must have belonged to a huge knight," Lori said. "I thought those people used to be short."

"Not all of them, I guess."

"You must be right. What about rust?"

"I oil it a lot, but maybe I should take it inside."

With a smile, Lori followed him past the armor and through the archway.

* * *

The wooden front door of Alex's "castle" bore a childishly scrawled sign which originally read "No Girls Allowed," but someone had altered it so that it read, "No *Good* Girls Allowed." This gave Lori pause. He was quite muscular, outweighing her by at least thirty kilograms. But as he turned and smiled in his disarming manner her fears dissipated and she followed him inside.

The interior of the apartment looked like a glorified child's fort, with poorly executed cardboard cutouts of medieval armor and other artifacts. She noted, however, how spotlessly clean it was, with a fresh lemon scent in the air. Here and there in clay pots and glass vases were silk artificial flowers, which she noted were of good, though not superior, quality.

"I have more armor in here," he said, "where it doesn't rust in the rain." He opened a walk-in closet, revealing two sets of armor, gleaming but looking very old and used, with dents and scratches on them, and evidence of repairs.

"Where did you get all of the armor?"

He shrugged. "Stuff that was already in Monte Konos when the women took over. I thought it was cool, but my Mom and the others didn't want it. They let me play with it."

Reaching into the closet, he dragged one set of armor out and after removing his short sword and scabbard put the armor on over his clothing, piece by piece. As Lori watched, fascinated, he moved with surprising speed, and in a few minutes he finally put gauntlets over his hands, followed by the armet, the headpiece. With his fingers covered by chainmail now, he adjusted the armet, so that could peer out at her, through the vision slit.

Playfully, Lori went into the graceful *t'ai chi* pose of a white crane spreading its wings, then flew at Alex and slammed the side of her fist into the breastplate of the armor, knocking him harmlessly onto a sectional couch, as she intended. It wasn't really the way her instructor would have wanted her to do it, but it was effective nonetheless.

"Whoah!" he said, sitting up and removing his headpiece. His curly hair looked disheveled. "Where did you learn how to do that?"

"My mother sent me to martial arts classes, so that I could deal with aggressive males." Lori smiled. "Like you."

"Aggressive? What does that mean?"

"A fighting person."

"Oh. I only fight for fun. And I never fight girls. That would not be chivalrous."

"So you do know some big words."

"Sure. I'm smart."

"I know." She helped him remove the armor and put it back in the closet.

Afterward, they sat together on the couch.

He lit a marijuana cigarette, took a long puff on it and handed it to her. "Marathon," he said in a dull tone, as gray smoke curled around his face.

Her hands shook as she lifted the crudely rolled cigarette to her lips, and she stopped short. She could smell the acrid smoke in the air, and sensed him watching her.

She remembered her mother, how she wouldn't have wanted her to take drugs. Now Mom was injured and Lori might never see her alive again. A tear formed in the corner of her eye, and she wiped it away.

"I can't do this," she said. She handed the coarse cigarette back to him and tried to compose herself.

"What is wrong, fair maiden?"

"I was thinking of my mother. I think she may be dying. . . the trouble involving your mother. We were attacked by soldiers and barely escaped."

He squeezed the burning end of the cigarette to put it out, and set it on an ashtray. With a big pout he said, "I don't like my mother."

"Because of the way she treats men?" Lori focused on the "roach," the marijuana remnant, and longed for a drag on it. She tried to put it out of her mind.

The words came slowly. "More than that."

"What do you mean?"

Fear slid across the dull features of his face, and he looked around. Then he said, his tone low, "She's dangerous if you make her mad."

"In what way?"

He bit his lower lip and said, in a childlike tone, "I don't want to talk about her any more. She's too scary."

Chapter 11

In The New Testament *there is internal evidence that parts of it have proceeded from an extraordinary man; and that other parts are the fabric of very inferior minds.*

—Thomas Jefferson

Dixie Lou Jackson and other UWW councilwomen watched an oversized video screen that showed a cargo plane off-loading heavy armored vehicles. The new order of war machines rolled down a spiral ramp to a chamber deep beneath Monte Konos, a freshly excavated area. There the equipment would be painted green-and-orange and emblazoned with the symbol of the paramilitary women's organization.

And from a dozen locales around the world, more military accouterment was being sent to them, paid for by wealthy contributors. She hoped it would be enough.

On Dixie Lou's lap lay a newspaper from Seattle, folded open to reveal a story about the mysterious helicopter gunship that attacked a house in the suburbs. If the Bureau could find her there, and Amy in Greece as well, they could find Monte Konos itself.

We must be ready.

* * *

At shortly before midnight, a lone figure in the uniform of a U.S. Army colonel—including jodhpurs, battle ribbons, white gloves, and (folded into a vest pocket) aviator-style sunglasses—prowled the corridors and rooms of the most important private residence in the nation. Many people with ADD–Attention Deficit Disorder–complained about it and considered it a handicap, but not Zack Markwether. He felt his own version of the malaise aided him in verifying security for the White House, since it literally compelled him to check and double-check everything–the door locks, the guard stations, the alarm system and all of the sophisticated surveillance electronics.

None of this was his official assignment, but by virtue of his status as the President's brother, he had taken the responsibility upon himself. His title–Special Adviser to the President–did not even entail specific duties or hours of work, but was instead a broad mandate accompanied by the highest security clearance–giving him full access to all federal buildings, including the Congress of the United States.

His background with the National Security Agency suited him perfectly for this, since he had been indoctrinated in the most advanced methods of counter-terrorism. Such training and experience wasn't nearly as glamorous as it sounded. In all his years of service in the Army and the NSA, most of it involved drudgery and office routine–unlike the romantic depictions of popular novels and films. Only once had he been personally involved in a car chase, and on only three occasions had he made arrests himself. He had, however, been responsible for the intelligence work that led to the apprehension of dozens of enemies of the United States.

After passing the Oval Office in the West Wing, Zack turned down the corridor and stepped into a private office. There he activated a computer at random, one of six work stations in the room. Running through the codes, he spent the better part of an hour reviewing e-mail messages sent by the staffer who ran this terminal, and did a deep encryption search to turn up any that might have been deleted. There were none.

He re-entered the corridor, popped a metab pill to remain awake. It had been a long day, but he needed to remain on constant alert. The less he slept, he always reminded himself, the better chance he had of catching the bad guys. Such security measures were beyond what anyone would consider necessary, but he took them on himself anyway. After all, he was the President's older brother, and felt it was necessary to protect him.

* * *

It was just before dawn of the third day since Consuela had fled from the church, and light was seeping back onto the verdant Mexican landscape so that she could see. As she stood on the side of the rutted dirt road she knew she was taking a big chance, trying to flag down the first vehicle she saw heading west toward the coast, where she wanted to go.

She had spent the night in the jungle, and her clothes were damp from a light rain. Nonetheless, she had managed to keep her baby fairly dry by huddling over the child, and now little Margarita, bundled in a *rebozo*, slept peacefully in the safety of her mother's arms. The first night, not far from her village, they had slept in an abandoned silver mine shaft, dating back to the days when the area had supported thousands of mine workers.

Now Consuela tramped along a dirt road where she had never been before, though she knew compass directions from the stars in the night and the movement of the sun in the day. Her father, a poor but intelligent man, had taught her how to do this and she was thankful for the knowledge. On other matters, despite her lack of formal education, she prided herself on her own natural intelligence.

From somewhere a burro brayed repeatedly in displeasure, and Consuela smelled the acrid smoke of a morning cook-fire. She longed for the warmth and security of her home, and was sorry to have run away without telling her parents where she was going. But there had been no choice. Not after the terrible events at the church, where demons had invaded the House of the Lord and gunfire had erupted.

She saw an approaching produce truck as it barreled along the dirt road, throwing up thick, swirling clouds of dust. At first she turned away from the vehicle, afraid to show her face. Then, hesitantly, she turned back and waved frantically, and moved out into the roadway.

* * *

On the viewing platform of a large underground grotto, Styx Tertullian and Nelson Culpepper watched their elite paramilitary squads pass in tight formation. The silver-and-black-uniformed men, wearing black jackboots, took high, stiff-kneed steps to military music, while keeping their heads turned toward their commanders. The front and rear rows twirled automatic rifles and saluted with sabers, while men carrying BOI banners tilted them forward sharply.

Behind them rolled gleaming small-rocket carriages, along with armored vehicles and customized weapons systems . . . and on wall screens around the grotto flashed video projections showing jets, bombers, and helicopters . . . all kept in chambers beneath the ground.

As the officials watched from their stationary platform, the floor with the squads and equipment slid smoothly beneath another floor, and an entirely new combat unit of men and hardware appeared. When this group had completed its pageantry, another unit appeared, and others afterward—until all of the forces stationed at BOI headquarters had been displayed.

It amounted to a small army, highly trained, well-equipped, and formidable.

Chapter 12

A woman will betray the Savior.
                    —Jewish Prophecy, 1st Century, BC

It irritated Styx Tertullian that he had to be in an underground office. Arguably the Bureau of Ideology was the most powerful private agency in the world, the maker and breaker of presidents, prime ministers, and even kings. Why then couldn't he and Minister Culpepper be ensconced above-ground, in the plush, ostentatious offices they deserved?

He knew the answers, but didn't like them. Three words provided the explanation: Security, security, security. Since its founding in 1932, the Bureau had always been obsessed about this, and history proved the wisdom of the paranoid world-view. While he understood it only too well, he didn't like it.

Seated at his desk, he watched a video report sent to him by the Vatican, which was requesting BOI assistance in investigating a break-in into one of their museum vaults. Priceless, irreplaceable treasures had been stolen, including paintings by da Vinci and Raphael, sculptures by Michelangelo, and a reliquary said to contain an ancient fragment of wood from the crucifixion cross of Jesus—the legendary "True Cross." The BOI, with its ability to investigate sensitive crimes committed against Christian organizations, was frequently called upon to offer its expertise.

According to the video, the UWW was suspected, as they were rumored to have a long-standing policy of stealing such artifacts and either hiding or destroying them—purportedly to undermine the sense of well-being in the evangelical world. In reality this was disinformation—a false story planted by the BOI to discredit their enemies. The Bureau had taken the religious articles, for what Culpepper called "safekeeping."

Styx flipped off the video, and was about to leave when the portly Minister entered, unannounced. "What are you doing about the Vatican request?" he asked. His girth seemed to grow larger by the day.

Standing by his desk, Styx didn't feel like answering questions from this irritating man. "I'll send some men to go through the motions. We'll put thumbscrews on the nuns until they confess."

"Don't try my patience."

"Look, I've got things to take care of," Styx said. "Can we continue this later?"

Culpepper paced the office. "You're sure the women will be blamed?"

"I know my job."

"Of course. Oh, I examined the inventory. Have the Raphael painting hung in my office, behind my desk."

Styx smiled in his unique manner, somehow forming a "V" with his lips. "You can trust me, sir." But he was thinking how sick he was of Culpepper's unethical scavenging.

As the Minister left, Styx was wondering, too, if a controlled blast might be set off inside the fat man's office, just enough to blow him up and all of his coveted things—after substituting forgeries for original religious masterpieces, of course. Styx took a deep breath, trying to calm himself.

He would only do that if God commanded it.

Chapter 13

Biblical scholars admit not knowing exactly which month, or even which year, Jesus was born. Naysayers try to dismiss The New Testament *because of this apparent discrepancy, but such thinking misses an immense truth: Jesus Christ walked the earth as the Son of God. Jesus was the greatest teacher of morals in all of history.*
—C.G. Anqui, *Voices in the Desert*

Monte Konos, an ancient hive of tunnel passageways and chambers, still bore evidence of numerous changes over the centuries as hard-working, enterprising monks continually made alterations. A walled over doorway here, a blocked stairway there, and beneath each building numerous abandoned and long-forgotten chambers where long-dead hermits once lived their austere lives.

With a detailed knowledge of this high-perched monastery, a man in dark clothing left the main passageway and slipped into an alcove. It was midnight, cold and wintry outside, cool and damp inside. He slipped a blade into a narrow opening between stones, causing an eight hundred year old concealed door to open. Almost noiselessly it swung inward, which was remarkable for its age, and the shadowy figure entered quickly. The door closed.

A familiar mustiness filled the sealed enclosure, an odor of moisture and bygone candle fires, because this room had once been accessible from the church above. Another odor mixed with the others, of decayed bodies whose wooden crypts had cracked open with age. Five long-forgotten priests had been sealed away here. The crypts contained few valuables, and no one was known to have removed anything from them.

Though it was pitch black in this windowless chamber, he knew the way by heart, and found the wall recess where a battery-operated lantern had been secreted. This was flipped on, causing shadows to scurry into the cracks between stones, where they would hide until it was again their time to come forth. On the ceiling a rectangular shape of dark stones was visible, showing where the original stairway had been covered over. Dark wood fragments from the ancient stairs remained, piled in a corner that had once been the altar.

A stone table stood in the center of the room, and upon it lay a black case. He zipped it open, revealing a laptop computer inside. He voice-activated it, and the keys clicked without being touched, typing a longer missive than usual. There was much to coordinate with the others.

Half an hour later he slipped out of the room, after leaving a microdisk in the usual place for pickup.

* * *

Lori lay half awake, having slipped in and out of troubled slumber all through the night. Sunlight streamed through a dirty window, illuminating a partially open doorway and a toilet. She had been provided with a small closet, stocked with clean clothes. On her right, a night stand held a small coffee maker, a cup, and a bowl containing packets of cream and sugar.

Rubbing sleep from her eyes, she pushed the covers away and swung her feet onto a cold stone floor. She wore a plain cotton nightgown. Her hands shook a little, and she lit a Greek cigarette, inhaled its rough, burning smoke. After exhaling for a long moment, she didn't feel any better.

Cold perspiration clung to her from a nightmare. Trapped in it only moments before, she and her mother had been back in the goddess circle again. Except this time Lori knew in advance what terrible events were going to occur, and could do nothing to prevent them. Again, the soldiers in silver-and-black uniforms attacked. Again, they shot her mother.

The Bureau of Ideology.

Whoever these enemies of United Women of the World were, and Lori had only minimal information on them, they were a deadly lot, not to be taken lightly. Her own narrow escape confirmed this.

The doorbell rang for several seconds, a short and unfamiliar ditty, perhaps Greek.

Upon opening the door, she was greeted by a smiling Alex Jackson. Wearing a white shirt with chain mail crudely drawn on it in black, he handed Lori a bouquet of silk daisies and cosmos. "This is how a knight should act," he said with a wink of his gray eyes.

"How do you know how a knight should act?" she asked. She accepted the artificial flowers, led the way into her apartment and located a vase.

"I read comic books," he answered. "Actually, 'graphic novels.' A graphic novel has a spine, you know."

"These flowers are beautiful," she said. "Thank you so much." As if playing a pretend game with a child, she put her nose to the silk blossoms and commented on the sweetness of their aroma. Then she resumed smoking, short, nervous puffs.

As they stood in the tiny kitchen she described the terrible attack on the goddess circle and the grievous injuries to her mother, and she told of a woman leading the attack group, the gender assumed because of the high-pitched voice. "Alex, your mom said they were with the Bureau of Ideology, a terrorist group masquerading as Christians. Do you know anything about them?"

He shrugged dully.

Lori was about to say something else when she stopped, her thoughts whirling back into the void of the dark, painful memory. She thought she heard the rumble of the attack helicopter again, and the brutal, staccato rhythm of gunfire.

"Quake!" Alex yelled. "Get under the table!"

Slow to respond herself, Lori felt him guiding her under the dining room table. She held onto her cigarette. On the floor, he circled his arms around her protectively.

The small chandelier rattled overhead, and window panes quivered in their frames. She kept expecting to hear glass shatter, but in a few moments the noises subsided and so did the shaking.

"Does that happen very often around here?" she asked, taking a quick drag on the cigarette, followed by another.

"I dunno. Sometimes, I guess."

Lori pulled away from Alex's arms and they sat cross-legged on the floor, looking at each other. Even though he was dimwitted, she felt like talking to him. He seemed receptive. Finishing the first cigarette, she lit another.

The teenager told him about her mother, who had resisted forming new relationships with men because of her fear that one of them might sexually abuse Lori. She related what little she knew of her father as well—the fragments of memory from her childhood that contradicted what her mother told her about him: how his laughter filled a room; the way he loved to wrestle with Lori and carry her around piggyback; the way he wore aviator-style sunglasses.

She kept talking to Alex, largely a one-way conversation. Because of his apparent inability to understand, she felt at ease telling him some of her innermost thoughts, as a person might talk to a favorite dog or a cat. While she spoke he nodded or grunted in affirmation, but not always at the right moments.

Then he surprised her, with an alert observation. "To listen to our moms," he said, "you'd think there are no good men in the whole world."

"Still, I wish I could listen to my mother again," Lori said. The girl broke down in tears, and he consoled her with simple, gentle words.

Part Two

THE HOLY WOMEN'S BIBLE

Chapter 14

It is said of Lori Vale that she is blessed with a holy talent.
—From *Saint or Sinner*, UWW Press

After knocking on the door of her son's apartment and receiving no response, Dixie Lou crossed a cobblestone street and took an elevator to a lower level, into the ancient catacombs of the monastery. She wore a metallic black dress, her sword-cross necklace, and gold-colored boots. Wondering where Alex was this morning, she decided to check back on him later. The earthquake, which had occurred an hour before, had not been strong enough to be a concern.

But as she stepped into a corridor she stopped suddenly, struck by a startling memory. She'd been in a place like this a long, long time ago, within an enclosure constructed of similar blackened gray stones, except it had not been a monastery. It had been something else, an entirely dark and gloomy place except for a narrow beam of sunlight that passed through a barred window and illuminated a bearded man inside as he knelt on the rock floor, praying.

A prison . . .

The prisoner turned his head, looked toward her through the bars of his cell. She squinted, tried to make out the details of his face, but the sunlight was too bright and she couldn't.

At a noise the image faded. She was back in the monastery, and saw a hooded figure in the passageway to her right, moving rapidly away from her. The figure bounded up a stairway, out of view. She couldn't tell if it was a man or a woman.

When Dixie Lou reached the base of the stairway she looked up, but no one was in sight.

Odd, she thought, wondering who it was. She would have the area staked out. There had been too many unusual occurrences recently . . . and annoying incidents of sabotage.

* * *

Following the time spent with Alex that morning, Lori had asked him to leave so that she could remove her robe and get dressed for the day, in blue jeans and a pink blouse. She hadn't worn the medical patch since the day before. The wounds on her forehead and temple were still pink, but only hurt a little to the touch.

Her eyes needed a little makeup. She searched through articles on the bathroom counter. A small container of personal articles had been provided for her with the apartment, but she didn't care for the eyeliner color, which was too dark a shade of blue. While washing it off with cold cream she heard the doorbell rang.

"Lori, hurry!" a man shouted through the door. She recognized Alex's voice. At first it irritated her that he had returned so soon, but then she remembered his disability, and resolved to be patient.

When she opened the door, she found him in a fever-pitch of excitement. "Come with me," he said. "I wanna show you a secret."

Within minutes they were hurrying down a stairway beneath the street, into a passageway. "I know a shortcut," Alex said, at a half run. He moved athletically, effortlessly.

Lori kept up, but had to breathe hard to do so. As she ran she felt a half pack of cigarettes that she had stuffed in a front pocket of her jeans. "Where are we going?"

"You'll see!"

They caught a rail car for a short distance, then ran into a tunnel. "We're almost there," he said, over his shoulder.

Lori was breathing hard behind him. "Why are we in such a hurry?"

"To get there before my mom does. I race her sometimes."

"I see."

A door slid open ahead, marking the apparent end of the tunnel. Bright lights shone. Guards in pale gold uniforms with green-and-orange shoulder patches waved them by, saluting Alex with W's as he passed. He and Lori climbed into an electric cart, which spiraled up a ramp. The small vehicle, which was white with a canvas top, exited into an immense room with a high ceiling.

"I think we beat her," Alex said, as they stepped out of the cart. "We're in a building where monkeys used to copy religious stuff into books."

On a wall, Lori read "Scriptorium Building," which was written in two languages, including English. She didn't recognize the other language.

"I think you mean monks," she said with a smile.

Alex didn't seem to understand. He led her to a guard station adjacent to a closed door. Two uniformed women greeted them.

"Good morning, Alex," one said with a broad smile. She looked at Lori, then back at him. "Your girlfriend?"

"We wanna go inside," Alex said.

"Now you know we can't permit that. We've been through that before. You always come here and we always give you same answer."

"But I wanna show Lori where my Mom works. This is her big job, huh? Right through that door, huh?"

A gray-haired woman approached from the side, at a purposeful gait. "Alex, what are you doing here?" she demanded. "Turn around right now and go home. We have important work to do." Her hands were on her hips, and her deeply creased face reflected displeasure. Her pale blue eyes glittered.

"You're not talking nice to me, Katherine," he complained, with a pout.

"Alex, I don't have time for this. Just go. We'll discuss it later."

With his face set in a stubborn expression, he shook his head. "This time I wanna go inside."

"We'd better leave," Lori said to him, grabbing hold of his arm.

"It's okay, Miss Pangalos," one of the guards said. "He always comes here and we always send him home. It's a harmless little game we play with him a couple of times a week. You go on inside, OK, and we'll take care of him for you."

"I don't see why he was even allowed to get this far," Katherine said. "Someone should have stopped him back there." She pointed toward the top of the entrance ramp, where several white electric carts were parked.

"Miss, he can't see anything from here anyway. His mother doesn't get mad about him getting this far, so we assumed–"

"Well you should never assume anything. Do you know who I am?"

The guard hung her head. "Yes, Miss Pangalos."

"Well I'm ordering you not to let this young man into the building anymore. Notify the other guard stations."

"Yes, ma'am."

Katherine grabbed Alex by the arm and pointed him toward the electric carts. "Young man, you are to leave immediately."

"What's going on here?" Turning, Lori saw Dixie Lou, who had come out of the door behind the guards. The teenager felt the familiar queasy feeling return, in the pit of her stomach.

"They're not being nice to me, Momma," Alex said, easily breaking away from Katherine. "Hey, how'd you get here before me? I went real fast."

Dixie Lou smiled at her dimwitted son. "Well your Momma is a little faster today." She looked at Katherine Pangalos. "What are you doing to my son?"

"Your stupid boy is wasting our time. He shouldn't be in here, and I've told the guards not to allow him this far again."

"I'm not stupid," Alex muttered, but only Lori heard him.

"Oh you did, did you?" Dixie Lou said to Katherine, her eyes fiery with rage. "Well did it ever occur to you to ask me first? In case you've forgotten, I'm Chairwoman pro tem, selected by Amy as her successor."

"And I brought in the first two special cases, not to mention the fact that I'm the largest UWW contributor. Ruffle my feathers, lady, and I stop your precious money flow. I have influence, you know."

"Even you couldn't stop our funding. We have plenty of other sources."

"You'd be surprised at what I could do."

"I don't care about any of that," Dixie Lou snapped. Affectionately, she put an arm around Alex. "This is my son and he's to be treated with respect, even by you. *Especially* by you, in fact."

"Such respect can occur elsewhere," Katherine said in a haughty tone. "There is critical work to be done here and these young people are interfering."

"We wanna go inside there, Momma," Alex said, pointing to the closed door.

"Out of the question," Katherine said. "I've never heard such a preposterous idea."

"And what harm could he do?" Dixie Lou snapped. "He's just a stupid boy, as you said."

"I'm not stupid," Alex repeated, louder this time so that all heard him.

"And her?" Katherine said, pointing at Lori.

"She goes inside, too," Dixie Lou said. "Lori Vale saved my life, which is more than you've ever done for me, Katherine. In fact, I'm not sure that you deserve to go inside any more. You're not even a councilwoman."

"Hrrmphh, just a technicality. I will be soon, and you know it. The next open chair has been promised to me."

To the guards, Dixie Lou said, "Until further notice *from me*, these young people are to be permitted inside, all the way to the cubicles."

"Yes, ma'am," they said, in unison.

"They're just young people," Dixie Lou said, as if trying to convince herself of the wisdom of what she was doing. "They can't do any harm." Leaning over, she flicked something off the top of one of her gold boots.

"You're responsible if anything goes wrong," Katherine huffed. She hurried through the door, followed by the others. . . .

Inwardly, as Dixie Lou led her son and Lori toward the cubicles, she was somewhat surprised that she was doing this, and hoped she wasn't making a big mistake. She had, after all, acted impulsively and out of anger, without fully considering the consequences.

"Thank you, Momma," Alex said. Smiling at her in his silly, carefree way, he passed a hand casually through his curly hair.

Dixie Lou looked at Lori, whose intelligence was far superior to that of her own son. The girl was somewhat defiant, but perhaps that was because she didn't understand the immensity of the project that was underway. After seeing this, her behavior was bound to improve.

But secrecy was of paramount importance, and Dixie Lou would discuss that privately with Lori. The girl would cooperate, *or else*, and there were ways of ensuring appropriate behavior. The Angkor Vow, perhaps, and put her on staff. As for Alex, it didn't much matter what he said to anyone, because no one took him seriously anyway. Besides, he wouldn't understand what he was seeing. Lori might, though, so she'd bear closer watching.

It'll all work out, Dixie Lou told herself. She took a deep breath, and began to appreciate the scale of responsibilities she was assuming as Amy's replacement. Was it only temporary? Would the Chairwoman return?

* * *

Lori absorbed her surroundings. The vaulted room contained cubicles and aisles and banks of computers. Men and women hurried up and down the aisles and stood at the machines, discussing what they saw on the screens. The air buzzed with activity.

Dixie Lou led Alex and Lori down one aisle and another, past modern tables and ancient rock-slab platforms that might have been used by monks at one time but which now held computer equipment. She paused by one of the glass-walled cubicles.

Lori was transfixed by what she saw inside the enclosure. A diminutive woman sat at a computer terminal, touching one of eight separate panels on an oversized screen that took up an entire wall. The panels contained words in an ornate script.

On top of a table in the center of the room sat a female child with olive skin and reddish-brown hair, being tended to by a rotund woman in a white dress, wearing a green-and-orange identity badge on her lapel. In a yellow play suit covered with camel and donkey designs, the little girl, perhaps a year and a half old, appeared to be pouting. The table had a safety railing all around it.

A peculiar feeling crept over Lori. The strange entwined with the familiar, an odd dance of sensations.

"Remain out here," Dixie Lou said. She entered the little room and crossed to the table. From the doorway Lori could see that the child had bright green eyes.

"This is Veronica, at her scripting station," Dixie Lou said, glancing back at Lori. "She's a very old soul. The woman with her is her matron. This is one of our special children, and her words are being recorded and entered into our computer system."

"Not much today," the matron reported. "None of the usual food or toy tricks are working." She looked inquisitively at Alex and Lori.

The toddler blinked her green eyes in Lori's direction, and looked sad. Then Veronica said a couple of words that Lori couldn't understand, and pushed away stuffed animals around her . . . toy camels and donkeys matching the designs on the play suit. Near her were little dolls resembling biblical men and women: a bearded man on a cross that must have been Jesus, and a male doll with short hair and a Roman tunic, with a single red stripe on the side of the garment.

"I want dolls like those." Alex said, his tone childlike.

Lori exchanged smiles with him, but felt troubled. She was not sure that she liked what she was seeing. Food and toy tricks? What did that mean?

"I'm glad they let us in," Alex said. He was shifting around on his feet, so excited that he could hardly contain himself.

Lori struggled to comprehend what was occurring here.

Upon noticing Lori through the glass of the cubicle, the child's expression changed, and she smiled and said something, which again the teenager could not understand.

The women in the cubicle exchanged glances, and the computer technician typed.

Hypnotized by Veronica's sad green eyes, Lori took a hesitant step into the cubicle, not removing her gaze from the child. But Lori was prevented from going further by the large matron, who moved toward her to block the way.

Dixie Lou waved the woman aside, and Lori approached the table.

Something ineffable drew the teenager forward, but she proceeded slowly, cautiously. As she neared the child, she felt a severe tingling of her own skin, as if the layers of flesh were vibrating against one other. It was an unsettling sensation, one that confused her and failed to provide her with confidence in the integrity of her own body.

The discomfiture increased as she drew nearer to the child, but it wasn't such that she wanted to turn and flee. Paradoxically, she felt a need to be closer to Veronica and eventually touch her, even if the result caused Lori to shatter into a billion irretrievable particles. What an odd thought. Why should she fear a tiny, innocent-looking child?

Lori reached Dixie Lou's side, and ever so carefully moved her hand to the edge of the table and rested it there. Lori's entire body was shaking.

Within the immense computer screen on the wall, the separate panels contained words, alphabet letters, and sentence fragments in an unknown language, and in English below that, with dots between the entries representing missing portions. The terminal operator scrolled the panels so that new sections came into view.

"How are you, Veronica?" Dixie Lou asked, with a broad smile. She clasped one of the child's hands in her own, commented that it was warm to the touch.

Veronica didn't reply, pulled her hand free and kicked the dolls and animals on the table. Some tumbled to the floor.

"She doesn't talk in the normal sense," Dixie Lou said. "None of the she-apostles do."

"The what?"

"She-apostles." Dixie Lou went on to explain to Lori that this child and the others like her were the reincarnated female apostles of Jesus—and that the children spoke in sentence fragments from a long-ago language, Aramaic.

Startled, Lori caught her breath. She didn't know what to believe. It didn't sound possible.

"This was one of the first two we found," Dixie Lou said. "She was born to Italian parents, who quickly took her to a doctor when she started babbling. It wasn't like normal baby talk, and frightened the parents." Dixie Lou stroked the hair of the child.

Veronica pushed her away.

"Be polite, little one," Dixie Lou said, in a soothing tone, "or we won't give you the little oranges you love."

At a signal from Dixie Lou, the matron brought out a small orange from one of her own pockets.

The child reached out for it, but the woman withheld it.

The child shook her head angrily, and scuttled to the opposite side of the table, away from her.

"I'm not the best person with these children," Dixie Lou admitted. "They're moody and unpredictable. Sometimes they talk, sometimes they don't."

"May I try?" Lori asked, reaching a hand out to the child, but not touching her yet. She didn't like the way Veronica was being treated, but didn't feel comfortable saying anything about that. Not until she figured out how to voice her complaint, and what to do about it.

"Don't let her," an urgent voice said. Peripherally, Lori saw Katherine Pangalos in the doorway.

"Go ahead," Dixie Lou said.

Gathering courage, Lori clasped the child's hand. Tiny fingers wrapped around the teenager's forefinger, and a sub-cellular earthquake shook Lori to the core, then dissipated, leaving her with a warm, infinitely calm sensation. She lifted Veronica into the air, and suddenly the child began to speak loudly and rapidly in a peculiar language, as if a faucet had been turned on.

"She's speaking ancient Aramaic!" Dixie Lou said excitedly. "Complete sentences!" She pointed to the woman at the computer. "We're translating to English on-the-spot . . . a rough translation that is refined later, after the recording is studied in more detail."

In their spoken form, the words sounded vaguely familiar to Lori, but she couldn't quite place them. She read the words on the wall screen, printed in ornate script:

"Our Lord Jesus loved and respected women. I, Veronica, and Mary Magdalene were among his twenty-four apostles. When the Savior was being led to his crucifixion, carrying his own heavy wooden cross, he stumbled and fell to one knee, near where I stood with Mary Magdalene in a throng of onlookers at the side of the road. As the Lord Jesus struggled to His feet, He gazed upon us and smiled. He was bloody and bruised from being beaten by the guards. I stepped toward Him and wiped His face with my veil. Gazing upon me tenderly He blessed me and said, 'You have my blood. I am with you always.' They took Him straight to the cross on the Hill of Golgotha and nailed Him there."

As the translator finished typing, Veronica held onto Lori's hand, and smiled at her. "The Catholic legend of Veronica," the translator said, "but the words of Jesus are new."

"Give her the orange now," Dixie Lou said.

The matron did so, and the child began peeling the skin off the fruit.

Standing and watching the she-apostle, Lori felt angered at this method of dealing with children, but held her tongue. She had heard of food deprivation techniques on animals, but never on human beings.

Dixie Lou glared at the old woman in the doorway. "Well, Katherine, what do you say to the latest?"

"It requires further study."

As the two women continued their discussion in sharp tones, Lori smoothed the child's reddish-brown hair, which was of a darker hue than her own.

"How diplomatic," Dixie Lou said to Katherine. "I'm surprised you're not accusing me of setting up a trick."

"I'm willing to admit I've been hard on you in the past," Katherine said. "We need to work together, so I'll try to be more understanding."

"How refreshing."

The elderly doctor's eyes flashed, but this time she made no retort.

"How do you know Veronica is reincarnated?" Lori asked, of no one in particular.

The translator spun on her chair, looked at Dixie Lou. "Shall I answer that?"

The Acting Chairwoman did not respond, and as she looked at Lori she seemed amazed by the remarkable effect the teenager's presence seemed to have had on the child. Dixie Lou watched them continue to interact, touching hands, smiling, sharing something in the looks they exchanged, in their eyes.

"There is no other explanation for the words they speak," the translator explained. "They are tiny children, using the ancient language of Jesus and no other tongue. At first, two female babies appeared, and informed us they were among a group of twelve."

"All females?" Lori asked.

"Yes, meaning Jesus had twenty-four apostles, twelve of each gender. When the special female babies and toddlers were brought in—we have eleven now—Amy Angkor-Billings began to call them 'she-apostles.'"

"Where is the twelfth—she-apostle?" Lori asked.

"Missing. Hasn't been brought to us yet, so we hope she is safe. With each additional child we learn new fragments of the story of Jesus, which we fit into place like puzzle pieces. Sometimes putting the children together causes them to talk more, but that stopped working several days ago, and they began speaking only sporadically, in incomplete sentences. Until you showed up."

Lori tried to understand. "These are *new* gospels?"

Finally Veronica pulled away, then hurled the doll of the Roman man across the little room.

The translator rose to her feet, crossed her arms over her chest. "In a sense, but they're actually *old*, brought to light again after being lost for centuries. We're assembling a new holy book, combining edited sections of *The Old Testament* and *The New Testament* with our *Testament of the She-Apostles*."

"This is a mind-blower," Lori said.

The woman nodded. "We quite agree."

"Have you learned anything sensational about Jesus?" Lori asked. "Anything shocking?"

"Such as confirmation of rumors that he might have been married, or something like that?"

"I guess so. Any dirt on the holy man at all? Did he always turn the other cheek, or did he ever get in a fist fight and give someone a bloody nose?"

"You have an irreverent manner of speaking," Katherine Pangalos said.

"I apologize for my directness," Lori said.

"No 'dirt' on him," the translator said. "To the contrary, we have new evidence that our beloved Jesus was completely nonviolent, and that he was celibate, too. Some of the rumors about his personal life are quite entertaining, and quite wrong. A number of biblical researchers have suggested that Jesus and Mary Magdalene were either lovers or husband and wife, and that children were born to them. There are even soap opera scenarios in which Mary Magdalene was not faithful to Jesus, or that he might have had multiple sexual partners himself. Some of these tales go back a long time. In the sixteenth century, Martin Luther discussed the possibility that Jesus might have been something of a ladies' man, and not in the platonic sense. There are even suggestions that he might have been married more than once."

"Wow!" Lori said.

"We don't believe any of that, of course. It's all nonsense, utter nonsense. Jesus loved and admired women, but he had no physical relationships with any of them."

"I'm glad to hear that," Lori said. "He wasn't gay either, I assume?"

She heard Katherine Pangalos mutter something in disapproval.

"No, he wasn't gay," the translator said, "and he wasn't asexual, either. He was celibate—one of the sacrifices he made when he took the form of a flesh and blood man."

"It sounds like you admire him," Lori said.

"All of us do, very much."

"But you have goddess circles, a She-God, and Jesus, too—I don't see how it all works."

"We're Christians, but obviously we're not in the mainstream."

"I'm sorry to ask so many questions. I'm just curious."

Smiling in a kindly way, the translator said, "You have every right, considering what we just saw with Veronica."

"I can't explain what happened."

"Well, it happened." She looked at Veronica. "Some of the information provided by the she-apostles is entirely new, while some of it—such as what this child said moments ago—is linked to information we already had. Last week, Veronica told us that Jesus loved Mary Magdalene most of all, a story that is very similar to the Gospel of Philip, one of the gospels that was omitted from the *Bible*. In the early centuries after Jesus died, a great struggle took place over the role of women in the church, and gospels favorable to them were destroyed. But some brave person hid copies near Nag Hammadi in upper Egypt, where they were found in 1945. Later there was an additional major discovery at Alexandria, with even more gospels that have been translated—gospels that contain fragments matching the new words of the she-apostles. This is further confirmation of our project."

The translator paused and glanced at Dixie Lou Jackson, who simply smiled. In Comparative Religion class, Lori had heard about the Apocrypha and other religious texts that were not in the *Bible* . . . but she didn't know much about them, or the reasons for the decisions.

"Why was the Gospel of Philip omitted from the *Bible*?" Lori asked.

"The framers of the *Bible*—powerful male clergymen in the first three or four centuries after Jesus Christ—didn't want any suggestion that he might have had a physical or even an emotional relationship with a woman. They had another overriding concern as well, wishing to conceal the high esteem Jesus felt for all of womanhood."

"Do you understand what you've done?" Dixie Lou said to Lori. "You've drawn more words from this she-apostle than anyone else, and we have ten others like her. What effect will you have on *them*?"

Lori shrugged. She was sensing something she couldn't quite identify, an inexplicable, mystifying feeling that was coming over her.

"Come back tomorrow," Dixie Lou said, "and we'll see what you can do."

The teenager was beginning to feel worse with each passing moment. She didn't respond. . . .

"But she could contaminate the memories of the children," Katherine protested, in a concerned tone.

"How?" Dixie Lou asked.

"Don't be dense. This is potentially disruptive to our entire program. It requires further study, the judgment of the entire council."

"So nice to see you back in your usual good humor."

"Think about it. At least admit when I'm right."

"Don't hold your breath." But inwardly Dixie Lou was beginning to agree with Katherine, and realized she may have acted precipitously in allowing her son and the girl in. This could be the work of the Devil, acting through an innocent-looking teenage girl.

"Do I need to obtain an emergency council order?" Katherine demanded.

"No," Dixie Lou said in an agitated voice. "I'll go along with you on this." Aside from her own concerns about allowing Lori in, Dixie Lou didn't want to risk weakening her own personal power base by going against the council on an issue where she would in all likelihood lose.

"Now you're making some sense."

"Lori Vale will be kept away from the children until the council approves," Dixie Lou promised.

"I'll see to that myself," Katherine said. . . .

"Thank you," Dixie Lou said, but Lori noted displeasure in her eyes, oddly mixed with fascination.

Lori noticed Alex outside the cubicle, watching silently with his gray-eyed gaze. In the midst of all the commotion, she'd almost forgotten about him. His relationship with his mother seemed peculiar to her. There was a playful aspect to the young man that surprised Lori— the race today, and other things he did. But the night before, he had confided that he didn't like his mother, and more. His exact words came back to her: "She's dangerous if you make her mad."

An overwhelmingly bleak feeling had settled over Lori, a dismal gloom. She felt alone and vulnerable, with a general sense of unease, that she was faced with important decisions but didn't have the wisdom or experience to handle them.

She thought she heard a whispering of women's voices, like a heavenly susurration on a cosmic, ethereal wind. Turning her head slightly, she saw Veronica's mouth moving.

Something clicked off in Lori's mind . . . or on. She wasn't sure which, but it was like a change of pressure, or the sealing of a vacuum chamber. She no longer heard specific sounds, not the mysterious murmuring and not the voices of Dixie Lou or the other women in the cubicle. The child's mouth continued to move, silently, and Lori saw that Veronica had one hand over the side of her mouth.

The lips made the same pattern of movement over and over. Word shapes, but not in English, and not in Aramaic either, she sensed. Closing her eyes, Lori envisioned Veronica's tiny mouth, framing something so carefully. A private message?

With a start she realized it was a single word, in a secret language that was unknown to the translators in this Scriptorium.

Iktol.

Somehow, inexplicably, Lori knew what it meant.

Murder.

But a secret language? How did Lori know that, and why couldn't she summon up any other words in that tongue? Surely, her mind must be playing tricks with her.

Opening her eyes she saw that Veronica was now gazing in another direction, away from Lori. From the side, Lori could see that her lips were no longer moving, and she had lowered her hand away from her mouth. The child's tiny hand had concealed the word from the others and especially from the camera in one corner of the room, so that no translator could read her lips on video.

Iktol.

Lori's thoughts spun wildly, and she wondered if her imagination had run amok. The incident certainly wasn't anything to mention to the others. They'd only think she was crazy, and maybe they'd be right.

Chapter 15

She-apostle babies and toddlers rarely smile, and never actually "play" with toys, in the usual sense of the word. They look at them occasionally, more out of curiosity than anything else, it seems, and then set them—or hurl them—aside. The children seem old in their behavior, and we understand why, of course, but there is something else about them that remains unexplained: an intense, abiding sadness.

—Note screen, UWW computer file

With Lori in the passenger seat, Alex drove the electric cart out of the Scriptorium and back down into the musty subterranean passageways. He accelerated through a long tunnel and took a banked turn at high speed. They went up a spiral ramp, then slowed and entered the interior of a large hall, where Alex parked the vehicle in one of several marked spaces along the perimeter, beside other small vehicles.

The hall was filled with stone slab tables and benches, a few of which were occupied by people in pale gold uniforms with UWW shoulder patches, or in dull grayish-brown robes with the hoods thrown back. Most of the diners were women. The men present, Lori had learned, were all "knights," because of the requirement that they fulfill the various needs of the women. There were serving knights, office knights, kitchen knights, and a variety of other job categories, including the popular stud knights. Even though Lori had grown up on the streets, she thought that the use of a stud service was depraved, without the personal commitment and responsibility that should be present in a relationship.

Even worse, the men of Monte Konos were held as slaves, without the right to make their own choices.

Lori noted a rectangular sign high on one wall: REFECTORY BUILDING. She and Alex seemed to be on the main level of the structure; through an open doorway another building, gray and weathered, could be seen on the other side of a cobblestone plaza.

"That's where we were," he said, noticing the direction of her inquisitive, lavender-eyed gaze.

"The Scriptorium?"

He nodded.

Lori wondered why they hadn't just walked across the plaza, and theorized that the fun-loving Alex enjoyed driving the electric carts. She smelled pleasant cooking odors, which made her hungry.

As the pair walked toward the dining area, Dixie Lou and a middle-aged blonde woman caught up and walked with them. Wearing a long black dress and glittering gold earrings, Dixie Lou moved to Lori's side. Upset that she wasn't being allowed to see her mother, and wasn't being told her condition, the teenager took a deep breath, but didn't say what was on her mind. Ever since arriving here, Lori had been asking about her mother; she asked guards, Dixie Lou herself, anyone she encountered. But no one gave her any answers. While Dixie Lou had initially said her mother's condition had stabilized, that had been the last piece of information Lori had received. After that, *nothing*, and she was feeling increasingly angry.

"The Refectory is much as it was in ancient times," Dixie Lou explained, in her Southern drawl. "Of course we've added modern cooking and refrigeration appliances and a few other touches for the sake of convenience. But if you squint, you can almost visualize monks here with their hooded heads bent over bowls of soup."

"How many monks were in the monastery?" Lori asked. She felt awkward being civil to this woman, whom she loathed, but if she was going to survive here—and find out about her own mother—it was a requirement. She would tolerate her, without getting too close.

"Four hundred twenty at the height of the facility in the fourteenth century. This dining hall seats a hundred and forty, a third of the population—so they ate in shifts." With a golden-ringed forefinger she pointed to a high bank of windows, on one wall. "If those windows were lower you'd see a magnificent view of the valley and Macedonian mountains, quite spectacular. But monks, being austere, did not partake in such hedonistic delights."

Dixie Lou selected a table near a buffet counter brimming with fish, lamb and salads, along with platters of dark breads and Greek cakes. Racks of wine lined a nearby wall.

Alex handed a luncheon menu to Lori. As he looked over his own copy, he tugged at an earlobe, thoughtfully.

She scanned the items, which were described in Greek, with English translations. There were no prices. Several types of baked fish and pilaf were featured, along with a stuffed squid sauté and, most tempting to her, a stuffed shoulder of lamb with eggplant. She loved lamb, but didn't feel like eating anything too heavy. Ever since the terrible events at the goddess circle her stomach had been upset, and she felt like she had lost several pounds.

"See anything you like?" Alex inquired.

"I'll have monk food," Lori said, finally. "Greek bread and a bowl of lamb broth soup." Her stomach wasn't so queasy around Dixie Lou now, but the sensation had been replaced by another. She didn't like anything about the woman.

"Ah yes," Dixie Lou said, in a tone of approval. "*Zomos arniou*, my favorite soup. It's best when served with boiled greens and slices of feta cheese. And white *retsina*, of course."

"*Retsina*?"

"Wine. There is no drinking age here. Even small children drink with their families."

"I'd better not," Lori said. "Alcohol has been a problem for me."

"Of course," Dixie Lou said. She discussed the food selection with the blonde who accompanied her, a woman who had not yet been introduced to Lori.

During the meal, a young female guard brought a message to Dixie Lou, in an envelope. The guard saluted—the three-fingered "W"—and left.

Lori stopped eating her soup and watched. As Dixie Lou read the transmittal something changed in her face, a complex interaction of emotions. Sadness in the expression, but in the eyes, something entirely different, and devoid of emotion.

"It's a coded Internet report from our operatives in the Bureau of Ideology," Dixie Lou announced, her tone somber. "Amy Angkor-Billings is dead, martyred like our Lord Jesus Christ."

At her table and those nearby, people gasped and began to weep, while Lori continued to watch the eyes of Dixie Lou Jackson—dark, simmering orbs that concealed so much. But not the anger when she noticed Lori studying her.

Abruptly Dixie Lou excused herself, along with the other woman, saying she needed to take care of important business.

* * *

The BOI had multiple sources of information concerning the operations of United Women of the World. On a bi-weekly basis they received encrypted Internet reports from operatives secretly placed around the world, as well as personal statements in other formats. All were of such importance that they found their way first to the Vice Minister of Minority Affairs, Styx Tertullian, for his review and dissemination.

So it was that Styx opened a coded e-mail file that had been forwarded to him by internal security.

The screen was blank.

With a barely suppressed expletive he pressed deep-access keys to find out why.

A computer voice spoke: "Erased, possibly by magnetic disturbance. A small amount of data retrieved."

Well, that's something anyway, he thought. He tapped the appropriate keys for retrieval, and the computer voice said something that was garbled. The following words appeared on the screen:

Your old way of life is dead.

—The Ladies

"I'll get you for this," he vowed, and slammed his fist on the desk.

He had something in mind, a plan he had recommended to Culpepper several weeks ago, and which had been approved. In recent months, the Bureau had been receiving coded reports that the "Ladies" had a mysterious preoccupation with unusual babies, having put out inquiries and dispatched people to a variety of countries to round them up.

Babbling babies. It almost sounded laughable, but the women were devoting considerable resources to a top-secret project involving them. What did it all mean?

Greece. An interesting country. Amy Angkor-Billings herself had been captured there, near the city of Salonika. Looking at a map, he placed a finger on the city in the northern part of the country. And his eyes wandered even farther north, to the rugged Macedonian mountains.

* * *

The next day, Styx Tertullian limped aboard a BOI Lear Fan 2100 prop-jet, which was hangared underground. An elevator lifted it to the surface, where hinged sections of ground folded open to make way. Other elevators raised a runway into place. The aircraft accelerated down the runway, took off in a hazy afternoon sky.

This was an antique plane from the century before, but entirely rebuilt. He liked it because of its unique look, with a propeller in the rear and a Y-shaped tail, and the fact that it represented another era, a bygone time when life was much more simple and women didn't raise such a ruckus about religion.

The comfortable interior, which had been customized according to Styx's exacting specifications, featured massive black leather chairs with individual entertainment centers and control panels that enabled a passenger to order a wide variety of foods and beverages from an automated kitchen and bar. The ceiling, of a black graphite material, had a soft, elegant sheen, as did the walls, which were silver. Beneath his feet, the Persian carpeting was BOI silver-and-black, dotted with blue Christian crosses.

In half an hour the plane touched down at Seattle's Boeing Field, just south of the downtown area. A Bureau car awaited him at the edge of the tarmac. After using a transmitter on his i.d. card to turn off the car alarm and unlock the doors, Styx located the keys above the visor on the driver's side.

The back seat was filled with grocery bags and other articles he had ordered, all of which had been placed there within the hour by BOI personnel.

The vehicle, a nearly new Hummer hovercar, was equipped with radar confusion devices on both license plates—thus giving the police garbled speed readings, making them think their radar equipment was acting up. It enabled him to drive twenty miles per hour over the speed limits without worry of apprehension.

Of course he wouldn't get a ticket anyway because of false government i.d. cards he could present if stopped, showing he was with the National Security Administration. Still, he didn't like to waste time with such matters. Every moment was precious.

Because of the speeds at which he was able to drive, he arrived at the small house in West Seattle one minute and fifty-eight seconds sooner than he would have been able to do otherwise, as calculated by the car's computer system.

After retrieving a bouquet of red roses and one of the bags of groceries from the back seat, he bounded up the creaky steps to the front porch. A note awaited him in shaky, familiar handwriting, inviting him to enter.

The home's alarm system beeped as he entered. Quickly, he tapped the five digit code into the control panel just inside the front door.

"Is that you, Styx?" a familiar, frail voice called out, from the rear of the house. "I'm in the bedroom, dear."

"Hi, Louise!" he called out in his high-pitched voice. "Just let me get a few bags of groceries into the kitchen and I'll be right up."

"Oh, you shouldn't have!" she said.

As Styx carried bags into the kitchen and made sure the perishables went into the refrigerator he thought about how much this elderly woman, Louise Bonham, had meant to his family. During his formative years he had lived in the bungalow next door, and Louise had been his mother's best friend. The two women had done everything together, from school fund raising events to art classes they taught at the community center down the street. When Styx's mother died six years ago she exacted a promise from him that he would take care of Louise.

In all that time Styx had done as she'd asked, for it had been her dying wish.

A wrinkled, angular woman, Mrs. Bonham was in her usual place in bed when he walked into her bedroom, picking up the odors of medicinals. An open, white-leather *Bible* lay on her lap, and an oxygen tank rested on a cart beside her bed, with its hose and mask within her reach. She needed oxygen at night when she slept. Well over eighty, she had steadfastly resisted all efforts by her son and daughter to place her in a retirement home. Styx admired her independence, and through the Bureau he had made arrangements with city officials to let her remain at home. Senior helpers and nurses were sent regularly to care for her, and every few weeks, whenever he could get away, Styx came himself.

She could get around on her own, but only with the help of a walker-frame, and only for short periods of time because she was weak and grew fatigued easily.

He leaned over to kiss her deeply creased forehead, and handed her the bouquet of flowers.

"Oh!" she exclaimed, drawing the roses close so that she could smell them. "You shouldn't have!"

She always said that, but never failed to show a little girl's delight at the gifts he brought. This was a God-fearing woman like his own sainted mother, not at all like the others who continually tried to stir up trouble.

He checked the gauge on her oxygen tank, and the tightness of the fittings. They were fine.

"Thank you, Styx," the old woman said. "You've always been such a dear boy."

* * *

Although it was only mid-afternoon, President Markwether lay on his bed in his suit, except he had draped the tailored gray jacket over a nearby chair. The White House staff had been notified that he was "incommunicado, working on a special project." He'd been trying unsuccessfully to take a nap, since he had not been sleeping well lately.

"Why are you so tense?" the woman asked, as she sat on the edge of the bed and massaged his muscular shoulders and neck. He had once been an athlete, a football quarterback. He wore a white shirt and red tie with the suit trousers. He kicked off his shoes. They thumped on the carpeted floor.

"The usual."

"Don't lie to me," she said, with a love tap on his back. "You're not very good at it."

Eleanor Markwether was not beautiful in the classic sense, but she had a quality about her that people found appealing, a charisma that made the citizens of the United States believe she really cared about the issues she championed: food and education for the poor, medical care for children and the elderly. Polls indicated she was fifteen points more popular than the President.

"That feels good," he said, as she continued to knead the muscles, like a masseuse.

"I'm concerned about you. I know you can't reveal national security secrets to me, but I'm not an idiot and I have given you good advice in the past."

"I know, and I appreciate that. There are many things weighing me down. My head is splitting and no pain relievers seem to touch it. I need to solve the problem and then I'll feel better. It's always that way with me."

"And the problem is?"

"An important private organization—my biggest campaign contributor—is demanding a lot of money. I'm having trouble getting it done."

"Wait a minute. If they're a campaign *contributor*, why do you have to give them money?"

"You know how politics works, darling. Money flows in more than one direction."

"I see. They contribute to your campaign, and you arrange for taxpayer money to go to them."

"I wouldn't put it quite that way."

"How would you put it, then? We are talking about a quid pro quo, aren't we?"

"In a sense."

She laughed, uneasily. "Is that all you can tell me about your problem?"

"Unfortunately, yes."

Then I can't do much more than this massage for you."

"I wouldn't say that." He turned around, and gave her a passionate kiss. Even after more than twenty years of marriage, they still had a spark for each other.

"Presidents aren't the only people who get headaches," she said, with a thin smile.

"It's against the law to use clichés on the Commander in Chief."

Now, he massaged her shoulders and back, as she lay on the bed.

As he did so, his thoughts remained on the crisis—which he had to solve if he wanted to be reelected next year. It didn't help that his approval ratings were down, so he needed all of the help he could get. He didn't tell his wife that he was having trouble with a clandestine agency, the Bureau of Ideology, and could never reveal to her any of the secrets within secrets that he knew about the organization. During a game of nine-ball in the White House game room that day, he had conferred with his brother Zack about the crisis, going into details with him that he could not reveal to his own wife.

Zack Markwether—two years the President's senior—was a de facto cabinet minister, resented by some and admired by others. He was a security expert, military liaison, troubleshooter, and much more. The President often said he couldn't get by without the assistance of his big brother. But Zack's overconfident manner, the way he strutted around using his influence, sometimes drew complaints and resignation threats from key staffers. Whenever that happened, the President would rein his brother in. For several weeks afterward Zack would be on his best behavior, but ultimately he would return to his old annoying ways.

In most respects the Markwether siblings were drastically different people—with Zack the organized one and Lowell the complete opposite, but adept at selecting good people and delegating. Among the few things in which they shared an interest were American blues (especially vintage 1930s and 1940s), microbrew beer, model trains, and games of pool. The men had a symbiotic relationship—a close association of different organisms—but they shared a deep respect for one another and a brotherly love that had endured for their lifetimes. They rarely argued about anything.

"I'm sorry I can't tell you more," the President said, as he did a deep muscle massage on his wife's back, working his hands underneath the clothing. "Politics is more complicated than you realize. There are interactions, obligations—" He despised both the Bureau of Ideology and their archenemy, United Women of the World, and wished they would blast each other off the face of the earth. Knowing the power that the BOI had over him, he wondered how much control they had over other government leaders, not only in his own administration but in other countries around the world. Such a complex web the Bureau maintained. They could ruin him if he didn't cooperate, and undoubtedly could ruin a lot of other important people, too.

"I understand," she said, with a sigh. It seemed obvious to him that she was thinking more of sensual matters now, and not of the weighty problems he had on his mind.

"I can't tell you too much," he said, as he laid down beside her and gazed into her gentle brown eyes. He smiled. "Or you would get worry wrinkles."

"What a sexist thing to say!" she exclaimed. She nudged him playfully, but her eyes narrowed as she recognized his lies and evasive behavior. This was something important, and the President would not discuss it with her.

Chapter 16

It is said of Lori Vale that her mother is not her mother and her father is not her father.

　　　　　　—From *Window to the Past*, UWW Press

On the elevated platform of the council chamber, which had once been the monastery's Byzantine church, sixteen councilwomen sat in black leather high-back chairs, including Dixie Lou Jackson and Deborah Marvel. The air was heavy with the perfume of burning incense. The chairs were arranged in a half circle, and in front of that, where the center of a complete circle would have been, sat an empty red leather chair. Each councilwoman—dressed in the black robe of mourning—held a single red rose wrapped in a green-and-orange ribbon.

On a high pedestal behind them rose the She-God statue, her oval face serene, her fathomless eyes turned heavenward. In her arms she held the sacred, legendary Sword of She-God, with its jeweled hilt glinting in sunlight that passed through a stained glass window.

The red chair, mounted on a swivel, had been turned away from the council, toward an audience of three hundred UWW members, all women, who sat in pews that had formerly been used for church services. Morning sunlight caused some of them to squint and shield their eyes. A closed-circuit television system broadcast the proceedings to the Scriptorium and Refectory buildings, where scholars, knights, and other personnel were gathered to watch.

At one side of the red chair, facing the audience, stood a lectern draped with the colorful vestment of United Women of the World. Overhead rose an ancient rock dome, and the walls were adorned with faded frescoes, depicting Christian religious scenes. The ones deemed controversial by the UWW had been painted over with whitewash. Among those remaining was a glorious depiction of Jesus in the Garden of Gethsemane, with the adult Mary Magdalene at his feet.

A buzz of anticipation filled the air. Several women were crying. Others vented their hostility with violently anti-male comments.

Dixie Lou tried to make herself look sad as she gazed at the empty red chair in the center of the platform. She watched the slender, middle-aged blonde Deborah Marvel place a rose on its cushion and then return to her seat beside Dixie Lou. Deborah wept openly, unable to suppress her sorrow. With a handkerchief, she dabbed at her eyes.

Visible to the council, but not to the audience because of their distance from it, an Internet computer scrolled through coded reports on clandestine UWW paramilitary forces in all of the major western nations . . . underground caverns filled with the most advanced stealth aircraft and armored cavalry units. The council had to remain in constant touch with such information. Also included were records of their personnel who were steadily infiltrating the armed forces of unfriendly nations—women (and a small number of trusted men) positioning themselves to obtain as much power and influence as they could. Because of recent events and reports of increased BOI funding drives, the council had ordered a sharp step-up in activity.

From a side entrance, Katherine Pangalos walked out in front of the council and faced the audience. Most of the onlookers grew silent, but a cauldron of simmering, seething anger remained. Katherine, in a long black dress, spoke tremulously, her voice amplified by a tiny microphone that hovered in front of her mouth: "I am old, and in my lifetime many dear friends have come and gone, women who have been abused by men and their violent systems."

Rage boiled over in the pews. Women screamed epithets against the male gender. Some called for an immediate military response, as well as the use of sabotage and assassination squads.

Inwardly, Dixie Lou seethed, since she had been forced into allowing this non-councilwoman, her principal foe, to speak prior to anyone else. But this had been the sentiment of the majority of the council, considering the many occasions when Amy had referred to Katherine as her closest friend. Though Dixie Lou had accused Katherine of betraying Amy, that had only been for effect; she didn't really believe it. The wealthy woman had no motive. Dixie Lou's feelings were complex, mixed. She was glad Amy was gone, since it cleared the way for her advancement to the chairwomanship, but now she had to deal with another obstacle, with this difficult, outspoken woman.

When the rancorous clamor settled down, Katherine continued in a weaker voice: "Seven years ago, Amy Angkor-Billings and her family were caught in a BOI attack while vacationing in Hawaii. After Amy's husband and children were murdered, she returned to the UWW a different woman than she had been before. She was more militant and focused, less willing to compromise."

A diminutive councilwoman, Jeanne Cousteau, handed a fresh tissue to Deborah Marvel, who was becoming inconsolable.

"She was our lighthouse," Katherine continued, "our beacon and our inspiration, and without her our lives are empty. Amy is gone, murdered by the enemies of every woman on earth."

More epithets were shouted against men, and vows of revenge.

As Katherine paused, each councilwoman placed a flower on the empty chair and briefly eulogized the remarkable leader of United Women of the World, who had guided its course for nearly twenty-five years.

Finally, Fujiko Harui, a tiny Japanese woman who was last to speak, said, in the saddest of voices, "Men have not only stolen our sacred gospels. They've stolen our precious Amy."

An eruption of fury shook the council chamber. If a man had been present—even an innocent one—he might have been torn to shreds.

"We must continue our work!" Fujiko shouted, over the din. "Amy wouldn't want us to give up, and we won't!"

While Dixie Lou clapped with the other women, she thought about the long-awaited *Holy Women's Bible* that would culminate their efforts, turning the Christian world upside down. As the new leader of United Women of the World, she would ride the crest of the immense, unstoppable wave.

In speeches broadcast all over the globe she would inflame passions by recounting the centuries of injustice women had endured at the hands of men. She would also draw parallels between herself and brave women such as Elizabeth Cady Stanton, who in the late nineteenth century published *The Woman's Bible*, which was not really a bible, but was instead a compendium of essays about biblical passages that related to women. In broad strokes, Dixie Lou would discuss the women's movement, showing how the civil rights of females had been enhanced in western nations, but not enough, since familiar systems remained in place, maintaining male supremacy. The male-written, anti-female King James Version of the *Holy Bible* was still in place.

Finally the noise in the ancient church edifice subsided, and Katherine took a seat in the front row of the audience.

"Who will lead us now?" a woman shouted. This was the traditional call for leadership when a Chairwoman had died.

"I will," Dixie Lou called out.

The room fell silent and all present closed their eyes in contemplation, as if the women were considering Dixie Lou's offer. Actually it was a *fait accompli*, since Amy had designated her successor in writing, as specified under the bylaws of the organization. If Dixie Lou had not spoken out, if she had not wanted the position, a different process would have been initiated, involving a formal vote of the council.

While she waited, Dixie Lou was thankful that Katherine Pangalos was not a younger woman. Had she been, by virtue of her position as Amy's closest friend, she might have been competition for the Chairwomanship.

Presently the women looked up, and each of them whispered Dixie Lou's name.

"Congratulations," Deborah finally said in her throaty voice, from a seat beside Dixie Lou. And from other council seats came more words of support. With intense focus, Dixie Lou chronicled the voices and faces, and judged which of them were sincere and which weren't. Along with Deborah, eight other councilwomen could be counted on to take her side most of the time.

A chill of excitement coursed Dixie Lou's spine. She stood in a humble fashion, shoulders sloped, head downturned. "I am your servant now," she said.

The old church erupted with cheering and thunderous clapping, though Katherine participated with a stony countenance. All rose to their feet.

As Dixie Lou walked across the stage, she did her best to appear somber, concealing the unseemly glee—riotous and ecstatic—that threatened to erupt within her. After all, this was not a happy occasion for the UWW, not with the death of their founder.

The audience noise continued.

Dixie Lou resisted an urge to say Amy was looking down on them from her place beside She-God, blessing these events, although such a comment would have had emotional impact. This was not Amy's moment, after all.

It was Dixie Lou Jackson's.

And so, raising her voice to be heard over the excited buzz in the church, she described her humble beginnings as an impoverished black woman whose Baptist mother forced her to memorize passages from the *Bible*. She also told of her mistreatment at the hands of men in her teens, when her stepfather and his brother raped her repeatedly. Presently she said, "Since I have been selected to lead you, I will carry a message to every man on earth." She paused for dramatic effect, then shifted her voice to a strong Negro dialect: "Massah Man, we ain't gonna be yo' slaves no mo'!"

Wild enthusiasm shook the ancient church, and in the buildings around the plaza it was the same. People were on their feet, applauding and cheering.

As Dixie Lou completed her remarks, someone in the back row called out, "Who will fill the vacant council seat?"

Again this was tradition, to fill the chair vacated by Dixie Lou Jackson. This process was even more involved than the one she had just gone through, because it was the full initiation of a new councilwoman into the inner sanctum of the order, a procedure Dixie Lou had already gone through years ago.

"I will," Katherine Pangalos announced. She smiled and stared at Dixie Lou, adding, "After I take the Vow of Angkor, of course. Would the Chairwoman like to administer it to me?"

Simmering with anger, Dixie Lou waited for the vote of acclamation in the chamber, the murmuring of Katherine's name. Then she motioned for the candidate to come up onto the platform. The old woman did so, and knelt in the proper fashion—head bowed, waiting—in front of her new superior.

With a barely discernible shrug of resignation, Dixie Lou rose and went to the high pedestal base of the She-God statue. At a control panel she entered a security code and punched in a command. Looking up, she saw the arms of the gray stone goddess tilt down with a grating creak, and the legendary Sword of She-God lowered slowly, supported by a nearly invisible wire cage. The mechanical fingers, usually cupped up slightly to support the sword on open palms, were gripping the weapon now.

When the cage reached her she removed the sword and carried it back to Katherine, who stared at it with palpable trepidation, perhaps wondering if Dixie Lou would kill her with it. Oh, how the new Chairwoman wanted to do that! But not now. The handle of the ceremonial weapon glittered with emeralds and fire opals, and sunlight sparkled from the gleaming blade.

Standing in front of the kneeling Katherine, Dixie Lou made her squint from the brilliance of the sun's reflection on the finely worked Spanish steel of the razor-sharp blade. "Look deeply into the Sword of She-God," Dixie Lou commanded, beginning the rite that she and all other UWW personnel had previously undergone. "Look and see the faces of all women who have come before you, and who will come afterward."

Shifting the weapon in her hands, Dixie Lou caused undulating waves of reflected sunlight to splash across Katherine's face, changing the character of the elderly woman's features by throwing them in and out of shadow. Transfixed by the light, Katherine stared into the gleaming blade and, in deep hypnosis, intoned the Vow of Angkor:

> Bonded to women,
>
> With hallowed secrets
>
> Of mind and heart,
>
> Sealed as one
>
> For the rest of time.

Her eyes still closed, Katherine kissed the blade, then fell silent. And for several moments, everyone in the assemblage closed their eyes and were entirely silent, in contemplation.

At the appropriate time the audience looked up, and each whispered the name of Katherine Pangalos again. She opened her eyes as well, and smiled softly. Then, one by one, the councilwomen, and even Dixie Lou Jackson, congratulated the newest member of their elite circle.

During the moments of this process, Dixie Lou considered the effects of the Vow of Angkor, how its mysterious powers—reputedly linked to the sacred Sword of She-God—now prevented Katherine Pangalos from revealing the existence of the organization to outsiders. The vow was curious, and many times Dixie Lou had considered the extent of its influence, wondering how it worked.

Did it operate through the power of suggestion, making a person *think* she couldn't break the oath, or was some other, more esoteric force, responsible? The wording contained no threat whatsoever, so what did a person fear, if anything? What was the penalty for violation? In any event, Dixie Lou had taken the vow herself, and while she felt bound by its strictures, it didn't prevent her from being secretly happy with Amy's death; it didn't stop internal UWW plots and intrigues; it didn't keep her from killing Katherine Pangalos eventually, if necessary.

At the very least, the leathery old woman would be a thorn in the side of the newly selected Chairwoman. Katherine would begin her duties with less support on the council than Dixie Lou's, but the old hag had wiles and would be constantly on the alert for weak links in her opponent's power base, for ways to undermine it.

Dixie Lou vowed to stop at nothing to protect her own position.

* * *

After the chamber had been cleared, Dixie Lou remained by herself. It was mid-morning, with sunlight still slanting through the stained glass windows, pooling bright light around the red leather chair of the Chairwoman of United Women of the World.

My chair.

She sat in it to get the feel of it, caressed the sun-warmed, timeworn leather armrests and inhaled the patrician smell of fine old leather. With a deep sigh of satisfaction, she held the Sword of She-God, and in the gleaming blade she saw her own smiling reflection.

"I am the Sword of She-God," she murmured. "Nothing can stop me now."

* * *

As Lori lay in bed that evening, she felt herself slipping into another dimension, but not of slumber. She was afraid to sleep. The mysterious word mouthed by Veronica, "*Iktol*," continued to disturb her, and she recalled the agitated expression on the innocent little face. *Murder.*

But how do I know what it means? And how do I know it is not Aramaic?

Being with the special child had triggered something Lori didn't understand. Something that terrified her. A chain reaction in the depths of her soul. She sensed it bubbling, percolating inside . . . growing, moving through her body back and forth, repeatedly traversing her cellular structures, intensifying. . . .

A powerful presence.

The new *Bible* project was big. *Huge*, in fact. Any doubts she had felt in the beginning, upon learning of the she-apostles, had been dissipated quickly by the evidence all around her. Lori felt as if she was in the eye of the most powerful hurricane in the history of the planet. It was relatively quiet at the center now, but a tremendous force was being generated.

She didn't know what her part might be in all of this, but knew she couldn't escape it. She needed to be with Veronica again, to protect her . . . and to shelter the other she-apostles. It seemed an impossible thought to Lori, the image of a teenage girl safeguarding the children against Dixie Lou and her cohorts.

Lori also wanted to question Veronica, to learn if the awful word had really been on her lips, or if it had only been imagined, some residue—a flashback?—of the drugs Lori used to take.

What do I know anyway? How could I possibly read the lips of anyone speaking an ancient, perhaps secret language? It's preposterous.

And yet, the presence-within was speaking to her now. Silently, but not in the same fashion as Veronica's message. This was a wordless communication within Lori Vale's cells, contained within every fiber of her being. It told her to sleep, to rest her troubled, fatigued brain.

She slipped into REM slumber.

And dreamed of being a baby herself, of struggling through her mother's birth canal, of trying desperately to reach the light. She felt large, strong hands around her, shifting her tiny, fragile form, guiding her to safety, and heard her mother scream out in pain, a muffled sound that was replaced by the cry of a baby. Her own voice.

I am born.

In Lori's dream she heard the urgent voices of women. Strangers in a shifting haze of light. They cut something, and she was no longer connected to her mother. The women spoke of a breach birth and their success at getting the baby turned around so that it didn't strangle on its umbilical cord. They said it had almost become necessary to take the mother's life to save the baby.

An odd comment, Lori realized, the reverse of what medical attendants usually said.

They were bathing her now, and Lori felt the cool, fresh wash of clean water spreading over her skin, like an ablution. Then something else, being rubbed all over her tiny body. A small amount touched her lips and she tasted it. Salt.

In her dream Lori was all things at once, a teenager and a baby, a person with knowledge of medical procedures, clean water, and salt, and a person who had never before experienced these things.

The newborn Lori was warm now, having been wrapped in swaddling clothes. A woman cradled her, murmuring, "*Tkehet erab, tkehet nahira.*"

She was speaking in the secret language of Veronica. The ancient, mysterious tongue.

Servant of darkness, servant of light.

From a nightmare, Lori screamed for her mother.

There was no response.

She awoke, pushed away the blankets and sheets. Much too hot. The pillow was wet; sticky perspiration covered her body.

Chapter 17

Think not that I am come to destroy the law, or the prophets: I am not come to destroy, but to fulfill.

—Jesus, in the Sermon on the Mount (Matthew 5:17, *The New Testament)*

BOI headquarters, eastern Washington State . . .

Styx was in quite a sweat. Not wearing his eyeglasses, he alternately pulled and pushed on the rubber-wrapped metal bar, and with his legs he lifted a connected bar, so that the abdominal machine did its best to harden his flabby stomach. It was part of a regimen Styx had been following for four months, and included the ingestion of fruit, vegetable, and protein capsules twice a day.

Located in a room adjacent to his office, this was a private exercise room that had formerly been occupied by a subordinate, and which Styx had appropriated for his own purposes. Equipment lined the walls, including weight machines, aerobics units, and an exercycle. Now he could work out any time he felt like it, followed by a refreshing shower in his private bathroom.

It was, admittedly, a rather retro collection of equipment, since there were new health maintenance techniques available, including fat-melting electronic fields, injections and implants, surgical procedures, and any number of ways to get physically fit without having to work hard at it. But he preferred old-fashioned ways and things. His antique Lear

Fan prop-jet was another example. Old things were available; you just had to search for them and have them rebuilt or constructed new, according to original specifications. That was how he felt about religion, too. The old ways were best, when women knew their place.

Exercise, Styx was discovering, had an unadvertised bonus: good ideas came to his busy, troubled mind as he worked out, apparently as his endorphin-relaxed brain developed solutions to complex problems that had been troubling him.

So engrossed was he in the machine now and in such thoughts that he didn't notice a uniformed orderly who appeared at his side and stood stiffly at attention, awaiting recognition. Receiving none, the orderly, a young man in the silver-and-black uniform of the BOI Quick Reaction Force, inched forward a little, until he was into the periphery of his superior's line of vision. When he finally caught the Vice Minister's attention, he spoke quickly and nervously.

"Sorry to interrupt, sir, but this appears to be important." He handed over a single sheet of white paper, but held onto an envelope.

A message in bold print proclaimed, to the Vice Minister:

> Glory be to She-God Almighty, Creator and
>
> Destroyer. Her power shall last forever.
>
> —Gospel of the Apostle Mary Magdalene, *Holy Women's Bible*

"The Apostle Mary Magdalene?" Styx roared. "There was no such apostle! *Holy Women's Bible*? She-God Almighty? What is this filth?"

"It came from an unknown source." The soldier handed him the envelope, which bore no return address and no post mark.

"Get out!" Vice Minister Tertullian thundered. He rolled the sheet of paper and the envelope into a ball and hurled it across the room, toward a wastebasket. It missed its target and rolled behind a weight machine.

* * *

In his office, Minister Culpepper read an e-mail report on what had transpired in the exercise room of the Vice Minister of Minority Affairs.

Voice activating it, the Minister read the blasphemous *Holy Women's Bible* quotation, which had been scanned into the system. With cigarette smoke curling around him, he looked out the window at the barren terrain. A large black vulture flew low in the sky, its wings flapping slowly as it searched the ground for prey.

With another voice command, he opened a folder and wrote an e-mail to Tertullian, saying : "Did you know about this women's *Bible*? What in the Hades is it?"

Forty minutes later he received a response: "Nothing to worry about. I'm taking care of it."

But gnats of worry swarmed through Culpepper's thoughts. These women were proving resilient and surprisingly enterprising. Maybe the Vice Minister wasn't up to the challenges of the job. He would bear even closer monitoring.

* * *

In the days following Lori's visit with the she-apostle Veronica, the Scriptorium hummed with increased activity. The anecdote related by Veronica in Lori's presence had only been the beginning, the translators reported. Suddenly all of the she-apostles were talking more, revealing additional stories from ancient times. The presence of Lori when Veronica poured forth new information was only a coincidence, the councilwomen were saying. The teenager had not been an influence on the child, after all.

One apostle, Abigail, told the Scriptorium scholars that their original *Testament of the She-Apostles* had been compiled and written during the lifetime of Jesus. During a period of persecution against women after the death and resurrection of the Christ, these gospels were placed in pottery jars and secreted in a cave. Subsequently they were found and destroyed by Sadducee priests. There were no other copies—except in the memories of the she-apostles.

With mounting excitement, editors organized the material into the burgeoning *Holy Women's Bible*. More than seventy new pages were added in a matter of days, to the less than forty that had existed previously. As part of this monumental project, Scriptorium editors were also revising the King James Version of the *Bible*, deleting and rewriting anti-feminine passages based upon the new information that was being received. When complete, the *Holy Women's Bible* would consist of three books, *The Old Testament*, *The New Testament*, and *The Testament of the She-Apostles*. It was a structure that had been set in place during the lifetime of Amy Angkor Billings, and many women in the monastery were saying it was a shame Amy wasn't here to see this glorious time.

Through it all, Dixie Lou had been reading and editing printed pages, instead of reading them on computer screens, because she found the hard copies easier on her eyes. She felt an increasing sense of unease, which she kept to herself. As head of United Women of the World, she directed the gospel recovery project, but everything seemed to have developed a life and energy of its own, entirely independent of her, a situation that didn't provide her with adequate credit. She could go to sleep or walk away and it would all continue apace. This bothered her immensely.

Stories surfaced about the demons who plagued Mary Magdalene before Jesus exorcised them—more details than the sketchy information provided by St. Luke in the New Testament. There were tales of Mary, mother of Jesus as well, who was not an apostle but was an inspiration for the other women. Sarah, who loved Jesus as a brother even though they were not siblings, was described. So was Abigail, whose frail child was nurtured and taught by Jesus, and Lydia, an adulterous woman who had been scorned by her villagers and cast out . . . and Kezia, Hannah, Esther, Rhoda, Priscilla, and Candace. Each she-apostle, it was said, had a special relationship with the Son of God.

Intriguingly, these eleven had even provided the name of the twelfth she-apostle—Martha of Galilee—who had as yet not been located in her modern incarnation.

It was revealed that at the age of ten a heroic Jesus saved an elderly couple from a fire, and as a young man he became involved with a Hindu mystic who was charged with sedition by the Roman government. Jesus helped the mystic escape imprisonment, and traveled with him to India, where the Son of God observed the ways of non-violent protest and studied the Hindu concept of karma and the resurrection of the soul.

Afterward he traveled to China, where he learned about Buddhism and the important links between humans and nature. In his mid twenties, Jesus returned to his homeland, where he became a follower of John the Baptist and later began his own ministry.

In the new information, the scriptorium scholars found many points of agreement with the traditional *Bible*, including parables of Jesus that matched, word-for-word. Other accounts of Jesus were either slightly different or previously unknown, with new beatitudes, admonishments, and stories that revealed his close ties with a variety of organized religions . . . and with women.

Then a most disturbing piece of information surfaced, involving Martha of Galilee, the missing twelfth she-apostle. Upon hearing it, Dixie Lou called for an emergency council meeting, in which she would move to suppress the material from the *Holy Women's Bible*.

Chapter 18

No one was happy about having to kill the Apostle Sarah's birthparents, but they refused to give us the child. We had no alternative.
—Report of the Commission on the She-Apostles

It was late afternoon, a frost cool day with wispy clouds drifting over the mountaintops. At the arched doorway of the old Byzantine church, Dixie Lou Jackson watched the councilwomen file past her and enter, wearing their dun-colored, hooded robes. It was the first council meeting under her new regime, and she felt exhilarated.

After following them inside she took a deep breath and strode to the red chair she had coveted for so long. She sank into its softly pliant padded leather, and slowly swiveled to face the others, as they opened their hoods.

"You're all familiar with the new material from the Apostle Lydia?" she asked.

"I'm not," the petite Fujiko Harui said. "I was helping out in the clinic." A former doctor, she had once managed the Monte Konos medical clinic, until her broader skills were recognized and Amy Angkor-Billings invited her join the council. Occasionally the clinic doctors still asked her for advice.

"Lydia says there's a She-Judas," Bobbi Torrence explained. Though not much taller than Harui, she weighed more than twice as much. "A she-apostle who conspired with Judas Iscariot to betray Jesus."

Several councilwomen shook their heads in dismay. Some, particularly Fujiko, appeared to be shocked.

Reaching into a pocket of her robe, Dixie Lou removed a sheet of paper and said, "Here are the sacred words of Lydia: 'Only with the testimony of Martha of Galilee will the gospels be complete, and only then will the identity of Jesus' betrayers be known. Judas Iscariot did not act alone. He and a female apostle conspired together.'"

"Lydia doesn't know which one it is?" Fujiko asked.

Dixie Lou shrugged. "She said only Martha can tell the story."

Katherine Pangalos folded her wrinkled, age-spotted arms across her chest. "Odd. She's not saying Martha did it, only that the missing child *knows* who did. Assuming Martha is innocent, that points to the other eleven."

"Or ten," Deborah Marvel noted, gesturing with a slender, long-fingered hand. "If Lydia was guilty she would never have brought the matter up."

"Don't assume anything," Dixie Lou cautioned. "This is a potential bombshell that could destroy our project. We can't let it leak out."

"No argument there," Katherine said.

"I move for suppression of the information," Dixie Lou said, "at least until we get input from the last she-apostle. All records of Lydia's remarks must be immediately removed from the Scriptorium, with everyone sworn to secrecy, under penalty of death."

"Including us?" Katherine asked.

"*Especially* including us," Dixie Lou responded, a razor edge to her tone.

Shifting in her chair, Katherine said, "Funny how this all happens after the appearance of the American teenager."

"It's just coincidence," Dixie Lou said.

"I'm not so sure. What if it was a chain reaction? When Lori was with Veronica, the child told us a new story. A short while later Veronica was playing with the other children, and new gospels flowed from *them*— more in a few days than in months before."

"We have no evidence of a link," Dixie Lou said.

"Every guard assigned to Lori says she's been asking to see the she-apostles," Deborah said. "She wants to see her own mother, too."

"Why don't you at least tell her the truth about her mother?" Deborah asked, "that she's *dead*."

"We may be able to control her by making her think her mother is still alive," Dixie Lou said. "Just a feeling I have. I always like to keep leverage, and potential leverage." She smiled. "You know me."

"Yes," Deborah said, with a grim smile. "Only too well, my friend."

Katherine: "I think we should allow Lori to see the other she-apostles, to see what sort of connection she has with them."

"What?" Dixie Lou said, so astonished that she half rose from her chair. "The last time we talked about this you said she shouldn't be with the children, that it was potentially disruptive to the entire she-apostle program."

"I changed my mind. A woman's prerogative."

Some of the women chuckled.

"Maybe Katherine has a point," Deborah suggested. "I mean, there might be a connection. And Lori could get more information out of the children."

A scowl crossed Dixie Lou's face, and she plopped back into her chair. "I can't believe you're saying that." A large black spider scurried along the floor in front of Dixie Lou. She tried to stomp it, but the spindly creature accelerated and got away.

"We should at least look into it," Bobbi Torrence suggested.

Dixie Lou fixed her with an angry stare, then sat silently as other councilwomen chimed in to agree with Katherine.

A long silence ensued. Finally Katherine spoke, locking gazes with Dixie Lou: "I move to affirm your request to remove Lydia's remarks from the Scriptorium."

"And everyone is sworn to secrecy, under penalty of death?"

Katherine nodded solemnly.

The entire council assented, and decided to put new resources into locating the last she-apostle. They needed to keep her story from falling into the wrong hands.

"And the matter of Lori Vale?" Katherine asked.

Considering her options, Dixie Lou realized she had been boxed into the awkward position of arguing against something she had personally allowed Lori to do in the first place. If Katherine had set this up by design, she was a more formidable opponent than anticipated.

A series of no-win alternatives—a Hobson's choice—faced the new Chairwoman, and she tried to select the one causing her the least personal damage.

"All right," she said at long last. "I'll go along with you on that, but let me set up a way to do it. And don't rush me." A shiver passed through her. Allowing Lori near the children again felt like a big mistake, and she almost wished she had never brought the girl back from America—the attempt to repay her for helping in the escape from the goddess circle. For now, Dixie Lou would stall, until she figured out how to deal with the matter.

As she voiced her conditional acceptance and the council ratified the decisions that had been made, Dixie Lou began to formulate a plan to get even with her principal opponents later, in a battle of her own design. A memory surfaced, something Amy had told her once, that Wellington had defeated Napoleon by luring him to an unusual, hilly battleground that was only familiar to the British general.

Katherine was moving quickly to solidify her new power base, and would need to be stopped.

For now Dixie Lou needed to clear her own mind. Utilizing another trick of leadership she had learned from Amy, she would make efficient use of her time by combining her daily workout program with something else she needed to do.

* * *

Shortly after sunrise in Washington state . . .

Styx Tertullian paced the length of his underground office, thinking back to the attack on the goddess circle, and his failure to kill or capture

Dixie Lou Jackson. Minister Culpepper had been displeased. It had been a smudge on Styx's reputation.

From a cabinet he brought out a large sack of effects taken in the raid and poured it out on his desk, as he'd done several times before. Wallets, purses, scarves, makeup articles, birth control pills, a plastic baggie of marijuana, cigarette paper, a drawing of a woman standing with Jesus . . . and the gray figurine of a different woman holding a sword-cross. This had to be their She-God, as Culpepper suspected. The sword-cross design was, after all, the symbol of United Women of the World.

He turned to the drawing of the other woman, which was captioned, "Mary Magdalene, companion of Jesus."

Styx's pulse quickened in anger. Because of his profession, he was well-versed in anti-Christian art and literature, including Satanic stories under the guise of scholarship that falsely linked the Savior Jesus Christ romantically with Mary Magdalene.

Lies.

Some documents purporting to be authentic—Gnostic writings not included in the *Bible*—claimed that the Savior kissed Mary Magdalene and that the Apostle Peter was upset by the closeness of their relationship. It was all garbage, of the worst sort. Jesus was pure. He was born of a virgin and lived his life in chastity. In like manner, Styx and other devout Bureau of Ideology men abstained from sexual relations.

The *Bible* said Mary Magdalene was a woman of ill repute—at least this was the interpretation Tertullian placed on Luke 8:2. The holy book also said that after Jesus cured her of demons he accepted her as one of his followers, into a group that traveled with him during the few short years of his ministry.

In disgust, Styx turned the drawing over so that he wouldn't have to look at it. Seething, he focused on the plastic baggie of marijuana, some of which had been rolled into cigarettes. More proof positive that these were evil women. Shoving the baggie aside, he stood the statuette up and gazed at it.

The women of the UWW were worshipers of idolatry, tramplers of the Ten Commandments and all that was holy.

The statuette had a benign face with a beatific smile, concealing the evil of its followers' souls. *She-God!* He spit on it and wanted to smash the figurine and the tiny sword it held, but decided against such a precipitous course of action. This was evidence, and might be useful at a later date.

* * *

A couple of hours before dinner, Dixie Lou led Lori down a worn stone stairway into the catacombs of Monte Konos. An escort of four armed guards followed them.

"What is it you need to discuss with me?" the teenager asked. She held a cigarette in her hand, which she had been smoking when Dixie Lou showed up at her door.

"Your uncertain future."

Nervously, Lori took a drag on the cigarette, blew smoke out through her mouth and nostrils, then coughed. The Greek tobacco was still coarse to her, and she didn't think she would ever get used to it.

In a rock-hewn tunnel at the bottom of the stairs, Dixie Lou removed her robe, revealing a black-and-tan jogging outfit and shoes with blue sports stripes. The guards climbed into two white electric carts.

"Think you can keep up with me?" Dixie Lou asked, looking appraisingly at the tall young woman.

"Keep up? You mean you're going jogging now? But I'm not dressed for it." While she did have on the proper shoes herself, she wore jeans and a blue-and-gold sweater.

"Those look like pretty good shoes to me. I know they are, as a matter of fact. They're one of my extra pairs, which I sent to your room. You're taller than I am, but we have the same size feet."

"Gosh, I don't know. Can't we just stand here and talk?"

"I never stand still!" Dixie Lou exclaimed, and she began running ahead.

Another runner approached, a blonde woman. As she passed, Dixie Lou gave her the "W" salute. "That's Deborah Marvel," Dixie Lou said. "One of the councilwomen."

"This is ridiculous," Lori protested. But she ran to catch up, and fell into stride beside the enigmatic black woman. The electric carts of the guards could be heard whirring behind them. The rock walls and ceiling were streaked in black, with illumination provided by widely-spaced halogen light fixtures. The rock floor was smoother at the center where it had been worn down by foot traffic, eons of robed monks going about their daily business.

"Here's the deal," Dixie Lou said, her short legs propelling her forward, making scuffling sounds on the rock. "You're not to discuss anything you saw in the Scriptorium or I'll have you killed."

"Well you don't need to kill me because I'm already doing what you want. After seeing the heavy security around the Scriptorium I came to my own conclusion about what I should do."

"Good. You're a smart girl."

God help me, Lori thought. *This woman's a lunatic.*

"When can I see my mother?" Lori asked, stumbling a little on the rough surface.

"We'll let you know when she's able to have visitors."

The girl felt her face flush hot. "I deserve better than that! I saved your life, and you won't let me see my mother?"

"You don't want to make me angry," Dixie Lou said. "Having trouble keeping up?" She increased her pace.

"Not at all." But Lori heard her own breathing grow labored and raspy. She flicked the burning cigarette into one of the gutters that ran along each side of the tunnel.

"If you never learn anything else from life, Lori Vale, remember this and remember it well: Things change. You must always be prepared for the unexpected. For example, no matter how pleasant I've just been, I could stop right now and order my officers to shoot you in the head. Or I could take one of their weapons and do it myself. What would you do then?"

"Die?" Lori said, with a winsome smile. She tried to display bravery, even though her insides were churning.

Caught off guard, Dixie Lou roared with laughter and slowed her jogging pace. "Yes, what else *could* you do?" Her glee faded. "There's no way to get away from here, or from me. I can guarantee you that, so for your own sake you'd better stay out of trouble and do as you're told."

"I understand." Lori stopped trying to conceal her labored breathing. She felt like saying a lot to this woman, but held her tongue.

"That's all," Dixie Lou said. She waved dismissively.

Lori stopped and moved over to one side to allow the electric carts to whir by her.

Dixie Lou ran on ahead of them.

Angrily, Lori watched the strange woman and her guards as they continued on their way. The way Dixie Lou treated her was infuriating—no matter who she was. Lori had more cigarettes in her pocket, and considered smoking them non-stop. But that would be an act of weakness, and she needed to be strong now.

Part of her wanted to attempt escape at the first opportunity, no matter the risk. But another part of her told her to stay here, for the sake of her mother, and of the children.

Something the translator had said stuck in Lori's mind. Of the twelve reincarnated she-apostles, one was missing.

There were layers to this mystery.

* * *

For more than a week, Consuela Santos had begged in crowded *mercados*, trying to obtain money and food for her baby. Like a village dog she foraged for scraps of food in the garbage and around the stalls of the market, and the best of what she found went to little Marta. Consuela never remained in one village for more than a day or two before moving along, usually on foot, sometimes risking rides from strangers. Always on the move and constantly on the alert, Consuela tried to frequent noisy, crowded areas where people wouldn't notice the odd sounds coming from her baby.

As days passed, the child had grown quieter, even when irritable or hungry. While this alleviated the fear of detection it didn't relieve the mother's concerns. On the contrary it heightened them, for she worried that the baby might be sick. Marta didn't seem to have a temperature, her eyes were clear, and her bowel movements appeared normal, but something was still wrong. Her smiles were lethargic and she moved listlessly. Consuela wished she could take her to a doctor, but even if she could find one who would not charge for his services she dared not, for the forces of Satan were everywhere and they were searching for her baby.

Consuela stood off to one side, away from a group of people who were on the edge of the village plaza, awaiting the first bus of the morning. This was one of the prettiest towns she had seen, with two fine Catholic churches and generous, friendly people who provided her with food, warm clothing for her child and a small amount of money. She especially enjoyed the mariachi bands in the evening. Sometimes, when she watched young women her own age engage in promenades and dances with handsome young men, she wished she could be like them, just beginning a relationship, without the burden of this child.

It had been a bad thought, one that shamed her, and for it she had gone to one of the churches that morning to sit in a confession booth and talk to a priest, thus expiating her sin.

Now she had just enough pesos and centavos to take the bus. She had asked how much it cost, and the exact amount was rolled up tightly in her fist.

Finally the old bus, dented and belching black diesel smoke, pulled up to the curb with a loud squeal of brakes. A stream of townspeople boarded, followed by Consuela. After paying the driver she found a tattered, patched seat in the back, by a farmer and his wife who had chickens in a small wire pen and a rambunctious, bleating goat that was tied to one of the seat stanchions.

With no idea what lay ahead, she prayed for safe passage and deliverance from evil.

Chapter 19

In this war of many levels, propaganda is employed, but not in the traditional form, owing to the requirements of secrecy. Instead, both organizations covertly fund a variety of smaller groups that espouse philosophies similar to their own. In all respects the competition is as clandestine as any war in history, and in view of the intense mutual hatred the conflict could involve the instantaneous destruction of the entire world . . . if either party gets nuclear capability.
—Classified White House report on the BOI and UWW

Lori spent much of the following day with a stocky, muscular female security guard that had been assigned to her—riding the rail car, walking, looking around, absorbing the ancient ambiance and the modern technology that had been brought in by the UWW and artfully concealed from prying satellite eyes and other technology. Though Monte Konos comprised what appeared to be a large area (much of it a subterranean hive of passageways and chambers), Lori was not permitted into many areas.

The guard would not answer any of her questions, and seemed to have a vocabulary limited to variations on the word "no" and the phrase "I can't comment on that," both of which she employed each time Lori asked about her mother or the she-apostles.

Finally, as they neared Lori's apartment, she said to the guard, "Your boss is the descendant of slaves, but she's made slaves out of those children. Why doesn't that bother her?"

"I only do what I am told, and you should do the same."

With that, the guard left Lori, but took a position a short distance away, where she could watch.

Outside her own front door, Lori found Alex waiting. He wore a light brown leather jacket and dark slacks. His long, curly black hair was neatly combed and wet.

"What time are you going to dinner?" he asked, glancing at his watch.

"The seven o'clock seating, I guess."

"We have a couple of hours, then."

She looked at him quizzically.

His pewter eyes were dull. "You wanna go with me?"

She took a deep breath, tried to maintain her patience. Despite who his mother was, he had been exceedingly pleasant to her, and she didn't want to offend him.

"Where?" she asked.

"I'm a better tour guide than that guard." He waved an arm expansively. "I'll show you the old monastery, where all the monkeys lived."

She laughed.

"I'm not stupid," he insisted, with a very serious expression. "I know the difference between monks and monkeys."

"I'm sure you do."

"I was just kidding you."

"I know."

"Hey, you want a cigarette?" He removed a pack from his pocket, extended it to her.

Though she wanted to accept, she fought the urge and shook her head. "Maybe I should quit. Those Greek smokes of yours may be the way I can finally do it."

"What do you mean?" He didn't seem to understand.

"The tobacco is coarse," she said, "too rough for a lady."

After pouting for a moment, he brightened. "How about some Marathon then? I could go in my apartment and get it."

"I should give up marijuana, too. My mother would want me to." She squared her shoulders. "OK, Mr. Tour Guide. Where to?"

"To see something really cool and really old." He led her around to a storage shed beside his unit, and rolled a yellow bicycle out. The bike, with fat balloon tires, had a front fender that was loose and rattled. A rusty horn and wire basket were secured to the handlebars.

She wondered what he was doing, but didn't say anything.

From the shed he retrieved a second bicycle, this one a bright red racer with gleaming metal accessories. "My brand new bike," he announced proudly. "Mom got it for my birthday. The other bike is my old one. I keep it for dates."

"I'm sure you're quite an operator."

The comment went over his head. "You can ride the new one, and I'll take the dented one. I'm a gentleman."

"I know you are."

Fetching two red helmets from the shed, he said, "We have to wear these. I was in a motorcycle wreck and hit my head, and afterward Mom said I couldn't ride motorcycles anymore, but I could ride bikes, as long as I always wear my helmet."

"Your mother is right." She realized that the accident might explain why he was dimwitted, or he might have been that way all his life.

"I still don't like her, though. She tries to fake like she's nice sometimes, but I've seen the other side of her, the bad side."

"What have you seen her do?" Looking around, Lori saw the guard watching them.

"Bad things. Like I said." As before, fear showed on his soft-featured face and he didn't provide details.

"Follow me," Alex said, after their helmets were secured, with the chin straps tightened. He led the way, walking the squeaky, rattling older bicycle across the cobblestone street.

She followed, with the bright red bicycle.

"I know how to lose that guard," Alex said, looking back. "But you'll have to keep up with me."

They carried the bikes down an ancient stone stairway to the tunnel where Dixie Lou had jogged. It was empty now, except for the two of them. But she heard footsteps behind them, following. Quickly, Alex climbed aboard his bicycle and headed in the opposite direction, riding in a weaving pattern, as if he were a child just learning.

Lori followed, but didn't get too close behind, for fear of running into him. Like her companion, she remained in the center, where the rock floor was worn smoother by the centuries-long passage of countless feet.

"Okay," he said, peddling harder. "Now we get to go real fast." His bike was only a three-speed, but he got it going more smoothly and at a pretty good clip. With her twenty-one-speed gear system, Lori had no trouble keeping up.

Laughing wildly, he led her around a turn in the tunnel, then made a series of sharp turns. At first they heard voices behind them, and then it grew quiet, only the sounds of their tires on the pavement and their heavy breathing. Finally they came to an abrupt stop at the edge of a precipice, with a barren, rocky valley visible beyond, hundreds of meters below.

In a panic she squeezed the hand brakes and prayed. He reached out and grabbed her bike, helping her to stop.

"Fun, huh?" he said.

Lori's heart raced, but she wasn't upset. They were at least three meters from the edge, not as close as she'd first thought. She had to admit it *had* been fun, and exhilarating. As much as the situation with her mother upset her, she still found it almost amusing that Alex's mother had taken her jogging and now he'd taken her on a bike ride. The Jacksons were an energetic family.

"It's beautiful here," she said, gazing out at the snowy gnome's cap of a ridge across the valley, beneath dark clouds. In the foreground, a flock of white-fronted geese flew lower than Lori's perch, winging gracefully off to the north, toward snow-capped mountain peaks.

She noticed now that the cliff on which she stood rose to a promontory on her left side, with some sort of a structure up there. A narrow, rocky path led to it.

"C'mon, I'll show you," he offered.

Leaving their bikes and helmets behind, he led the way over an uneven surface that was around a meter from the edge. Lori had no fear of heights, and looked over the drop-off several times without concern or ill effect. Still, it was a long way down.

The tiny wood and stone building atop the promontory was open air, with a roof but no walls. An attached deck cantilevered out over the edge of the cliff. A heavy-duty block and tackle mechanism loomed overhead, with thick hemp rope connected to a platform that appeared capable of being lowered over the edge. The rope looked relatively new.

"This is the old lift system," he said, striding out onto the cantilevered section. "Monks brought food, animals, and military equipment up on it."

The deck looked sturdy enough, with some evidence of modern repairs, and was surrounded with a railing, so Lori followed him out onto it. Reading from a brass plaque adjacent to a huge rope drum, she learned that the lift system had been restored ten years ago, by hermits who lived on Monte Konos. Alex explained that the work was done shortly before the UWW took control of Monte Konos. The platform had a primitive gate that slid to one side in wooden grooves. According to the plaque, the mechanism had been rebuilt many times over the centuries, always according to the original specifications.

"I know how to make it go up and down," Alex announced, proudly. "You wanna take a ride with me?" He swung the gate open.

Looking down the face of the high cliff, Lori felt her stomach lurch, but it was a pleasurable feeling, a thrill. She'd always been a risk-taker, and wondered, as she had before, if this might have been a trait of her father's. Her mother certainly had not been that way, despite the manner in which she had been so badly injured . . . and perhaps even killed. Lori hated to imagine that possibility, and clung to a slender thread of hope. No one could have suspected it would be dangerous to attend a women's meeting, a goddess circle, in a wealthy suburb.

Lori placed a foot on the platform, then looked at Alex and saw sudden alertness in his gray eyes and a slight, mischievous smile. "Go ahead," he urged.

Something about him gave her confidence at this moment, a sense that he was knowledgeable in ways that were not easy to perceive. Sometimes, such as now, he seemed surprisingly intelligent, and not slow at all.

Bravely, she stepped onto the platform by herself. Looking down over the side she saw the scarred rock face of the cliff in waning sunlight, with hardy, clinging plants in crevices, and the shadow of what might be an opening in the rock several meters down. The platform swayed slightly on its rope tethers, then a little more, in a frigid gust of wind.

"Now you," she said.

As he stepped aboard and held onto a hand rail, the contraption creaked, but held together. He rested his hand on the control lever of a pulley and gear mechanism that controlled the lift and descent ropes, then paused, looking at her. "I really like you," he said. "To me, we're on a date today."

The comment struck her as odd, but she smiled gently. The platform rocked in the wind, giving her a queasy feeling.

"I haven't exactly been straight with you," he said, his words coming rapidly, and his voice seemed to have changed slightly, becoming more alert. "I'm not really simple minded at all, not the court jester I've been playing. And I know things about your mother."

She glared at him. The dumbness that seemed to permeate his facial expression before had all but disappeared. "The truth? Where is she? She's alive?"

Alex grasped her hand, and his grip was warm in hers. He looked into her eyes with warmth and compassion. "A friend of mine can tell you more."

He lifted the control lever, and the platform began to descend slowly, creaking and swaying. They passed windows into unoccupied, stone-walled rooms. Presently, Alex brought the device to a stop at a wide ledge, with a large wooden door in the wall. It looked like a loading dock, from untold centuries past.

Using a stick with a hook on it, Alex pulled the platform closer and then tied it to heavy cleats on the ledge.

As he did this, the door creaked open, revealing a bearded man.

* * *

Elsewhere in the complex, Councilwoman Deborah Marvel paced a low-ceilinged stone room nervously, sharply alert to the slightest unusual sounds from the passageway outside, indications of trouble. Her short blonde hair was windblown, from her having been outside when the weather turned bad. She and fifteen other councilwomen were in a food storage room beneath the Refectory Building, in the midst of large bags of rice stacked in neat piles.

Deborah didn't like this one bit, meeting without Dixie Lou's knowledge, but the other councilwomen—especially Katherine Pangalos, Fujiko Harui, and Bobbi Torrence—had insisted upon it. The UWW Charter, designed with checks and balances in mind, allowed them to meet without the knowledge of the Chairwoman, as long as a majority of the councilwomen were present. No minutes or other records would be kept, and they were free to say anything. Title 6.19.2 prohibited any of them from disclosing the contents of the meeting to an outsider without the unanimous consent of the council.

"We know you're not pleased to be here, Deborah," Katherine Pangalos said, "but you must agree our new leader has been behaving strangely."

"So, what else is new?"

"I mean, worse than ever. Even the guards are saying so. She goes around carrying the Sword of She-God, acts like she's on some kind of a bizarre movie set."

"I've seen her," Fujiko Harui said, nodding. "Sometimes she just walks right by me and doesn't say a thing—hardly even looks at me. She's incredibly focused."

"Or crazy," Katherine said.

"She's trying to take Amy's place," Bobbi Torrence added, "but no one can do that." A heavy woman with a jowly face and a dark, overhanging brow, she had expressed grave concerns to Deborah about the Chairwoman.

"Strange behavior doesn't translate into guilt," Deborah countered.

Tilting her head back, Katherine gazed down the bridge of her nose. "Dixie Lou hardly mentions Amy's name anymore. The rest of us talk about her all the time, how much we miss her, but she doesn't do that. It's as if she wants to forget Amy's sacred memory, as if she thinks she's more important."

"I'm sure that isn't the case," Deborah opined, passing a hand through her hair. "She's just busy with her new responsibilities, taking them seriously. I know her, and she looks toward the future, not the past. Admittedly she could be more diplomatic, more polite at times, but don't forget she was raised in the most desperate poverty. Besides, we aren't here to crucify—uh, attack—her for personality defects."

"Let's talk issues, then," Fujiko Harui snapped, from Katherine's side. "She may have had Amy killed."

"You can't prove that," Deborah said.

Katherine raised her voice. "Based upon this, she's either guilty or negligent." She lifted a piece of paper, an anonymous tip that had been slipped under the door of her apartment earlier in the day.

"We don't even know who wrote this," Deborah said.

Katherine was scowling. "But the information is most shocking."

"I still think we should tell Dixie Lou about it."

"We will, after our little ambush."

Deborah pursed her lips, but nodded.

* * *

The paunchy man had a reddish beard and horn-rimmed glasses. Lori could not determine his age. With his unlined, pallid skin, he might be twenty-five, or forty. He seemed agitated. Dressed in a pale green smock, he stood in a large, dimly lit room filled with medical supplies and equipment.

"This is Dr. Yonncy Zakheim," Alex said. "He tends to the stud knights, keeps them in top working order." Pausing, Alex added, "I'm sorry. I don't mean to be facetious. We're here to discuss something much more important."

"You know about my mother?" Lori asked, of the doctor.

He gestured back, to doorways that opened into other rooms, all dimly lit. Men could be seen moving around in one of them, and she heard their voices. "There are two clinics on Monte Konos," he said, "one for women and one for men. The male doctors are not as well trained as our female counterparts and we don't have the best equipment, but somehow we manage to—"

"I'm sorry to interrupt," Lori said, "but what does that have to do with my mother?"

"For some reason they brought your mother to the men's section. We did the best we could."

"I want to see her."

After exchanging uneasy glances with Alex, Zakheim said, "I'm sorry to tell you this, but your mother is gone. She arrived here barely alive, and died two days later." From his smock, he brought out a photograph and handed it to the shocked girl.

Shaking, with tears streaming down her face, Lori looked at the picture. It showed Camilla Vale lying on a hospital bed, with life support systems connected to her. Her face was pallid, her eyes closed. She appeared to be barely alive, and only sustained by the equipment—which they must have decided to disconnect eventually, without Lori's knowledge or input. Her death was an outrage, on so many levels.

"I knew it," Lori said. "Dixie Lou was stringing me along. But why? Why in the name of God would she do that?"

"For her own filthy reasons. Maybe she wants something out of you, or thinks she might need to get something out of you in the future."

"Your ability with the she-apostles?" Alex asked.

"Where is her body?" Lori asked, tasting the bitter salt of her own tears.

"Cremated," Zakheim replied. "By order of Dixie Lou Jackson."

"How considerate of her," Alex said.

"How do I know you're telling me the truth?" Lori asked, of Zakheim. "Photos can be faked."

"What motive would we have?" the doctor asked. "Come with me, please," he said, leading the way into an adjacent room. With Lori and Alex behind him, he went down a corridor for a short distance, and entered an office.

Opening a desk drawer, Zakheim brought out a clear plastic bag filled with jewelry and other personal articles. As Lori accepted the bag from him, her heart sank when she recognized her mother's jade ring, gold necklace, and a monogrammed cigarette lighter.

"I wish it were not true," Zakheim said.

"So do I," Alex said. And in an icy voice, he added, "I lost my mother, too, a long time ago. Dixie Lou Jackson may have given birth to me—or that could be one of her many lies—but no matter what, I don't consider her my mother."

"We have one more thing to tell you," Alex said. He left for a moment, and when he returned he was accompanied by three young men and two young women. As they stood in the office, he introduced them by name, including a redheaded food service worker named Mila Bennett.

The very serious-looking Bennett appeared to be in her early twenties, and she quickly took charge of the room. The others seemed to defer to her.

"You've been vocal about how the UWW has been mistreating the children," she said, to Lori. "And we have a solution."

"We're taking a risk telling you anything," Alex added, "but life is about taking chances, to one degree or another."

"Our resident philosopher," Bennett said. "Lori, when you and Dixie Lou arrived, an explosion blew up a rail line."

"I remember," Lori said. "She was very upset. You did that?"

Bennett nodded. "Originally, we wanted to break the stud knights out, since they're no more than sex slaves."

"Not all of them want to leave, though," one of the men said.

"Some do," Bennett insisted. "In any event, we have a more important cause now, since the she-apostles arrived. We're going to rescue the children, get them out of here, out of the hands of those crazy Dubbers."

"That's what we call the UWW women," Alex explained.

Bennett continued. "Maybe the children really are reincarnated apostles, and maybe they aren't. No matter, we need to get them in the hands of more responsible people. Not these religious fanatics."

"I'm with you," Lori said.

"We hoped you would say that," Alex said. He clasped her hand in a new form of friendship and camaraderie.

Chapter 20

Jesus Christ was generous, loving, forgiving, brilliant, and filled to overflowing with the spirit of God Almighty. The earth has never seen anyone who even came close to matching the influence of this Savior who walked among us.

—Lori Vale, from a dream

The subterranean conference room featured mirror walls and liquid crystal picture panels projecting morning views from topside. Styx sat at the head of a gleaming oval table, with Minister Culpepper on his right and the Vice Minister of Finance, Tommy Lee Chang, on his left. The rest of the large room was empty.

Waiting for Chang to distribute copies of his report, Styx watched a panel embedded in the mahogany table top as it changed, displaying the location of known UWW paramilitary squads, as well as those controlled by known UWW allies. He wanted to attack all of them at once and take them out, but the Minister insisted on a more careful approach, since some of his advisers felt they might be traps.

"Aren't you going to begin?" Culpepper asked, in a raspy, irritated voice.

Startled, Styx looked over the first page of the report. The Minister was having him run this meeting, as he did frequently, saying he wanted to make certain Styx learned how to lead. Actually, Styx thought, the old man was just lazy. He should retire, but hung on stubbornly instead.

"Highlight this for us, please," Styx said, to Chang.

"Just give us the bottom line," Culpepper interjected. "Has everyone paid?" He was referring to a Special Funding Request that the Bureau had sent to all of their supporters around the world.

A Chinese-American who was a whiz with figures, Chang began nervously. "Well, we got another two hundred million from the Spanish crown and triple that from the British Parliament. The American Congress approved three billion in secrecy, and the Pope has agreed to . . ."

Culpepper half rose out of his chair. "I told President Markwether *four* billion."

"He said he's working on it."

"The man's a weakling and a fool," Culpepper snarled.

Styx chewed on a fountain pen. "We should get rid of him," he said in his high voice, with a dangerous edge to it.

"Next election."

"Sooner would be better." Styx meant by assassination.

"Now don't be too anxious," the Minister responded, in a paternal tone that Styx found particularly irritating. "You can't go around flying off half-cocked."

Styx rolled his eyes toward the ceiling, reminded himself to be patient. Eventually his time would come, and then things would be *violently* different. He wouldn't coddle people the way Culpepper did, wouldn't play politics with them. They would do exactly what he told them to do, without hesitation.

* * *

Consuela Santos rode the old bus as far as her pesos took her, to the Pacific coast of Mexico in the state of Jalisco. It had been noisy and smelly the whole way on the clattering, dented vehicle as it traversed rough mountain roads, carrying animals, produce, and families with children. She was thankful for the camouflage of constant commotion. Several times a day, whenever her baby nuzzled against her, she opened her blouse and allowed Marta to suckle the warm milk from her breasts. None of the other passengers paid any attention.

In a seaside fishing town, the bus came to a squeaky, jarring stop, and the driver pulled a lever to open the front door. Consuela, who had been seated near the rear, awaited her turn and stepped off onto the unaccustomed luxury of a concrete sidewalk, in front of a freshly painted white stucco bank building. Cradling her baby in her arms, she stood by the immense plate glass window of the bank, gazing in at well-dressed people as they conducted transactions with tellers. With all they had, their lives seemed separated by a universe from the possibilities open to her. They were merchants and fishermen and farmers and domestic workers. There were even some who looked like tourists, dressed in shorts and bright shirts and blouses. In sharp contrast to all of them, Consuela and her baby had nothing.

"Are you all right, dear?" a woman inquired.

Startled, Consuela turned to see a *mestizo* woman in a tattered black and red dress, with a charcoal gray shawl wrapped around her head, covering most of her silver hair. Her face was deeply creased and weathered, but her eyes remained clear and bright nonetheless, as if this impoverished Indian, despite hardships, was able to see a side of life that Consuela could only imagine.

"I don't have much," the woman said, removing a few centavos from the pocket of her dress. She extended the money to Consuela.

"Oh no, *señora*, I couldn't."

"Do you want to eat?"

In her arms, the six-month-old Marta whimpered, and Consuela knew that she would have to eat so that she would have at least minimal nutrients, enabling her baby to nurse at her breasts.

Accepting the coins, Consuela murmured, "*Gracias.*"

As the woman adjusted her shawl and left, Marta babbled more of the strange, unintelligible words.

At a tiny store on a dirt side street, Consuela purchased tortillas and beans, then found a doorway in an abandoned building where she could eat. She crouched in the shadows, out of the direct heat of the sun.

* * *

During her first hours in town Consuela surveyed the citizens, and noted a number of foreigners of lighter skin who appeared to be Americans or Europeans. The village seashore, lined with weathered fishing boats, was picturesque, she had to admit. Rich people came to this place, which gave her an idea.

Just outside of town, at the end of a chuckhole-filled driveway, she found what she was looking for, an isolated stucco house with an unlocked

bedroom window. The home sat on a knoll and might have offered a fine view of the aquamarine sea, if not for jungle growths in the way. This led her to believe that the owner either rarely came around or had abandoned the place. Entering through an unlocked window, she found the interior quite dusty and overrun with mice and fat cockroaches, and noted a newspaper that she couldn't read, except for the year-old date. Basically illiterate, she nonetheless had a good understanding of numbers and simple calculations, which had been taught to her by an uncle years ago.

In a large storage room off the kitchen, she located cans of food and tins of crackers. A box of cereal and several soft packages of soup were infested with cockroaches, so she threw them in a garbage hole she'd dug outside in the yard, at the perimeter of the property. Since she couldn't read or write she saved all of the packages and cans that had been opened, as a method of keeping track of her debt to the people who owned the house. She was not a thief, and was only protecting her baby.

The light switches didn't work. At the back of the house she experimented with various settings on an electrical panel, but to no avail. Soon she began to clean the house, and washed the curtains in a nearby stream. In this way she felt she was earning her room and board, almost as if it were a real job.

The ample brick-floored kitchen featured a wood-burning stove with a cast iron top for heating pans, but she didn't dare use it during the day, for fear of smoke that could lead to her being discovered. So, over ensuing days, Consuela only lit the stove at night when she thought no one would notice.

In the food storage room she noted several large steel drums, and opened them. They contained uncontaminated grains and corn meal, perhaps for making bread, and in one she found a large quantity of salt, which she theorized may have been used for curing fish.

To ward off evil spirits, she sprinkled a thick line of salt all around the bed where her baby slept. She also borrowed red votive candles from the local Catholic church (intending to pay for them when she could), and lit them each night, after carefully covering the windows so that no light escaped. In a dresser drawer she located a necklace with a gold crucifix on it, which she shortened by knotting the chain, so that it could be hung about her daughter's neck . . . a further effort to thwart the evil ones who wanted her baby.

As each day passed Consuela felt a little more secure in her squatter-abode, and harbored faint hopes that perhaps she might live here for several months or longer, hiding Marta for as long as possible, so that no one could hear her strange, dangerous talk. In this idyllic retreat, Consuela also wanted to remain until she got her bearings and found a way of earning a living. She kept the premises spotless, and organized the labels and empty food containers meticulously, to record the items she had consumed. She intended to pay all of it back and return the home to its owner in better condition than it had been when she'd found it.

Chapter 21

There are several signs of demonic possession. One is to speak in a strange tongue, a language that is not of the person's experience.
— *The Rites of Exorcism*, a Roman Catholic handbook

Midnight . . .

Fear washed through Lori as she slipped down the stone staircase, just behind five shadowy figures: Alex Jackson, Yonney Zakheim, Mila Bennett, and two men whose names Lori couldn't recall, each of them dressed in dark clothing. The group moved with urgent purpose, and Lori felt instilled with the feeling that she had to do this, no matter the danger. Wearing only a thin black blouse and jeans, she shivered.

At the bottom they slid furtively along a wall, not walking boldly through the corridor. The two women carried pistols, while the four men had automatic rifles.

Overhead, electric lamps flickered on and off, casting eerie shadows. The wall of the passageway was moist against her arm, and bore the odor of mildew tinged with a chemical, perhaps something that had been sprayed on it to kill the growth. Somewhere she heard rainwater running through ancient gutters, a familiar sound to her now.

Glancing back, she thought she saw movement in the shadows behind them, and whispered a warning to Alex, just ahead of her. He passed the information forward, and Mila called them to a halt.

"What did you see?" Mila whispered, moving close to Lori.

"I'm not sure. Maybe it was a trick of my eyes, or of the light. I thought I should mention it."

"You did the right thing."

In her pocket, Lori closed her fingers around a small handgun. Glancing back, she didn't see anything now, and neither did her companions. Cautiously, they continued forward.

*   *   *

"We're almost there," Alex whispered to Lori. He hoped that it wasn't a mistake to bring her on this important mission. In these catacombs, ghostly shadows and unexplained sounds had a way of playing tricks with the mind. Some people said the spirits of the dead haunted the remote mountain, the revenant forms of monks who had dwelled here in centuries past. Over the years there had been numerous sightings and strange noises that people tittered and whispered about, but always with a nervous edge, as if they weren't quite certain.

Normally Alex and his companions might have taken the rail car for a short distance, but they couldn't risk it this time, because of the chance of discovery. The operation had to go smoothly, on a tight schedule. They had to coordinate with other people coming from different directions, converging on the exact same spot.

Ahead of him, Mila picked up the pace, while Alex thought back to earlier in the evening, when he had met with the others, including Lori Vale, the newest member of their clandestine group. . . .

*   *   *

"Tell me again what she said to you," Yonney Zakheim had said. The paunchy, bespectacled man had been leaning across the rectangular table in his own studio apartment, glaring at Liz Torrence, a computer programmer who was the niece of a councilwoman. She'd been sitting next to Alex in an apartment that was a windowless room, used in centuries past by cenobite monks.

A slender young woman with the long, elegant fingers of a piano player and green eyes, Torrence had responded, "But I've already told you. Jen said she wasn't feeling well, that she was going to consult with one of the musers."

"Those old men?" Zakheim had said. "What do they know?"

"She thinks the monks know things, ancient healing methods. They do trace back to the original inhabitants of this monastery."

"And no one here has seen any sign of her since?" Zakheim had then asked, looking around at everyone except Lori, who didn't even know Jennifer Aldrich. "Doesn't it bother any of you that she knows our complete plan and no one knows exactly where she is? What if she turned us in to Alex's mother?"

"What if Alex is a spy for his mother himself?" Liz Torrence said. "What if, what if? If we worry about everything, nothing will change around here. The children will never be rescued from those crazy women."

Others had been seated with them at the table: their leader Mila Bennett, strangely silent; Dan Rhodes, a muscular laborer; Siana Harui, daughter of another councilwoman; and Christine Brickowski, whose older sister was one of the Scriptorium scholars working on the *Holy Women's Bible*.

"At least Jen doesn't know when we plan to make our move," Siana Harui said. She had short black hair, and a small bone structure like her mother. "We're deciding on that right now."

"She knows enough," Zakheim said. "She knows all of our names, and what we intend to do. It doesn't ring right. Why isn't Jen here?"

Torrence heaved a deep sigh. "You worry too much."

"I don't like it. I just don't like it."

"Jen did look feverish, and her face was sweaty."

"I hope it wasn't nervous guilt," Zakheim said.

"You're always so paranoid," Torrence snapped. "Every one of us is sick of it."

"So you're all against me, is that it?" His eyes feral, Zakheim looked from face to face.

"No one's against you," Bennett said. She placed a reassuring hand on the doctor's arm. With the man's coat off, Alex saw the shoulder holster he wore, and the composite pearl handle of a pistol. Nearby, a black automatic rifle leaned against the wall. The other men, including

Alex, had similar weapons, and every woman—including Lori—concealed a pistol in her purse. All of the guns were constructed of new ceramics and plastics, and could be folded into innocuous shapes, making them undetectable by surveillance equipment.

"I say we make our move tonight," Bennett said. "If we delay, it only increases our chances of being discovered."

They had split into two groups, approaching the target from different directions. . . .

* * *

Thinking back on the meeting, it troubled Alex that no one had located their dark-haired companion Jennifer Aldrich, that she wasn't participating in the operation. A rail car maintenance employee, Jen was in a key position to cause serious disruption to the Monte Konos transportation systems, and had successfully sabotaged the rail lines twice without being caught.

Now Alex and his companions hid in the shadows of the corridor beneath the Scriptorium Building. Through a high-arched doorway, a guard station was visible to them in a pool of illumination, and beyond that, the bullet-proof glass doors of the living quarters of the she-apostles.

Alex glanced around nervously. A little ahead of schedule, they had several minutes to wait for the next guard shift to take over, the women they had paid off. A short distance down the corridor, on the other side of the guard station, he saw movement along the wall, and a light that blinked once. The rest of the rescue team.

"Everyone is ready," Mila Bennett said in a subdued voice, remaining in the shadows.

Lori moved closer to Alex. "I'm not afraid," she whispered.

"I know that. You're tougher than I am." He checked the clip on his automatic rifle, snapped it back into place.

"It would be nice if we could just give the children back to their families," Lori said, "and forget about having any so-called experts look them over and prod their minds."

"It's a complicated matter," Alex said. "These kids are from all over the world, and we need to turn them over to the appropriate authorities first."

"I suppose so," Lori whispered. But she wasn't even sure if she agreed what she had just said, about what to do with the children. Morally it seemed wrong to keep the children away from their families any longer than necessary, but what if they really were reincarnated apostles of Jesus? The thought frightened and exhilarated her. She had to admit that she had felt a visceral connection to Veronica, and even, for some odd reason, to Dixie Lou herself.

"We're rescuing them," Alex said. "The UWW kidnapped them, and we're reversing it."

"I should be mad at you for tricking me," she said. "For playing the fool—and playing me for a fool."

"Are you? Mad, I mean?"

Her eyes danced across the shadows of his face, only inches from hers. "I haven't decided."

Focusing on the guard station beyond him, Lori watched the arrival of four women in pale gold uniforms. They were talking with the other guards. Alex looked at his watch. "Five minutes to shift change," he said.

She noted increased nervousness around her.

"If it makes you feel any better," he said, "I fooled a lot of other people, too, including my mother." Lori felt the warmth of his breath against her face.

Following a moment's hesitation, she asked, "How did you deceive your clever mother?"

He smiled, but warily, alert to his surroundings. "So many questions, so little time." Again, he glanced at his watch.

Moments later, the guards changed shift. At a signal from Mila, the two groups of rescuers joined forces, and they removed child carrier backpacks from a large sack, strapping them onto their backs.

Lori ran forward with the others. They opened the heavy glass doors and hurried inside.

* * *

Lori stood in what appeared to be a lounge, furnished with black leather couches and chairs. On a wide wall ahead of her were eleven closed doors, each with the name of a female apostle written in golden script over it, the same ornate lettering style she had seen on the Scriptorium computer.

One of the doors was designated "Apostle Veronica," and on each side of that were inscribed the names of the others, Mary Magdalene, Abigail, Sarah, Lydia, Kezia, Hannah, Esther, Rhoda, Priscilla, and Candace. A twelfth door was unmarked.

Pursuant to the plan, Lori's companions opened the doors and began loading children onto the backpack carriers. A toddler with black hair whimpered softly as she was lifted into place on Yonney's back. Lori saw her kicking and waving her chubby little arms, heard her protests increase in volume. Some of the other children began to fuss as well. They were a variety of races and combinations of races.

Lori's assignment was to protect the escape route, remaining near the entrance. At a counter on the right a white-uniformed attendant dozed in her chair, her head drifting toward the counter top and then bouncing back every few seconds. She snored, made intermittent snorts. Even the commotion of the children failed to waken her.

Yonney Zakheim disconnected her videophone, used the receiver to smash the plastic connector, so that the phone could not be used.

Now the woman sat straight up, her eyes open wide and filled with terror. Around fifty, she had a bun of gray hair and a high forehead. "What's going on here?" she demanded.

"We're taking the children," Zakheim said, identifying himself as a doctor.

"I need to call for approval," the attendant said. She lifted the videophone receiver, but he put his hand on hers.

"It doesn't work," he said. He was larger than she was, and stronger. Taking her firmly by the arm, he led her to a storeroom and locked her inside.

When all of the rescuers were gathered, with children on their backs and in their arms, Lori scanned the young faces, searching for Veronica, the one she had been with in the Scriptorium. To her surprise she didn't see her, though she counted all eleven children. A sinking feeling set in.

She met Alex's startled gaze. He had noticed the same thing.

"These aren't the real she-apostles!" he shouted.

"Are you sure?" Mila asked.

Alarms sounded.

"It's a trap!" Lori yelled.

"Leave the kids here!" Mila commanded. "Everyone outside, fast!"

As the would-be rescuers emerged into the corridor, their guns drawn, the guards attacked, firing automatic weapons. More guards appeared from hiding places.

Chapter 22

Any understanding of the Bible *must begin with the stark realization that men have written it, as they have written history. Most of the stories of women are missing. The sacred gospels of the she-apostles are missing . . . stolen.*

—From a letter written by Amy Angkor-Billings, a copy of which was turned over to the Bureau of Ideology

As Dixie Lou lay in underclothes atop her bed, the well-built man undulated to throbbing music, dancing for her, moving his hips suggestively. He removed his tight silk shirt, leaving on only a pair of black bikini pants. Outside, windblown rain pelted the panes of the apartment windows.

Giovanni Petrie, one of the stud knights kept to provide sexual favors for the UWW leadership, was no more than twenty, with light brown skin and a shock of long blond hair. All of the males in his position were young and virile, but few had the brains required for intelligent conversation. So dumb were they that some of the women referred to them as "himbos"—male bimbos. Giovanni was a decided exception. She found him bright and interesting, and he was a great lover. But he drank too much *retsina*, the resinous Greek wine, and on occasion this made him obnoxious.

At Dixie Lou's voice-command, the night stand lamps dimmed. Her eyes pleaded with him to come closer.

Instead he stretched his body backward, touching his head to the carpeted floor, by his own monk's robe that was draped over a chair. Unable to wait any longer, she leaped from the bed and wrestled him down. They finished disrobing, and coupled in a frenzy of passion.

When Dixie Lou's appetite had subsided she lay next to him on the floor while he massaged her back with powerful hands that worked deeply and relaxingly into her muscles.

Giovanni's robe, still draped over the chair, was within reach, and from a pocket of it he removed a flask of *retsina*, from which he drank. A slip of paper fluttered to the floor from his robe.

"What's this?" she asked, picking up the paper and reading it. "A passage from the *Holy Women's Bible*?"

Hesitation. Then: "I was just reading it. You showed it to me and I liked it."

"But you shouldn't have removed it from my room. This material is Most Secret!"

"I was excited about it." He smiled nervously. "You're going to publish it anyway."

"But not yet, you fool. We're not ready!"

An alarm klaxon sounded. Three long blasts followed by a short one.

Dixie Lou and Giovanni exchanged surprised glances.

She knew the signal. It meant trouble in the quarters of the she-apostles.

Dixie Lou dressed hurriedly and removed a short barrel .38 from a holster on her desk, then spun the chamber. It was loaded. She put the holster on, connecting the straps across her right shoulder and under her left arm, then voice activated a computer keyboard beside her desk. On the monitor appeared images of the entrance to the living quarters of the she-apostles.

Injured guards lay sprawled on the ground, with another guard tending to them. Nearby on the stone floor were two motionless bodies. Beyond them, on the other side of the glass entrance doors, children were on the floor, many of them crying. Some were in backpack carriers. Others crawled around or walked about in a state of confusion. She didn't recognize them. They weren't the she-apostles, though they were around the same age and all appeared to be girls.

Two of her guards moved into the view of the camera, and began tending to the children. Women in robes appeared. She recognized Deborah Marvel, Fujiko Harui, and Katherine Pangalos. The sight of Katherine made her blood boil.

What were the councilwomen doing together, and why were those children in an off-limits area?

Waving the sheet of scripture under Giovanni's nose, she said to him, "I'll deal with you later." Without giving him the usual parting kiss she ordered him to return to the stud harem.

Dixie Lou ran from the office, into the hallway.

* * *

As Lori and Alex burst into the tunnel, a klaxon sounded its alarm: three long blasts and one short, repeating. In the midst of their companions, they ran into a din of gunfire, firing back. Bullets ricocheted off the ancient stone walls.

While pulling the trigger, Lori prayed.

* * *

With her gun drawn, Dixie Lou took the stairs two at a time to the main floor of the Refectory Building, where she stopped for a moment to determine the best way of reaching the living quarters. She considered crossing the plaza but decided against it because of the bad weather, and instead took the stairs to the next level down and then ran through a tunnel toward the basement of the Scriptorium Building.

Her mind spun with questions. She worried about the she-apostles. The monitor had shown different children. Why?

The klaxons continued their desperate alarm. In a matter of moments, people would be rushing in from all directions.

Rounding a turn, she saw a fallen security guard. The woman was moving slowly, stumbling, clutching a shoulder wound. Dixie Lou ran past her, reaching the entrance of the living quarters. Blood pooled on the stone, but the injured guards she'd seen on the monitor were sitting up and appeared to have suffered only minor injuries. Peering through the bullet-chipped but impenetrable glass she counted five councilwomen now, along with half a dozen security guards. In the background, matrons in white dresses were holding the unknown children, trying to calm them.

The stocky Dixie Lou pushed both doors open and strode through. She asked Katherine Pangalos about the children.

"Kids of our staff," she replied, "plus some we brought in from outside as decoys. We heard about a kidnap plan and decided to set a trap. The she-apostles are safe."

"Did you know about this?" Dixie Lou asked of Deborah.

"Yes," she replied. With her large blue eyes, she fixed a nervous stare on Katherine.

"Why wasn't I informed?" Dixie Lou demanded.

Katherine's expression was filled with disdain. "Security leak close to you. We acted under Title 14 of the charter, permitting the council to—"

"I know about Title 14. What's this security leak?"

"A report that your favorite stud knight has an unsavory background. We needed to check him further."

"Giovanni isn't a conspirator, you idiot. You think I didn't check him out myself before I invited him into my bed?"

"You may have overlooked a few things," Katherine countered. "He's been carrying around printed excerpts of our new gospels. Do you have any idea where he got them?"

"None at all," Dixie Lou said, lying. She might have to kill Giovanni now, in order to protect herself.

"This is serious," Katherine said. She exchanged an uneasy glance with Deborah.

"Do you have evidence linking my stud knight to the kidnappers?" Dixie Lou demanded.

"Not exactly," Katherine admitted, "but—"

"You should have discussed your suspicions with me privately before setting up a sting."

"We're sorry that wasn't done," Deborah said.

"This whole operation looks mixed up to me," Dixie Lou thundered. "Do we have any prisoners?"

"Not yet," Deborah said. "A couple of the kidnappers are dead. A food service worker, a gardener—"

"Names?"

"Insignificant in their case, but others aren't. Uh, Liz Torrence may be involved, and—" She hesitated, glanced at Fujiko Harui, who stood nearby. "—and Fujiko's daughter, Siana. Guards have identified them."

The little Japanese woman gasped.

Without another word, Dixie Lou whirled and hurried down the corridor, back the way she had come.

"We should have told her the rest," Katherine said, to Deborah.

"I know."

* * *

On a section of slick stone, Alex slipped and fell, twisting his ankle and dropping his rifle, making a clatter of noise. Lori helped him to his feet. As he got up, he picked up his weapon and tried to continue, but said his ankle was throbbing. With her help, he ran on it anyway, but not well. She saw his anguished features in the yellow light of an overhead lamp.

Unaware of his injury, Mila Bennett and Yonney Zakheim ran ahead of them, and disappeared into shadows.

"We have to hurry," Alex said.

Lori ran beside him, holding onto his arm so that he wouldn't fall.

Chapter 23

Men fear women. This is why they've set up so many structures to control the activities of the fair sex. The Bible *is one of those structures.*
—Note screen, UWW computer file

Security guards ran toward Dixie Lou, and saluted her with W's as she passed them.

A down-staircase veered off to the right. On a hunch, she took it. At a landing she found a fallen man with a head wound, blood pooling around him. He appeared to be dead, but in the low light she didn't try to identify him. Slender and bald, he wore a black coat and trousers. Something familiar about him. One of the knights, a laborer? Yes, she'd seen him doing tile repairs the week before.

She continued a long way down the staircase, and at the bottom encountered one of her security guards lying injured and bleeding on the rock floor of a chamber. It was a heavyset woman whom she recognized as Linda Cutler.

The victim's eyelids flickered as she fought to stay conscious. For a few seconds she gazed up at Dixie Lou with glassy eyes, then smiled weakly and said, "Thank She-God it's you, ma'am." She tried to salute but didn't have the strength, and passed out.

Glancing around, Dixie Lou saw no one. Feeling Cutler's neck, she got a strong pulse. The woman moaned, and Dixie Lou saw a wound on her right side. It might not be life-threatening.

Dixie Lou looked around again, satisfying herself that no others were in the chamber. No security cameras to worry about in this section either, no eyes to see what she was about to do, except her own.

Pointing her gun at the back of Cutler's head, she fired once, causing an echoing percussion.

The body jerked.

Dixie Lou leaned over and rechecked the pulse. This time there was none.

It left the newly elected Chairwoman in a position she liked, for with at least one dead guard she could insist upon the death penalty for the kidnappers. Of course she had the authority to condemn or reprieve anyone involved in the plot anyway, but this gave her more control over the situation, and potentially more councilwomen who would vote with her. The daughter of Fujiko Harui and niece of Bobbi Torrence were involved, and in the past neither of those councilwomen could be counted upon to vote with Dixie Lou. If she could lay a trail showing the daughter and niece were responsible not only for kidnapping but for murder, it would give her two additional council votes. In exchange for their support, Dixie Lou would spare their family members.

It was just politics.

She stepped around the body and crossed the cavern. Down a little incline she located the entrances to three tunnels. Cold, forbidding darkness lurked inside each of them. If she wasn't careful she could get lost in the moldy passageways of this ancient monastery.

She hurried past the dead security guard, ran back up the stairs.

* * *

From their hiding place in the shadows of an alcove, Lori and Alex watched.

"I told you she was dangerous," Alex said, his voice agitated.

"But why one of her own guards?"

"Who knows?"

Carefully, Alex and Lori crossed the cavern, to the side of the fallen guard. Alex limped slightly from the twisted ankle, which he had wrapped tightly in a strip of cloth. Leaning over the body, he removed a radio handset and a small flashlight.

Lori heard a noise behind them, on the stairway.

"Halt!" a woman shouted.

Looking up the long flight of stairs, Lori saw two security guards running down the steps. One shined a bright light on them.

Alex and Lori fled across the cavern, with the guards shouting after them. A bullet ricocheted off the wall, whistling by Lori's ear.

"Alex Jackson! Stop!"

Lori and Alex disappeared into the middle tunnel and ran for their lives.

* * *

On the sheer rock western face of Monte Konos, where centuries ago a medieval monk leaped to his death, a rope ladder dangled, writhing like a living creature in the wind-blown rain. Overhead, a transport helicopter throbbed, as its pilot fought to maintain control. Simultaneous with the kidnapping attempt, the conspirators had disabled the monastery's air defense system, an effort aided by the storm.

For Greek pilot Philikè Metaxas, the storm was a double-edged sword. He didn't like the way the wind was picking up, reaching levels so dangerous that he might not be able to stay in the air. He glanced at his watch, then cursed as a gust buffeted the craft, causing the ladder below to whip violently against the cliff face.

Where were Mila Bennett and the others? This was supposed to be a split-second operation to rescue the abused children, but it was nearly ten minutes past the deadline. He couldn't afford to wait much longer.

The strongest wind yet slammed into the helicopter, and Metaxas barely kept control of the craft. He ordered his crew to winch up the ladder. Mission aborted.

Then a rocket hit the craft, and a ball of fire slid down the cliff face.

* * *

In a basement room of the Refectory Building, Liz Torrence, Siana Harui, and Yonney Zakheim were cornered. They threw their weapons down, and emerged with their hands raised high.

Security guards collected the weapons and snapped handcuffs on the failed kidnappers.

* * *

On her way back to the quarters of the she-apostles, Dixie Lou overheard a security guard shouting over a radio handset, and a voice on the other end saying all of the fugitives had been captured with the exception of Alex Jackson and Lori Vale, who'd been seen at the body of a murdered guard.

Dixie Lou felt empty in the pit of her stomach. Had they seen anything?

* * *

Lori's flashlight beam played off the rock walls of a wide passageway, throwing eerie reflections. The sides of the corridor were cut irregularly, leaving protruding rock shapes that looked at times like human heads and bodies, and from some angles like ferocious gargoyles. She had to keep shining the light directly at them to reassure herself. It smelled moldy in here, and she saw grimy green and black streaks of moisture on the walls, and gutters of shallow water on each side.

"I've never been this far," Alex said, from her left. Limping, he carried the automatic rifle, which glinted dully in the shadows. In the darkness he had dropped and broken the radio handset before they'd been able to use it to eavesdrop on the conversations of the guards who were bound to be pursuing them.

The fleeing pair were somewhere in the maze of passageways at the heart of Monte Konos, where rail cars and lifts didn't go. Hoping to find an exit at the base of the mountain, they had been attempting to descend for an hour, but at times couldn't tell up from down, since some of the inclines were so slight. Lori felt disoriented.

Hearing a noise, she flipped off the flashlight and froze in her tracks. Alex disengaged the safety of the automatic rifle, making a soft click beside her. Lori's ears probed the cold, damp darkness.

She identified footsteps, the percussion of boots on hard rock. More than one person, she thought. Guards? She struggled to determine direction but an echo effect made it difficult. She concentrated harder.

Whoever was approaching seemed to be behind them, so maybe she and Alex should run ahead. But she wasn't sure, and that could hurtle them right into the wrong hands.

"Which way are they coming from?" she whispered.

His response was only a little louder. "I can't tell!"

Lori shivered in the dank cold, hugged her arms against her chest for warmth. A hardpack of Greek cigarettes bulged in a pocket of her jeans. Though she'd gone cold turkey the day before, vowing to quit smoking, she hadn't thrown the cigarettes away. Now she felt her hands shaking, and not from the low temperature. A cigarette—even a bad one—might calm her nerves, but she didn't dare light one now. She also couldn't use the small flashlight in her hand. . . .

Paramount in Alex's mind, he wanted to protect Lori, since she didn't belong in this mess. No lights came from either direction of the tunnel. Were the guards wearing night vision goggles? He'd heard the UWW had them, for use in certain contingencies. Was this one of those occasions? Could they see him now? His sore ankle throbbed.

The sound of footsteps grew louder, but still he could not confirm direction.

He pulled Lori back against a rock wall, seeking an alcove or indentation behind which they might conceal themselves. With one of his athletic shoes he felt the contours of a gutter on the floor and considered lying in it, with his gun ready.

Alex detected a little trickle of water, which seeped through the fabric of his shoe. Probing more with his foot he slipped, and as he fell his rifle clattered noisily onto the rocky floor.

"Are you OK?" Lori whispered.

Frantically Alex felt around and finally located the weapon, by a wide hole in the gutter. The opening was wide, and he could barely reach across it. But how deep was it? Sticking his rifle inside, he couldn't find the bottom. A musty, rotten odor filled his nostrils.

"I found a hole, a big one," he whispered to her. "I think it's a storm drain, but the cover is off, if it ever had one."

In Lori's ears, footsteps seemed to be coming from all directions. They echoed off the ancient rock walls. Louder, closer. Then she saw a play of lights coming from her right, the direction she and Alex had been heading. She had been correct not to run that way. Behind the illumination of flashlights she made out three human shapes.

Too late to run.

"Into the hole!" Lori husked.

"I couldn't find the bottom."

"We'll get inside and hang onto the edge," she said.

With her heart pounding fiercely, Lori slipped her small flashlight into a back pocket of her jeans. Even though she couldn't see, she bravely lowered herself into the hole, grasping the edge with both hands. The surfaces were moist and slippery, but with both shoes she found purchase on a protruding stone.

She heard Alex sliding in beside her, and hoped he could hold onto the rifle without dropping it down the hole. It worried her that they hadn't found the bottom. They didn't dare use the light now. She felt cold wetness on her fingers, water from the gutter. It ran down the sides of the hole, soaking her blouse and jeans all the way to her skin.

Overhead, light touched the top of the orifice, and her fingertips, over her head. She held her breath, saw Alex's eyes glint beside her, in a flicker of light.

The footsteps seemed to slow. *Have we been seen?*

They picked up pace again, making punctuating noises on the ancient rock floor that once had been traveled by religious hermits. The intrusive, approaching footsteps seemed to be right beside them now.

Lori's nose twitched . . . a powerful, unstoppable sneeze coming on. She wrinkled her nostrils in the dense air, sniffed as quietly as she could. Water splashed across her hands and against her face. A rush of water could be heard, getting louder very quickly, and she tried to firm up her handholds and footing.

"Must be raining like hell up there," a woman said.

The water grew louder, a mounting roar.

Cursing under her breath, Lori wanted to be anywhere but here, in the monastery's storm-drain system. Unable to suppress her sneeze, it cut loose just as a torrent of frigid water inundated her and Alex. Lori's feet and fingers slipped. She tumbled into the hole, letting out an involuntary cry.

She thought she heard shouting but couldn't be certain, because the sound and substance of the water consumed her, sweeping her downward. Alex seemed to be below her, because seconds before, she had bumped into him.

Her lower back slammed painfully into a rock at the side of the hole, and she groped and kicked, trying to find some way to arrest her descent. This only succeeded in skinning her knuckles and knees.

Struggling to breathe, Lori sucked in a lung full of air and water, making her cough. The water was carrying her down feet-first, flowing with her, bouncing her painfully against the rough rock sides of the storm drain. Trying to protect herself, she put her hands over her face.

* * *

In the darkest hour of the night, a robed figure hurried down a passageway beneath the Refectory Building. The smell of rotting garbage from the cafeteria filled Dixie Lou's nostrils. Her powerful flashlight illuminated the way. She could have gone a different way, but this was a shortcut.

At a heavy metal door she pressed her hand against a security plate and the door opened. She slipped through and the door thunked loudly behind her. No matter. She wasn't trying to be quiet. No odor of garbage here.

She was in a wider corridor, one of the main pedestrian arterials of the hivelike monastery. Spotting her, two slender female guards came to rigid attention and saluted. Dixie Lou passed between them, into the stud harem.

A faint red glow illuminated a large room containing more than forty beds, some with curtain dividers between them. Casting yellow light ahead of her with a flashlight, she walked down the main aisle. Some of the forms on the beds stirred. Giovanni was on the right, at the end.

Reaching him, she stood and looked down at him as he lay on his back, snoring gently. She directed a beam of light at his eyes, leaned down and husked in his ear, "I should kill you right now."

His eyelids twitched, and opened. He tried to sit up, but she pushed him back down roughly.

"Do you want to die in your sleep?"

He rubbed his forehead, as if that would produce clear thoughts. "What's wrong?"

"As if you didn't know. The innocent little boy. You know perfectly well what's wrong: The *gospels*. Give me everything you have. *Immediately*." She studied the adjacent beds, satisfied herself that the occupants were asleep.

"You got it, the last time we—"

With a backhand across his face, she snapped, "The council told me you've been carrying around excerpts of the gospels."

"A few sheets, that's all I had. You showed them to me, remember?"

"And then you *took* them."

"You didn't seem to mind."

"Keep your voice down. You're going to forget all that, if you want to live."

Looking fearful, he nodded.

"Give me all the copies."

Giovanni climbed out of bed. He wore only black bikini underpants, but this time Dixie Lou wasn't aroused. Lifting the mattress, he said, "This is where I kept them, but they're missing."

"Under the mattress," she muttered. "What an original place to hide something. You aren't as smart as I thought you were."

He hung his head, awaited her next command.

"You have no idea who took them?"

"No."

Again Dixie Lou studied the nearby beds, and saw no signs that any of the stud knights were awake. She stepped close to Giovanni, so that she could smell the musk of his cheap cologne. "You're expendable, do you understand?"

"Yes, ma'am. Do you still want me to visit you?"

"That's the least of your worries."

With that remark she whirled and strode off, but didn't get very far before she felt faint and almost dropped to her knees. Grabbing the headboard of one of the beds, she remained standing but images assailed her mind. The walls seemed to close in around her, constricting to a more austere enclosure, one with less beds, less sleepers. Rough, black-streaked stone walls, without adornment. Different shadows.

A prison cell, she decided, a relatively large one . . . The sound of a rodent chittering in the darkness. Dizziness, and suddenly she was moving between beds with a knife, stabbing the sleepers through the blankets, over and over. Hurrying between beds, killing everyone before they could awaken and stop her.

Reliving the moment, an enormous sensation of satiated revenge swept over her. It was done!

The images faded, and her mind pulled one way, then another. A new image took shape before her. She stood on a platform and was dressed in a white robe, made to appear whiter by the intense blackness of her skin. She fingered a metal pendant that dangled on a chain from her neck. Beside her stood a man in a similar robe, with a glittering pendant matching hers on his chest, shining like a star. With an icy expression he gazed down on a bearded prisoner who stood serenely before them, looking ragged but proud in the polished elegance of the room. The prisoner was answering a question that had been put to him.

Dixie Lou despised the prisoner's arrogant manner, the way this impoverished man held his head high like a king and said anything he pleased, without fear of the consequences. The man beside her was questioning him again, and Dixie Lou remembered her companion's face and name.

"Joseph Caiaphas," she murmured in the darkness.

Suddenly he leaped down from the platform, ripped the prisoner's clothing, and hit him hard on the side of the face. "Blasphemer!" Caiaphas shouted. "We have no king but Caesar!"

The images faded, and as Dixie Lou looked around, she felt as if she was awakening from a deep sleep. She stood in the stud harem again, and around her the men were sleeping peacefully. Continuing uncertainly down the aisle, she reached the corridor. For several moments a feeling lingered that she had killed many people back there, but the rational side of her brain told her this had not happened.

I'm going mad.

Chapter 24

Thus saith the Lord She-God; Remove the diadem, and take off the crown: this shall not be the same: exalt her that is low, and abase him that is high.

    —Ezekiel 21:26, as amended in the *Holy Women's Bible*

Lori was underwater, surging feet-first through the current in the storm drain. Struggling to find air, she tried to dog paddle, and managed to lift her head clear. This permitted her to gasp a little breath, but she choked and coughed when she was dragged under again. The torrent slammed her sideways and her lower back hit something hard. She cried out in pain.

The roar of rushing water filled her ears, but somehow she was no longer moving with the current, was no longer immersed in the water. She lay on her side, then sat up, coughing and spitting out foul-tasting fluid. In her back pocket she located the flat flashlight, and almost dropped it. Lori flipped the switch, was relieved when a beam of light revealed the gray rock walls of the tunnel.

Shivering, she sat on a narrow ledge inside a section of horizontal tunnel, with water at least a meter deep rushing by her feet. With the light she saw a black drop-off not far away, where a waterfall rushed over a precipice.

Alex lay a short distance from her on the same shelf of rock, struggling to sit up. His black hair was disheveled and pressed flat and wet against his scalp. Relieved that he appeared to be all right, except for scrapes and bruises like her own, Lori helped him up.

As she did so, she thought about how much she liked him, and how there had been no time so far for her to consider her feelings. But this was no place, or time, to develop a relationship.

The ledge was narrow, with most of the water roaring around their perch and some of it splashing their faces. In the illumination of the flashlight the air was misty, and quite cold. She prayed the storm would let up, hoped the torrent would not sweep them away again.

Hearing what sounded like voices, she flipped the light off, and moments later saw flickers of illumination from high above them—possibly the flashlights of guards in one of the passageways that was not a storm drain. Had they seen or heard something?

The voices of the guards, already weak because of the noise of water, faded with their light, and all around Lori it grew pitch black.

* * *

In the terrifying darkness, Lori heard the ominous sound of water increase. More frequent and larger splashes hit her.

"It must be raining harder up there!" she shouted, to be heard over the noise.

Alex held her close against him. His arms were strong, and he made her feel safer, but only a little. "Don't be afraid!" he yelled.

"I'm not!" But this wasn't true.

Moment by moment, more water entered the storm drain system from above, and became a deafening roar in Lori's ears. She and Alex backed up against the tunnel wall behind them, and she found a hand grip. It felt like a metal railing.

She guided his hand to it, then released her hold for a moment and reached over the wall, touching the surface. Feeling an indentation, she wondered if it might be the edge of a service door for the tunnel. She was about to pull the flashlight out of her pocket when water roared against her, covering her up to her waist.

Alex pulled her close, and she held the railing with her free hand.

But the railing was coming loose.

And she remembered the drop-off.

* * *

As Dixie Lou hurried across the plaza in the night, heading for her apartment, she felt a loss of control, that she couldn't keep all the important pieces of her life together, and portions of it were slipping from her grasp. Unexpected complications were making things difficult; her list of secrets was growing larger. In addition to the murder in the tunnel, she would have to conceal the stud knight's thefts from her office safe: money, a pistol, and, worst of all, a recent printout of the in-progress *Holy Women's Bible*. She cursed Giovanni, and herself as well, for allowing him to get too close to her. A *man*. As Chairwoman of United Women of the World, she should have known better.

She took a rock-hewn staircase down one level and caught a rail car.

* * *

The water was up to Lori's chin, and the railing in her grip felt as if it might break loose at any moment.

"We'd better let go!" Lori shouted. "Before the tunnel fills and we have no air!"

He yelled something in response that she couldn't make out, and she hoped he understood her.

With great difficulty she removed the little flashlight from her back pocket and flipped the light on. It revealed only a few centimeters of airspace left, and a torrent of water rushing toward the drop-off.

With the beam of light she pointed down-tunnel, then tugged on the arm Alex had been holding around her waist. He nodded.

Fighting the current, Lori replaced the flashlight in her pocket, hoping she and Alex would live to use it again.

They let go of the hand rail, tried to hold onto one another.

And went over the drop-off in a thundering torrent of water.

Chapter 25

After being sentenced to death by crucifixion, the Lord Jesus Christ faced Pontius Pilate in his palace without fear and said to him, "I forgive you, for you are not evil but are on a path set for you by others." Upon hearing such love from a man condemned to die, the Roman governor wept, and then sent Jesus away to be crucified.
—Gospel of Lydia 22:14–15, *Holy Women's Bible*

The women of the council were seated in the half circle of black leather chairs, facing a stony-faced Dixie Lou Jackson as she addressed them from the historic red chair.

Through clear window panes edging a magnificent stained glass centerpiece, Dixie Lou saw the mountains of Macedonia with puffy clouds scudding beyond. She glanced at her watch: 9:22 AM.

"The conspirators include my son Alex," the Chairwoman announced in a somber tone, "as well as Siana Harui and Liz Torrence—in all a son, a daughter, and a niece of our own select group." Her gaze moved to the petite Fujiko Harui and to the jowly Bobbi Torrence, each of whom looked at her with anguish in their eyes. "I smell the BOI in our midst."

"Nonsense," Katherine Pangalos said, her tone contemptuous. "If the Bureau knew where we were, they'd blow us off the face of the earth. They wouldn't infiltrate us and try to steal the she-apostles."

"Wouldn't they?" Dixie Lou snapped back. "Maybe they want the children for reasons we can't imagine."

"I doubt that, but in the list of conspirators don't forget Lori Vale, the little drug addict you brought from America." Katherine Pangalos's tone was as frigid as the mountains across the valley. Casually, she picked at something in her ear. "It seems that *two* of the kidnappers were close to you."

"I wasn't *close* to either of them," Dixie Lou snapped, leveling a fierce gaze at her constant adversary. "From what our informants are revealing, Alex was never actually retarded. He fooled me and every member of this council, too. As for Vale, I don't think she was ever a hard-core drug addict, just smoked a little weed—but she has street smarts and the two of them got into trouble together. No matter what their relationship is, if you're trying to connect me with this—"

"Maybe *three* instead of two. Giovanni, Alex, and Lori. You must admit, it's hardly been an auspicious beginning for your regime."

"Shall we deal with the matter at hand?" Dixie Lou demanded, fighting to maintain her composure. "Alex and Lori have not been captured, but Siana, Liz and two others have. They're undergoing testing and interrogation at this very moment, *with BOI involvement suspected*." She paused, arched a thick, jet-black eyebrow, stared Katherine down and added, "I seek no special treatment for my son, nor will it be granted to others."

Around the half-circle, some of the councilwomen nodded.

"Alex was seen near the body of the murdered guard," Katherine said. "No disrespect intended to your family, Madame Chairwoman, but that killing—a bullet in the back of the head—sounds like the vicious act of a man. If your son did that, perhaps the other kidnappers should not be blamed, including the Vale girl, who may have been drawn in."

"I see no distinctions among them," Dixie Lou said, in the iciest of tones. "Even if only one of the kidnappers killed the guard, the others are still accomplices. Right now I could charge every one of them with murder and order immediate executions."

The councilwomen listened silently, for each of them knew from Title 8 of the UWW Charter that the Chairwoman was empowered to act as the sole judge in cases of treason, which this most certainly had to be. In that forum Dixie Lou could evaluate evidence as she saw fit, declare guilt or innocence, and pass sentence. This could include pardoning her own son but not the others, and no one could appeal or reverse her decision.

"What about the injured guards?" the pudgy Bobbi Torrence asked of no one in particular. Are they better?" Bobbi had a history of voting against Dixie Lou on matters before the council. With Bobbi's niece in trouble, Dixie Lou was looking forward to the first opportunity to change that.

Katherine Pangalos answered. "It looks like they'll pull through."

The meeting drew to a close with no decisions made. Before drawing conclusions, the councilwomen said they needed more information from ongoing interrogations of the captured kidnappers, including Alex and Lori, if they could be located.

The last to depart the council chamber, Dixie Lou pressed a button on a hand-held transmitter to deactivate a video camera hidden behind one of the eyes of the She-God statue. Giovanni had set it up for her, using surveillance skills he had acquired in the United States while working with an equipment manufacturer. Later that evening Dixie Lou intended to view the tape of the council members, in private. She would watch it over and over, evaluating words, facial expressions, and body language to determine whom she could and could not trust.

Trust, she had long ago decided, was a constantly changing, highly fragile equation. A person who could be counted upon one moment might not be there the next, for any number of reasons . . . a better offer from an opponent, a new view of the situation, a pique of anger over some seemingly minuscule matter.

No one could really be relied upon entirely, in Dixie Lou's way of looking at the world, not even those councilwomen who were closest to her, Deborah Marvel, Nancy Winters, Jeanne Cousteau, and Wendy Zepeda, or any of the other five councilwomen who normally voted with her. All relationships were no more than games . . . sleights-of-hand performed by the participants in order to obtain favorable

positions and valuables. Everyone in the political arena harbored ulterior motives.

To survive, one had to excel at the game.

* * *

In a subterranean chamber Dixie Lou huddled with three much taller female guards. Blueprints were spread across the table in front of them, along with photographs of Alex Jackson and Lori Vale.

One guard, a burly woman with a dark mole on her chin and oversized eyeglasses, leaned over the papers, pointing as she talked. She was Lieutenant Sears, third in command on the force. "We searched Sectors One through Thirty-Seven," she reported, "blocking off each, moving deeper and deeper into the mountain. It's all been covered, but somehow they got away."

"This does not please me," Dixie Lou said. She glared up at each of the guards. Accompanying Sears were guards Ellison and Robson. Ellison was tall and pencil-thin, while Robson was as large as Sears but not as masculine in her features.

"Uh, there is one place we haven't looked," Ellison offered, hesitantly. "Umm, we were on our rounds in Sector Five, ummm, two nights ago during the storm. Water was starting to fill the storm drain system, and we were walking by the end of an open pipe. My partner thought she heard a human voice in the pipe. I didn't hear it myself, and seconds later water was rushing through the system. We didn't see anything unusual."

"The storm drains, eh?" Dixie Lou said. With thick fingers she rifled through the blueprints.

"Those schematics aren't here," Sears said.

"Why not?" Dixie Lou snapped.

"It didn't seem possible for anyone to be inside the storm drains. I mean, not the way water rushes through them. No one could survive."

"Get me the plans," Dixie Lou snapped. "Fast!"

* * *

Lori came to consciousness with a stench in her nostrils, the odor of festered vomit, or worse. She was lying on her side in shallow water, staring with blurred vision at a furry gray lump only inches from her face. The lump had two dark spots on it. She had been dreaming . . . something about a foul, concealed odor in her house.

With difficulty she shifted position and sat up, all the while trying to breathe through her mouth. Her clothes were soaking wet and torn at the knees and elbows, with red, scraped skin beneath. She had a crashing headache, and winced with pain as she touched her forehead. A swollen, sore area.

Her eyes came into focus, and in horror she scuttled away, then looked back. The dark spots on the lump were the dead, sightless eyes of a large rat, staring at the eternity beyond Lori. A huge bloated rodent, soggy and drowned.

And no sign of Alex.

Carefully, Lori checked her injuries. She moved her arms and legs, flexed fingers and toes. Nothing was broken that she could determine, but her knees, elbows and knuckles were scraped and her muscles ached. On her forehead she probed a bump with her fingertips—carefully, since the spot was sore—and felt crustiness, which came off on her fingertips to reveal dried blood. Her lower back felt bruised and painful. She was thirsty and hungry. From a pocket of her jeans she brought out a waterlogged pack of cigarettes and matches, and tossed them away.

She hoped Alex was OK.

How long had it been since they had tumbled down the storm drain? She glanced at her wristwatch. Through a cracked dial (with moisture droplets on the underside) she noted that the timepiece was still working. On the digital display she noted that more than a day and a half had elapsed.

Beneath her, a wet concrete surface sloped off to a pool of dirty water. Some sort of drainage spillway, she decided. Overhead loomed a rock cavern ceiling, a streaky gray and black vault. Low light filtered in from an unseen source. She was inside a large chamber.

Even though Lori was now some distance from the dead rat, the rotten stench of it lingered in her nostrils. Normally she wasn't queasy, but she didn't like the thought of the filthy creature bumping against her in the torrent of water. Maybe its decaying corpse had been against her face as she lay unconscious and dreaming, and she had pushed it away. She wiped her face on her wet blouse.

Walking carefully down the incline, trying to avoid slippery surfaces and remain on rough, grainy concrete, she made her way to the pool of water. Rectangular and perhaps the size of a residential swimming pool, the bottom wasn't visible. Little pieces of scrap wood and leaves floated in the murky water, along with the mangled, headless body of a gray and red bird.

Lori wished she could drink or wash her face, but the pool was brackish and unclean. It reeked. On the other side, the water swirled in a slow circle, perhaps from a poorly functioning drain.

Turning, she studied water that trickled down the sides of the spillway into the pool. On the left side, at the top of the spillway, she noted a dark opening against the rock that might be the storm drain through which she had traveled on a torrent of water.

Could Alex still be in there? She worried about him.

Climbing up to the opening, afraid of what she might find, she knelt and peered inside the end of a large concrete pipe. Water in there made an echoing gurgle. On top of the pipe she saw something clinging, greenish-black and slimy. Algae? On the bottom the surface was smooth, apparently from the force and flow of water. A trickle coming off the end of the pipe looked clean enough, and she caught some of the liquid in her hands and splashed it on her face, then drank. It tasted bad, but she swallowed anyway.

Leaning into the pipe, Lori listened carefully to the water. Bringing out her remarkably durable flashlight, she shined it inside the murky tube. The limited illumination didn't reveal much, just a long reach, rising at a gradual slope.

If she crawled into the pipe, she risked being inundated again, and even drowned, but she could think of no other options. She couldn't remain here. Since her knees were already skinned and the concrete was hard, when she entered the orifice she avoided crawling and instead scampered on all fours, like an animal.

The concrete tunnel rose at a modest incline, into pitch blackness. Periodically she brought the flashlight from her pocket and probed ahead with its beam, then put it away and scrambled in the ebony darkness to the limit of what she had seen. Once, her hands touched something long and slimy that didn't move, like a dead snake. She shuddered and kept going. After a distance the pipe curved to the left and the ascent grew steeper. Her jogging shoes provided good traction but she worried what she would do if the pipe ever became vertical.

The surface dipped, then rose steeply again. She slipped, bumping her knees and chin, but resumed climbing. Finally she became short of breath and had to stop. In the Stygian tunnel she heard her own labored, jagged breathing.

A portentous, increasing sound intruded. Rushing water? Shining the light ahead, she saw only empty pipe.

Should I turn and run back down?

On impulse, she scrambled to a higher elevation.

The rushing sound grew louder, and the concrete pipe around her trembled, like an earthquake. But she sensed something else.

Desperately, Lori scrambled higher, rounded a curve and reached a flat, muddy area. In the beam of her light she saw a black metal hatch with a handle. She tried to lift the handle, but after moving it only a little, it stuck.

The flashlight fell from her grasp into the mud, but remained on, casting eerie yellow illumination up the tunnel.

The sound of rushing water grew unmistakable, and deafening. Out of the corner of her eye she saw movement. Something *big* and approaching. She gave the handle a mighty tug. It lifted, and she pushed her shoulder against the hatch, as hard as she could. She felt resistance from spring-mounted hinges, but tumbled through an opening and sprawled onto a hard surface.

The door slammed shut behind her automatically, and on the other side she heard the roar of passing water, a deluge.

"Oh there you are," a woman's voice said, a familiar Southern drawl that made Lori's heart sink.

The teenager saw fancy gold boots and a black woman's legs. With trepidation, she looked up.

Dixie Lou Jackson held a pistol in one hand and a rolled set of blueprints in the other. The gun was pointed down, directly at Lori. The fierce little woman was flanked by two female guards, carrying automatic rifles.

"What are you gonna do," Lori asked, "kill me like you did the—"

In front of her eyes, a blur of movement, a glittering boot. It slammed into her forehead, against one of the wounds she had suffered earlier.

Pain enveloped her, followed by darkness, and she thought she heard Alex's voice, calling her name.

Chapter 26

The She-God is my light and my salvation: whom shall I fear? The She-God is the strength of my life; of whom shall I be afraid?
—Psalm 27:1, as amended in the *Holy Women's Bible*

"Gimme shum more wine!" Giovanni Petrie called to the waiter, in drunken English. He lifted a nearly empty bottle of *retsina* high in the air but tipped the bottle over sloppily, dumping the contents on his head. The resinous wine seeped into his eyes, stinging them.

He wiped himself with a cloth napkin, while fellow *taverna* patrons looked at him disapprovingly from their little bistro tables.

Giovanni had been in the city for a day, since escaping from Monte Konos in the middle of the night. The Chairwoman had terrified him and he knew he would have been killed if he'd remained—so he'd broken into her office and taken money and a pistol from a safe, along with a recent printout of the new gospels, which were not yet complete. He'd read them on the train and found them most intriguing, enough so that he had formulated a plan for them. A profitable one.

On the other side of the *taverna* a waiter in a white shirt and apron shook his head. This was one of the expensive tourist establishments fronting the gulf in Salonika, the second largest city in Greece. It had been raining all day long, and now, in the early evening, streaks of water covered the interior tile floor from foot traffic. Wet coats and umbrellas hung from hooks on the wall.

"I shedd more wine!" Giovanni boomed, so that all the patrons and employees turned toward him. He pushed away plates of *souvlakia*, dark bread, and Greek salad.

Without moving, the waiter stared at him. The short, swarthy man had deeply set olive-pit eyes with dark circles beneath, and a downturned nose. Stubbornly, he folded his arms across his chest and mouthed the word, "No." At the table moments before, he had been speaking rapidly in accented English.

A black-haired man at the next table told Giovanni to be quiet, in Greek, which the stud knight understood. The other patron said he wanted to hear the *rebetika* music of a young man who was on stage playing a *bouzouki*, a stringed instrument.

Giovanni could speak a little Greek himself, and grasped even more when he heard it, but he acted as if he didn't understand, and repeated his slurring call for more wine.

Again the waiter shook his head, and the man at the next table grumbled.

The waiter's attitude made no sense to Giovanni. Since escaping from Monte Konos he'd been spending good American dollars here, and if he wanted more wine, by the heavens he would have it! He hadn't liked this waiter from the beginning anyway, for the cur had been cheating him on the exchange rate. A duffel bag full of stolen items sat under Giovanni's table, with his foot resting against it for security.

The waiter turned his back and went to clear a table at the rear.

Impulsively, Giovanni shambled to a rack of wine bottles by the bar and grabbed a bottle of *retsina*, with its amber elixir visible through clear glass. He took it and a corkscrew back to the table.

Before he could sit down and open the bottle the waiter and the business owner, a fat, balding man whose apron was covered with food spots, stood over him, chattering angrily in broken English. The owner tugged at the wine bottle, while Giovanni resisted and shouted American insults at him. The man at the next table got into the fray, too, yelling at Giovanni in Greek.

The owner lost his grip on the bottle and his footing, and slipped to the floor. This made him even more angry. The waiter helped him to his feet.

Giovanni pressed a fifty dollar bill into the palm of the owner and told him to keep the change and leave him alone. Grumbling, the man did so, leaving the waiter behind.

"Look, mister," the waiter said, "don't you think you should eat some of your dinner? You haven't even touched it."

"I did'n come 'ere ta eat," Giovanni said. He pulled the cork himself and refilled his wine glass.

"In Greece we do not drink without eating, mister. It can lead to public embarrassment. The food keeps you from getting drunk. Eat some of your *souvlakia*, it's good. Eat and drink, eat and drink. That is the Greek way."

Giovanni quaffed the glass of wine, downing it like water. He poured more. "Well ish not *my* way," he said, pushing the food plates to the edge of the table. "I letchou bring shlop over shince you inshishted, but zhere's no law shaying I hafta eat it."

"No, mister, there's isn't, but—"

"Do you shee dis bag at my feet?" Giovanni asked. He kicked it out a little from under the table.

The waiter looked down, said he did.

"Well iss fulla money, good hard 'merican curren-shy. I got it 'cause I knew where a bunch of crazhy females kep' it. Ever heara United Women o' da World?"

The waiter shook his head.

"I got shumpin' elsh in the bag, too," Giovanni said in a conspiratorial tone, "a manushcrip'. Zose women are holed up onna mountain writin' a new version o' the *Bible*. Imagine nat, a *Holy Women's Bible*."

"I never heard of anything like that, mister."

"Sho? Lishen, you know a priesht?"

"Sure." He puffed out his chest proudly. "I go to church every week."

"You're Greek—Orchadox?"

"But of course. This is Greece, mister."

"No offench, but I need a pipeline to da big guy in Rome, da one wid all the money. Not your Pate . . . Pate—"

"Our Patriarch of Constantinople?"

"Yeah, zhat one."

"The big guy in Rome? You mean Pope Rodrigo, mister?"

"None other. I wan' you to fine me a *Roman Cash'lic* priesht and bring 'im back 'ere."

The olive-pit eyes narrowed. "Yes, I know one. He is a good man." The waiter smiled. "He is from America, too."

"Good. I wanna shee 'im right away."

"I'll get him for you after my shift is over. You'll pay me?"

"Onee if you bring 'im now."

"But mister—"

"I'll give your boss 'nother fifchy dollars. It'll be OK." Giovanni handed two matching bills to the waiter. "One for easha you."

The waiter discussed the situation with the owner, and money changed hands. Finally, the waiter removed his apron and hurried out the front door.

Two hours later, an overweight man in a black robe and white collar sat at Giovanni's table, reading the manuscript. By now Giovanni was almost sober, since he had important business to conduct. He'd been drinking strong black coffee and eating breath mints. Presently the priest said, "This is most disturbing, and *dangerous*. I must show it to my superiors."

"Not so fast, tubby." Giovanni took the pages and stacked them neatly on the table, away from the priest. "I don't give this away for free. Tell your superiors to bring me cash, and lots of it. No funny stuff, either, I'm talking dollars, not drachmas."

"Where can we reach you?"

"Right here. This is my office."

Chapter 27

For centuries the Swiss Guard had been the Pope's most trusted military force. Comprising three hundred men, they saw to it that no one except a short list of people obtained an audience with the Vicar of Christ. The President of the United States was on that most exclusive of all lists.

President Lowell Markwether surveyed the large waiting room, which he'd heard had been redecorated recently, with art works and antique furnishings brought in from storage, replacing what had been here before. Two aides sat nearby, one carrying the nuclear codes briefcase, and the second—his white-gloved brother Zack Markwether—holding a parcel wrapped in paper bearing the Presidential seal. Zack, a powerfully-built man with auburn hair and a narrow chin, wore his brown and tan US Army officer's uniform, with colorful ribbons on the chest. He stared straight ahead.

The President thought back on the events that had placed him and his brother here. Zack—two years older—had been a basketball star in high school and a Rhodes scholar in college, graduating Magna Cum Laude. Everyone expected him to be the most successful of the pair—he'd always been the more popular and had achieved much more in school, with his Attention Deficit Disorder closely monitored and controlled by medication.

But subsequent events, when the two of them were adults, had been quite different. Unable to hold a civilian job, Zack had, by his mid-twenties, enlisted in the Army. In that career he had excelled, attaining the rank of full colonel and a coveted investigator position with the National Security Agency. During that time, Lowell Markwether had founded a successful Internet company, and with his fortune had bankrolled a victorious US Senate campaign for himself. This led in turn (by the time he was forty-six) to the Presidency, where he was now in the third year of his initial term.

On the other side of the waiting room sat a Cardinal in a ceremonial scarlet robe and skullcap; he avoided making eye contact with the President, and instead fussed with an embroidered edge on his garment. The door through which the President had entered moments before was open, and just outside stood two Swiss Guards in sixteenth century body armor with royal purple and gold leggings and red headdresses. Each man carried an antique rifle. On the President's right, just inside the room, two more of the papal guards stood at attention by another door, leading to the Pope's temporary office—which he was using while remodeling was being conducted in his own office.

The waiting room, with gold-embossed arches and doors, featured the original paintings of great masters, depicting a number of the most important cardinals of history. The mosaic tile floor was the finest workmanship President Markwether had ever seen. He sniffled from a cold that had been sneaking up on him in the last couple of days. To ward it off he'd been loading up on vitamins, but today he felt the malaise gaining on him, as if he were opposed by an inexorable enemy, with an army of persistent bacteria.

The door to the inner sanctum opened, and a tall, elderly man in a white vestment emerged, walking energetically. He held one hand on a golden cross that dangled from his neck. In his late-seventies, the olive-skinned Pope Rodrigo was still in excellent health, which he attributed to a vegetarian diet and mild activity regimen. He had a full head of thick black hair, with dignified streaks of silver. President Markwether and his aides rose to greet him.

"So nice to see you, Mr. President," the Pope said, extending his age-spotted, ring-bejeweled hand.

Markwether kissed the hand. "Thank you for seeing me, Your Holiness."

"This way, please," the old man said. He led the way back into a private study, where his morning espresso and Segovia cookies were being served by a nun.

Just before going inside, the Pope conferred briefly and privately with the nun. At this time, Zack passed the wrapped parcel to the President, saying as he did so, "Maybe I should stay with you." He nodded toward the man carrying the nuclear codes. "And him, too. Security doesn't look too good around here. Did you notice how old the guards' rifles are? Sixteenth century, I'd guess. I wonder if they even fire, or if they're strictly ceremonial."

The President smiled with a lack of concern. "I saw other guards with automatic weapons—out in the corridor and in St. Peter's Square."

"You don't understand security the way I do, Brother. This place is full of holes, like a sieve. It's dangerous. Let me come inside; I'll give the Pope a few suggestions."

"Don't be presumptuous. Go back and sit down." As the Pope finished talking with the nun, she scurried away and the President followed the holy man into his office. The door closed behind them.

"You have brought a bomb?" the Pope inquired, looking at the parcel. He spoke English with a slight Spanish accent. Waving an arm, he designated where he and his visitor were to sit, in seventeenth century Spanish chairs with a *papelera* in between, a hand-carved wooden chest with drawer compartments.

"Of course not," the President replied, amused at the pontiff's unpredictable sense of humor. "Although it could make you blow up somewhat physically. It's a box of North Carolina chocolates, made at my family's factory."

"Ah yes, one of my favorites!" he said. A mischievous expression crept over his creased face as he accepted the gift. "I shall have to hide this where the nuns won't find it. They say I eat too much chocolate, and keep trying to make me cut back."

"One can never eat too much chocolate, Your Holiness."

"My sentiments exactly." Pope Rodrigo set the box on the table. "Now what is it you wish to discuss, the matter that could not be mentioned on the phone or by letter?" He lifted a golden scepter from a stand and examined it casually.

"There are matters of utmost sensitivity that you cannot mention to your Cardinals and I cannot reveal to my Cabinet. We are alike, you and I."

"So true, although I envy you your pretty wife."

"You don't mean that, Pope Rodrigo."

The men exchanged smiles, but the President's was uneasy, and he came to the reason he had requested this audience. "The Bureau of Ideology is causing problems for me."

The Pope nodded understandingly. He replaced the scepter on its stand.

"How do you suppose they spend so much money?" the President asked. He sipped a little demitasse of espresso.

The Pope chuckled, but unpleasantly. "Ah yes, their latest funding request—sort of like a municipal levy but without the option of voting on it. It's hard to say where all of it goes, but I can think of better uses for it."

"So can I. Did you pay the latest demand?"

"Yes, but to do so we had to divert funds earmarked for new churches in Africa and Asia."

"Well I didn't make my quota, and Culpepper's not happy about it. His attack dog, Tommy Lee Chang, has been crawling up my backside."

The Pope nibbled on a chocolate cookie, nodded. "Their Vice Minister of Finance. Most unpleasant fellow."

"He certainly is."

"I shall pray on your behalf."

"Maybe we should send money to the women instead," the President said, solemnly. The words had barely escaped his lips when he regretted them, but his host showed no evidence of being offended.

"What a choice," the Pope mused, "United Women of the World or the Bureau of Ideology. One extreme or the other." His eyes twinkled. "What is it you call those organizations in private?"

"Oh, you wouldn't want me to say that here, Your Holiness."

"Sometimes, humor relieves tension."

"We call them United Whores of the World and the Bureau of Idiots."

"How about the Bureau of Idiotology? Or the Bureau of Insanity?"

The President grinned. "Those work too. Sometimes I wish they would just blow each other up and get it over with." Then Markwether sat silently, considering the problem. In recent years the BOI had grown too large, too powerful to be controlled.

"The UWW is just as bad as the Bureau," the Pope said, "but on a smaller scale." He smoothed his robe across his lap. "I'll bet the ladies are putting the arm on several third world countries right now, with their own funding demands."

"Probably so. They're a tough bunch, from what I hear."

"We must be careful ourselves," the Pope mused, "or the women will have our jobs one day." He scratched his ruddy chin. "Reports have reached my desk that these women are an offshoot, fanatical branch of Christianity, but followers of Jesus Christ nonetheless."

"I've seen their strange emblem, the cross misshapen into a sword."

"Just the tip of the iceberg." Crossing the opulent office to his desk, the Pope retrieved a brown sheathe and passed it to the President.

"What's this?"

"A present. You were kind enough to bring a gift for me, and here's one for you as well. I purchased it a couple of days ago for a pittance, nothing worth mentioning. This is your copy."

President Markwether thumbed through the pages. "*Holy Women's Bible*? A UWW project, it says. But I have heard nothing of this."

The Catholic patriarch nodded. "Nor had I, until recently."

After studying it further, Markwether said, "This looks like blasphemy to me, Your Holiness, with twisted biblical passages."

"It's that, and much more, Mister President. From your perspective it's a bargaining chip, a document you can sell to the BOI for a substantial sum—" He winked. "Perhaps for the one billion dollars of your funding shortfall."

"How do you know the exact amount?"

"The ways of God are mysterious."

Nodding, the President listened while the pontiff continued. "One of our priests spoke with a runaway from Monte Konos, the headquarters of the rebellious women. The runaway was a sex slave to them, what they call a stud knight. A despicable practice, and the young man was lucky to escape with his life. He says this computer printout represents only part of an immense project, a new *Bible* that will incorporate *The Old Testament, The New Testament*, and the sort of blasphemy you hold on your lap. He says reincarnated apostles are dictating the new gospels, in ancient Aramaic."

"Is that so?"

"And that's not the most intriguing part. He says the modern apostles are all females."

"But Jesus had no female apostles!"

"I know that. The stud knight—Giovanni Petrie—said the women are insane. Apparently they've come to the belief that Jesus had twenty-four apostles, not twelve—and there were a dozen of each gender."

"This is the worst sort of heresy, Your Holiness. But why do you entrust such a document to me? Wouldn't you prefer to keep it secret and deal with it yourself?"

"You are the President of the United States, leader of the most powerful Christian nation on earth. My friend, I trust you implicitly. This will help you, as I have suggested, and when it is turned over to the Bureau the women will be—shall we say?—dealt with."

"The Bureau does get rather excited about heretics, doesn't it?"

"Yes, it does."

The President smiled. "I shall have to bring you a much nicer gift next time."

Moments later, as Markwether and his aides were being escorted to the visitors' apartments by a nun, Zack Markwether whispered to his brother. "Look down the corridor there—those guards are standing around chatting."

To the President it did appear that Zack was correct in this instance. Upon seeing the approaching dignitary, the guards straightened, and stopped talking. They stood at attention on either side of a doorway, as the nun led the visitors past them.

"These guys need to be shaped up or shipped out," Zack said. "Just be glad the White House isn't operated this way."

* * *

Heads bowed, they stood in a prayer circle on the grassy expanse of Gasworks Park, at the northern perimeter of Seattle's downtown core. These were the rejects of society, hardened youths who lived on the streets and endured the underbelly of human existence: stabbings, drug overdoses, venereal diseases, miserable, impoverished deaths. Dressed in tattered jeans and denim shirts, they wore their hair in radical, brightly-hued spikes and frizzy cuts, or they shaved all the hair off. Metal rings pierced their ears, noses, lips, tongues, and belly buttons. These were the dropouts, misfits, malcontents, and dissenters who didn't fit into structured employment, school, or home environments. They didn't care a whit what others thought of them, with the exception of their peers.

By evening, the Seattle Police would be out as usual in this public area, making arrests for the sale and consumption of methamphetamines and other illegal drugs. Some of those in the prayer circle would likely spend the night in jail.

Only moments before, a young man in military surplus clothes, who had been Lori Vale's boyfriend before she left him for another, had spoken emotionally of her compassion for the downtrodden, how she had reached out to help others, even when she was hurting herself. Lori never passed a person sleeping on the street without leaving something for him or her: money tucked in a pocket, gloves fitted over freezing fingers, a pair of used shoes, a wrapped sandwich. A teenage girl with orange hair, Alicia Koppel, mentioned parties they had attended together, and heart-to-heart talks lasting far into the night.

It had been almost three weeks since Lori disappeared, and those who missed her feared the worst—but hoped for the best.

* * *

The door of Styx's office swung open hard, and Minister Culpepper strode in, holding a sheet of paper. "President Markwether wants to make a deal. E-mail from one of his aides."

Styx read the encrypted document. It was a request to reduce the funding demand by one billion dollars, in exchange for an unfinished manuscript—the *Holy Women's Bible*. Several passages were quoted from the book, along with an excerpt from the introduction. Feeling his face flush hot, he said, "Who cares what that stupid book says? It's garbage, like the first quote we saw."

From one corner of his mouth Culpepper had a cigarette dangling, which remained there as he spoke. "A sex slave—a stud knight, they call men like him—sneaked the manuscript out of a place called Monte Konos."

"Monte Konos? Where is that?"

"Greece. The Macedonian mountains. We have it under satellite surveillance now."

"You didn't order an attack yet?"

"Not until we learn more about what the heretics are up to, why they're creating a sacrilegious book with words from what they call 'special children.' It's all very strange."

"But if we delay they could escape."

"We're moving forces into place right now. Don't worry. They're trapped in their den of iniquity."

"Let me handle the operation, sir. Please."

Culpepper shook his head. "No, I'll handle the movement of our forces. I want you to notify President Markwether that we accept his offer."

Staring at the e-mail, Styx said, "The President is not a very good negotiator. He already gave us the location in Greece, and that's worth a lot more than the blasphemous manuscript. We don't need to pay a billion dollars when we already have the most important thing."

Opening his eyes wide in displeasure, the Minister said, "I'm surprised that you'd say something so dishonest, Styx. You should be ashamed of yourself. We are not crooks!"

Styx reddened. "But sir, the heretical book isn't even complete, and it certainly isn't the only copy. The price is too high."

"You have my instructions."

"A billion dollars would be better spent on missiles."

"Do as I say!"

Styx glared at his superior, but remained silent.

Chapter 28

Blessed are the women, who have been meek: for they shall inherit the earth. Blessed are the women who hunger and thirst after righteousness: for they shall be filled.

    –Matthew 5:5–6, as amended in the *Holy Women's Bible*

The red security phone on the Chairwoman's desk made a doleful mew like a kitten, a carryover from the previous occupant of this office, Amy Angkor Billings, who had loved felines. With a grimace, Dixie Lou realized her change order had not been carried out.

She loathed cats, since she considered them disloyal, sneaky, and arrogant. In her childhood, the family tabby had secreted a foul substance all over Dixie Lou's skirt and blouse (which had been on a shelf), so that she nearly gagged when she tried to put on the clothing. For that heinous transgression she had tortured and mutilated the animal, tying it down and ripping off its legs one by one (with a knife and tools) while it was still alive. The screeches and squeals of pain still clung to her memory, giving her renewed delight.

Papers were spread in front of her, a UWW budget report that compared actual and projected operating expenses for the past month. The room air was chilly due to yet another problem with the Monte Konos heating system, so she wore a thick wool sweater.

She swallowed one last forkful of her dinner, a middle-eastern lamb stew that was a little too spicy for her taste, then pushed it away and washed it down with strong Greek coffee. The videophone rang, and she answered.

It was Lieutenant Sears, reporting from the guard station at Lori Vale's cell. She said the teenager was conscious, and showed her image on the phone-projection screen.

"She's to speak to no one," Dixie Lou snapped. Through a small window she watched the contrail of a distant jet as the aircraft ascended at a steep angle in the golden, sunset-washed sky, heading away from Monte Konos. She was sure that her defense unit was tracking it.

"I understand, ma'am. As you can see, we're looking at her through the door glass. She's sitting up in bed, rubbing her head. Looks kinda dazed."

Hearing background voices that were off-video, Dixie Lou asked, "Who's with you?"

"Two councilwomen. Katherine Pangalos and Fujiko Harui. They've asked permission to interview the girl, but I told them you left orders to route all requests through you."

"Hold them off," Dixie Lou drawled. "I'll be right there." She hung up the phone, and hurried to the door of her office. In her mind she reviewed the provisions of Title 8 of the UWW Charter, the section that allowed her to act as sole judge in cases of treason. That included jurisdiction over evidence gathering, which encompassed the interrogation of prisoners.

As she strode into the corridor she ran into the stud knight Marcus Aaron, arriving at his appointed time to service her on the office couch. The replacement for Giovanni Petrie, he wore a tight shirt and baggy trousers. Every golden hair was combed in place. Glistening muscles rippled. He moved like an exotic dancer.

"Return to the stud harem," Dixie Lou commanded, with a sneer. She forced her way by him, locking the door behind her.

* * *

Feeling dizzy, Lori sat on the edge of her bed. She wore a sleeveless, moss-green gown. Her forehead throbbed, and the muscles in her arms and legs were sore and aching, covered with scrapes and dark blue bruises.

The walls and ceiling of the room were rough-textured stone, painted white and yellow. She had a vague memory of being struck by something. A gold boot.

I was kicked. Dixie Lou did it.

Lori heard raised voices outside her room. Through a small wire glass window she saw Dixie Lou Jackson, Katherine Pangalos, and Fujiko Harui, all engaged in heated conversation. Dixie Lou was doing most of the talking, quoting some sort of law or rule.

Finally the commotion died down and the door opened. Dixie Lou entered, wearing a pair of her trademark gold boots. She held a small electronic device, with blinking blue and red lights on it. She scanned it around the cell, and presently the lights turned green.

"First, let's set some ground rules," Dixie Lou announced in a terse tone. She stood over Lori, who still sat on the bed. "You're not to talk to anyone except me. I'm the only one empowered to investigate the attempted kidnapping."

Not saying anything, Lori stared down at Dixie Lou's boots.

"Do you understand?"

A slow nod. Her lavender eyes were hard, angry. Lori felt like leaping to her feet and attacking her.

"What was your part in the kidnap plot?"

Looking up, Lori answered, "I have nothing to say."

"And my son?"

Lori's heart raced. "Is he all right?"

Dixie Lou narrowed her eyelids. "He hasn't come to, yet."

"You mean he's in a coma?"

"Not sure, maybe just unconscious. What was his involvement in the attempted kidnapping?"

"I'm sure he doesn't know anything about that."

"Who was the ring leader?"

Lori shrugged. She hoped Alex was not seriously injured.

"Tell me about the BOI."

The teenager didn't intend to answer these questions, wanted to go to Alex and do what she could for him. "I don't know anything about the BOI," she finally said, "only that they're against everything you stand for."

"And what about you? Are you against everything I stand for, too?"

"My mother's dead! You lied to me!"

"So you know about that, eh? Well, we did the best we could for her, but her injuries were too severe."

"Liar! You turned her over to the male doctors and their third-world medical clinic. You let her die!"

"The male doctors took care of her? This is the first I've heard of that."

"Liar. You think you can say anything to me, don't you?"

"I'll order an investigation of your mother's death."

"A lot of good that'll do."

"Listen," Dixie Lou said, in an urgent tone. "It would be in your best interest to cooperate with me, Lori. This is not just a failed kidnapping. A guard was murdered. Get smart, and I'll see what can be done to spare your life."

"But you're the killer! I saw you—"

Lori's words were cut off by a sharp slap across her face. "No one will believe you." Dixie Lou grabbed the girl by the bare arm and shook her. "If you say that again, I'll—"

Suddenly, while Dixie Lou was touching her, Lori cried out in pain, and her world split, an out-of-body experience. Inexplicably, Lori was looking at herself from across a room.

Unclothed, she lay supine in bed, with a bright, amorphous shape hovering over her, preventing her from moving, numbing all of her physical sensations, transfixing her with its presence. The shape surrounded her, encompassed her, flowed through her entire body like a mist of otherworldly light.

A baby cried out, and Lori felt the comforting warmth of a tiny form that she held against her breast, an auburn-haired girl-child. The bright shape was no longer there.

Now Lori became aware of a woman's presence, backing away from the baby, staring at it in terror and confusion. The woman had a broad, deeply-tanned face and dark eyes. She gripped a knife, and blood was spattered all over her white dress, but Lori and her baby were not harmed. The weapon clattered to the floor. . . .

The startling mental picture disappeared, and once more Dixie Lou was shaking Lori by the arm. The images had blasted through the girl's consciousness in a fraction of a second. Looking at Dixie Lou now, she saw her face register terror and confusion, the identical expression she'd seen on the other woman . . . no knife or blood this time, but the dark eyes were the same, too.

Her mouth agape, Dixie Lou backed up, then turned and fled the room.

* * *

Torn by internal conflicts, Styx paced the length of his underground office. A flat screen on one wall projected a series of daytime images of the town, thirty-one levels above him. It was nearly noon. An unopened, unexamined parcel lay on his desk, along with a number of colored folders.

Minister Culpepper had selected him above all others for promotion to second in command of the Bureau, and more than that, the old man had been a father figure. Six years ago, following the death of Styx's mother from a lingering illness, Nelson Culpepper had consoled him with biblical passages and prayers. Old Culpepper could be tough, though; Styx had never known anyone tougher.

But the Minister had soft spots—perilous for a man in his position, since enemies could work them to their advantage. Delaying the attack on Monte Konos was the latest of those weaknesses to surface, leaving the Satanic women a place to thumb their noses at the forces of God, continuing to perform their witchery, assembling their heretical book.

Styx cursed his boss for his stupidity. The doddering old fool was moving too slowly, might never institute the necessary attack. Those whores could escape.

Pausing at the desk, Styx flipped the parcel over so that he could read the address label. It was from elderly Mrs. Bonham, mailed to a post office box in the nearest city—set up so that non-Bureau people could send messages to Styx.

With a smile, he tore the brown paper from the box and scanned a brief note written in erratic penmanship, as she said she was looking forward to their next visit. Pictures of them together were enclosed, along with a tin of homemade lemon squares. He nibbled on one, and as he absorbed the familiar sweet tartness, he began to feel better.

* * *

All day long, dark clouds had hung over Salonika, dumping their contents on the northern Greek city, drenching it. Now it was well past midnight, and the few pedestrians out at this hour were bundled against the rainstorm.

Giovanni Petrie emerged from the *taverna* that had become his favorite haunt in recent days, moving slowly and uncertainly because of the *retsina* wine he had been drinking and the deluge inundating him. For a moment he couldn't recall the direction of his hotel, and he paused in the shelter of a doorway. Then, noticing a landmark white tower on the waterfront, he went back the way he had just come, passing the *taverna* and continuing on. He had been going in the *taverna* every evening to dine and drink, after that first day that had yielded such a nice payoff from the Catholic Church—$600,000 down in exchange for the only copy he had of the manuscript, and a contract for another $200,000 a month over the next year. Eager to share in his good fortune, the staff of the tourist establishment was being very attentive to him, and he'd been giving them generous tips.

Giovanni had opened a local bank account, and had hidden more than $30,000 of the remainder in his hotel room. With his newfound riches he had been looking for a house to rent in Salonika, and he'd met a couple of interesting women, including a wealthy middle-aged widow who had offered to let him move in with her. But he wasn't sure if he wanted to do that; his own money was giving him an independence that he was enjoying.

Soaking wet, he waited at a crosswalk while an old American car passed, its windshield wipers flopping furiously.

But as Giovanni stepped into the crosswalk he became aware of a vehicle approaching from the side with its headlights off, going fast. A truck. In the darkness he hadn't noticed it, and in the downpour he hadn't heard it. He tried to run but the truck loomed over him, only swerving at the last moment. A fender hit him, knocking him to the pavement. Money and a handgun flew from his jacket pockets.

The truck screeched to a stop. Entirely black, it was a flatbed with raised wooden sides and a canvas canopy.

As Giovanni lay on his side, stunned, he saw three women emerge from the vehicle. His shoulder and hip ached. The women lifted him and shoved him unceremoniously into the back of the truck on a cold metal floor, then slammed the tailgate shut. Before he could protest or figure out what was happening, the vehicle was underway, careening down one street and another, as if it were being chased. A staccato of rain pelted the top of the canvas canopy.

"What are you doing?" he said. "This must be a mistake!"

"Keep quiet," one of the women said, in an American accent.

The engine roared over the noise of the storm as the driver pressed hard on the accelerator. Brakes squealed as the vehicle took turns. The truck went over bumps, maybe sidewalks. Giovanni was bounced around painfully in the rear compartment. In the shadows, broken by occasional city lights and the headlights of other vehicles, he saw three women holding onto side rails, their eyes black as pits. Cold, wet, and terrified, he shivered.

Keeping hold of the rail, one of the women opened the rear flap of canvas to peer out. "I think we lost 'em," she said.

* * *

As the truck left the city heading west on the motorway, a midnight blue Volvo van followed from a distance, its headlights off. At the wheel of the vehicle the driver, a man wearing a headset and night vision goggles, received satellite relay instructions. His name was Pierre Sandoval, an overseas agent of the Bureau of Ideology. Three other men sat silently in the car, holding snub-nose automatic handguns. The windshield wipers worked furiously.

"We have you in sight," said the voice of the dispatcher, Marc Hoodek. "The truck, too." He was looking at the vehicles through an infrared camera attached to a BOI satellite orbiting the earth.

After stopping at a toll plaza, the truck crossed a bridge over the broad Axiós river, whose waters originated in the rugged Macedonian mountains to the north. When Sandoval passed through the toll plaza he had his headlights on and his headset and goggles off. His passengers concealed their weapons. Soon the Volvo's lights were off again, and once more the driver was looking into the night through the military goggles.

The truck and its stealthy pursuit vehicle passed farms and orchards, and a sign marking a turnoff to the ancient ruins of Pella. Sandoval glanced at a computer generated map on the console, which in its illumination showed the ruins, with a caption that Pella had been the capital of a unified Greece at the time of Alexander the Great. It was from this region that Alexander had set out to conquer the known world.

Ahead, the truck turned south onto a two-lane highway, and after several kilometers it turned west again, onto a winding road that climbed steeply past the terraced hillsides of small farms. Reaching a plateau they passed through a quaint little town. Automatically, the computer provided more detail. Near here at Mieza, the philosopher Aristotle had tutored the young Alexander.

Soon the truck turned off again, onto a narrow, winding highway that ascended even more steeply. Sandoval saw on his computer monitor that the road led to the ancient monastery of Monte Konos, known from a new intelligence report to be the headquarters of the UWW. The dispatcher reported additional BOI units moving into position ahead.

The rain let up for a few minutes and then resumed, worse than before, so that Sandoval could no longer see the red tail lights of the truck. He sped up, then heard the bark of the dispatcher, telling him the satellite was losing contact in the storm. The dispatcher asked for Sandoval's coordinates, but heavy static cut into the message.

"On the road to Monte Konos," Sandoval said into his headset. "I'd estimate forty kilometers to their defense zone."

Radio static filled the air.

Uncertain if his transmission had been received, Sandoval nudged the accelerator with his knee. As his turbocharged van rushed forward, the tail lights of the truck came back into view, a short distance ahead. He backed off on the accelerator, maintaining a distance that barely enabled him to see the truck.

This separation remained constant for several kilometers, as they went through a narrow mountain pass and then down a steep incline, after which the road leveled and straightened somewhat, with the turns less sharp. The truck increased speed.

Sandoval restrained his urge to accelerate. Just a little more pressure on the accelerator and he could blow right by the truck, as if it were parked. He watched the tail lights disappear around a turn. His windshield wipers flopped, but it was no longer raining.

When his own van reached that turn, he again saw the lights of the truck, far ahead on a straightaway.

Noticing the wipers scraping dry glass, he switched them off.

And saw something, a dark shape moving in the air between him and the lights of the truck. The shape grew larger as it drew closer. It was above the road, skimming it. An aircraft? His pulse quickened, and he called for the satellite dispatcher, but received only a broken response, and more static.

One of the passengers behind him cursed.

Lances of blue light erupted from the shape, soundlessly illuminating the darkness. It was a beautiful sight, Sandoval thought, just before he died.

* * *

During the attack the black truck had pulled off the road, behind the cover of a massive rock. Now, catching the women off guard, Giovanni jumped out of the rear of the vehicle and tried to run away. The beam of a spotlight found him and he was ordered to stop.

He didn't.

One of the women fired a gun, apparently on impulse, and Giovanni fell in the middle of the road, a .45 caliber bullet in the back of his head. He didn't move.

"There'll be trouble over this," one of the women said. "Dixie Lou said to bring him back alive."

Chapter 29

It is said of the traitorous she-apostle, the She-Judas, that she went with Judas Iscariot and testified against Jesus before the Sanhedrin, the supreme council of the Jews.

—The Apostle Lydia; information set aside by Dixie Lou Jackson and not included in the *Holy Women's Bible*

It was early afternoon. In the cool half-light of her catacomb cell, Lori Vale lay on the uncomfortable bed, immersed in private thoughts. So far today she hadn't been contacted by anyone, and as each moment passed she wondered more and more if she would ever be free of this confinement, if she would ever again see Alex, or her old friends back home, especially Alicia Koppel. Sometimes the two of them used to sit up late at night talking about important things. She missed that.

Lori was terribly worried about Alex, and perplexed by the curious chain of events that had taken place. In her memory the image of Dixie Lou's terrified face played over, and the vision that preceded it: The bloody knife clattering to the floor, Lori and her baby unharmed.

Did Dixie Lou share that vision with me?

It seemed impossible, but somehow Lori sensed it had really happened, a vision experienced by the two of them simultaneously.

A chill ran down her spine.

My baby? Is that woman a threat to a child I'm going to have?

Suddenly, more than anything, Lori wanted Dixie Lou dead. She wanted to do it herself, to watch her die painfully so that she could be certain of her baby's safety. But these were crazy thoughts, she realized quickly. Wild products of her imagination.

I have no baby to protect anyway. I'm only fifteen years old.

But the look on Dixie Lou's face, and the way she had departed so quickly. The scene was indelible in Lori's memory, and played over and over in her mind.

Something happened between us.

Lori lay on her back on a hard, thin mattress, staring at the elongated pattern of window bars on the opposite wall, created by a yellowish light in the corridor outside. Her forehead remained sore where Dixie Lou had kicked it. She heard water dripping, from an unreplaced faucet washer in an adjacent bathroom, which was the only other room she could enter freely. The separate toilet area was strange in a cell, she thought, but at least it afforded her some minimal privacy.

The dripping water seemed to grow louder. Each drip was like a life, she thought, for water and life had been inextricably linked for billions of years. A human being could go without food for up to thirty days, but nowhere near that long without water. She knew from her science class in high school, which seemed like an eternity ago, that each droplet of water, when viewed through a microscope, revealed a micro-world teeming with living organisms.

There had been uncounted molecules of water since time immemorial and an unending stream of children as well, and with the kerplunk of each drop Lori imagined the birth of a fresh, clean baby, heard its cry, and saw the unending cycles of water and life, the continuous flow of fluids from earth to sky and back down in the form of rain, and from person to person and from animal to animal.

She sat up and held her stomach with both hands, where one day she might carry a baby, as the vision had suggested. Though she felt special in an undefined way, she reminded herself she was like all other girls, biologically and emotionally designed to become mothers, carrying seeds in their wombs to protect and nurture, permitting new life to grow and ultimately to thrive.

One of her pearl-and-gold earrings fell off, and she replaced it on her ear, securing the pin in its clasp. She liked to wear this pair, especially with everything that had been happening recently, because they reminded her of her mother, who had given them to her.

With a long sigh she laid back on the mattress and closed her eyes, blocking out the shadow of the bars on the wall. Using her fingers she tried to plug her ears and block out the dripping of the faucet.

A thought sparked and Lori whispered, "Dear God, what do you have in mind for me?"

She heard no answer, only the steady dripping of the faucet, which now made her think of blood dripping from a body, of life ebbing away . . . .

* * *

A day passed, without the appearance of the twelfth she-apostle. In the council chamber of United Women of the World and in coded conversations over the worldwide computer web, women conjectured that any chance to locate this important individual may have died with the murder of Amy Angkor-Billings. In Mexico, the child and its mother seemed to have vanished. Had Amy hidden the baby someplace before her own death, they wondered, or had she taken some other action to suppress dangerous revelations?

Sitting silently in the red chair, Dixie Lou recalled the three highly realistic visions she'd experienced . . . one in which she saw a bearded man praying inside a prison cell . . . another in which she stabbed sleeping forms, in a larger prison cell . . . and yet another in which she held a bloody knife and was backing away from Lori's baby in shock, without harming it. The visions seemed connected, but how?

She focused on the most recent one, and recalled the bright, amorphous form over Lori disappearing, replaced by the teenager holding a baby tightly against her bosom . . . a child that terrified Dixie Lou. But why? The scene replayed in her troubled mind, as it had several times since experiencing it, but she came up with no answer. It frightened her even now, just thinking back.

She gathered her composure, felt strength returning. It was all foolishness, she convinced herself, nothing with which to concern herself and certainly nothing to reveal to anyone else.

I do not fear a baby!

Dixie Lou thought of her own son, Alex. Not long ago he'd been small like that, too, and far less complicated. He was a troublesome young adult now, and she might just sentence him to death in order to get him out of her way. Even if she did that out of political expedience, she assured herself, it wouldn't matter much. The women of the UWW were her family now, and at long last she was the mother of them all, to be revered one day as the holiest of all living women.

Chapter 30

*Behold, the She-God cometh out of her place to punish the men of the
earth for their iniquity.*
  —Isaiah 26:21, as amended in the *Holy Women's Bible*

Wearing a black pants suit with red pockets, Dixie Lou hurried
through the tunnel, toward the worn rock stairway that led to Alex's cell.
It was a couple of hours before dinner, but she thought she might skip it
today and have food sent to her office later that evening.

She was a woman of secrets, of mysteries, of intrigues and death.
Her past was rife with such events. Born Betsy Rae Collins in backwoods
Mississippi, her studies carried her no further than the sixth grade. At
the age of fourteen she ran away from home, after being raped and
beaten by her stepfather and his brother. She'd headed north for the
promise of a better life, just as her slave ancestors had done following the
Civil War. In her case, the war had been in her own household, and she,
only a child, had not been in possession of the strength necessary to
survive against much stronger male opponents.

In recurring nightmares throughout her adult years, she was
revisited by the sweating, stinking bodies of the men as they took turns
with her, as if she were no more than a piece of meat, without feelings or
personal worth. Worst of all, they were black men. How could they do
such a thing to a girl of their own race? It made a lie of what Baptist

ministers said in church every Sunday, that "black folks" should stick together and help each another out.

For six difficult years Dixie Lou had lived on the streets of Baltimore, first as a prostitute and later (so that men would not paw over her anymore) as a thief. At the age of twenty-two she found herself in Cleveland, having hitchhiked there. In that city she was arrested for shoplifting, and jailed for a month before the judge let her go with a stern warning.

Other cities followed, and numerous arrests and aliases. In Chicago she murdered a drunken black man and got away with it. The incident occurred in the middle of the night on a bridge, where the drunk stumbled into her and then apologized, in a voice that reminded her of her father's. Not liking the way he sounded or smelled, she'd pushed him off the high deck, then laughed as she watched him disappear into the darkness, where he undoubtedly drowned. A short while later, she robbed and murdered a cab driver in Milwaukee, stabbing him to death. In those days she often slept on cold sidewalks and under freeway ramps, bemoaning her misfortune and vowing to overcome it.

Eventually she ended up in New York City. There she found a home for the first time, under an alias that was a combination of names from the Bronx phone book: Dixie Lou Jackson. On Staten Island, she met Amy Angkor-Billings and gradually wheedled her way into a position of trust with United Women of the World, in which she was given responsibility for the handling of donations. This provided her with the opportunity for skimming, and Dixie Lou amassed a tidy fortune in the process. She manipulated, cajoled and bribed her way up, eventually becoming a councilwoman, and now Chairwoman, of the most important women's rights organization in the world.

Now she negotiated three stone steps and reached another passageway, with a lower ceiling. She hurried through it, noting that it smelled musty.

Yes, Dixie Lou harbored a great many secrets, and she had a more recent one to conceal, the murder of one of her own security officers. Lori Vale had seen her do it, meaning Alex had either seen it, too, or knew about it. Should she terminate Lori herself in lieu of a public execution, to keep her mouth shut? All day long, Lori had not been permitted out of her catacomb cell, and only Dixie Lou's most trusted guards had been posted to watch her—guards who wouldn't talk if Vale said anything to them.

The Giovanni Petrie matter was a problem, too. He was missing, and that infernal Katherine Pangalos was requesting a special session of the council to address the serious questions that had arisen.

Still, this collective Sword of Damocles over Dixie Lou's head could have two edges. If she seized it and redirected it properly, she could make others bleed. She would turn it into the Sword of She-God, visiting death upon her enemies.

With short, powerful strides she negotiated a long, shadowy stairway that led down to the catacomb cells, including the one where Alex was being kept. Ideas churned and frothed in her mind, stemming from her visions . . . She thought of another prison cell . . . a large one in which she'd moved from bed to bed, stabbing the forms that lay there so peacefully. Where had it been, and when? Was it only a dream? But it was so vivid. She hated thinking of it, but knew she must, that she could not escape it. Again she saw the dream-baby of Lori Vale and the blood all over herself as she fled in terror. It had been so real she'd actually *smelled* the blood, the metallic, coppery odor.

* * *

When Dixie Lou arrived at Alex's cell, she found Katherine Pangalos awaiting her, standing in front of the door, arms folded across her chest. Beside her, councilwomen Fujiko Harui and Bobbi Torrence looked nervous. Two guards stood at attention nearby, along with Lieutenant Sears.

"We heard you were on your way," Katherine said, in a snotty tone.

Dixie Lou narrowed her gaze as she focused on her key adversary, staring up at the taller woman. "I'm here to see my son."

"He's unconscious," Katherine said. The crease lines in her aged face seemed to deepen.

"I want to see him anyway."

"We'll go in together, just in case he comes to."

"I'll see him alone, thank you. He's my son."

"That would not be appropriate," Katherine countered. "This is council business, not a family matter. You had no right to disable the listening devices in Vale's cell—a little trick you undoubtedly intend to employ here, too." She looked at one of the bulging pockets of Dixie Lou's pants suit, where a hand-held signal muter was concealed. "Mmmm, Giovanni used to work for a surveillance equipment manufacturer."

"That's no secret. I've mentioned it in council, and you've seen all the devices he's obtained for us."

"Rather a talented stud knight," Katherine mused. "Too much so, some say, which casts certain suspicions."

Dixie Lou's lips became thin, hard lines, as if drawn by a pencil. "Since you seem inclined to deny a mother the simple human right to be with her seriously injured son, I must inform you that as Chairwoman of United Women of the World I will not be treated as a guilty party. I had nothing to do with the plots against our organization."

"No one said you did."

"You said I was close to two of the kidnappers, and perhaps to a third, insinuating that I was involved in their actions. Now get away from the door." She pushed her way through, shoving Katherine aside.

"Hey!" Katherine exclaimed angrily. A much larger woman, she got in front of Dixie Lou.

But the Chairwoman was younger and stronger, and pushed the old troublemaker aside. "I'm going to see my son!"

As Dixie Lou tried to use a key card to release the lock on the door, Katherine still interfered, trying to push her hands away. "Your son is charged with murder and treason!"

"Do you have any evidence incriminating *me*?" Dixie Lou demanded.

"Nothing direct, but—"

"In matters of treason against our organization, the Chairwoman— that's me, in case you've forgotten—has the right to conduct an investigation, with or without the assistance of the council. The discretion is mine."

"But you have a conflict of interest."

"Our charter mentions nothing about that. Besides, have I said anything about sparing my son?"

"No, but–"

"No buts about it. Stay out of my way on this, or risk your position on the council. Are you prepared for the consequences of your actions? I warn you, Katherine, don't test my patience anymore."

The elderly woman's mouth moved, but words seemed to stick in her throat. Finally, shaking her head in exasperation, she turned and walked away. Fujiko and the heavier Bobbi followed her.

Dixie Lou fumbled with the key card, couldn't get the door open.

"Sears, get over here and help me with this door," she commanded.

The big lieutenant hurried to comply. She removed the key card from the lock, tried it again. The door beeped twice, swung open.

Dixie Lou removed a short barrel .38 from her shoulder holster. She went inside the cell, motioned for Sears to remain outside. The heavy door clanked shut behind her.

* * *

The door to Lori's cell squeaked open, and a matronly female attendant lumbered in, carrying a tray of food. The dinner smelled good, causing Lori to salivate. She tried not to look at it, though, or think about it. Instead she thought back to the last time she'd smoked a cigarette. It had been more than a week, and she was feeling better each day about the decision to quit. Every time she resisted lighting up she felt stronger, and though she was shaky at times, this discomfiture had been subsiding. She was determined to succeed, not only for herself, but for her mother, who had always opposed what she called a "filthy habit."

"What have we here?" the puffy-faced old attendant asked, noting the uneaten lunch on a simple wooden table by Lori, who sat on a stone bench. The woman, so corpulent that she experienced trouble walking, had an Irish accent and reddish-brown hair streaked with gray. "You must eat to maintain your pretty figure."

"I don't want anything," Lori mumbled. She didn't like the woman. She had an irritating habit of speaking in a sweet, grandmotherly tone that concealed her true nature. The eyes, deep purple and malevolent, concealed something. The food was probably drugged, something to control her. Or worse.

"Well, maybe you'll change your mind. I'll just take this lunch away and leave your dinner. Fresh lamb stew today. Specialty of the house."

"Take everything with you."

The woman paused at the doorway, shook her head. Her voice hardened. "You'll eat it, or—"

She paused, as Lori grabbed the dinner tray and hurled it against a wall by the door, smashing dishes and spreading a brown splash across the wall and floor. She had intentionally thrown it several feet away from the woman, intending to startle her but not hit her.

It worked. With a squealing string of protestations, the attendant fled the room, slamming the door behind her.

Chapter 31

What more wondrous and heavenly act can there be than a woman bearing a child in her womb? It's no wonder that men, out of envy and gynophobia, have sought to diminish the status of the female.
  —Amy Angkor-Billings, *The Goddess Arisen* (unfinished manuscript)

As Dixie Lou sat at her son's bedside, she held his hand, just in case anyone might look through the window in the door. Appearances, perceptions. Always so shallow, like a reflecting pool, but so critically important. It was quiet in here, with only the sounds of Alex's regular breathing. She wondered what he would say if he returned to consciousness, if he knew about the murder of the guard. She had to assume he did, and this made him dangerous to her.

Parting his unkempt, curly black hair, she saw a little redness on the scalp, and newly forming scabs. He didn't look too bad, and the doctor, a woman, had told her that he should recover. She had given Alex something to hasten the process, an injection.

But do I want him alive?

She could lean over as if to kiss him, but secretly block his breathing and hold him down, just in case he awoke and fought back. He was injured, and she was strong. Dixie Lou had given Alex life, and she could just as easily take it away. It was a mother's right.

Then she chastised herself for worrying about what others thought, and for trying to rationalize her actions. She was Chairwoman of United

Women of the World, and her son was suspected of treason and murder against the organization. High crimes. She wore a .38 pistol in a shoulder holster, and could shoot him on the spot, or do away with him any other way she pleased, and no one would question her actions. There would be no surveillance recording of it, because she had used the hand-held signal muter that Giovanni gave her—but it didn't really matter if anyone saw her execute the prisoner.

If she disposed of him, though, there would be no opportunity for her plan. It was a wild design, one that had occurred to her on the spur of the moment, perhaps without thinking it through adequately. Now she had time to think, and recalled her strange visions, especially the one she apparently shared with Lori. The Chairwoman had never heard of a shared paranormal experience, but from the odd expression on Lori's face she suspected it had actually occurred, and that Lori knew it, too. If that was the case, did the girl understand what had occurred?

Does she know things I don't?

Dixie Lou focused her memory, and again recalled seeing the bright, amorphous shape with the teenager. At first it had been separate from her, and then it had seemed to merge with her and encompass her, like a ghostly mist flowing into her body. Why did this seem so much clearer to her now, revealing things she hadn't noticed before? Did some memories work like that, coming back more vividly than the original experience? Or was this particular memory flawed?

Not flawed. There is something more to remember.

Her head pounded from the effort, but nothing came. The vision-image blurred, becoming charcoal fuzziness, and then nothing at all.

She tried again, but it only made her head hurt more.

She was missing something, *forgetting* something. But what?

On the bed Alex stirred, and his eyelids flickered. Then he drifted back to sleep.

Dixie Lou reviewed more details of the memory, and became increasingly disturbed. Lori with a shadow-shape . . . a baby is born . . . Dixie Lou backing away in terror.

Frustrated, she pounded her fist on a table.

At the noise, Alex stirred again. His gray eyes opened and stared at her. Did he recognize her? His lips quivered but no words came out. He grimaced in pain, then closed his eyes and slipped back into slumber.

* * *

Like a concerned mother, Dixie Lou stayed with him, and that evening Alex returned to consciousness. His light black skin was scraped and cut, but she wasn't thinking about his injuries.

"We have things to discuss," she said, in her soft drawl. "You're not a slow-witted dolt, are you? Not what we've been led to believe you are. Instead you're a sneaky, treacherous kidnapper, a rotten little traitor."

Warily, he glanced at a short-barrel gun on her lap, by her hand. Her right forefinger rested inside the trigger guard, behind the trigger. His own mother with a gun? It seemed incongruous, and yet, he'd seen her do terrible things.

"*I'm* not what I appear to be?" he snapped. "You should talk! I'm not like you at all. No matter what you say, I'm not as bad as you are. I haven't murdered anyone!" The top of his head throbbed.

She narrowed her gaze menacingly, adjusted the gun so that its fat barrel pointed at Alex. "So this is your real voice," she said. "That was a nice acting job, the slow speech, the simple vocabulary and dull gaze. You recovered fully after that motorcycle accident in Athens, didn't you? The things you said to the doctors were faked, weren't they? You're with the BOI. What sorts of tricks did they teach you? The art of assassination, perhaps? Were you assigned to kill me?"

"If I had been, you'd be dead."

"Maybe we've been watching you longer than you realize, Alex."

He didn't respond, wondered how much his mother had discovered about his secret life, if she knew he was involved in sabotages at Monte Konos, or the clandestine efforts to improve conditions for the stud knights. If so, she must think it was a BOI plot, which was totally wrong.

He met her gaze, saw questions in her dark brown eyes, and uncertainty. No, he decided, she didn't know very much about him; she might try to bluff, but he wouldn't tell her anything.

"Answer my questions," she demanded.

"Your questions are unimportant," he said, in a flippant tone. "Lori and I saw you kill the guard."

A nasty smile curled her lips. "You bumped your head in the storm drain, causing you to imagine wild, untrue things."

Alex described the subterranean passageway in detail, how he and Lori had been hiding in shadows, watching Dixie Lou shoot the guard in the back of the head, perhaps with the gun she now held.

As she listened, Dixie Lou shook with suppressed rage, and her eyes flashed. "Witnesses saw *you and Lori* by the body of the guard."

"Two other witnesses saw *you* kill her."

Running a finger over the gun barrel, Dixie Lou said, "You're mistaken about what you think you saw."

"An hallucination caused by my head injury?" He touched his head lightly, felt a sore bump and rough, chaffed skin.

"You're beginning to understand." She leaned closer, said, "I can influence the council to spare your life."

Alex shook his head at her lie, lowered his gaze. He knew about Title 8 . . . the clause in the UWW charter that gave its Chairwoman the power to determine the fate of an accused prisoner. He decided to prod her a little before mentioning this.

"Am I being charged with murder?" he asked.

"Not yet."

"Where are my friends?"

"Not your concern," she drawled. "Worry about yourself, Alex."

"Have you brought that gun here to kill me?"

"Just keeping my options open, sliding from moment to moment. Perhaps I'll let you tell your story to the council, and I'll tell what I know, that it wasn't a guard I killed. It was a provocateur, an enemy agent like you."

"A BOI agent dressed like a house guard? You're making things up, Mother, lying. You think you're good at it, but I can tell."

She smiled. "It would be so easy to have both of you executed for the murder of the guard. Or I could just throw you and your little friend off the cliff."

"You'd do it, too, wouldn't you? Your own son and an innocent girl. I'm ashamed to admit you're my mother."

Dixie Lou felt a compulsion to strike out at him, but suppressed it. For the moment. In a low, urgent tone she said, "The council has decided to confine the kidnappers in cells of two, for observation."

"What do you mean?"

"There will be eavesdropping equipment in each cell, and we will analyze the conversations to determine degrees of guilt."

Her son looked at her blankly.

"Your cellmate will be Lori Vale," she said. "Siana Harui and Yonney Zakheim will be in another cell, and the rest of your robber band will occupy other cells, two by two. Each of you will have only one person to talk with, and we will decide which of you is the more or less guilty."

"More or less guilty? What are you talking about?"

With a crafty smile, Dixie Lou replied, "Each cell is a little courtroom, and in that courtroom one of you will be declared more guilty than the other. That person will be executed, and the other will be saved."

His head jerked back. "That's not justice. You're insane."

Her eyes sparkled with a fanatical gleam. "Maybe so, but I'm also smart. And you, Mr. Sanity, are my prisoner. Which is better, then, to be sane or insane?"

Disgusted, Alex shook his head.

In reality, Dixie Lou had made up this form of incarceration and punishment herself, without council approval. She didn't know if she would execute one person from each cell after all, or if she would inflict some other form of creative punishment on the kidnappers. Whatever she decided, she was confident that she had the council votes to prevail.

With her gold-ringed hand she patted Alex on the arm. "Don't worry, Son. You're a good actor, and maybe you can make Lori look more guilty than you are."

"I won't do that to a fifteen year old girl! Lori is the most guiltless of all of us. Saving the she-apostles is the only mission she's ever been on."

"Each of you will have to prove your comparative innocence. We will be watching, and listening."

"Between me and Lori, the guilty one is obvious. Why don't you kill me now?"

"And spoil the fun? No, I'd rather do it my way, in my own time."

"Let me speak directly to the council. I'll tell them the truth about Lori's innocence."

Her upper lip curled, a snarl. "Speak to them from your cell. They'll be behind the two-way mirror."

Dixie Lou was enjoying this moment immensely. Her thoughts swept inward, transporting her away from the conversation, to an entirely different realm. She had been thinking things over on the way here while traversing the corridors and stairways of the ancient monastery, trying to figure out where the mysterious Lori Vale fit into the mysterious events surrounding United Women of the World. The Chairwoman expected to learn more by observing her in the cell.

Dixie Lou's belief system was complex and personal. For her, the occult held dominion over the world, a supernatural force (or combination of forces) that she couldn't explain and which guided her and all living creatures along the paths of their lives. Convinced that she received warnings and commands from this alternate realm, she always followed her own gut feelings; she did what her instincts told her to do.

She believed Jesus existed as a historical figure, and that he rose from the dead following his crucifixion . . . a process that could undoubtedly be explained by the occult, or even by science. Similarly she believed in the she-apostles and in their modern incarnations. Dixie Lou did not, however, subscribe to the Christian view of a bearded God in Heaven, and had seen no evidence proving Jesus was the Son of God.

All such contentions sounded like wild speculation to her, insupportable by common sense or written evidence. Likewise, she did not think the She-God actually existed, despite the fact that some she-apostles had spoken of this entity. To her the concept of She-God was merely a tool, a unifying figurehead for United Women of the World to use, enabling them to advance their goals. The she-apostles certainly understood this, and so did she.

But at times she wavered, and found herself leaving the door to another world open a crack. Maybe, just maybe, there really was a God. But even if a deity existed—God, She-God, or whatever—the possibility of a heavenly entity watching her never gave her any feelings of regret for the people she had killed. All had deserved to die anyway, having foolishly placed themselves in her path where she had to slaughter them.

But now, with the door of her belief system open just a little, an intriguing new thought surfaced in Dixie Lou's consciousness, like an object bobbing to the surface of a pond, from way down deep. What if her own actions were the product of an opposing, Luciferian, force? That might offer a more plausible explanation for some of the strange events in her life.

It also suggested fascinating possibilities for the missing twelfth she-apostle, the "She-Judas" who in collusion with Judas Iscariot was said to have done a bad thing, damning her soul for all of eternity, along with her more notorious male cohort. This suggested that the two of them owed an allegiance to Satan.

A shiver of raw pleasure coursed Dixie Lou's spine.

Chapter 32

Have mercy upon us, O She-God, have mercy upon us.
    —Psalm 123:3, as amended in the *Holy Women's Bible*

Profiled in the low morning light, she resembled a black witch as she entered the cell and looked around. Her long nose was downturned, with a prominent chin and bony cheekbones. But when she faced Lori, her features softened and she smiled.

"Someone is here to see you," Dixie Lou announced. She wore a long black dress. Glittering gold earrings dangled from her ears.

Lori had been lying on her bed, off to one side of the doorway. In her confinement, she had lost track of time, but thought it must be sometime in the afternoon. She sat up now, and stared past Dixie Lou at the doorway. "Who?" she asked.

"Why I am, dear," Dixie Lou said.

"No, I mean who else is here?"

"Why you are, dear."

"Don't tease me." The bantering surprised Lori, and she tried to figure out Dixie Lou's mood. It wasn't quite cheerful; instead it had a cruel, scornful edge to it.

Placing her hand on the girl's shoulder, Dixie Lou said, "Patience, child. Some things cannot be rushed."

"What do you mean?"

Dixie Lou turned and left.

Moments later a much taller form filled the doorway. "Hello, Lori," a man's voice said.

Her heart raced. With corridor lights behind him she couldn't see his face, but there was something familiar in the voice.

He stepped into the room.

The door closed behind him. A lock clicked.

Lori suppressed a cry. It was Alex Jackson. He wore a navy blue coat zipped halfway up, and jeans. His pewter eyes were flat, emotionless. Scratches and bruises covered his face and hands.

"Are you OK?" she asked.

"I was knocked out for awhile, slammed my head into something in the storm drain system. How about you?"

"I was out cold, too. Then, when I found a way out of the storm drains, your sweet mother kicked me." Lori pointed to her own forehead, which was still red and chafed.

Her gaze riveted on his as he moved closer to her. His eyes were probing and intelligent, his movements lithe. She began to tremble.

He touched her hand. "It's all right," he said, a gentle tone.

Lori couldn't stop shaking. "I'm glad you're better," she said, because she'd been worrying about him.

He knelt in front of her. "I wish things could be different between us, that everything wasn't so complicated."

"What do you mean?" The teenager's heart pounded against her chest. She saw Alex's pewter eyes darken, and in the poor light she couldn't read them. . . .

Alex was in a quandary. He wanted to stay near Lori, to defend her, to save her life if necessary. But not under these circumstances. He wasn't sure how to save her from execution; his mother didn't care about anyone but herself. She was worse than ever, now that she was the Chairwoman of United Women of the World.

"I'm here to protect you," Alex said. He ran his fingers through Lori's auburn hair, which hung loosely around her shoulders. It was a gesture with which he intended to comfort her. Noticing the red area on her forehead, he commented on it as he removed his hand.

"I'll be all right," Lori insisted.

Alex struggled with his anger toward his mother. The woman had to be stopped . . . any way possible.

The teenager, so innocent and so strong despite the hardships she faced, smiled at him.

He leaned close and was about to whisper in her ear, telling her the latest plan in his mother's twisted mind . . . only one survivor per cell. Then he had a second thought, and pulled back. No, it would be better not to do that. His mother would only find a way to make things worse. He didn't believe for an instant that someone would be eavesdropping impartially, rendering a "fair" judgment on who was the most guilty and who was the most innocent. . . .

"What's the matter?" Lori asked, looking at him intently. She touched his hand.

"A great deal," he said. She saw his eyes mist over, and he looked away.

Lori seethed. The witch-mother had something to do with it. Oh, how Lori hated that woman! Why had she sent him here, and why was he behaving so oddly?

Still on his knees, his head slumped against her leg, and he began snoring; he had fallen asleep. Low voices came from outside the door. Lori couldn't make out the words but thought it sounded like women, perhaps the guards who had been posted at her door ever since the attempted rescue of the she-apostles. Then she heard an unmistakable drawl. Dixie Lou spoke Lori's name, and Alex's, but the rest was unclear.

Presently the catacomb cell grew quiet, leaving Lori to consider her predicament. She was being forced to share this confined space with the Chairwoman's son, both of them prisoners.

Closing her eyes, Lori tried to bring to mind the image of the baby's face she had seen almost three days before, in the strange vision shared with Dixie Lou. *My baby*. Now something began to materialize, a child's countenance which subsequently filled in with details so that she could make out the features: Large blue eyes, prim mouth, stubborn chin.

The image moved her, and with each passing moment the face grew brighter and more alive, suffused with illumination like the moon in the night sky.

Yaloda, she thought . . . an ancient word, she realized, though she didn't know where she'd heard it. *Innocent child*.

The glowing image faded away. In its place was something she found unsettling, an intense blackness, of a deep and disquieting hue. Like a hole cut in the fabric of the universe.

Something bumped into Lori, jolting her, and she opened her eyes. One of Alex's arms had flopped against her leg. He was still asleep but snoring fitfully, as if experiencing a nightmare.

She eased him onto the floor, put a pillow under his head and blankets over him.

Chapter 33

The gospels of the she-apostles were missing for nearly two thousand years. In 1945, a fragment of the Gospel of Mary (Magdalene) was discovered in a buried earthenware jar at Mt. Jabal-al-Tarif near Nag Hammadi, Egypt. Later, more female manuscripts were found in ancient catacombs at Alexandria, also in Egypt. And recently, the reincarnated she-apostles began to appear miraculously, in the form of children. One by one we obtained custody of them from their parents.

–UWW press release, timed to coincide with publication of the *Holy Women's Bible*

Alex sat on a bench inside Lori's cell, staring at her as she slept, worrying about her safety. She was beginning to stir. He saw her eyelids flicker, and open. Her lavender eyes were strikingly beautiful, filled with surprise at first, and then irritation.

"Good morning," he said.

"Now tell me what's going on."

"I don't really know."

"Let's start with what you *do* know," she said in a low tone. She swung out of bed in her pajamas, stood looking at him with her arms folded across her chest. "Your mother ordered you to be with me. I'll have my explanation now, please. Are you supposed to be my stud knight? Is that it? They've turned you into a sex slave?"

Shaking his head, he said, "That's not it at all."

"Then what is? You also said you're here to protect me. Are you some kind of a personal bodyguard, then, one who sleeps in?"

"No. I want to protect you from them."

"Them? I presume you mean the UWW—"

"Right." He broke gazes with her, wished he might say something that would make the eavesdroppers pick her to survive, and him to execute. But he didn't believe that whole scenario from his mother, and didn't want to play her little game any more than he had to. He didn't want to tell Lori, either, or she might try to act heroic and incriminate herself. She had that type of personality: impulsive, defiant, and brave. No, silence was best. Dixie Lou would do what she intended to do anyway.

"You're hiding something, Alex. Don't play dumb with me. Save that act for the others."

"I'm not hiding anything. As for my act, they're on to me."

"Well so am I." She paused, chewed at her lower lip.

"I don't like this any better than you do."

"Do you know your own feelings?" she asked. Lori rose to her feet, began pacing the small room.

"Sure, I guess."

"Do you find me attractive?"

"Sure I think you're attractive. You're smart and pretty and I like you. It's just that I have other matters that are requiring my attention."

"You're only seven years older than I am. Not so much."

"Not so much later, but now it's a lot. I'm a man and you're still a child."

"Don't be condescending to me."

"Sorry, I'm only trying to be realistic."

"Alex, I'm a *woman*, not a virgin. I've already had several experiences."

"I don't know how to break this to you, Lori, but there's more to being a woman than having sex."

"I know that!" She smiled disdainfully, but her expression faded into a scowl. "I don't like you or your mother. You *use* people, lie to people. It's how you were raised, isn't it, Alex? You're both manipulative."

"I'm ashamed of that woman," Alex said. "I hate her. I'm not like her at all."

Lori laughed. "Oh, but you are, Mr. Big Shot Child 'Napper, using everybody for the cause. Maybe you're a BOI agent, trying to get the she-apostles for them. How's that so different from your mother and her UWW? Everyone is secondary to the Cause, with a capital 'C.' In your family there are no real personal relationships, are there?"

"You have it all wrong. As I told her, I have nothing to do with the BOI. As for my mother, she always thinks of herself first and the UWW second. I'm somewhere down the line, around the level of a pet."

"However you look at it, neither of you are capable of love."

He arched his thick eyebrows. "And you're an expert on the subject?"

"More than you, obviously."

He stood in front of her, and with a gentle hand moved her long hair out of her eyes. "Lori, I—"

She pulled free of him. "Get away from me. In fact, get out of here. Now!"

"I don't have the key."

Furious, she turned her back on him.

* * *

Styx Tertullian took a deep breath, hesitated. His entire body was shaking, and he felt feverish.

If he went through with this, things would never again be the same between him and Minister Culpepper. There would be no way to conceal the gross insubordination, because only he and his boss knew the codes.

This was no small matter, nothing to be overlooked or forgotten.

It's him or me after this. I die, or he does.

Perspiration ran down his brow. He trembled as he voice activated the computer. Styx was in his own office, but acting like a thief there, an intruder. It was the middle of the night, as still as a graveyard.

Seconds of trepidation elapsed that seemed like hours. Then urgent impulse guided his fingers and he tapped in the deep-access military codes, a combination of numbers, accent marks, and umlauts. Someone might stop him if he didn't hurry.

The screen came to life in a silvery glow, with a border of black BOI crosses and a heading that read in bold letters, "Most Secret. For Eyes Only."

Key-stroking for a deeper, even more secure code, he brought up a red-bordered screen with a golden circle in the middle. Within the circle he typed a series of words in phonetic English, directing Bureau paramilitary forces in Albania and Bulgaria to coordinate a powerful strike against Monte Konos.

Styx's screen flashed three times, confirming that the messages had been received.

He tapped the codes to exit the system, and shut off the computer terminal.

* * *

"We need a golf course up here," Dixie Lou said, as she gazed through an open patio doorway at a grassy field outside the Refectory Building. "Then we can discuss business on the links, the way men do." Thick clouds were socking the monastery in, with rugged mountains barely visible to the south. A dark gray rainstorm could be seen approaching from across the valley.

She was seated at the head of a long table in the Refectory's private dining room. The entire council was present with her, a working luncheon. The aroma of exotic spices, butter, and seafood wafted through the air.

"Too much slope," Katherine Pangalos said, as she set down a glass of iced tea. "The balls would roll off the cliff. Not enough room up here, either. We could only fit in three or four holes."

"We won't have to hide on this mountain forever, ladies," Dixie Lou said, watching a black, wild goat negotiate a treacherous path along the top of the cliff. "When the *Holy Women's Bible* is published and women are empowered, we'll take the world by storm! Men will hide from *us*!"

The women were quiet as they watched Dixie Lou attentively. One of them got up and closed the door, since a cold wind was picking up outside.

"I've been thinking about our new book," Dixie Lou said. "and I have a funding issue to propose." She noticed the rain clouds getting larger, darker, and closer, dominating the sky.

"What about the kidnappers?" Bobbi Torrence asked. "Are you prepared to discuss the evidence with us?" Nervously, she dropped a napkin from her lap, but because of her girth couldn't reach down to pick it up.

"Do you mean the *murderers*?" Dixie Lou asked, leveling a cold stare at her, since Bobbi's niece was one of the accused. "I'm compiling evidence and will render my decisions in due course. Nothing in Title 8 says I have to discuss evidence of treason with the council."

"The final judgments are yours," Bobbi agreed, "but we thought you might want our advice at some point." Her jowls quivered as she spoke.

"I've decided to go it alone," the Chairwoman said.

"Oh," Bobbi said, in a small voice.

"As for my son Alex, as I've said before, he will receive no special consideration. Each of you knows I will have him executed if I decide to do so, and I might even do it myself."

None of the other councilwomen said anything.

"My investigators are preparing reports for me," Dixie Lou added, "and I'll review them privately."

This was not true. There were no investigators—Dixie Lou's judgments about the young people didn't rely upon evidence that might be assembled in such a manner. Her decisions were dependent, instead, upon how much cooperation she received from her son and from Lori—

and from the councilwomen at this table concerning issues she would present to them.

Dixie Lou could see any number of reasons why she might delay her announcements about the rebels' fates. The longer she waited, the more funding votes would come up in the interim, and the more leverage she would have. It was all politics, the skillful management and manipulation of power. If two votes swung to her side—those of Bobbi Torrence and Fujiko Harui—it would mean a great deal on a sixteen member council. Then she would have ten votes in her camp out of the sixteen, a clear majority that would not require her tie-breaking vote as Chairwoman.

The sentencing possibilities available to her made Dixie Lou smile as she nibbled on a vegetarian sandwich, sprinkled with feta cheese. Gazing down the table she noted nervous, quick glances in her direction, and considerable indigestion. Fujiko Harui popped a little yellow tablet as she sometimes did when she was upset, an antacid from her pharmacopoeia.

"We will now discuss funding the completion of our most important project," Dixie Lou said, "the *Holy Women's Bible.*"

All eyes were riveted on her. The clinking of silverware and dishes ceased.

"We have a little problem with the project, don't we?" Dixie Lou drawled. "Our missing twelfth she-apostle? I don't suppose any of you are hiding her?" She took a small bite of the moist sandwich, swallowed.

Nervous laughter traveled around the table. Someone coughed.

Dixie Lou raised her voice: "What are we supposed to do, hold up the release of our book until Martha of Galilee makes her grand entrance?"

"I don't see what other choice we have," Katherine said.

"Maybe that's why I'm the leader and you aren't," Dixie Lou said. "Let's review for a moment. The *Holy Women's Bible,* as we have envisioned it, consists of *The Old Testament* and *The New Testament*— both edited to make them more female-friendly—and fanfare please!—ta ta!—*The Testament of the She-Apostles*! The only trouble is, we're missing a small portion."

"Are you suggesting that we publish what we have?" Katherine asked.

Dixie Lou shook her head, picked a bone out of her salmon. "No, something far more interesting."

Perplexed expressions surrounded the table.

"What if we bring in a baby—and say it's the twelfth?" Dixie Lou asked.

"What are you driving at?" Katherine inquired.

"We bring in a baby; it doesn't matter which one. Then we write a new gospel on our own, and say it's from—" She paused as a male waiter opened a door and entered the room. He refilled the cups with strong, steaming coffee, and left.

After the waiter closed the door, Dixie Lou continued. "Don't you see?" Her dark eyes glittered with excitement. A vein at her temple pulsed. "This is the best thing we could possibly do. We create a logical story for the twelfth she-apostle. We already have her name, Martha of Galilee, and make up events that might have occurred in her life—excluding anything about the betrayal of Jesus by a 'She-Judas,' whoever that might be. Then we print our new holy book and spread it all over the planet—in bound copies, recorded books, and e-books."

"You mean *fake* it?" Katherine asked.

A wry smile worked at the edges of Dixie Lou's mouth as she said, "I'm just talking about exercising a little creative license for one teeny-tiny little gospel. Men have done a lot worse to us. They suppressed and destroyed *all twelve* of our gospels, and rewrote others to put women in a bad light! They stole our heritage!"

Outside, rain began to fall, a sudden onslaught. The wild goat was gone, having disappeared down one of the trails scarring the cliffs of Monte Konos.

"But what if the real Martha is brought to us?" Tamara Himmel asked. A soft-bodied woman with an undersized head and pinched face, she had always sided with Dixie Lou in the past, but seemed agitated now.

"Simple," Dixie Lou said. She nibbled on an olive, and shoved her plate away. "If we have her and she talks about a woman who betrayed Jesus, we suppress her gospel. If we don't have her and she says those things, we condemn her as a liar."

"And an instrument of Satan," Councilwoman Nancy Winters added.

"Right!" Dixie Lou exclaimed.

"We can't fake the *Holy Women's Bible*," Katherine protested. "We are charged with a sacred task, and must perform it honestly." The rain intensified outside.

Murmurs of concurrence went around the table.

But Dixie Lou asked, with her gaze burning directly into the eyes of her principal opponent, "What about the Apostle Lydia's statement concerning the She-Judas, whose identity is known only to the real Martha? We voted to suppress the She-Judas material, remember? What do you call that, Katherine?"

"A temporary and reasonable action," came the response, "until we can obtain verification from the last she-apostle."

"As long as I sit in this position," Dixie Lou said, "our publication will never include anything about a *woman* betraying Jesus! You folks can vote to fund until cows go to college, but I have the final word on whether we actually proceed with any project."

"Your proposal is too dangerous," Katherine said. "If we're caught in a lie over the last she-apostle, our enemies will extrapolate and say the entire *Holy Women's Bible* is fraudulent. It's a matter of credibility, in the court of public opinion. We need to hold off until Martha of Galilee appears, and include her gospel. We must be truthful!"

"What if the reports from the other she-apostles are wrong?" Dixie Lou asked, "and there are only eleven females instead of twelve?"

"If that's true," Katherine said, "it casts doubt on all of the gospels of the she-apostles. Believe me, we don't want to open up that can of worms. No, there are twelve, not eleven."

"I see a bigger picture than you do," Dixie Lou said.

"That's why you're the Chairwoman, right?" Katherine said, her tone acidic.

Dixie Lou nodded. "If we delay, the wrong people could get wind of our project and suppress it, maybe even killing all of us in the process. As for your comment about being truthful, why should we be more truthful than men have been? Let's do whatever it takes to tip the scales in our favor!" She slammed her fist on the table, causing silverware and china to bounce.

"Maybe someone has kidnapped the Apostle Martha," Tamara suggested, "or worse. Maybe she's been murdered."

"If she's dead, we're better off," Dixie Lou said. "Well, ladies, time to vote, and I motion to fund the immediate editing of the final gospel. We'll keep it sparse. Let's see . . . We can say the last she-apostle was a quiet, shy person, and she revealed only a few pages of material. We can assimilate it into the text in a few days. "

Ten hands went up to pass the measure, with Katherine and five of her associates in opposition. Bobbi Torrence and Fujiko Harui, who could formerly be counted on to side with Katherine, changed sides this time and voted with Dixie Lou, for obvious reasons.

Katherine stormed out of the room, followed by her allies. Among others, Bobbi and Fujiko stayed behind.

Muttering an oath under her breath, Dixie Lou stared at the remains of her lunch on the table. She vowed to get even with the six who continued to oppose her.

* * *

Southern Bulgaria, near the village of Skrût . . .

In the early morning hours, a squadron of twenty BOI warplanes took off, heading southwest into Greece. They had been concealed underground, beneath what appeared to be a fig grove from the air. The aircraft bore no distinguishing emblems, no way of tracing them to their owners, in case they were shot down. A similar BOI base lay on a plain in southern Albania, and was dispatching another attack squadron.

Headquarters had ordered destruction of the target at any cost, no matter the consequences. Now they only had to wait for the weather to improve. Greece, Albania, and Macedonia were engulfed in a severe storm, with high winds and torrential rains.

Chapter 34

*Those close to Dixie Lou Jackson speak of her disturbing psychosis.
She imagines what particular people might look like dead.*
                                –Confidential UWW memorandum

For eleven days Consuela had been caring for the house on the knoll as if it were her own. Better than her own, in fact. From her perspective as an impoverished Méxicana peasant, she felt as if she had become the caretaker of a great estate, and that she was fortunate in this position, since it provided a shelter for her growing baby. She considered this duty–albeit one she had assumed without permission–an almost sacred trust, one in which she strove to improve the condition and cleanliness of the property.

Actually the house was not large–and certainly not what would commonly be considered an estate–but it had many fine appointments, including tile counter tops in the kitchen and in the two bathrooms, a stereo music system (that she couldn't use, because the power was off), prints of famous Mexican murals, and handmade area rugs with Aztec Indian designs on them.

In the smallest of three bedrooms, which she considered most appropriate for herself and her child, she had set up a basket for the baby, with thick red-and-green towels for a mattress and blankets. It was mid-afternoon, and she knelt over Marta, who fussed as she slept, as if having a bad dream.

Something thumped in another room, twice. She heard voices. Consuela caught her breath.

Quickly she placed little Marta's basket on a table, then opened the window. The hinges squeaked, but not loudly. She climbed outside, onto the soft, loamy dirt of the garden, then reached back in and removed Marta from the basket. The child awoke and was about to cry, when Consuela placed a hand over her mouth, and quieted her by offering a warm, comforting breast for her to suckle. The baby drank hungrily.

As she hid behind a saguaro bush, the young mother realized that the voices she'd heard were those of children. Creeping around to the other side of the house, Consuela peered through a window into the master bedroom. Two boys, around ten years old, were rifling through drawers and an oak armoire, searching for valuables.

Rapping on the window, Consuela shouted out, "*Andalé, niños!*"

Startled, the thieves ran. One knocked over a large black clay urn, which crashed to the floor and shattered. As the boy stumbled, he dropped a jewelry box, scattering its contents on the floor.

Consuela set her daughter down on the ground and ran around to the front door. When the would-be burglars emerged she kicked one of them in the seat of the pants, and swung a hard fist against the back of the other, sending him careening down the steps.

Crying out in pain, the failed criminals fled into the jungle.

Consuela spent the rest of the day cleaning up the mess. She put broaches, rings, and earrings back in the jewelry box and replaced it where it had been before, on an armoire shelf. The large clay pot seemed beyond repair, but she carefully scooped up all the pieces and put them in a wooden box, just in case it was possible to glue it back together. It bothered her that it was broken, especially since she had startled the boy who did it. But she felt good that she'd been there to stop the burglary in progress, preventing the loss of valuables.

Now she could truly say she had been of service to the owners.

* * *

Minister Culpepper was not a particularly eccentric or colorful man. In fact, those who knew him best might even call him pedestrian. In his behavior there was, however, one notable exception. His Internet connection was not only hacker-proof and state-of-the art, it *was* art. One day it generated one marvelous thing and another day, something else entirely. Not only that, it didn't remain in one place for long.

Now a figure danced in front of his eyes—a computer-generated three-dimensional ballerina, about half a meter high. The hologram twirled and pirouetted, pleasing to the eye and to his childhood imagination. Presently, however, she paused and spoke a message to him that he found disturbing:

"Pursuant to your instructions, our squads in Bulgaria and Albania have been activated," the ballerina reported in a sweet computer voice, "in preparation for Mission Monte Konos. Your warplanes are circling above the cloud cover, waiting for the weather to clear."

Culpepper rose out of his chair, sweeping papers from his desk and sending the faux ballerina fleeing to a safer distance. "I didn't order anything like that!" he roared. "Mission Monte Konos? What is going on here?"

"You are displeased, sir?" The computer voice sounded confused. . . .

Moments later, Styx Tertullian hurried into the office, having been summoned. "Minister?" he said with a slight bow. Peripherally, he watched the ballerina hologram, which was nearly motionless in the air in the middle of the room.

"Tell him what you told me," Culpepper demanded, of the Internet messenger.

She did so, after which Styx said in a convincing tone, "I am astounded, sir, and confounded. It must be a computer error."

"I make no errors!" the ballerina protested, a squeal that was no longer sweet. "I am integrated with a Mayberry III mainframe, linked to the Bureau's own—"

"Well you've made an error anyway!" Styx insisted.

"Not possible!"

With a shrug, Culpepper shut off the ballerina's voice. The diminutive figure continued to mouth silent protestations.

"You must be right, Styx," he said. "Find out about this. Now."

"I will, sir, and the responsible technicians will be *terminated*."

* * *

"I know you're upset with me," Alex said, "but you don't understand everything that's going on." He scratched the back of his neck.

"Stow it," Lori said. "I'm not interested." She heard water running on the other side of a wall, and earlier had heard a guard mention a problem with storm water leaking. . . .

Alex and Lori sat on the floor at opposite corners of the cell, glaring at one another across the space. Under the circumstances, he thought, they couldn't get any farther apart than this. A series of arguments between them had escalated, and this morning even Alex wanted out of the cell. He tried to tell himself he no longer cared what happened to the girl, or to himself. But he knew this was only half right. He was extremely worried about her, especially the way she wouldn't go along with anything he told her, the way she kept getting more and more upset with him.

Not so long ago, she seemed to have liked him, might even have had sex with him if he'd wanted to, but now she seemed to consider him anathema. Who knows what she was really thinking? For a fifteen-year-old, she certainly was complex. In some ways she was mature beyond her years, but in others, especially in matters involving relationships with boys, she seemed decidedly naïve. . . .

As Lori glared at Alex across the short expanse of floor she wondered about his true motives. He'd faked the role of a dimwit, had gotten her involved in the unsuccessful kidnapping attempt. Was Alex as brave and gallant as he wanted her to believe, or was he duplicitous? He certainly was full of himself.

"How am I supposed to know when you're lying and when you're telling the truth?" she asked.

"Well I can understand why you say that, but consider this. Even liars tell the truth sometimes. Even liars have feelings and can do honorable things. Do you believe that could be possible?" He scooted over by her. Even though they were the same height, he sat taller than she did.

"I think you and your mother set up the whole kidnapping episode as an excuse to lock me up. The switched children, the trap. It was all a big scheme."

"That's ludicrous. I had nothing to do with it."

"Sometimes when I look at you, I see her in your features." She paused. "How much *are* you like her, Alex?"

"Not at all! Where do you get such ridiculous thoughts?"

Lori didn't really believe the accusation she'd just made against him, but she had thrown it out as a trial balloon anyway, to see how he'd react, to watch the expression on his face. His voice and features had betrayed nothing but apparent sincerity to her, but he was known to be skilful at deception. There were dimensions to him that intrigued her, but she sensed danger there. She didn't like to be manipulated, by him or by his mother. The teenager longed for the comparative simplicity of high school in Seattle and her life on the streets. She felt as if she were caught in a whirlwind.

Looking confused and angry, Alex crossed the room, to the corner where he had been. This time he didn't look at her.

"I don't even want to think about you," he said.

* * *

Through a one-way monitor concealed in the mottled rock of the ceiling, Dixie Lou watched, but couldn't hear their words. Leaking storm water had shorted out the surveillance equipment in the cell, and replacement parts were on order.

For three days she had been observing and recording them (until the equipment failed), hoping to learn something important about Lori Vale, something she might use to understand and control the mysterious, difficult teenager. But the girl's arguments with Alex were just that, arguments. They didn't provide the Chairwoman with any insights.

In her mind's eye, Dixie Lou envisioned killing both of them with her bare hands, so that she could experience the pleasure of their flat, dead eyes staring into oblivion.

Chapter 35

Women, being smaller and less muscular than men, must use their brains more in order to compete. The brains of men, in disuse because of their reliance upon brawn, have atrophied to a dangerous, almost dysfunctional level.

—Introduction to "A Woman's Survival Guide," a satirical UWW play

The blonde-haired baby had a rather large head, almost giving it a hydrocephalic appearance, with the skull out of proportion to the body. Employing mock secrecy and staged security, Dixie Lou had the child brought into the quarters of the she-apostles one day and placed in its own room, with a matron. A name was posted over the door, in ornate script: "Martha of Galilee."

Dixie Lou met privately with the child, and purportedly from these sessions, words and events were added to the text of the *Holy Women's Bible*. The "good news" spread quickly throughout the monastery complex: The last she-apostle had been found and the *Holy Women's Bible* was nearing completion!

But in her innermost thoughts the Chairwoman brooded, wondering about the real twelfth she-apostle, and if it might be the baby she saw with Lori in the shared vision. Lori's baby. Uncertainties bothered Dixie Lou, working like an infection at her innards. Were powerful forces at work—human or otherwise—concealing the information in the possession of this she-apostle, controlling its dissemination?

And in her personal torments Dixie Lou debated about whether or not to discuss the shared vision with any of the councilwomen. The first name that occurred to her as a potential confidant was Deborah Marvel, but she quickly ruled her out. Deborah might think she was out of her mind, which could result in the council attempting to remove her from the red chair.

* * *

Liz Torrence stood at attention, her toes on the edge of a rock precipice that overhung the valley floor. A biting wind whipped her hair, and rain misted her face. All morning and afternoon the storm had continued. On each side of her stood the surviving members of her group, also at attention. They were dressed alike, in gray denim jeans and shirts.

Her thoughts flashed back to minutes before, when the would-be rescuers had been in a subterranean room, having a blinding light shone in their eyes by a tall, exceedingly heavy female security officer.

"You will go outside and stand on the edge of the cliff," the officer had said, "and in that position you will either tell us everything we want to know or you will be pushed off."

Liz felt a heavy hand on her shoulder now, pressing a little, and heard a smooth, flowing voice in her ear, as if the wind were whispering to her . . . questions about her involvement in the kidnapping conspiracy. She didn't feel brave or rebellious, and only wanted to pass this test, one of many she had already endured.

"We met regularly at Yonney's apartment," Liz shouted, to be heard over the storm. Unable to stop the flow of words, she rattled off the names of her comrades, along with everything she knew about their involvement.

Simultaneously, she heard the others talking. On her right, Christine Brickowski told of surreptitiously copying documents from the Scriptorium, and how her sister, a Scriptorium editor, had not known about it. On her left, Dan Rhodes told how he had obtained handguns and rifles constructed of composites that could not be detected by surveillance equipment.

Liz felt the pressure on her shoulder diminish and finally disappear. Glancing peripherally, she saw no one behind her, or behind anyone else. She'd only imagined it, or . . . and this made more sense to her . . . they'd used a power of suggestion on her, and undoubtedly on the others as well.

The voices ceased. All had been said.

Feeling a sudden compulsion, Liz turned and led the way back through mounting wind and rain to the underground room, where she found the security officer waiting for them.

A video screen beside the officer flashed on, showing Liz and the others on the edge of the cliff, their backs to the camera. Their voices could be heard, speaking simultaneously. Then a filtering system eliminated storm noises and separated each voice, so that they were heard individually in their complete statements, and recorded.

While watching this on the screen, the conspirators shuffled uneasily on their feet. Presently the security officer removed a tiny microphone from the lapel of each of them, and the group filed out of the room, followed by the officer.

Each day it had been something different, a new method of probing their thoughts and reactions, of tormenting them into utter and complete submission. Liz wondered what unbearable cruelty she would be required to endure tomorrow.

* * *

Styx Tertullian had never done anything nearly as difficult as this. He was a man who had led countless commando raids against heretical females, killing them, taking them prisoner and torturing them without compunction. All these things he had done for the sake of his beloved Bureau of Ideology, for the benefit of the glorious Christian cause and all that was eternally good and moral. He was certain that God in His infinite mercy understood, even condoned, the things Styx had been forced to do.

This time, though, it was different, and Styx wasn't certain if God would understand, wasn't certain if this course of action would dispatch him to the fiery realm instead of through the pearly gates. The problem had more to do with a difference of opinion, with disparate views of the future of the Bureau, and a disagreement over how best to handle the heretical women at Monte Konos.

Styx had tunnel vision when it came to those women. Every morning when he awoke they were the first thing on his mind, and every night he thought about them as he drifted off to sleep. He was constantly thinking about them, working through plans to annihilate them, imagining all of them stone-cold dead.

For years he'd been upset that Minister Culpepper had never trusted him to lead a large scale military operation. Styx was tired of the small assignments he'd been given, even though one of them had been to question the leader of the hated women, Amy Angkor-Billings. Torturing and killing her had not been enough. He wanted more. According to word that had reached BOI headquarters, the women had replaced her with that black witch, Dixie Lou Jackson, and the women's operations were proceeding with even more fervor than before.

The *Holy Women's Bible* . . . Thus far Styx had only seen excerpts from it, but Culpepper had accepted the offer from President Markwether to reduce their funding demand in exchange for a computer printout of the unfinished manuscript. That had been six days ago, and the manuscript was expected to arrive any moment now. What a foolish way to spend a billion dollars. In any event, such lousy decisions would soon be a thing of the past.

The women had to be stopped quickly, at any cost.

As Styx stood by Minister Culpepper that fateful morning, peering over his shoulder at the computer screen, the Minister was using voice commands to order updated reports from paramilitary forces in and around Greece. A pair of Raphael and da Vinci paintings were on the wall behind the Minister, and on his credenza stood a reliquary box said to contain a fragment of the "True Cross" on which Jesus was crucified—all items secretly removed from the Vatican by the BOI, with evidence falsified to make it look like the UWW did it.

"This is no computer error," Culpepper said. "I've received independent corroboration. Someone has ordered our forces into position for a strike. Who overrode my authority, and why?"

Scowling, the fat man wrote an e-mail countermanding the earlier orders, and was about to send it. He reeked of angry sweat. At a sound from Styx, he stopped and looked up at him.

Tears streamed down Styx's face, and he barely suppressed a sob. He had his right hand behind his back.

"Son, what is it?" Culpepper asked. Then he saw the hand coming around from behind, with something glinting in it.

Unable to look, Styx closed his eyes, slamming the knife into Culpepper's side, penetrating the rib cage and piercing the heart. The big man gasped, slumped to the other side, and toppled from his chair.

Moments later two aides rushed into the office. Styx had paid them off.

"Remove him," Styx ordered, "and spread the heart attack story."

As they dragged the heavy Minister, groaning from his weight, Styx erased the e-mail and wrote one of his own, for distribution to important political, and religious leaders around the world, including the President of the United States and the Pope. All would be informed of the unfortunate, untimely death of Minister Nelson Culpepper, following twenty-nine years of service and dedication to the Bureau.

"The Lord Almighty called him home," Styx wrote at the end of the e-mail. A line he liked very much.

In ensuing days, falsified medical reports would be released to key leaders, purported evidence that Culpepper had been suffering from a heart condition for years, exacerbated by high blood pressure and a quick temper . . . it was a medical condition that he supposedly took great pains to conceal. A personal notation by his doctor would say it was a wonder he had lasted as long as he had. Even the autopsy would be falsified . . . *doctored*. Styx smiled at the wordplay, and it eased some of the tension he had been feeling.

Through meticulous planning and preparation he had set up the means of disposing of the body and obtaining the medical reports, through men who were steadfastly loyal to him, men who would serve his new regime as it blazed a glorious path into the future. He felt the sadness for Culpepper dissipating, replaced by a welling sense of euphoria. Now he could proceed with full force against Monte Konos.

Nothing stood in his way. He already felt the winds of God against his back, propelling him forward.

Chapter 36

Behold, the new things do I declare: before they spring forth I tell you of them. Sing unto She-God a new song, and her praise from the end of the earth. Let the wilderness and the cities thereof lift up their voices in joy; let the inhabitants of the earth sing, let them shout from the tops of the mountains. Let them give glory unto She-God, and declare her praise forever.

—Isaiah 42:9–12, as amended in the Holy Women's Bible

On the fifth day after bringing the counterfeit Martha in, Dixie Lou went to her own office on the top floor of the Refectory Building. It was shortly before 7:00 AM, her customary time of arrival. She found Fujiko Harui waiting in the shadowy corridor by the office door, pacing the floor.

"Did you get my message," Fujiko said, "that I need to discuss my daughter with you?"

"Make it short," Dixie Lou said. "My patience has limits."

"I don't want favoritism, only simple human decency for Siana, fairness for her. The kidnapping wasn't her fault. She didn't know what she was getting into. They talked her into it, didn't tell her everything that was going on."

"I'm not granting any favors for my own son, so why should I listen to you?"

"Because Siana just went along with the others. She didn't plan any of it."

"How do you know that?"

"A mother knows her own child." The small Japanese woman had a facial tic on her left cheek, one Dixie Lou hadn't noticed before. Apparently it was stress-induced.

Fujiko started to say something more, but Dixie Lou waved an arm dismissively and voice-activated codes on the control panel of the door to open it. "We'll discuss this another time," she said. "I'm busy right now."

She stepped past the councilwoman, pushed the office door open.

"You don't have any right to do what you're doing," Fujiko said. "Two in each cell, and one dies?"

"Where did you hear that?"

"The council needs to decide the fate of the prisoners, not you."

"Don't push me on this," Dixie Lou said.

"All right. I'm sorry, but I'm just worried about Siana. As a mother, you can understand that?"

Dixie Lou didn't respond.

"Bobbi is just as worried about her niece, who's innocent, too. Bobbi wants me to tell you that she'll vote with you on any council issue, whatever it takes."

"I never had any doubt of that. What about you?"

The eyes flared and almost produced tears, but Fujiko said, "You can count on me, too. I already voted with you on faking the twelfth she-apostle."

"Oh did you?" the Chairwoman said, with a tight smile. "I didn't notice." She entered her office and slammed the door, then heard a muffled retort out in the hallway, and the thump of a fist or shoe against the wall. Presently it grew silent and Dixie Lou turned her attention to the report on her desk, concerning her escaped stud knight, Giovanni.

The report didn't have much new information in it, so she sighed and pushed it aside, then pulled a thick stack of papers toward her, the latest computer printout of the *Holy Women's Bible*. Her false Gospel of Martha had been incorporated into the manuscript.

Thumbing through the pages, she found no major changes that needed to be made. By the following morning she would receive the final copyediting suggestions. The book was almost ready to go to press.

* * *

In a dune buggy with two surfboards on the top-rack, Gilberto Inez drove over a cobblestone street and brought the car to a stop in front of a small adobe building. A weathered wooden sign with faded red letters hung unevenly over the door, identifying this as the power and light company for the region, which encompassed this seaside market town and two smaller nearby villages.

Gilberto and his brother José—a year younger than he—got out in the bright sunlight and went into the office. The young Méxicanos were dressed in shorts and American surfer tee-shirts. For months they had been riding waves on the western coast of México, from Baja California to the Guatemala border.

The office clerk, a woman with a huge mole over her eyebrow, was pleasant enough, but to Gilberto smelled as if she hadn't showered in weeks. Hearing the request from the boys, she checked a large ledger book. "Seven Avenido de los Cruces, you say?"

"That's it," José said. "Our parents' house. They want us to have the power turned on and get it ready for them. They're arriving at the end of the week."

The taller of the two despite being a year younger, José had blue-black hair like his brother, but his face was long and narrow, more their mother's features. In contrast, Gilberto stood shorter and blockier, favoring the paternal side of their family, and had long sideburns with dark, baby fine hair on his upper lip.

"Oh yes, here it is." The clerk looked up at José. "Your mother is Professor Inez, isn't she?"

"That's right."

"My nephew is an intern at the clinic here. He said he studied under her in México City, and that your mother is quite brilliant."

"That's true," José said.

"Okay, boys, the power will be turned on this afternoon. Do we bill the usual place, the postal box in México D.F.?" She was referring to Mexico City, in its federal district.

Gilberto answered in the affirmative.

A short while later the dune buggy rolled up the long driveway to the house. "Place looks surprisingly good," Gilberto observed. "Did Mom and Dad hire a gardener?"

"I don't know. They must have."

The boys toted heavy duffel bags into the front parlor, set them down with a thump on the terra cotta floor and looked around. "They must have a maintenance man, too," José said. Through a window he saw a ladder leaning against the house. "Hey *hermano*, what do you say we go down to the beach this afternoon and check out the waves?"

"Sounds good to me."

Gilberto heard what sounded like the cry of a baby. He exchanged puzzled glances with José.

In the smallest bedroom they found a woman asleep on the bed, with a baby in a basket by her. The woman stirred. Her eyelids fluttered. She was dark-skinned and round-faced, perhaps one of the reclusive, rarely seen mountain *indios*. Her cheeks were flushed, and beads of perspiration covered her brow. She wasn't much older than the boys.

"*Señorita*?" Gilberto said.

She sat straight up. The bedding slipped to her lap. She wore a caramel brown dress. "Oh!" she exclaimed.

"Who are you?" José demanded.

Her eyes were huge with fear. "Consuela Santos. I haven't stolen anything. My baby Marta needed a place to stay. I have worked hard, repaired the doors and windows, cleaned the yard and the entire house. I planted vegetables, but the seeds are old and some didn't sprout. Every day I work, but today I'm so tired. I fell asleep."

She took the baby to her breast, letting the child suckle hungrily for several minutes. Out of courtesy, the boys left the room, and returned when Marta was finished.

"Come with me," Consuela said after a time, putting the child in the basket. "I will show you what I have done here."

"How did you get in?" José asked, as the boys followed her into the kitchen.

"I found an unlocked bedroom window." She hung her head. "We have eaten some of your food, but I have a detailed list of everything, and I will pay it all back."

She showed them several cardboard boxes filled with empty cans and packages that she had opened. All had been cleaned and neatly organized.

"Why didn't you just write it all down?" Gilberto asked.

"I do not write so good," she answered. "I can't read, either, mostly numbers."

"The house looks very nice," Gilberto admitted, "but we aren't sure what to do with you. Our parents will be here in three days."

"I understand. I will leave right away. You won't call the *policia*? I promise to give you all the information on who I am, and I will not fail to make regular payments for the food."

"It looks like our parents owe you money," Gilberto said. "Did you fix this screen door?" He noted where a patch had been placed skillfully over a hole in the wire mesh.

"Yes," she said. "I found a torn piece of screen in the storage building and cut it to fit, then wrapped wires to tighten it in place."

"You've done a fine job. I can hardly notice the patch. I only know it's there because I knocked a hole in it the last time I was here, and it was one of the things I was supposed to fix."

"I think we should let her stay," José suggested, "at least until Mom and Dad get here."

"*Bueno*," Gilberto said.

Consuela heard Marta in the other room, babbling with the strange sounds that had proven to be so troublesome.

José noticed it, and commented, "Sounds like your baby wants to talk. She's trying to make words."

Consuela smiled prettily, but she felt nervous. She wasn't sure if she should remain here any longer. For her, the safety of her baby was paramount. These youths didn't seem to have heard about the search for her daughter, but their parents might have. The young peasant woman wanted to leave right away, but was afraid it might be more dangerous somewhere else.

"Say, you look like you need some rest," Gilberto said. He touched her arm gently. "Please, *señorita*, go back to bed."

"You are too kind," she said. Moments later she collapsed back into bed, and fell fast asleep.

* * *

Underground aircraft hangar, BOI headquarters . . .

As Styx Tertullian disembarked from his Lear Fan prop-jet he was approached by the Vice Minister of Doctrine & Faith, a tall, distinguished-looking man with an oval, unlined face and perfectly combed black hair. Nearly out of breath, Kylee Branson said, "This just came in. I saw you land, and since you're Acting Minister I thought you should see it right away."

A graduate of the finest Ivy League schools, Branson had an irritating habit of staring down his long nose through half-lidded eyes, as if he were peering at an insect. He did this no matter the comparative rank of the person with whom he was speaking; he had done the same with Minister Culpepper, and he was doing it to Styx now.

Styx scowled as he accepted a single sheet of paper bearing the BOI logo on top, a black cross on a silver background. He studied it. The report, transmitted over a secure frequency, read, "Weather not optimal for mission."

"Satellite connections are down, sir," Branson announced, "and this is all we can get. Shall we tell them to call off the attack? The weather is playing havoc with our equipment."

"Call it off? I warn you, don't say such foolish things around me. I have no time or patience for stupidity." A fly buzzed near Styx's face and he swatted it away. He started toward a bank of elevators.

Falling into step beside his superior, Branson said, "Uh, sir, I apologize if I'm speaking out of place, but I must tell you that some of the, uh . . . officers of the Bureau are worried about the plan to attack Monte Konos. Some fear it will create an embarrassing international incident, and others want to know more about the heretical religious texts there before they are destroyed."

"And you? How do you feel about it?" Despite his personal dislike for Branson, he had to admit he was extremely competent and loyal to the Bureau. For this reason Tertullian had placed him in charge of the attack on Monte Konos.

"Oh, I support the mission, sir. I'm just passing information on to you." He smiled nervously, revealing a set of flawless teeth.

"Tell me the truth. I don't like liars, and I don't tolerate yes-men." Styx brushed crumbs from his uniform, the remnants of an egg salad sandwich he had eaten onboard the aircraft. With irritation, he noticed an oily mayonnaise stain.

Branson reddened, an uncharacteristic crack in his eggshell skin. "Uh, apologies, but I'm worried, too, sir. Minister Culpepper is concerned about such a large attack inside the sovereign nation of Greece. We've never done anything on this scale before."

Styx stepped on a pressure plate to order an elevator. "You're forgetting one thing."

"What's that?"

"The Bureau of Ideology doesn't exist."

A perplexed expression formed on Branson's unlined face. "But if word of the attack gets out to our congressional friends and wealthy contributors it could jeopardize funding sources."

"Who's going to tell them? *You*?"

"No. I would never do that!"

Above the elevator door, red-and-green lights blinked. Watching the pattern, Styx said, "We don't exist and none of it happened. Got it?"

"Yes, sir."

The elevator arrived and Styx stepped aboard. The Vice Minister didn't try to follow.

Holding the door open, Styx barked, "Have our operatives dropped into the Macedonian mountains, and continue with the mission schedule. And don't tell me our warplanes can't fly in bad weather. We're going in, and nothing is going to stop us. Do you understand?"

"Yes, sir."

The elevator doors closed with a percussive thump, and the car descended. On the ride down to his office level, Styx anticipated what would happen next. Soon his agents—those that survived the perilous trip through the storm—would be infiltrating the caves, tunnels and catacombs of Monte Konos . . . killing guards, rigging explosives, destroying defensive military materiel and fortifications, poisoning the ancient water cisterns that were still in use. In the ensuing full-scale attack these BOI operatives, unbeknownst to them, would be sacrificed. Good men would be lost, and this was a pity, but unavoidable.

The blasphemous *Holy Women's Bible* made it all necessary. Styx wanted to cut off the cancer at its source, before it had a chance to spread any more. He hoped he was in time, that the unfinished version stolen by the stud knight was the only one to have gotten out.

In his private office the computer screen displayed a map of Greece, with a blinking red dot marked "Monte Konos." Flashing yellow dots in Bulgaria and Albania designated the locations of BOI strike forces that were being dispatched.

He sat back in his chair and sighed. By the grace of God this mission would not fail. With every fiber of his being Styx loathed those women, and in prayer he requested fiery, painful deaths for all of them.

There could be no reasoning with such people. Like rabid dogs, they had to be destroyed.

Chapter 37

At the trial of Jesus before the Sanhedrin a number of serious charges were leveled against Him, including sedition and claiming to be the Messiah. Evidence was also presented that Jesus, in attempting to elevate the status of women to equality with men, was violating tradition and holy law, which dictated that men were supreme and were to be obeyed by women.

—Commentaries on the *Testament of the She-Apostles*

In a hooded robe, Katherine Pangalos hurried across the plaza, heading for the ancient Scriptorium Building. Two lights on the front of the structure illuminated the plaza, but not brightly, so that she had to watch her footing on the shadowy, wet cobblestones. In the past hour the storm had let up, and the air smelled fresh and clean.

She climbed a short stairway, pushed open a wooden door and entered the building. Beyond a foyer lay an immense high-ceilinged room that had been divided into cubicles having walls that did not extend to the ceiling. Looking in the cubicles, she saw computer equipment and what looked like oversized computer monitors. Something sparkled on a table, and she moved closer.

One of Lori's pearl-and-gold earrings lay there. She picked it up.

Suddenly a roar filled Katherine's ears, and through a window she saw the plaza bathed in blue light. An explosion rocked the building, and the ceiling caved in on her.

* * *

Working late in her office, Dixie Lou heard the huge blast. The floor shook. An alarm klaxon went off, followed by another, and then all of them sounded in the monastery complex, a screaming din of sound, desperate electronic voices.

Beside the laptop, a security computer cast amber light from its monitor, and its built-in speakers blared, "ALL-SECTOR ATTACK! ALL-SECTOR ATTACK!" The screen showed a schematic of the monastery, as seen from the air. Red blips marked the approaching enemy aircraft. There were no green blips whatsoever, representing defense aircraft.

She cursed, slammed a fist on the desk. "Why aren't our ships getting up?"

With shaking fingers she tapped a deep-access code on the security computer's keyboard. The large words " EVACUATION ALERT" filled the screen.

Hangared in the base of the mountain were three long-range helicopters and a vertical takeoff and landing plane—a VTOL. These four stealth aircraft could safely accommodate forty-one passengers, and had firepower. The system would automatically notify the nearest outside UWW forces, but Dixie Lou didn't have time to wait for them.

Quickly she hooked the modem to her laptop computer, intending to transmit the *Holy Women's Bible* as it was. The introduction was basically complete, giving far more credit to herself than to anyone else, but she'd been in the process of rearranging paragraphs and polishing them up. Now she couldn't risk not sending it out.

But the system would not go on-line for her.

She shouted at it, tried again. No luck.

An explosion in another sector of the monastery shook the building and rattled the window glass. In an adjacent room something crashed to the floor.

On the security computer she spoke rapidly into the voice activation system, updating a list she always kept. It contained the names of those who would accompany her on any forced evacuation: Her council, but only her supporters—Deborah Marvel, Nancy Winters, and eight others, including Bobbi Torrence and Fujiko Harui—since they had switched their allegiance to Dixie Lou. Katherine Pangalos (whom she did not know had already been killed) and her five council allies would be left behind. That was part of the update. Every she-apostle would be evacuated, split among the aircraft so that they were not all subject to one crash. Lori and Alex were included in the special group as well, for the unfinished business involving them. The other conspirators who were imprisoned would remain behind, with the exception of Bobbi's niece and Fujiko's daughter . . . in order to keep those councilwomen in line.

Dixie Lou still wondered if the kidnapping attempt had been a BOI plot. Just another piece of information that she would have to extract from the remaining conspirators. Whatever it took, she would find out.

After making her final preparations she tapped the code keys to authenticate her orders. She then made four computer disk sets of the *Holy Women's Bible*. The three additional sets would go with other councilwomen, on separate aircraft.

She tried the laptop again, through voice-activation and a backup startup key. It still wouldn't go on-line. An explosion rocked the building and broke a window in her office. She saw a fire burning in the Refectory Building. Shaking with rage, she aborted the attempt to use the laptop, snapped the lid shut.

With the computer, backup disks and a hard copy of the manuscript in her briefcase, Dixie Lou ran from her office into the corridor. She heard warplanes and gunfire. Through a window at the end of the narrow passage she saw four dark shapes landing outside in the plaza, showing no lights. The aircraft she had ordered.

* * *

The door of Lori's cell burst open, and two female guards carrying semi-automatic rifles filled the doorway. Lori sat on the edge of the bed, and Alex on a hard chair. Just before the interruption they'd been struggling to converse, awkward with one another. Both wondered what the muffled explosions were.

When the guards burst in, Lori thought they were going to shoot her and Alex. But instead one of them commanded, "On your feet! Let's go!"

Chapter 38

A woman is a rock, and a man a reed swayed by the wind.
—Sign posted in council chamber, UWW headquarters

"Get inside!" Dixie Lou exhorted. "Hurry!" Wearing a dun-colored robe with a pants suit under it, she stood in the entry hatch of a black helicopter, waving frantically to the evacuees, shouting orders. Three helicopters and a vertical takeoff and landing craft were in an underground hangar beneath the main plaza. A stream of robed women hurried aboard the command helicopter, some of them carrying the she-apostle babies and toddlers.

On the pavement at the base of the entry ramp, a youthful guard pushed Lori forward. Lori wore khaki jeans and a heavy knit sweater. "Where does this one go?" the guard asked, looking up at the Chairwoman. The guard, who looked as young as her teenage prisoner, carried a sleek, silver-colored assault rifle.

"'Copter Three," Dixie Lou said, pointing to another craft. "I want all the she-apostles with me."

Glaring up at Dixie Lou, Lori said, "You shouldn't risk all of the she-apostles on one craft. You should split them up."

"Split them up?" Dixie Lou exclaimed. "You don't give the orders here!"

Pausing beside Lori, Deborah Marvel held a baby in her arms. "Maybe she has a point," Deborah said. "You did put computer copies of the holy book on every aircraft. We don't want to risk killing all of the children in a crash."

"Our She-God will not allow my personal helicopter to crash," Dixie Lou said, indignantly. "The apostles are safest with me." Explosions sounded from somewhere in the mountain complex, causing people to look around nervously and shout to each other.

Large hangar doors opened, and rain blew inside the enclosure, borne on strong gusts of wind that buffeted the hair and clothing of the people. The storm was picking up again.

"I beg of you," Lori said, "Think of the best interests of these children, and of the UWW." Gently, she reached out and touched the baby in Deborah's arms, the Apostle Martha.

Dixie Lou glowered. "I always do!"

Curiously, Lori didn't detect any extrasensory sensation from touching this she-apostle, not like she'd felt earlier with Veronica. But beyond that, something seemed ineffably different about this child, something that troubled her.

"Even our She-God cannot protect you all of the time," Lori said, meeting Dixie Lou's glare. "With all due respect, I must remind you that powerful demons are aligned against you." Staring hard at the black woman, Lori thought she saw fear flicker in her eyes.

"This is no time for a debate!"

"There *are* demons all around," Lori insisted.

"I agree with her," Deborah said.

Exasperated, Dixie Lou said, "All right." She waved an arm. "Put four children in each 'copter. Quickly!"

"And Martha?" Deborah asked.

Another explosion sounded, closer.

Hesitation. "She goes with me. And so do you. Bring her inside!"

"As you wish, Chairwoman."

Women hurried to distribute the children as ordered. Shots rang out, causing some of the adults to duck for cover and protect the children. A matron tripped, carrying a toddler with pale, flaxen hair, sending both of them sprawling. Apparently uninjured, the child stood straight up and looked in the direction of the shots, as if she had no fear.

Lori saw men in silver-and-black uniforms at the top of a stairway, firing automatic weapons. An older woman, one of the Scriptorium translators, fell near a service vehicle, half her head blown off. UWW guards, stationed around the aircraft (including hers), fired back. Two BOI soldiers tumbled down the stairs.

To Lori's horror, the flaxen-haired she-apostle walked directly toward the attackers.

"Candace!" the matron shouted, struggling to get up. She ran to get the child.

Just then, a volley of shots rang out. In horror, Lori thought she saw bullets flying through the air, toward the tiny, brave girl. Lori didn't see how this could be possible, but the bullets looked as if they were moving slowly, almost floating.

Calmly, the toddler stood in the path of the deadly projectiles, with a slight smile on her cherubic face.

Lori heard a soft click, and what felt like a pressure change around her.

Just as a hail of bullets was about to hit Candace, the toddler vanished. The bullets passed through the space where she had been, and thudded into a wall.

Unable to believe her eyes, Lori squinted.

As she did so, Candace reappeared, in the same place, in the same posture. It was if the eye of time had blinked, shifting the child into an alternate dimension for a moment and then returning her to this one.

Suddenly, everything was going quickly again. The matron scooped Candace up and ran with her into a helicopter. UWW guards fired on the enemy soldiers and they dropped, splattering blood and torn flesh.

Glancing over, Lori also noticed Dixie Lou staring, seemingly transfixed, toward the hatch where Candace had entered the aircraft.

Did she see what I saw?

In apparent answer to her question, Dixie Lou met the teenager's gaze, and Lori knew that they both understood. They had seen the same thing.

Abruptly, as if snapping to awareness, Dixie Lou ordered Alex and several guards into the VTOL, and again told Lori's guard to put her in the third helicopter. Lori thought the Chairwoman wanted to keep away from her in order to avoid touching her, after what had happened to them before.

She's afraid of me.

After Lori boarded and took a seat beside her guard, she watched four she-apostles and their caretakers taking seats. Two of the children, Mary Magdalene and Veronica, had councilwomen with them—the diminutive Fujiko Harui and the much larger Wendy Zepeda. The other two children were attended by wiry-thin matrons.

Lori looked out a porthole. In the adjacent VTOL, she saw Alex looking back at her, through a wide window. They waved to each other nervously. She wasn't sure why, but she sensed that he was trustworthy, that he had her best interests in mind. She was sorry she had ever doubted him, and hoped he made it to safety. Lori also noticed Liz Torrence and Siana Harui in the aircraft, at portholes on the same side as Alex.

Lori's aircraft rose into the darkness third, with two companion vessels above hers and one below, fast-rising shadow shapes illuminated by the explosion-wracked monastery below. Strong winds buffeted her vessel, giving her a sick feeling in the stomach. She didn't like to fly, and always felt edgy whenever she had to do so. In the present circumstances it was far worse.

She saw flames below, and angry red streaks of tracer fire in the air. One of the monastery buildings—the Refectory—was consumed by flames.

Beside her, the female guard did not look like she was feeling well, with her eyelids hovering just above the lower lids. Through slits, she peered over at Lori for a moment before looking away, her eyes dull, as if she had taken a drug. Across the aisle, another guard sat, not paying any attention to Lori. Both of the uniformed young women looked like high school students to Lori, and she wondered how they had gotten into such a dangerous profession at their ages.

These were the only two guards aboard. The other passengers were councilwomen, matrons, a translator, and four of the she-apostles.

Lori's guard wore a sidearm that was only centimeters from Lori's hip, and she thought it might be possible to release the flap of the holster and grab the handle of the weapon. The guard's eyes were closed, and as moments passed, she began to snore softly.

This may be my only chance, Lori thought, remembering the shooting lessons her mother had given her the year before. Camilla Vale, always concerned about the danger of attacks—particularly from men—had taken her teenage daughter out in the woods for target practice one day, using a handgun and a rifle. Curiously, it had been one of the few times in recent memory when the two of them had gotten along well. They'd spent hours lining up pine cones on a log and shooting them off.

The following morning, Lori had commented about how masculine their day had been, in contrast to the feminine ideals Camilla professed to hold. With a sharp glance, Lori's mother had said, "It is necessary to know the art of violence in order to defend ourselves against men."

And maybe I can use those skills now, Lori thought.

Carefully, moving centimeter by centimeter, Lori's hand drew closer to the guard's holster flap. Ever so slowly, she lifted the flap. For a moment the snap stuck, then released. The guard stirred. Her eyelids fluttered.

Lori pulled away.

Presently, she heard the gentle snoring resume. Looking peripherally, she saw the black handle of the gun, exposed and ready for her to take. She hesitated. If she failed at this, it could mean her death. Probably would, in fact, in the flurry of a few seconds, if the guard across the aisle lifted her automatic rifle and started firing. If Lori didn't do this right, the children aboard could be injured or killed, too.

And the teenager felt something else as well, a sudden spark of awareness deep in her soul. She had something important to live for, something significant to do with her life. It was her life, and she deserved to direct it herself, to success or failure. She would not be controlled by others any longer.

Moving quickly, her fingers darted toward the gun, grabbed the prize and withdrew it. No reaction from either guard.

She released the safety and cocked the weapon.

At the click, her guard jerked her eyes open. Lori shoved her into the aisle and shouted to the other one, "Get on the floor with her! *Now!*"

When the two young guards were down, Lori ordered a matron to give her their weapons, and to tie the women with electrical cord. Just ahead of Lori, Wendy Zepeda sat with the she-apostle Veronica, "This will not please Dixie Lou," Zepeda said. The toddler with her was crying.

"I didn't do it to please her," Lori said, standing in the aisle. "I'm in charge of this helicopter now. Now take care of that child."

As Zepeda did as she was told, the other councilwoman onboard, Fujiko Harui, made her way along the aisle toward Lori, coming from the rear.

"That's close enough," Lori said, waving the handgun at her. She had the other guns beside her.

"I want to help you," the tiny Japanese woman said. "But watch out for Wendy." Hearing another child cry in the rear of the cabin, Lori glanced back. One of the matrons was trying to calm her.

"I already know about Wendy," Lori said. "The way she always votes with Dixie Lou Jackson."

"Have you heard how I vote?" Her voice had an edge of anger.

Lori nodded. "You switched to Dixie Lou, but not until she threatened to harm your daughter."

"That's right. Now if you'll excuse me, I must tend to Mary Magdalene." The diminutive woman made her way back along the aisleway.

* * *

Inside Dixie Lou's command helicopter, the seats were arranged two on each side of a narrow aisle. The ceiling was mirrorlike, enabling the Chairwoman to look down on the other passengers through reflections. She sat alone at the rear, watching everyone, trusting none of them . . . and still excited about the harrowing escape from Monte Konos. She still couldn't believe that Candace had not been hit by those bullets. Under other circumstances, she might have thought her eyes had played tricks on her. People didn't vanish into thin air and then reappear. But since the discovery of the she-apostles, strange events had been occurring, and she worried about being able to keep things under control.

Just ahead of her, a baby fussed, and Bobbi Torrence spoke to her in a soothing tone that immediately caused her to quiet down.

On her lap, Dixie Lou held a laptop computer, the screen casting pale gray light. It was time to disseminate the *Holy Women's Bible* via the worldwide net. The first editions to reach the public would be in the form of free, downloadable e-books in more than a hundred languages, and she would also transmit the manuscript to secret UWW printing establishments all over the world, so that that bound editions could be assembled on a rush basis and given away.

But now, as she tried to connect with the Internet on their encrypted line, she couldn't get the system working. It was extremely frustrating to her.

Presently Dixie Lou gave up the effort and stared glumly out a porthole on her left. In the Scriptorium Building that was fading into the distance, UWW military information was being erased from the computer system, an automated security procedure. Somewhat similar to Lori Vale's line of thinking concerning the children, micro-cylinder copies and printouts of the *Holy Women's Bible* were aboard the Chairwoman's vessel and the VTOL, so that all UWW assets were not in one basket. The teenager was highly intelligent. No question about that.

All four of the aircraft in her squadron had long-range fuel tanks, enabling them to fly for great distances without refueling . . . more than three thousand kilometers if necessary. They were also stealth, constructed in the last year with the latest materials and designs, but this gave her only small comfort. She'd heard that stealth capability was a continually evolving technology, one that kept becoming obsolete and then changing as a result of new detection equipment. There had, in fact, been a disturbing incident only three months before, in which a stealth UWW plane had been shot down over the Mediterranean Sea.

That was roughly where they were headed now, on a southwesterly course that would take them out over the Mediterranean, heading for a secret UWW base in Tunisia, on the north coast of Africa.

Dixie Lou wished she'd been able to get off an Internet broadcast of the book, and wondered if the storm had anything to do with her difficulties. Strapped to a wall bracket beside her was the sacred Sword of She-God, with the inlaid emeralds and fire opals of its hilt dancing in reflected light.

Unfortunately, the two guards aboard this craft, and some of the other guards as well, were not the ones she'd specified in her evacuation list. Most of them were only the greenest of trainees, but they would have to suffice. In the confusion of the surprise attack, there had been little choice.

With an exasperated sigh, she stared at the laptop, containing her precious *Holy Women's Bible*, undoubtedly the most earth-shaking publication in history. She envisioned special hardcover editions with ornate script and gold embossing, giving her tome the same stature as traditional holy books—and she had numerous companion projects in mind as well. But first Dixie Lou needed to get the gospels disseminated around the world, before they could be suppressed by BOI operatives.

All was in readiness.

* * *

Lori sat in the low illumination of the cockpit behind the pilot, having closed and locked the door to provide security from the other passengers. She held the handgun on her lap, and had other weapons stored in a locked cabinet near her. The control she had exerted over this one small aircraft seemed minuscule in the midst of all the huge events whirling around her.

Outside the window, she saw the angry red streaks of tracer fire, and heard hissing and popping sounds. It seemed surreal to her, more like something she'd experienced in a virtual-reality movie or a holo-game than reality. Lori's life since the goddess circle and the tragic death of her mother seemed not her own, as if a force much larger than herself—like a cosmic tidal wave—was thrusting her forward into an uncertain, dangerous future.

About the Author

Brian Herbert, the son of Frank Herbert, is the author of numerous *New York Times* bestsellers. He has won many literary honors and has been nominated for the highest awards in science fiction. In 2003, he published *Dreamer of Dune*, a moving biography of his father that was nominated for the Hugo Award. After writing ten DUNE-universe novels with Kevin J. Anderson, the coauthors created their own epic series, HELLHOLE. Brian began his own galaxy-spanning science fiction series in 2006, TIMEWEB. His other acclaimed solo novels include *Sidney's Comet; Sudanna, Sudanna; The Race for God;* and *Man of Two Worlds* (written with Frank Herbert).